LOST PROOF

A NATE SHEPHERD NOVEL

MICHAEL STAGG

Lost Proof

A Nate Shepherd Novel

Copyright © 2023 by Michael Stagg

For more information about Michael Stagg and his other books, go to michaelstagg.com

Want a free short story about Nate Shepherd's start as a new lawyer? Hint: It didn't go well.

Sign up for the Michael Stagg newsletter here or at https://michaelstagg.com/newsletter/

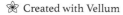 Created with Vellum

SEPTEMBER

1

The first time anyone ever tried to kill me was during the Logan Carver case. I'm telling you about it, so they didn't pull it off, but it was still a relatively unpleasant experience.

I didn't realize what had happened at the time—I mean, I realized I could've been killed, but I didn't realize that someone had done it on purpose until later. Even more time passed before I figured out the message that went along with the attempt but, unfortunately, by the time I worked it all through, the consequences had already occurred.

You'd think that someone who dealt with murder all the time would be more prepared to be on the receiving end of it, but I wasn't. I guess that's one thing I had in common with the victim in that case—Christopher Marsh didn't expect to be robbed and beaten to death in his home, and I didn't expect someone to take a run at me while I was defending the man accused of doing it.

I didn't know that's where all this was headed when I found Wendy Carver waiting for me in my office. But that's where it started.

Daniel Reddy met me the moment I walked in the door.

"Your appointment is here, Nate," he said.

"For the associate interview? She's early."

Danny frowned. "No. Your client meeting."

"I didn't think I had one this morning. Certainly not this early."

Danny and I are a two-man shop. My last name is on the door of the Shepherd Firm and Danny is my associate. So far, I'd resisted hiring a legal assistant so this kind of conversation happened more often than it should.

"In the conference room?"

Danny nodded. "With coffee. Do you want me in there?"

I shook my head. "I promised you were out of the criminal work. If it's something else, I'll let you know."

Danny hesitated, nodded again, then went back to his office. I grabbed a coffee and my laptop and went into the conference room.

A woman was sitting on the far side table gripping a pen and a handkerchief, her hands resting on a plastic-covered check book. Her head jerked up as I entered, and she put her hands in her lap. She had brown hair, cut short so that the ends curled around her chin. Her skin was pale and her eyes that particular tint of red that indicated chronic allergies or recent tears.

"Good morning," I said.

She stood and extended a hand over the table. "Mr. Shepherd?" She was dressed in a white shirt with a black tie, a black skirt, and black tights that had the look of a uniform.

"Nate, please," I said as I shook her hand.

"I'm Wendy Carver. I'm sorry I don't have an appointment."

"Well, that's a relief, Wendy, because it means I didn't forget." I smiled, motioned, and we both sat. "How can I help you?"

"It's for my son. He's been arrested."

"Where?"

"In Carrefour. On the Michigan side."

"For what?"

"They're saying he killed someone. But that just can't be true. Logan has his problems, but he's not violent. He would never hurt anyone."

Wendy Carver looked to be in her mid-forties. "Is your son over eighteen?" I asked.

She nodded. "Twenty-four. He's been on his own for a few years now." She wrung the handkerchief, twisting it around the pen.

I nodded. "So what happened?"

"I don't know," she said.

"What are they saying happened?"

"They say Logan broke into a man's house and killed him."

"Who do they say he killed?"

"A young man. I don't know his name." The handkerchief twisted. "Logan would never do that."

"Why do they think Logan did it?"

Wendy Carver shook her head. "I'm not sure. The sheriff

won't talk to me. Logan said something about the sheriff trying to get him to confess, but Logan said he didn't do it."

"You've spoken to Logan then?"

Wendy Carver nodded. "He called asking us to post bail."

"Alright, I can put the wheels in motion to start the bond—"

"—I can't afford to get him out," she said. "I can only pay you to defend him."

"Wendy, if he's accused of murder, that means he could be held for a long time before trial."

"I know." She wrung the pen. "We...His stepdad and I...Logan has..." Wendy Carver stopped, took a breath, and said, "Logan hasn't gone down the best path and it only got worse after his dad died. We, Logan's stepdad and me, thought it best if Logan go live on his own three years ago. I know he hasn't made the best decisions sometimes, but I also know my son wouldn't kill someone. How much would it cost to hire you?"

"For a murder case?" I told her.

She took another breath. "I can afford to pay you then. But he'll have to figure out the bond himself."

"Are you sure? Bond companies will take an interest in—"

"—We lost everything when his dad died. My husband and I are barely keeping the lights on."

"I understand." I thought for a moment. "When was Logan arrested?"

"Yesterday."

"Ash County jail?"

"Yes."

"He's been arrested before?"

"Yes."

"For what?

"Robbery. Or burglary. Whatever they call stealing."

I hesitated, not crazy about the idea of representing

someone who may have killed someone while robbing their house.

Wendy Carver watched me, then said, "Mr. Shepherd, Nate, my son is...easily led. I'm sure he's stolen things. I'm just as sure he hasn't killed anyone. Will you represent him?"

"I'll need to talk to your son. He has to agree to the representation."

"He will. I told him I'd pay for it."

"Then I'll go talk to him and find out."

Wendy Carver took a huge breath and sat up straight. She relinquished her grip on the handkerchief and clicked the pen. "What do I owe you?"

We talked about retainers and fees and expenses, and, as she started to write the check, I held up a hand. "Let me talk to him first. I'll go up to see him this afternoon, then let you know if he accepts the representation."

Wendy Carver stood and thanked me and shook my hand at the door with a gratitude I felt I had not yet earned.

As soon as the door clicked, Danny emerged from his office. "What was that about?"

"Murder, I think."

"Why wouldn't it be?" said Danny.

"Don't worry, you're in the clear as long as this interview for the new associate works out."

Right on cue, Emily Lake opened the door.

S he stopped with the door halfway open and looked back
and forth between us. "Uhm, Nate Shepherd?"

I realized Danny and I had been hovering in the
entryway and took a step back. "That's me."

"Emily Lake." She stepped forward with a hand extended.

Emily Lake had thick reddish-brown hair that hung to her
shoulders, a sprinkling of freckles, and hazel eyes that were
giving me a steady, earnest stare as she shook my hand. She was
wearing what we would call a prosecutor suit—neutral color,
well-made but off the rack, and designed to deflect notice and
not offend the widest possible range of jurors.

"So you worked for Anne?"

Emily Lake blinked, then nodded. "Two years for Judge
Gallon, yes, then two more years in the Carrefour prosecutor's
office."

"How do you feel about murder?"

"I'm against it."

"How about defending those accused?"

"Do we go to trial?"

"Sometimes."

"Then I'm in."

"Are you licensed in Michigan?"

"Yes, but I've never tried a case up there."

"Are you willing to learn?"

"You bet your...yes, I am."

I pointed. "This is Daniel Reddy. He's a hell of a trial lawyer, but he is going over to the dark side."

Emily nodded and shook Danny's hand. "The prosecutor's office?"

Danny smiled. "Worse. Estate planning and business."

"Really? I mean, great."

Danny grinned. "Someone has to pay the rent around here."

"So, when can you start?" I said.

Emily blinked. "I brought my resume."

"I read it."

"No interview?"

"You just had one. Do you have any more questions, Danny?"

"You said you want to try cases, right?" said Danny.

"As many as you've got," said Emily.

"Hire her."

I nodded. "So, when can you start?"

"That's really it?"

"I talked to Judge Gallon and she said if I didn't hire you, I was a—what was it, Danny?"

"An empty-headed whizz-nozzle."

"She is a poet." I turned back to Emily. "You'd support both of our practices—corporate research and filings for Danny but mostly trial support for me."

"What's the pay?"

I told her. "Still interested?"

"I'm in," she said.

"Great. How much notice do you have to give the prosecutor's office?"

"Two weeks."

"Take whatever time you need to wrap up your cases. Then take another week or two after that."

She scowled. "Why?"

"Because the time between jobs is the only true vacation a lawyer gets. Enjoy it."

"I don't need it."

"You will. I have to go up to Dellville. I'll write up a formal offer to you and send it over tonight."

"What's in Dellville?"

"A meeting with our new client for a murder case we might be handling."

She grinned. "Can I go? I took the morning off."

I smiled. "You're still an officer of the State of Ohio. I don't think I can have you in a private conversation with my potential client just yet."

"But if I'm coming here—"

"—Then you'll have plenty of time to get up to speed when you do."

Emily looked disappointed but nodded.

I realized we were all still standing by the door and that this had gone off in a far more half-assed fashion than I'd planned. I offered her coffee, showed her around, and took her into the conference room where we chatted about some of her cases and what Danny and I did. After we had spent what felt like a respectable time, I checked my phone and said, "I'm sorry, Emily, but I do have to get up to the Ash County jail."

"You're sure I can't go?"

"Positive. Are you sure you're interested in our job?"

"Positive."

"Then I'll send you the offer sheet tonight."

"I'll give them my notice this afternoon."

I smiled. "Why don't you wait until you get the offer sheet just to make sure."

Emily shrugged in a way that said *no promises*.

We shook hands, she said goodbye to Danny, and left.

I ducked into Danny's office. "I'm heading up to Dellville."

Danny was grinning. "Looks like I won't have to."

I smiled. "It does."

"I knew Judge Gallon was wrong."

"Yeah?"

"You're not empty-headed."

"Thanks."

With that affirmation of my existence, I headed up to Dellville to meet Logan Carver.

C arrefour is a small city that sits on the Ohio-Michigan border not too far from Indiana. The southern two thirds of the city is in Ohio while the northern third is in Michigan which creates two separate jurisdictions and court systems.

Logan Carver was accused of killing someone on the Michigan side of the line. That meant Logan had been arrested by the Ash County Sheriff and taken to the Ash County jail, which was located in the town of Dellville about twenty minutes north of Carrefour. That also meant I had to deal with Sheriff Warren Dushane, the chief law enforcement officer for Ash County.

I caught up with Sheriff Dushane eating lunch in his office, a meatball sub by the looks of it. Sheriff Dushane smiled, licked some marinara off his fingers, then wiped them before shaking my hand.

Sheriff Dushane was a cinderblock of a man in his early sixties with a salt-and-pepper mustache, thick arms, and a barrel chest. His gun belt had loosened a notch or two over the years, but he still looked like he could hold a tackling dummy at a youth football practice, which was no coincidence since he continued to do it every fall.

"Nate!" he said as he gripped my hand. "I was just on the water with your dad last weekend."

"He mentioned it. How'd they bite?"

"To the limit, which is all you can really ask for. I see Tommy's team is off to a good start."

My older brother, Tom, coaches the local high school football team. The last case Sheriff Dushane and I had been involved in together had dealt with Tom's star quarterback, Tyler Daniels, and his brother Colton.

I nodded. "You don't lose a quarterback like Tyler without some growing pains. I think he's going to have to do it with defense this year."

"There's more than one way to win a game." Sheriff Dushane settled back down into his chair and waved at one for me. He held up his sandwich. "Do you mind? I have to go down to Carrefour this afternoon."

"Not at all. I'm the one interrupting your lunch."

"What can I do for you, Nate?"

"I've taken a new case. Logan Carver."

Sheriff Dushane took a big bite of meatball and wheat bread, chewed, took another bite, and then chewed some more.

I waited.

Eventually, he set his sub down, wiped the sauce out of his mustache, and sighed. "Nate, we've gone around like this on two cases now."

"We have, Sheriff." He was referring to Tyler Daniels' case and one before that where I'd represented Archie Mack.

"I feel like you keep giving ammo to my election opponents."

"Nobody's actually got the stones to run against you, do they?"

"Not so far. That doesn't mean it can't happen."

I waited.

Sheriff Dushane stared at me some more before shaking his head. "What do you want to know?"

"Whatever you're willing to tell me."

"What do you know?"

"Very little. I'm on my way to see him now and thought you might fill me in."

"It's not fair to ask me for help doing your job, Nate."

I raised my hands. "I don't want help. But I think it's fair for me to ask what you've arrested him for."

Sheriff Dushane wiped his mouth with a napkin, then said, "Murder."

I nodded. "May I know who?"

Sheriff Dushane stared at me, as if thinking, then said, "On Friday night, someone broke into the home of Christopher Marsh, a young reporter for the *Ash County Torch*. They stole some things, mostly electronics. They also beat Christopher to death with a bat." Sheriff Dushane shook his head. "He was only twenty-four years old."

"And the connection with my client?"

"Your man sold electronics Friday night that belonged to Christopher Marsh. That was enough to lead us to him. When we picked him up, we found the murder weapon in his car."

"Motive?"

"Being interrupted during a robbery seems like enough."

"Forensics?"

"Nice try. Now if you'll excuse me," he stood, "I have to get back down in Carrefour. Have a meeting with—" he stopped, smiled "—I have a meeting."

"No problem. Thanks for seeing me."

"Anytime, Nate. But next time, make it fun; maybe join me and your pops on the boat."

"That does sound like fun. See you around."

"I expect so."

So much for Wendy Carver's insistence on innocence, I thought, and crossed the street to the Ash County jail.

5

When I entered the interview room, Logan Carver was already waiting for me. He was young, in his early twenties, with brown hair that was limp and long enough on top to fall over his eyes. He was neither fat nor thin but that middling soft that comes from habits that haven't yet caught up to the young. He was wearing jail-issued orange and was sitting on both of his hands, rocking a little from side to side.

"I didn't kill anyone," he said as soon as I walked in. I was struck by how young he sounded.

"Okay." I sat down.

"They need to let me out because I didn't kill anyone."

"That's not going to happen right now, Logan."

His eyes were wide. "My mom sent you, right? To get me out?"

"To represent you, Logan. Do you want me to?"

"Yeah, now get me out."

"To get you out, you need money to post a bond. Do you have money?"

"No, I don't have money that's why...no I don't have money! My mom does though, so get me out."

I shook my head. "Your mom told me she doesn't have money for a bond."

Logan rocked. "That's not my mom, that's Dick talking."

"Dick?"

"My stepdad, Rich. He won't give me anything."

"Do you have money or property at all for a bond?"

"I got an old car."

"You're in for murder, so that won't be enough."

"Mom really won't pay for it?"

I shook my head. "She says she can't. She said you'll have to arrange bond on your own."

"But I don't have anything!"

"Is there anyone else you can ask?"

"There's nobody. She knows that."

"Then I'm afraid you're going to be in here for a while."

"How can they...I didn't kill anyone!"

The bond conversation was going nowhere, so I said, "Tell me what you know about this murder."

Logan's eyes got even wider as he rocked faster. "I got nothing to tell you! I didn't kill anyone! Are you stupid? Don't you ever listen?"

"Logan!"

He stopped yelling, but he kept rocking.

"Do you know who they're accusing you of killing?"

Logan Carver shook his head.

"It was a man named Christopher Marsh. Have you ever heard that name before?"

Logan Carver looked at me, then shrugged.

"Were you in Christopher Marsh's house that night?"

"I didn't kill him."

"I didn't ask that. I asked if you were in his house."

Logan's head was down, but he glanced up, like a dog deciding whether you could be trusted to give him a biscuit.

"No one can find out about what you tell me," I said. "Not the police. Not your mom. And I need to know it if I'm going to have a chance to get you out of here."

Still silent.

"Were you in Christopher Marsh's house?"

Logan shrugged.

"Were you in *a* house."

Logan nodded.

"Did you take things?"

Logan nodded again.

"How did you get in the house?"

"Through the door."

"What did you do?"

"I looked in the easy spots."

"What are the easy spots?"

"Places where people keep good stuff."

"Did you find good stuff?"

Logan looked down, rocked back and forth, and nodded.

"What did you find?"

"A PlayStation and some Beats headphones."

"What did you do then?"

"Put them in my bag and left."

"You had a bag?"

Logan nodded again. "A gym bag."

"How long were you in there?"

"You shouldn't stay long."

"You shouldn't?"

"Nope. Just circle around to the easy places and out."

"So how long did it take to circle around to the easy places?"

He frowned. "Not long. Once I had the PlayStation and the Beats, I had enough."

"And no one was there?"

"Nope."

"Did you see anyone outside?"

"Nope. I just walked a little ways to my car and left."

"How did you pick that house?"

Logan shifted, then shrugged. "It didn't seem like anyone was home, and I could see a huge TV in the window, so I figured it would have some good stuff."

"You just happened to see it?"

He shrugged again. "There was a big window. And it was a big TV."

"What time was it?"

Logan shook his head. "Don't know. I didn't have my phone with me. After eight, maybe."

"Where was your phone?"

"At home."

"Forgot it?"

"Never take your phone." The words snapped out.

I couldn't argue with that. "What did you do next?"

"I was thirsty, so I got a couple of shakes at McDonald's."

"You were driving?"

He nodded.

"What kind of car?"

"An old Honda Civic."

"Then what?"

"Uhm, then I went, then I went to Second Chance Electronics."

"To sell what you had?"

Logan nodded. "The guy screwed me. I should've gotten more."

"For the Beats and the PlayStation?"

Logan nodded again.

"Then what?"

Logan shrugged. "I went home and hung out."

"What does 'hang out' mean?"

"Gamed. Drank. Ate. Why do you care?"

"I care because anything you were doing would be evidence that you were doing it."

"There was no one else there."

"When did you get up the next day?"

"I don't know."

"When was the first time you were with anyone that day?"

"What day was that?"

"Saturday."

"I don't think I saw anyone."

"When did the sheriff come?"

"That night, Saturday."

"What did they tell you?"

"Not much. They asked if I'd been to Second Chance and I said no. So then they looked in my car and there wasn't anything in there and then they looked in my trunk and there was a bat and I told them right away that it wasn't mine, so I don't know why I'm in here."

"Logan, this is important—did they ask you if they could look in your car?"

Logan nodded. "I knew there wasn't anything in there, so I said go ahead."

I felt a flash of disappointment. "Did they ask you about the trunk too?"

"Yeah, I didn't put anything in there. But they arrested me anyway."

"Between the time you left Marsh's house until you were arrested, did you get into the trunk of your car?"

Logan shook his head. "I threw the gym bag in the front seat next to me."

"Do you own a bat?"

Logan laughed. "I can't even play Mario baseball."

"And you never saw Christopher Marsh that night?"

"I told you, I don't know who he is."

I nodded and made a few more notes. I checked them, then said, "Alright, that's enough to get me started. Which McDonald's was it?"

"The one on Eighth Street." Logan stopped rocking. "What happens now?"

"You're going to be in here for a few months until we have a trial."

"Months?!"

"I'll let you know when we have a date, and I'll keep you updated on what's happening. And I'll need to meet with you sometimes like this to prepare."

"I can't stay here for months!"

"Logan, if they convict you of murder, you'll be in here for years."

Logan blinked. "I didn't kill anyone."

"Let me get to work on that."

As I rose to summon a guard, Logan said, "Mom really can't get me out?"

"No, Logan. You'll be here for a while."

He sat there, then nodded.

"And don't talk to anyone in here about what happened."

"Friends don't tell other people what they talk about."

"No one in here is your friend on this, Logan."

Logan said he understood. I wasn't sure so I repeated it. He said he understood again, the guard came, and I left.

I'd seen real fear in Logan, and real confusion, and some mental tracks being replayed over and over again. It was enough to make me call Wendy Carver and tell her I'd represent her son. She gushed and said she'd send the check.

6

I t was midafternoon by the time I was headed back to
Carrefour, which meant that I'd have to drive right past my
house in order to arrive back at the office, and honestly,
who does that? So instead, I decided to drive to the Brickhouse.

The Brickhouse is an old warehouse that has been reno-
vated into a gym by two of my oldest friends. Besides running
the gym, Olivia Brickson is an investigator and her brother,
Cade, is a bail bondsman. It was Olivia that I needed to
see now.

I parked my Jeep, grabbed the gym bag which was my price
of admission, and headed in.

Cade was behind the desk. He had short dark hair and wore
a black t-shirt that looked like it hid softballs on top of his shoulders. As he swiped my card, I said, "Is Liv around?"

He jerked a thumb. "Mobile iron class. Starts in five
minutes."

I thanked him and hustled to the back.

Olivia was sliding plates onto a small bar, wearing running
pants and a tank top that exposed the tattooed sleeve that
covered her left forearm. She had bleached white hair that

swooped up and half mirrored sunglasses that turned toward me as I approached.

"Shep!" she said. "Have we finally dragged your soft ass to my class?"

"Still not man enough, Liv. I brought some work."

She nodded. "I've got five minutes. Help me set up and I'll listen."

As we retrieved a series of small straight bars, rubber weights, and plastic steps, I said, "New murder case. I need research on the client and the victim."

She nodded and handed me two bars. "Have I heard about it?"

"Not sure. It was recent. Christopher Marsh is the victim. He was a reporter for the *Ash County Torch*."

She nodded. "They posted a big story on their site this weekend. Who's the client?"

"Logan Carver. He's got priors."

She nodded.

"Sheriff Dushane said Logan pawned some electronics, so we'll need to get that eventually. I'll email you the names and spellings to confirm and see what I can find out on my own but—"

"—But you want it done right, so you need me."

"Always."

"Done." Olivia put her hands on her hips and looked at the neat rows of three. A group of women and men were gathering off to the side.

She pointed. "I have room for one more."

"I've decided I need to be able to walk tomorrow."

"Walking is overrated."

"So I've been told."

"You should be running anyway."

"Bye. I'll text you the stuff."

I heard a hrumph and then the crack of Olivia's voice inviting her victims—I mean her clients—to load up their bars.

I got out of the way.

WHEN I CAME HOME LATER that night, Roxie was waiting for me. She didn't get up from her plush dog bed by the couch, but her short tail thumped when I walked over to give her a scratch. She still laid there on her side, but her tail thumped faster which, some days, is all you can ask for.

Roxie is a brindle boxer. She was a service dog until her owner passed away, but now she's retired and lives with me. When I asked her if she wanted to go outside, she pushed up and made her way to the back door. Roxie was nine so there was no sprinting involved, but she waited as I opened the door, waited again for me to open it to let her back in, then followed me to the kitchen where I made us both dinner.

It had been an adjustment, but as you can see, her training of me was going quite well.

I was just clearing the dishes before our evening walk when my phone buzzed. The number was in my contacts, but I hadn't talked to the caller in a while.

Ted Ringel, senior reporter for the *Ash County Torch*.

I took a deep breath and answered. "Hi, Ted."

"Tell me you're not going to represent that scumbag."

"Who's that?"

"You know who I'm talking about, Shepherd. That piece of shit that killed Chris."

"I don't know that he did that, Ted."

"Then you're the only one. They caught him red-handed."

"I'm just getting into the case."

"Let me save you some time. Your guy broke into Chris's

house and killed him for his video game system."

"I'm sorry for your loss, Ted."

"Don't give me the fake sympathy. If you cared about Chris, you wouldn't be representing the asshole who killed him."

"Everybody deserves—"

"—And save the constitutional crap. Yes, everybody deserves representation. But lawyers can, lawyers should, decide who they're going to give it to."

"We do."

"And you're going to give it to someone who robbed and killed my friend?"

I almost replied that just because someone steals something doesn't mean they killed someone when I realized that whatever I said to Ted would end up as a quote in the paper. Instead, I said, "Ted, I just took the case. How did you hear I was involved?"

"Why? Are you ashamed of your murdering client?"

"No. I just mean I haven't even filed the paperwork yet to show that I'm handling it."

"Get used to it, Shepherd, because the *Torch* will be covering this case wall to wall. Let me give you a little preview of what's on tomorrow's front page—the obituary complete with a listing of Christopher Marsh's accomplishments along with quotes from his family who loved him, his friends who miss him, and the people he helped."

"I'm sure he was a good man."

"How the hell would you know? Your client killed Chris before you could meet him. Which is what we'll report right underneath the obituary—an update that a man has been arrested in connection with the murder, complete with your client screaming FU at all of our readers."

"What do you mean FU—" I said, but Ted had already hung up.

7

Ted Ringel was as good as his word. The next day, the front page of the *Torch* was filled with a profile of Christopher Marsh. Son of local teacher Jerry Marsh and caterer Sylvia, Christopher had grown up in Carrefour before attending North High School where he was captain of the cross-country team, a trombone player in the school band, and a National Merit Scholar. He received an academic and track scholarship to Northwestern where he plowed through an undergrad program in journalism and economics while making All-Big Ten in the 800 meters. He had come home for two years to gain some practical experience with the *Torch* and had just been accepted to return to Northwestern for its journalism master's program, where he already had an internship with one of the major Chicago papers lined up.

"Chris was always on top of things, whether it was to shine a light on a problem being experienced by one of our readers or to feature one of their accomplishments," read a quote from Ted Ringel. "Chris reported with enthusiasm and insight that was a credit to our paper and our community." The article went on to highlight several of Christopher Marsh's stories, from a local child's Make-A-Wish journey to his recurring Carrefour "Business of the Month" feature to an exposé uncovering a contractor who victimized seniors with fraudulent home repairs.

It ended with a quote from Christopher Marsh's father, Jerry, stating that he couldn't understand how anyone could want to hurt his son.

Which, of course, led to the second article.

Right below the tribute was a headline that blared "Burglar Arrested for Murder of Local Reporter." Some of the facts I had already heard—Logan Carver's arrest after selling items stolen from Marsh's home, a bloody bat found in his car, a history of minor theft convictions. There was one fact I didn't know though—a prescription bottle made out to Christopher Marsh had been found in Logan Carver's garbage can. Great.

They, meaning the *Torch*, topped it all off with Logan's mug shot. His eyes were half-closed, his lank hair messed, and he looked even worse than when I'd seen him. To top it off, Logan was wearing a grey crew necked sweatshirt that said "FU" in huge purple block letters across the chest.

Ted Ringel hadn't been kidding. The "FU" reached out and screamed at you.

I shut my laptop, said goodbye to Roxie, and left for work.

MY OFFICE IS on the third floor of a suburban building made of steel, glass, and brick that houses small groups of lawyers, doctors, and accountants. It's nothing fancy but it gets the job done. As I walked in, Danny was waiting.

"We have a problem."

"Good morning to you too, Danny."

"I mean, *you* have a problem."

"A common sentiment."

"We need to set up an office for Emily."

I stopped. "I suppose we do."

"We need another computer too."

"True. Could you—"

"—And by we, I mean the owner of the business. Which is you."

I opened my mouth, closed it, then nodded. "Damn corporate lawyer."

Danny smiled. "Speaking of which, good news."

"Oh?"

"I have two new business clients—one who wants me to set up their company, and another who wants me to look at a purchase contract."

"Good work! Who are they?"

"A yet to be named skincare business and Tri-State Nursery."

"Nurseries of kids or trees?"

"Trees. They're buying a greenhouse to grow stock."

"Outstanding. Need any help?"

"Can you give it?"

"Nope, but I thought I'd ask."

Danny smiled. "I'll manage. Speaking of which, are you going to be able to manage with the new case until Emily gets here?"

"I should. I have Olivia doing some research and I'll be able to hold down the fort on filings for the next couple of weeks."

"Four weeks."

"Four?"

"You essentially told her to show up in four weeks."

"I guess I did. It'll be fine."

"I'll still help on anything short of a trial."

"I know. Thanks."

I grabbed a coffee, fired up my laptop, and checked my

email. I smiled as I read an acceptance email from Emily Lake at
9:47 p.m. I'd sent her the employment offer at 9:45.

I was putting together a list of things I would have to buy
before Emily started when Olivia called.

"See the paper today, Shep?"

"Couldn't miss it. I think there's going to be a lot more of it." I
told her about my call with Ted Ringel the night before.

Olivia chuckled. "The FU sweatshirt did stand out. So I don't
have any more on Marsh right now—I basically found the same
background as what was in the paper. I did find more on your
client, though. It's not great."

"How bad?"

"Convictions for possession of stolen property, breaking and
entering. Also, one arrest for entering without breaking, but it
looks like that one didn't stick."

"So consistent with robbery, but not necessarily murder. Any
history of violence?"

"One arrest for disorderly conduct at a Meijer between him
and another customer, but it looks like charges were dropped all
the way around. That's it on the violent end."

"Tell me more about the theft convictions."

"Looks like one set stems from breaking into a construction
site and stripping out some copper wiring, then selling it. He
was caught when he hit the same site for the third time. The
other was possession of a stolen smart phone that still had the
'Find My Phone' feature enabled."

"That's all consistent with what his mom told me. Some
wrong choices, but not violent."

"What do you want next?"

I prioritized. "Could you keep an eye on Ted Ringel on social
media and in the *Torch*? He's pissed and I get the sense I'm not
going to be able to keep up."

"He does sound pissed."

"And please research who owns the house Marsh was living in. I'd like to get in there as soon as possible."

"Done. Why don't I check out the shop where Carver sold the electronics too."

"Perfect. Thanks, Liv."

We hung up.

I still had a bunch of questions about the crime scene and the murder and how the Sheriff's office had tracked Logan down so quickly. The law is slow, though, and it's hard to get any information right away. I started that process by drafting discovery to the prosecutor asking for access to anything the State had collected so far. I filed it by the end of the day, but I knew I wouldn't get answers for a few weeks.

Just as I was leaving, Olivia texted me that she'd found the owner of the Marsh house and he'd agreed to give me access to Marsh's rooms the next morning. The only hitch was that, given the situation, the owner wanted a sheriff's deputy with me when I was there.

It wasn't ideal, but I couldn't blame him. I texted Olivia that I'd be there and that she was great.

She agreed.

8

A s you might've guessed from the name, Carrefour was founded by the French as they explored out from Detroit and the upper Great Lakes. State lines didn't mean anything at the time, because there weren't any, but after the state boundaries were finalized and the Toledo War of 1835 bloodlessly fought, the Old North Quarter of Carrefour's original downtown wound up being located on the Michigan side of the line.

Today, the Old North Quarter was filled with large, magnificent houses that were built during early boom times and had fallen into disrepair in the century or so after. Now, artists and students and young people had taken to moving in and renting a floor of one of these old, rundown, grand houses for half the price of an apartment while getting twice the space.

Christopher Marsh had lived in just such a place, so, at seven a.m. the following morning, I was driving through the Old North Quarter and spotted the Ash County Sheriff's vehicle in the driveway just ahead. I found a place to park in the street and walked up the driveway.

The house was three stories tall with streaked black shingles faded white, wooden siding of chipped green paint, and a covered porch supported by ornately carved wooden posts that might once have been yellow. A sheriff's deputy stood, arms crossed, waiting for me in front of the door.

I climbed the stairs of modestly buckled hardwood and extended my hand. "Nate Shepherd," I said.

He wore the brown shirt and pants of the Ash County Sheriff but wasn't wearing his hat, so I could see his close-cropped blond hair. He was a little over six feet and looked to be in his early thirties. His arms remain crossed as he said, "I remember you."

I cocked my head, then remembered. "Deputy Pavlich, right? You testified in the Colton Daniels trial. How have you been?"

Deputy Pavlich was not there to exchange top 'o the mornings. "Sheriff Dushane says I have to let you inspect the place. You can take pictures, but you can't touch anything and I'm to stay with you."

"Sounds good." I had won the Colton Daniels trial. Deputy Pavlich seemed to remember.

Deputy Pavlich handed me a set of latex gloves. "We're done printing the place but wear these anyway." I put them on, and we went in the old wooden front door.

"He lived on the first floor?" I said.

Deputy Pavlich grunted.

Where the outside seemed dilapidated, the inside was actually striking. Old hardwood floors, battered but refinished and beautiful, extended throughout, along with broad trim, crown molding, and ten-foot ceilings. I turned the light on and what had once been a parlor or dining room was now set up like modern day family room complete with full leather couch, small low coffee table, and big screen TV.

I saw an entryway to a kitchen and said, "Is the front door the only access point?"

Deputy Pavlich stared at me.

I held my hands out. "I want to get out of here as much as you."

Deputy Pavlich stared at me a little longer before he said, "There's a door to the rear stair from the outside that goes straight up to the apartments on the second and third floor. There is a separate side patio door that gives access to this suite."

I walked over to the TV, which was sitting on a cheap console, its doors open. Wires and a surge protector tumbled out of the opening. A few game cases, some of which I recognized due to my nephews, were still in there, along with a controller. The sound bar and the big screen TV were still there, I figured because those were too big to carry out in a gym bag.

The other half of the family room was set up as a makeshift office with a desk, a lamp, a laptop docking station, a monitor, and a printer. Papers were strewn about on the desk.

The thing about looking at a scene after the police have been there is that you don't know what the thief took and what the police did. "I take it you have an inventory of everything your office took?"

Deputy Pavlich grunted a yes.

I walked toward the kitchen.

"Watch where you step," said Deputy Pavlich.

I stopped in the opening. Red brown stains and an acrid tang identified the dried blood smeared on the floor and spattered across the cream-colored cabinets. I stopped short of the nearest streak and squatted down. "This where you found him?"

"You'll see the pictures," said Pavlich.

"How do you think the killer got in?"

Deputy Pavlich did not reply.

I stood and walked around the smears, noticing that the spatters went up a good six feet on one of the walls. A wooden door led to a small side porch. It was one of those doors where the bottom half was solid wood and the top half was filled with nine panes of small windows. The pane of glass nearest the door handle was broken.

"Did you find my client's prints anywhere?"

Deputy Pavlich crossed his arms, watching me.

I circled around a small hall with two doors, both open. A bedroom and a small bath.

I went to the bathroom. The medicine cabinet mirror hung open, but there was nothing unusual inside—toothpaste, razor, stuff like that.

Last, I went to the bedroom. A no-nonsense bed without a headboard and a single nightstand with a clip LED light and a phone docking station.

"Did you recover Marsh's phone?"

"The Sheriff and Mr. Stritch will provide you with our inventory in discovery."

The closet was opened and I looked—work clothes and casual shoes on one side, piles of athletic clothes on the other with a plastic bin of dirties in between. Nothing that seemed unusual and no sign of ransacking.

"Any cash in his wallet?"

"Sheriff Dushane and Prosecutor Stritch will give you an inventory with discovery."

I went back down the hall to the kitchen, coming at it from the other end. It looked like the spatters were going toward the kitchen cabinet drawers, as if Christopher had his back to the room.

"What kind of bat was it?"

"The Sheriff and Mr. Stritch will provide you with our inventory in discovery." I was getting the impression that Deputy Pavlich had memorized it.

I took a few pictures on my phone, basically for reference until I received the Sheriff's more detailed inventory and photos.

"Thanks, Deputy Pavlich. I'll let you know if I need to get back in after I speak to the Sheriff and Mr. Stritch about their inventory in discovery."

The statement was lost on Deputy Pavlich, who just stared.

I left, going out the side door this time. As I did, I smelled the distinct odor of weed. I looked around then looked up to a tiny third floor deck built out from a small open door.

No one was on it.

9

A few days later, I appeared in the Ash County courthouse for Logan Carver's formal Circuit Court arraignment. The Ash County courthouse was a tan brick building with brown metal trim and painted orange railings that came straight out of the last decades of the twentieth century. I went through the busy metal detectors to the cramped elevator that grudgingly carried me up to the third floor to the courtroom of Judge Eliza Jane Wesley.

I had appeared before Judge Wesley before, back when I had represented a farmer who was accused of beating his sister-in-law half to death. I remembered Judge Wesley as being formidable—a stickler for the rules who was happy to correct attorneys who didn't follow them. One of my colleagues had told me that she was an easy-going person off the bench, but the same wit that made her fun at parties could be deployed mercilessly in her court.

I waited in the courtroom as it filled up with other attorneys and family members and before long, the bailiff told us to rise, and Judge Wesley took the bench.

She had wide shoulders and wore her long black hair piled

up on her head, held in place with two silver-tipped black hair sticks, which made her seem to tower even higher above the court. "Please be seated," she said and waited until she made sure that everyone had.

When we had complied, she asked the bailiff to call the first case which just happened to be *State of Michigan versus Logan Carver.*

A young attorney I didn't recognize took the prosecutor's table as I stepped forward for the defense. "Tim Stevens for the prosecution, Your Honor," the young man said.

"Mr. Stevens, I expected Mr. Stritch to be here today given the severity of this case."

"He had a prior scheduled appointment, Your Honor," said Tim Stevens.

"That wouldn't happen to be the Rotary Club candidate breakfast, would it?"

Tim Stevens stuttered. Judge Wesley stared.

"Well," he said finally. "Since I'm here, I guess any comment on Mr. Stritch's whereabouts would be hearsay."

Judge Wesley chuckled. "Well done, Mr. Stevens. And Mr. Shepherd, welcome back to our court."

"Thank you, Your Honor."

"Will you be representing Mr. Carver?"

"I am, Your Honor."

"Have you had an opportunity to meet with your client so that you can enter a plea?"

"Yes, Your Honor. As soon as he's brought here, I'd be happy to do so."

Judge Wesley sighed. "Mr. Shepherd, when we finished our last trial you were doing reasonably well understanding and obeying our local procedures. It appears, though, that I must remind you, like last time, that you are responsible for knowing our local processes if you appear in our court."

I honest-to-goodness did not know how, in the space of two sentences, I had already screwed this up. "Of course, Your Honor."

She stared at me. "You don't know what you did, do you?"

"No idea."

"We now conduct our arraignments by video from the jail. We've had that capability for six months."

A huge video screen on the left side of the courtroom, which those in law enforcement would've called a clue, flared to life. "My apologies."

"No apologies, Mr. Shepherd, just brush up. Bailiff, please connect us."

The screen blinked and a split screen of Judge Wesley on one side and Logan Carver on the other appeared.

"Mr. Carver, can you hear me?" Judge Wesley said.

"Yes, ma'am."

"Mr. Stevens, what are the charges?"

"Your Honor, Logan Carver is charged with home invasion in the first degree and murder in the first degree as it was an intentional killing committed in the course of said home invasion." Timothy Stevens then read the formal charges, which carried the possible sentence of life imprisonment without the possibility of parole and added a few theft-related offenses like breaking and entering for good measure.

"Mr. Carver, could you hear that?"

"Yes, ma'am. I didn't kill him."

"Mr. Carver, please don't offer any statements. How do you wish to plead, Mr. Carver?"

"Is this where I say not guilty, Nate?"

"Yes, Logan."

"Not guilty, ma'am."

"The plea of 'not guilty' is accepted," said Judge Wesley. "Mr. Shepherd, if you would like to move for a bond hearing you may do so. Since it has been some months since you've been before the Court, I would remind you that the uniform bond schedule is available in our local rules."

"Understood, Your Honor." I knew Logan didn't have the money, so the schedule made no difference.

"Has discovery been submitted?"

"Yes, Your Honor."

"See that the responses are timely, Mr. Stevens."

"Yes, Your Honor."

"And tell Mr. Stritch that I hope his candidate breakfast went well."

"I will, Your Hon—" Timothy Stevens hung his head.

Judge Wesley smiled as she dismissed Logan, and his half the screen went blank. "See you soon, gentlemen. Next case, please."

10

It took most of two weeks before I could get access to the materials that led to Logan Carver's arrest. In fairness, the prosecutor, a man named T. Marvin Stritch who was just as uptight as his name, could've waited another week but sent the discovery responses over to me as soon as he had the materials compiled.

There were photos of the crime scene, but I decided to save my breakfast and set those aside for now. There was also an inventory of items that the police had taken as evidence and items they had identified as potentially significant but left at the house. I would go through those later too. What I was interested in right now was the stolen property that had supposedly led the sheriff to arrest Logan Carver.

Under "Items the State claims belonged to Christopher Marsh found to be in possession of Logan Carver," the prosecutor identified: 1) one PlayStation 5 game console; 2) one PlayStation controller; 3) one pair of Beats by Dr. Dre headphones; and 4) one empty prescription bottle for Adderall.

I cross-referenced over to his answer regarding potential witnesses and saw the name of Sam Perkins, Second Chance

Electronics. A quick search on my phone told me that was a place to buy and sell used computers, TVs, and, yes, game systems. I loaded the address, yelled to Danny to hold down the fort, and left.

SECOND CHANCE ELECTRONICS was in a strip mall just north of the border, situated alongside a gold dealer, a cannabis dispensary, and a diner, with a chain drugstore serving as the anchor at one end. I parked my Jeep and headed in.

The door beeped as I entered and I had an immediate impression of narrow aisles stacked with devices and pegboard walls filled with hooks of chargers, power blocks, and accessories of all kinds. Before I'd taken two steps, a man popped out of the back, took a place behind the front counter, and said, "Buying or selling today?"

"Looking and asking, if you don't mind."

"Not at all. What product can I tell you about?" He waved a hand. "We have just about anything you could find at a big box store for half the price."

The man leaned on a glass counter, his wiry, veiny arms sticking out from the sleeves of a black My Chemical Romance t-shirt. He had sandy brown hair, a little long and prematurely thinning, and was probably in his late thirties. He gave me a squinty smile as I approached.

"I have some questions about a PlayStation 5 game system."

The man shook his head. "You and everybody else, mister. Those are hard as hell to get new and the people who have them aren't giving them up yet. I do have some PS4s and Xbox 360s if you're interested. I've also got a nice selection of Nintendo Switches if you'd like something more mobile."

"No, I'm sorry—I mean, I have questions about a *particular*

PS5. I represent a man named Logan Carver. I understand he sold you a PS5 here a few weeks back?"

The man took a couple of steps back and held up his hands. "I run a clean shop here, man. I called the police right away."

"I understand that. I'm not with the police. I just need to know what happened the night the man sold you the PS5."

"I don't know anything."

"The police say you do. They've listed Sam Perkins as a witness."

"Oh, for Christ's sake. Listen, I run a clean shop."

"You mentioned that."

"I don't need to get hauled into court to talk about customers. It's not a good business plan."

"I'm not with the police, and I don't have anything to do with law enforcement. I just need to know what you told the police."

"Can I do that?"

"Did they tell you not to?"

"No."

"There you go."

"I run a clean shop here."

"So I've heard."

"I provide a valuable service. Most people can't afford a first run computer or a game system and I let them buy birthday presents and Christmas presents without going broke, you know?"

I nodded. "I have nephews."

"Then you know what I'm talking about, man. Hell, you can't even order a meal at some restaurants without a smart phone anymore—they make you get an eight-hundred-dollar phone to order a seven-dollar meal! It's crazy."

"Sure is."

"So, phones, game systems that are one or two generations behind, those are my bread-and-butter, and there are all sorts of people who might be looking to unload those. And if I help them make it to payday, even better. I provide a valuable service."

"Sounds like it. So do you remember a guy trying to sell you one a few weeks ago when you called the police?"

Sam Perkins stared at me for a moment, then said, "Yeah. A couple of hours before close, this guy comes in sporting a sweatshirt with 'FU' on it and I think well this should be rich. But the guy's got a gym bag, and he takes out a brand-new PS5 system and a controller, and a set of Beats headphones that he wants to sell. I check the Beats and those are fine but I tell him I have to run a diagnostic on the PS5 to make sure it works. He's kinda jumpy and tells me he's running late and can't wait. I tell him I have to check it to buy it. He says how much can you give me for it now? I tell him I can give him fifty bucks now but if he wants to come back the next day after I check it, he can get the rest. He says fine. I say what's your name and he hems a little bit, then says Christopher Marsh. So I say, 'Here you go, Christopher,' and give him the money and he leaves."

I smiled. Offering a deposit was certainly one way to characterize the transaction, but I just said, "So did you check out the PS5?"

"I did but not 'til the next day. I powered the PS5 up and it was still logged in to the gaming account and I see the ID for the machine is 'MarshRules.' Now I don't know the guy who sold it to me the night before, but he said his name was Christopher Marsh and that matches the ID on the machine so that's good enough for me and I expect he'll come in sometime that day to get the rest of his money. So I make sure the game system's working and it is so there's no way I'm going to put it out on the floor. Instead, I post it for sale online for way more than new because nobody can get their hands on these things. Then I don't think any more about it until I see a local news report that some guy named Christopher Marsh got his head beaten in and killed the night before. And I think 'Oh shit,' and I take down the sale, and I call the cops."

I had been curious why the owner of this particular establishment would voluntarily call the police. Getting in front of publicly advertising the sale of property linked to a murder wasn't a bad reason.

"Did you tell them what happened?"

"I did."

"But you didn't know the name of the person who sold it to you, right?"

Sam Perkins shook his head. "I thought it was Christopher Marsh, man! But I remembered that 'FU' sweatshirt because it was right out there in your face and I had the video footage."

"Video footage?"

"I have a camera outside in case anyone tries to break in."

"Nothing inside?"

"Er, uhm, no. I don't need one inside."

"I see. What did the cops do?"

"Asked the same kind of questions you did, then took the game system and the Beats. Said it was evidence. Didn't pay for them either, so I'm out that cash."

"I see. Do you remember anything else?"

"Isn't that enough, man?"

"Just asking. Thanks, Sam."

I turned to leave.

"Christmas will be here before you know it," he said. "And nephews can be hard to buy for."

"Good memory." I paused, thought, and went over to the video game section where I picked four games that I thought matched my nephews' game systems.

As Sam Perkins rang them up, he said, "You said you're a lawyer?"

"I am."

"We have laptops and tablets back there, too."

"I think I'm all set."

Sam Perkins smiled. "You don't make the sale if you don't ask."

"You do not. Thanks, again."

"And you tell the sheriff I run a clean shop."

"I'm sure he knows."

I left Second Chance Electronics knowing that the State had video of my client selling Christopher Marsh's game system on the night he was killed. I headed back to the office to find out what other fun facts had been produced.

11

I heard rustling in the conference room, so I walked over and said, "They have evidence that our client sold Marsh's game system—"

Danny wasn't standing in the conference room; Emily Lake was, leafing through a stack of papers.

Emily grinned. "Danny had to leave. Something about a meeting with a landscaping client."

"What are you doing?"

"Keeping myself busy until you got back. Have these been scanned in yet?"

"No. And no, I mean, what are you doing *here*?"

"Not much of a reception, Boss."

"We weren't expecting you for another couple of weeks."

She frowned. "Why?"

"You said you had to give two weeks' notice."

"Right. It's been two weeks and a day."

"You were going to take a couple of weeks off."

Emily shook her head. "No, you *advised* me to take a couple of weeks off. I ignored that."

"We're not set up for you yet."

"So buy me a laptop and let's get rolling." She held out a stack of papers. "I'll scan these while you go get that laptop. How do you like them organized?"

I showed Emily what to do and then left to buy her a computer.

I RETURNED at the same time Danny came back from his meeting. I had an armful of boxes, Danny's hands were full of files, and Emily was running back and forth between stacks of paper and the scanner. I set down the boxes, contemplated the administrative tasks that awaited us that afternoon, and made an executive decision. "Let's go get a welcome lunch."

Both of them agreed.

OUR OFFICE WAS a stone's throw from a bunch of restaurants that you can find scattered in any suburban business complex. We picked one that was local and featured seafood.

"Huh," said Emily. "I had you pegged more as a deli guy."

Danny laughed. "He is. He's putting on airs."

I shrugged. "Can't let you realize your mistake on the first day."

"Don't switch things up on my account," Emily said.

"Don't worry about that," said Danny.

As soon as the server had explained the specials and dropped off the menus, Emily said, "Dan said you were out interviewing a witness?"

I nodded. "Owner of an electronics resale shop." I told them about my meeting with Sam Perkins.

"Was our client there after the murder?" said Emily.

"He said it was a couple of hours before closing."

"The sheriff is putting the killing at around eight-thirty," she said.

I raised an eyebrow.

Emily gave a little grin. "I can read and scan."

"So the video will show our client with an item stolen from Marsh's house *after* Marsh was killed?"

"Looks like."

"What does our client say happened?" said Danny.

"Logan says that no one was home and that he didn't kill anyone."

"But he robbed the place?" Emily said.

"Yep."

"And confirmed it was him that sold the PS5?"

"And the Beats."

"Yikes."

"On the bright side, he said he never saw the murder weapon."

"The bloody one in the trunk of his car?"

"Exactly."

"So a thief but not a killer?" said Emily. "Tough sell."

I nodded. "Once we get the new materials sorted, why don't you start creating a timeline of where Logan was on the night of the murder."

"Will that help?"

"We won't know until we know."

Emily nodded. "What about Marsh's activities?"

"I'll put an investigator on that."

"Who?"

"Olivia Brickson."

"Cade's sister?"

"You know Cade?"

Emily chuckled. "I worked at the prosecutor's office. Everybody knows Cade."

I shook my head. "Don't tell him that."

"Wouldn't think of it."

Our meals came and I couldn't help but notice the look on Danny's face.

"What are you smiling about?"

Danny picked up his knife and fork. "I was just thinking about what a wonderful conversation I had with a nursery owner about buying a facility with forty acres of greenhouses."

"Honestly?" said Emily.

"Yep." Danny took a bite of whitefish. "Let me know if you have questions. Or need any forms."

"You have some?"

"Dozens. And I'm happy to give them all away."

The rest of the meal was spent with conversation about Emily's last days at the prosecutor's office, Danny's daughter Ruth's reluctance to sleep, and the waiting IT crisis back at the office.

EMILY WAS A WHIRLWIND. By the time I hooked her computer up to our network and set up her office, she had half of the Carver file scanned and sorted.

And yes, it is more efficient to just produce things on a thumb drive or by Dropbox or by any other kind of electronic method, which is why the prosecutor gave us boxes of paper.

I was watching the piles shrink on one side of the table and grow on the other when Emily said, "I think you'll want to see this," and flipped me a newly stapled stack of paper.

It was a calendar.

It was not an actual physical calendar; instead, it looked like someone had printed out a monthly electronic calendar from a phone or computer. When I saw a "*Torch* editorial meeting" marked every Monday at eight a.m., I assumed it was Marsh's.

There were no appointments listed for Friday, the day Marsh was murdered. Earlier in the week I saw two calls scheduled— one said, "Lacombe Distillery call" and the other "Ringel— Paxton Plating."

Lacombe Distillery sounded familiar, but Lacombe was also a pretty common name around here so I couldn't be sure. I looked it up and found the distillery was right here in town, just north of Carrefour on an old farm. Its website featured a picture of a man standing next to a barrel, a small glass in his hand, with a caption that read, "André Lacombe celebrates his first barrel. Photo courtesy of the *Ash County Torch*."

I skimmed through a summary to the bottom of the page where there was a link that said, Full article here. I clicked through to the website of the *Ash County Torch* which showed an article about Lacombe Distillery written by Christopher Marsh.

The article was part of a monthly series highlighting local businesses. A quick check of the dates showed it was published the Sunday before he died. The focus seemed to be that André Lacombe, the descendant of a family of farmers that had settled in Carrefour a few generations back, was reviving a whiskey brand using old family recipes.

Then I did the same thing with Paxton Plating. I found the company website—it was an electroplating operation with five locations in North America, one of which was in the middle of Ash County. The Ash County location specialized in the plating of automotive related parts and employed hundreds of people.

I searched a couple of different ways but didn't find any published articles by Christopher Marsh on Paxton Plating. I knew one thing—Ted Ringel wasn't going to tell me voluntarily what he'd discussed with Christopher Marsh about Paxton

Plating that day, so I thought for a moment more, then gave Olivia a call.

"Hey Shep," she said. "I don't have much more on Marsh yet, but I should in a few days."

"I have called not to dip from your bucket but to fill it."

"You sound like you're full of something. What have you got?"

I told her about Christopher Marsh's calendar and the calls he had scheduled for Lacombe Distillery and Paxton Plating, then said, "Could you go through the calendar for the last few weeks, match it up with any other articles, then do research on anything that seems interesting?"

"Interesting as in has a potential connection to his death?"

"You got it."

"Looking to see if anyone had a motive to come after Marsh?"

"Exactly."

"How are you going to explain all of the evidence at the crime scene?"

"As a good friend explained to me once, one brick at a time."

"She sounds wise. And will your good friend see you at a house built of bricks today?"

"Today or tomorrow."

"Today." Then she hung up.

I looked at one of the tabs on my computer that I'd just been looking at and decided there was a bit of research I could do on my own. I called Cade Brickson.

"What's up, Shep?"

"How do you feel about whiskey?"

12

The Lacombe Distillery gave tours every Friday and Saturday; so that Friday afternoon I left the office early and went out to see it. You notice I didn't say that I left work early because what I was doing was, in fact, work.

Yeah, Danny didn't buy it either.

I drove north across the state line and picked up Cade at the Brickhouse. Then we drove out of Carrefour itself into the rolling hills and woods that lay between Carrefour and Dellville.

Cade and I had a chance to catch up on the way—I told him about the Carver case (he agreed that nothing could be done about Logan's bond), and he told me about some of his new bonds, including a guy who had been caught smuggling cigarettes into Ohio.

"Cigarettes?" I said. "From where?"

"Indiana," he said.

"But they have cigarettes in Ohio."

Cade shrugged. "The taxes are a lot less in Indiana. People buy them there and unload them in Ohio."

"How much did your guy have?"

"Not sure. Whatever fits in a van."

"That's a lot of cigarettes."

"It was a lot of bond. There it is." Cade pointed.

A sign hung from a squared post announcing, "Lacombe Distillery," so I followed the green arrow pointing up the gravel drive into the woods. Our view was blocked by trees on either side until we drove about fifty yards, at which point we came to a weathered covered bridge that crossed a stream with deep banks on either side.

Once we crossed, the tree line stopped and a large clearing opened up. There were acres of farmland on our right, an old white farmhouse with a large wraparound porch directly in front of us, and an enormous green barn off to the left where the trees started up again. I parked my Jeep on a gravel lot that was big enough to hold twenty or thirty cars and currently held four.

Another sign had an arrow pointing to the barn that said, "Distillery and Warehouse" and a second arrow pointing toward the house that said, "Tours and Tasting Room."

"Check out the tour?" I said.

Cade shrugged. "I'd rather taste whiskey than see it."

As we climbed the steps, I noticed how big the house was, wide with a wing on either side and a covered porch that wrapped around both corners that had an array of chairs and small tables scattered about. We opened the double door and entered a foyer where a woman with blond hair wearing a blue Oxford shirt with "Lacombe Distillery" on the pocket was standing behind a small wooden stand.

She smiled. "Good afternoon, gentlemen." Her voice had a pleasant rasp to it. "I'm afraid our tour just left, but you're welcome to take a look around the history rooms and have a tasting in back until the next one."

"Perfect," said Cade and made his way toward the back of the house.

"Just go right on through those back doors to the porch."

Cade held a thumbs up as he walked away.

"And how about you?" The woman was in her late twenties or early thirties and her smile went right to her blue eyes.

"You say you have a history room?"

"A couple of them right here on the first floor. My great-grandfather saved all sorts of things from when he first started distilling and so we've set some of them out."

"No kidding."

She nodded, came around the stand, and guided me to a room. "Right over here. You'll find all sorts of things going all the way back to the early 1900s. Are you a history buff?"

"I saw the *Torch* article and it made me curious. I didn't know you were here."

She smiled again. "We've been here for over one hundred years." She held out her hand. "Marie-Josée Lacombe."

I took it. "Nate Shepherd. So the family decided to revive the brand?"

"My dad André did, yes." She led me into what had once been a living room and was now filled with yellow pictures, tattered paper, and old bottles. "My family started as rye farmers and eventually kept a bit for themselves to make the first Carrefour Classic Rye. These are things from when they started the brand."

"It's amazing you kept all this."

"My great-grandfather, Jean-Jacques, hung on to everything. We're lucky."

There was the sound of footsteps and voices from the back of the house and Marie-Josée Lacombe put her hand on my arm and smiled. "One of the tours is back. If you'll excuse me, I have to man the gift shop. Be sure to head back to the taster." Then she hustled off, and I heard her sunny greeting of folks in the next room.

I took a slow walk around the room, absorbing black-and-white pictures of an old still, a warehouse lined with barrels, and a horse-drawn wagon stacked with barrels being driven by a man with a sharp black beard. There were some old empty bottles and a painting of a ravine with a stream running through the bottom of it. I kept walking around a glass case that held yellow papers with faded ink that looked to be recipes and notes, but I didn't stop because none of it had anything to do with what I was interested in, which was their most recent contact with Christopher Marsh.

I went back to the main hallway and past a room that I assumed was the gift shop since I heard Marie-Josée's voice, and out the door to the back porch.

A small bar like you would see at a cocktail party or wedding was set up crossways with three bottles on one side and a small chalkboard on the other. I walked up as Cade sniffed over a glass.

The man behind the bar nodded. He looked to be about my father's age and was tall with a sharp hawkish nose and a mop of steel gray hair that appeared unwilling to be fully subdued. "Smell the difference?" the man asked.

Cade nodded and took a sip. "I like the second one better."

The man behind the bar smiled. "That's why we make them both! The Seared Rye has a spicier finish."

Cade finished the glass, then held out his hand. "It's delicious, André."

"Thank you, Cade. Tell your friends."

Cade pointed at me. "Here's one now."

As Cade moved inside, André Lacombe turned to me with eyes that were the same bright blue as his daughter's. "What would you like to try?"

"I have to admit I'm not sure."

André clapped once. "The sampler it is! This is our Classic Rye, which is aged four years, our Seared Rye, which is a little spicier, and our Eight-Year Special Reserve, which is aged for eight years and finishes as smooth as a mill pond." André filled three small glasses on a wooden paddle and slid it forward.

Now just so we're clear, I tend to drink barley and hops in cold twelve-ounce cans, so I don't know a bourbon from a rye, and I certainly can't tell you whether to spell whiskey with an "E," so I'm not going to be able to relate to you the details of the finishes that André explained to me. I can tell you that the Classic Rye had some heat, the Special Reserve was smooth, and the Seared Rye let you know that you could pleasantly withstand more heat than you thought. If you want more details than that, you're going to have to go talk to the folks at the Lacombe Distillery yourself.

What's important for our purposes was that, as I picked up the Classic Rye, André Lacombe said, "So how did you hear about us?"

"The *Ash County Torch* article."

"You're the third group today. Chris did such a nice job with it." André Lacombe shook his head. "Did you see the news about the *Torch* reporter that was killed?"

"I did."

"That was him. So terrible."

"It was."

"And I talked to him just a few days before."

"Oh? For the story?"

"Sort of. I'd given him my great-grandfather's journal with all of his recipes for the rye whiskey and the mash and things like that. We normally display it out there in the case, but I let Chris take it with him to give him some flavor for the article." André smiled. "With a promise that he would never print the recipes or the mixes, of course. He was calling to apologize that he hadn't gotten it back to me and said that he'd bring it over the next week." André frowned. "I never did get it back and now I'm not even sure how." He looked up. "It's not important, not with what happened, but it would be a shame to lose it."

"You might want to check with the Sheriff's department."

"I don't think we need to ask the police to look for it."

"No, I mean if it was in this reporter's house, they might have taken it as evidence."

André cocked his head.

I shrugged. "Sorry. Lawyer."

"That's not a bad idea...What's your name?"

"Nate," I said as we shook hands, but just then there was the clump of shoes on planks as more people climbed the stairs of the porch.

"That would be the tour group," said André. "Can I answer any more questions for you about the whiskey, Nate?"

"No, thank you, André. Great stuff."

"Tell your friends."

I nodded and stepped back as a group of four couples crowded around the bar and André started pouring samples and answering questions.

I wandered into the gift shop and, in a development that surprised no one, found Cade talking to Marie-Josée Lacombe. She was smiling and Cade made a comment that got her laughing. She put her hand on his forearm and told him he was terrible, then looked over and saw me. "There he is. Did my dad answer your questions?"

"He did."

"You'll have to come by for the whole tour next time."

"Sounds good."

As I took a step away, Cade held up his Lacombe Distillery bag. "So which ones are you buying?"

I nodded a quick thanks for his catching my thoughtlessness. "I'll go with one Classic Rye and one Seared Rye."

"Fantastic," said Marie-Josée Lacombe as she grabbed a bottle of each.

"Tom and Mark will love those," I said to Cade.

Cade nodded. "Seems rude to get your brothers a bottle and not your dad."

Marie-Josée's back was still to me, so I raised an eyebrow at Cade.

He stared back. "Seems like a father deserves the best one."

I sighed. "Better add a bottle of the Special Reserve too, Marie-Josée."

"Great!" She grabbed the third bottle.

As she put the bottles in a custom bag, she said, "So how about you, Nate? Do you go to plays very often?"

"Not really. But I enjoy it when I do."

"Cade was just telling me he had tickets to the Carrefour Grand Theatre tomorrow."

I nodded. "My brother and sister-in-law went last week and said the production was something else."

Marie-Josée Lacombe finished loading the bag, handed me my receipt, and said, "Well, I look forward to seeing you."

I didn't know that I'd be coming back to the distillery anytime soon, but she was altogether too pleasant, so I said, "Me too."

As we walked away, Josie said, "Six o'clock, Cade?"

"Perfect," he said.

As the two of us walked out to the gravel lot, I said, "Taking her to the show tomorrow?"

"No. You are."

I stopped and looked at him.

Cade shrugged. "I had four tickets." Then he kept walking.

13

I tried to avoid going to the office on Saturdays but I needed to on this particular morning to handle some administrative work, especially with Emily starting early. I was surprised to find Danny standing at the coffee pot.

"What's going on?" I said.

"Working on the purchase of that greenhouse business. The zoning is more complicated than I thought. You?"

"I need to finish Emily's paperwork."

Emily popped out of her office. "Find anything at the distillery?"

"What are you doing here?"

Emily smirked. "Good to see you too, Boss."

"You know what I mean. You don't have to work on Saturdays."

She waved at Danny and me. "Clearly."

"I mean, unless we have something going on."

She shrugged. "I wanted to finish setting up my computer and get started on the Carver timeline. Do you have a few minutes to talk?"

"Sure." We went into her office and sat down. "Shoot."

Emily checked her notes. "From what you told me, Logan robbed the house, but we don't know when except that it was maybe after eight."

"Right."

"Then he goes to McDonald's for shakes, goes to Second Chance Electronics, then goes home?"

"So far as I know."

"Then he's home all day on Saturday until he's arrested Saturday night?"

"Yep."

Emily stared at her notes. "Seems like odd things to do after murdering someone."

"I'm not sure what someone does after that, but I think I agree. If Logan's not a criminal mastermind, and I don't think he is, there should have been signs when he went to those places. Why don't you try the McDonald's and see if you can find any witnesses."

"Do you think they'll talk to me?"

"No idea. It's the one on Eighth Street."

Emily nodded then said, "So. The Distillery?"

I told her about André Lacombe's call with Christopher Marsh about returning the journal.

"So nothing there."

"No. I have Olivia looking into Paxton Plating, but the best source for what the call was about won't talk to us."

"That's this Ringel guy?"

"Right."

"Because he thinks our client did it?"

"Exactly."

"What if we subpoena any communications between Marsh and Ringel for a couple of weeks before the murder?"

I thought about it. "He'll raise hell about impinging on a free press."

Emily shrugged. "So we let him redact any protected material. Any info would help."

"That's a good idea, Emily. Let me call Ted first as a courtesy to see if he'll give us any materials voluntarily then if he turns us down, like he probably will, we can subpoena it."

"On it, Boss."

"Don't draft the subpoena today, though. Go ahead and get out of here for the weekend."

Emily shrugged. "As soon as I'm done. I don't have to be anywhere until three-thirty."

"Yeah? What's going on?"

"I'm going to my fiancé's house to watch the Buckeyes."

"Big fan?"

"Never miss a game."

I stood and went to the door so I could look into both offices. "You're fired, Danny."

Danny didn't look up. "Why now?"

"You were in charge of screening resumes."

"And?"

"She's an Ohio State fan."

"Stands to reason."

"Why?"

"Since she graduated from Ohio State. You did read the resume, didn't you?"

"I talked to Judge Gallon."

"So that's a no?"

"I skimmed it."

"Don't worry," said Emily. "I'm very discreet."

"Yeah?"

"Yeah. You won't hear a peep out of me when we whoop Sparty."

I snorted.

"Again," she said.

"I blame you for this," I said to Danny.

"Your name's on the door."

"O-H," said Emily.

I pointed. "That's too far."

"*I-O*," Emily mouthed.

I went to my office, vowing aloud to pay closer attention to future hires. Neither of my associates were impressed.

Even though it was Saturday, I knew Ted Ringel would be working, so I gave him a call. He didn't answer, which didn't surprise me. I left him a message asking him to call, then wrote a follow-up email, asking if we could have copies of Christopher Marsh's emails and notes with *Torch* personnel for the last two months without issuing a subpoena.

About half an hour later, I received an email back from Ted Ringel, telling me that the *Torch* would not be providing Logan Carver's defense team with any information voluntarily and that all further correspondence should be directed to the *Torch's* attorney, Fred Pressfield, whose contact information was attached.

A moment later, my phone buzzed. It was a text message from Ted, encouraging me to go right off and develop an intimate relationship with myself.

"Emily?" I said.

"Yeah?" she called back from her office.

"Draft that *Torch* subpoena Monday."

"You got it."

"So we're a yelling office now?" said Danny from his.

"What?" I said.

"No funnier though."

14

J ust before six that night, I met Cade at the bar of a nice
steak house on the west side of Carrefour. I ordered a
beer, then said, "So what's with all this, anyway?"

Cade sipped his drink. "All what?"

I waved at the bar. "This."

Cade shrugged. "You need to get out. I know her friend."

"I've been out."

Cade stared. "With someone who doesn't live here anymore."

"She might come back."

"So just have dinner."

My wife Sarah had died a few years ago. This past summer, I
had dated a woman named Kira, but Kira had moved away, and
we'd agreed before she left that that was probably it. Cade had
apparently decided that there wasn't going to be another
mourning period. I suppose he wasn't wrong. Still irritating, of
course, but not wrong.

Cade raised a hand and a tall woman with dark hair at the
door returned the wave. Marie-Josée Lacombe appeared next to
her and gave me a quick smile. We stood and the dark-haired

woman greeted Cade with an enthusiasm that indicated they were acquainted.

Marie-Josée rolled her eyes. Her blond hair was down and her blue eyes were bright enough to be distracting, which was saying something given the blue dress she was wearing. "So you didn't bale once you heard the plot?" she said.

I smiled. "Happy to be fooled. But I'd like to think I could've managed it on my own."

Cade snorted. "In a year."

I ignored him. "What would you like?"

Josie (which she preferred to Marie-Josée) ordered a white wine while her friend (who turned out to be Amelia) took a Moscow Mule complete with the copper mug. We'd made it through the introductions—Amelia and Josie worked at the same hospital here in town and Amelia had met Cade a few months back when she was working at the Detroit car show—when the lights on our pager started flashing.

"That's us," said Cade, and the four of us headed over to the hostess stand. As Cade handed her the pager, the hostess said, "Two for Shepherd?"

"That's right," said Cade.

Josie and I stopped and stared. Amelia giggled as Cade put his arm around her and said, "Have a good night, kids." Amelia waved and the two of them left.

"Right this way, please," said the hostess.

The two of us looked at each other, laughed, and followed.

Once we were seated, Josie said, "Nate, I wasn't in on that part. I thought we were all going out together."

I smiled. "Your turn to bale if you want."

"No, I don't mean that, I mean..."

"I'm happy to be here, Josie."

She smiled. "Me too."

The server gave us a brief break from the awkwardness by

telling us about the specials. After he'd left, I said, "So, if you're a respiratory therapist, you don't work at the distillery full-time?"

She shook her head. "No, I just give my dad a hand over there when I'm off."

"Is that the house where you grew up, at the farm?"

"No, the farm belongs to the whole Lacombe family. I grew up in another house a couple of miles away."

A name clicked. "Are you related to that guy running for state rep, with the initials?"

"JP Lacombe?"

"That's it, JP. His signs are everywhere."

Josie nodded. "He's my cousin."

"Is he involved in the distillery too?"

"No. He's busy running his campaign. The distillery is Dad's baby."

The server stopped by for our order, after which Josie said, "But that's enough whiskey talk. How about you? Amelia said you're a lawyer?"

"I am."

"What do you do?"

"I've done all sorts of trial work. The last few years, I've mostly been doing criminal defense."

"Oh, yeah?" Her eyes sparkled. "Representing any murderers?"

"Uhm."

"You're kidding."

"I am not."

I had a choice here. I could play it off and avoid talking about what brought me out to the Distillery the other day or I could let her know up front what had happened and see if my dinner for two became a dinner for one. I decided life's too short to screw around.

"Actually, that's one of the reasons I was out at your place the other day."

Josie tilted her head. "Why?"

"I'm representing the man accused of killing the reporter who did the story on your distillery."

It took her a second to process. Then she did. "You're representing the man who killed Chris?"

"The man accused of it. They've arrested my client, but I don't know that he did it."

Josie looked concerned. I didn't blame her. "What does the Distillery have to do with it?"

"Turns out nothing. Your dad had an appointment with Marsh the week he died, but it turned out it was just a call to get some materials back from their interview."

"That's it?"

"That's what your dad told me."

Josie was frowning, spinning the stem of her wine glass back and forth when her face cleared. "Wait, Cade and I set you up on this date."

"You did."

"Then Amelia and Cade dumped us."

"So it appears."

"You're the only one who wasn't in on us having dinner."

"That's right."

"So our date can't be related to your case."

"I wish I were that good."

She smiled. "Well, that's okay then."

"I'm glad."

"But we can stop talking about death and whiskey?"

"I'd prefer it."

Something clearly occurred to her.

"Uh-oh," I said.

"As long as we're dealing with awkward topics..."

I smiled, raised my beer to her, and drank. "Shoot."

"I was married."

"Me too." I paused. "My wife Sarah passed a few years ago."

Josie blinked. "Really?"

"Yes."

"So did my husband Peter."

"I'm sorry."

"Car accident. Sarah?"

"Accidental overdose."

Things were quiet, but only for a second.

"How are you doing?" I said.

"Better than I was. You?"

"Same. It took a while to get on top of it though."

"Same here. Good friends made a difference."

"All the difference. Family too." She looked down for a moment. "I hope you'll forgive this question, but have you dated anyone since?"

"This past summer was the first time."

She smiled. "Last winter for me. And that makes me more optimistic about dinner."

Then the server came and delivered a ribeye, a filet, and two large dishes of asparagus and potatoes to share.

"It smells delicious," Josie said, but she didn't pick up her knife and fork.

"It does."

"Do you miss her?"

"I do. You?"

"Every day."

Then she handed me the asparagus.

I am very aware that this all sounded like the absolute worst possible beginning to a first date. But I can't begin to tell you how strange it was to always avoid talking about a major portion of my life, to constantly be confronted with a wave of awkwardness or sympathy when someone learned my history for the first time. And I can't fully describe what a relief it was to *not* have that hanging over my head, to not be worried about an out-sized reaction to some small detail just because it's tied to that history, and what a joy it was to jump right into a free-flowing conversation of our shared acquaintances, experiences, and interests.

We ate every bite and even ordered dessert.

15

The next day was a Sunday in September, so that meant Roxie and I piled into my Jeep and headed up to my parents' place on Glass Lake. It was a little ways north into Michigan, nestled between rolling hills and a wooded state park with distinctive groves of trees. My dad loved the water and my mom loved attracting grandkids, so the place was perfect for them.

The pro football season was underway, so that meant our Sunday afternoons on the water were replaced with watching the Detroit Lions, although my dad's cook out remained the same. My whole family was usually there—my older brother Tom, his wife Kate, their daughters Reed, Taylor, and Page, and little Charlie, their son. My younger brother Mark would be there with his wife Izzy, and their three boys Justin, James, and Joe. It can be confusing with all of the Shepherds running around making a ruckus, but if you remember that the girls go with Tom and Kate and that all of the "J" boys go with Mark and Izzy, you won't go wrong. To be honest though, none of us will mind if you make a mistake.

As I pulled in, it looked like I was the last one there, so I grabbed the chips and dips that were my assignment and hurried in with Roxie. James, Joe, and Page flung open the door to meet us and immediately hugged Roxie. Take that for what you will.

As the kids pulled Roxie into the yard, I ducked into the house where the game was on and my family was scattered about. I gave my mom a hug, took the bowls she offered, and filled them with chips. As I popped open some French onion dip, my brother Tom said, "How is the guy with no kids and the least stuff always the last one here?"

"Sorry. Roxie had a conference call with the Boxer Association."

"Hear that, Mark? It was the dog's fault."

Mark shrugged. "Lawyer. Always shifting blame."

Izzy smacked her husband Mark's leg. "Leave him alone." She grinned. "He's probably exhausted from being out late last night."

"That's me. Just a regular party animal."

"Uh-huh." She smirked. "So, how was the show?"

I focused on opening a jar of salsa that was giving me trouble.

"And who was the blond?"

The jar popped open. "Sweet Jesus, Izzy, it hasn't even been twenty-four hours. How do you..." I stopped, but it was too late.

Izzy cackled and pointed. "It *was* you then! Corey wasn't sure."

I had no idea who Corey was in Izzy's apparently vast network of spies and I wasn't going to ask. I decided silence was the best course.

"Hear that, Kate?" said Izzy.

Kate rounded the corner from the kitchen. "I did." She handed a pop to Tom and opened a seltzer for herself. "Spill, mortal."

Now if I said her name, hordes of Shepherds, well, two in particular, would launch an electronic and social investigation that would put J. Edgar to shame, so I said, "It was a blind date. Cade asked us to double with him and a date for the show."

Izzy kept grinning. "Oh? Corey didn't see Cade."

I nodded. "He wasn't there. They baled."

"So it was just the two of you?" said Kate.

"And two thousand other people marveling at the rotating stage, yes. Speaking of which, when are you going?"

Kate elbowed Tom. "When are you going to take me?"

"Did you see what they're charging for tickets?" said Tom.

"Worth every penny," I said. "Right, Mark?"

Mark nodded. "Best money I ever spent."

Tom visibly squelched his desire to kill his brothers. "Maybe next time it comes through, honey. You know how it is during football season."

"I do," Kate said and kissed Tom's cheek.

"And how about you, Nate?" said Izzy. "Will there be a return engagement?"

"They're about to kick off," said my dad.

I shrugged at Izzy, pointed to the TV and my dad, and we all watched the ball soar into the air of Ford Field.

IT WAS HALFTIME BEFORE I remembered my gifts. "Be right back," I said, and went to the Jeep to retrieve the bottle bag. As I came back in, I handed a bottle each to Mark, Tom, and my dad. "I was out at a distillery this week for work and picked up a few bottles."

My dad peered at the label. "Thanks, son. What is it?"

"It a special reserve rye whiskey that a local distillery makes.

Supposedly, it's based on an old family recipe that goes back a few generations."

My mom came out of the kitchen, plate in hand. "What distillery is that, son?"

"The Lacombe Distillery. It's just north of here."

My mom nodded. "That was thoughtful of you." Then she put the plate on the table and disappeared back around the corner.

"Thanks, son," said my dad with a glance at the kitchen.

"What's Seared Rye?" said Mark.

"It's spicier than the regular stuff. Thought you'd like it."

"Absolutely."

"Is it too expensive to mix?" said Tom.

"You can drink it anyway you want."

"Game's on," said my dad and put the bottle on the far side of his chair next to the wall.

IMMEDIATELY AFTER THE GAME (AN ENTERTAINING, heart-breaking, last-second loss in case you're wondering), my dad went out to the deck to fire up the grill for some chicken. Since Izzy's attention seemed to be circling back around to the theater the night before, I decided to join him.

It was sunny and warm for a fall day with only the slightest crisp of the chill to come. I looked out at the lake and said, "Keeping the dock in for a while yet?"

My dad nodded. "I should be able to take the boat out for a few weeks yet. Don't want to waste it."

As he scooped up leg quarters with his tongs and laid them out over the flames, he said, "You know, speaking of waste, why don't you take the bottle of rye with you when you go?"

"Really?"

He concentrated on lining up the chicken to get the most out of the grill space. "Yeah, I just don't have the stomach for rye anymore. Got sick on it some years ago and really haven't been able to drink it since."

I smiled. "You? Sick?"

He gave me a half-smile. "There was probably kryptonite in it. Happens to the best of us. Anyway, I'd hate to waste it. I know it's expensive."

"I don't mind that."

"But I do."

The chicken was arrayed, just like it was every Sunday, but my dad still adjusted it, getting the perfect angle for the flames.

"No problem."

"I do appreciate the thought though, son."

"Sure, Dad."

So before I left that afternoon, I found the bottle of the Eight-Year Special Reserve Rye still laying between my dad's chair and the wall and took it home with Roxie and me.

OCTOBER

16

The following Monday, I was in my office when my phone buzzed with a number I hadn't seen in some time.

"Nate? This is prosecutor T. Marvin Stritch."

"T. Marvin! I missed you at the Carver arraignment the other day. How are things?"

"Very well indeed, Nate."

"Your Assistant Prosecutor let slip that you were at a candidate breakfast."

"Young people are not as circumspect as they once were."

"That's the truth. I didn't think there were any judge races this year. Are you considering something else?"

"There weren't, but I find that it never hurts to keep your name in the forefront of people's minds."

"True enough."

"And my foresight has been rewarded."

"How so?"

"I don't know if you've heard, but I am going to be elevated to the bench."

"I had not, T. Marvin. Congratulations! Very well deserved."

"I am certainly the most qualified to take the seat, but it is still gratifying to know that the appointment is coming through."

"I bet. Who's leaving?"

"Judge LaPlante."

"He's not sick, is he?"

"My no, he's fine. He's decided to take a job with a regulatory company up in Lansing."

"I didn't think he had his years in yet."

"He's just a few short, but apparently this opportunity was too good to pass up."

"Good for him. When's the big day?"

"Judge LaPlante is leaving in a couple of weeks and his docket is quite full, so they anticipate my getting the appointment within a couple weeks after that. Of course, I will be even-handed with both defense counsel and prosecutors, so you need not worry about any bias from me."

"Hadn't crossed my mind, Your Honor."

T. Marvin Stritch paused, then chuckled. "You're the first one to call me that."

"First of many. So who will be taking over the Carver case?"

"That's why I wanted to call you. Once I take the bench, my fellow circuit judges and I will have to appoint a replacement prosecutor who will serve out the rest of my term. I know of a few candidates, but I'm sure my brother and sister judges have thoughts as well."

"I'm sure."

"So it may be a few weeks while this sorts itself out. We're still quite a ways from trial so I don't think it will have any real impact right now, but I just wanted to let you know that things might be delayed for a time."

"I understand."

"But I assure you, you will have our DNA and forensic

testing as soon as it's done. I will leave detailed notes and instructions for my successor."

"I appreciate that. Thank you."

"As I said, unbiased. We won't be on opposite sides anymore, but I look forward to having you appear before me."

"Sure thing. And congratulations again, Your Honor."

"Oh, come now Nate, we've tried a case against each other. You can still call me T. Marvin in private."

"Thanks, T. Marvin. Take care."

I hung up and shot Emily an email telling her what happened. I had no idea who would be replacing T. Marvin, but it sounded like I would have a couple of months to continue putting the case together before that person got involved.

I went back to work, contemplating the delight that it would be to try a case in front of T. Marvin Stritch someday and being grateful that we were in front of Judge Wesley right now.

THAT NIGHT when I walked into the Brickhouse, Olivia was waiting for me.

"Mr. Shepherd, just in time. Would you like our New Member Tour?"

"Hi, Liv."

"We can show you where all the equipment is, explain gym protocols."

"I'm good."

"We've also found that the tour helps old members get re-acclimated to our environment after a protracted absence."

"Liv, I was here two days ago."

"And you wouldn't want that kind of absenteeism to become a habit now, would you?"

"I'll manage."

"Well, don't be shy about asking for a spot, especially if you try squats with those baby colt legs of yours."

"I do work, you know."

"Yes, you're the only one. Speaking of which, I have some information on Paxton Plating."

It took me a moment to recall the Paxton Plating entry on Christopher Marsh's calendar. "So what do we know?"

"You know they're an electroplating company that finishes parts for the auto industry?"

"I do."

"The factory here is one of five in North America. Guess what was announced over the weekend?"

"No idea."

"A four-hundred-million-dollar acquisition of Paxton Plating."

"That much?"

"Five facilities and a premium on top. By all accounts, the market has come together to create a one-time opportunity."

"And Marsh was doing something on Paxton last month."

"Exactly."

"Sounds like I really need to get a hold of his *Torch* file."

"I think you do. And when you do, give it to me, and we'll do some real investigation."

"Perfect. Thanks, Liv."

As I took a step toward the locker room, she said, "So, how was the show?"

"Did someone take a billboard out or something?"

"I am an investigator, you know."

"It was good."

"And the company?"

"Also good."

"And beautiful I hear."

I sighed. "She was very nice."

I stood there. So did Olivia.

She broke first and smiled. "Is there anything else you'd like to tell me about her?"

"Not right now, no."

"Okay. Well, when you do want to talk about Marie-Josée Lacombe of the famous Lacombe family, I'm always here for you."

I realized that what I'd mistaken for a smile was actually an evil smirk. "Could we maybe see if we get to a second or third date first?"

"I'll just check on my own then."

"Honestly, that's obnoxious."

"Honestly obnoxious is part of my charm. The weights are that way."

"Thanks."

I had peace for the first half of my workout before Cade came over.

"Did you two hit it off?"

"Yeah, actually."

"Amelia thought you might."

"Thanks for the tickets."

"Wouldn't have used them. Are you going to call her on your own or do I have to arrange that too?"

"I can handle it."

"Don't wait too long."

"Why's that?"

"If you found a sack of money on the sidewalk, would you pick it up or circle back around the next day to see if it's still there?"

"I'd call the police to see if there'd been a robbery."

Cade sighed. "That's why you can't handle it alone." Cade glanced at the bar I was using. "I'll let you finish your warm-up," he said, and walked away.

I cursed him, added ten pounds to the bar that already held damn near all I could lift, and thought about finding new friends.

WHEN I CAME HOME that night, I took Roxie for a walk first thing. There was an inordinate number of rabbits hopping about so she was pulling more than normal. I think her service training had kept her from doing that at first, but either she had gotten the memo that she was retired or she'd come to associate me with play. The joy was fun to see.

When we got home, Roxie flopped down on the kitchen floor next to me as I started making dinner for one. I flipped the TV on, more for noise than programming, and was considering the merits of chicken thighs versus pork tenderloin when I heard the news report.

"State representative JP Lacombe joined members of the medical and education communities today to announce a campaign against vaping."

A different voice said, "These products are targeted at our children. Why else would they make flavors like berry and apple and vanilla? I stand here with teachers and doctors— dedicated professionals who are seeing kids use these products and seeing kids get sick from them. If re-elected to the House, I will introduce legislation to eliminate the most egregious products from the market, raise the age of purchase, and impose a greater tax on adults to reduce the use of these harmful products."

I peeked around the refrigerator door at the screen. A tall man with blond hair and a gray suit stood in front of a group in white coats. He looked about my age and had one fist on a lectern as the screen flipped back to a news anchor.

"JP Lacombe is widely considered to be on the short-list for Michigan's Speaker of the House if he wins re-election."

The newscast went to commercial, right into an ad for JP Lacombe asking, *Who will represent you in Lansing?* With the election only a month away, I knew the ads would only get worse.

The Bricksons and the commercial put Josie Lacombe on my mind. I texted if she had time for a call. She said sorry, she didn't, she was on shift right then.

Now I was stuck. I hesitated for a moment since a text really didn't seem like the right way to do it, but I was now under a blinking, three-dot time bomb, so I asked if she wanted to go out Saturday. Pretty quickly, she texted back that she was working Saturday but was off Friday. I told her that sounded good to me. She said great, let's talk Thursday for details. I sent a cringeworthy "great" right back then put the phone down like a hand grenade with the pin pulled out, which I suppose is terrible analogy because it means I would've been blown to bits ten seconds later, but honestly, negotiating all this dating etiquette was about all I could handle.

Roxie flipped over and sighed.

17

W hen I entered the office the next day, Emily and Danny were talking by the coffee maker. They abruptly stopped.

I smiled. "What plots are being hatched here?"

"Emily just took a call from the new prosecutor in the Carver case," Danny said.

"Really? Stritch just told me about the change yesterday. He said they weren't appointing someone for a couple of weeks at least."

"They appear to have moved faster. "

"Okay. So who was it?"

Danny tilted his mug at Emily, who said, "Silas Winford."

I scowled. "Does he have a son or something?"

"No. *The* Silas Winford."

I blinked.

Emily nodded. "He said you can call him Sye, though."

I continued to process. "You're telling me Silas Winford is the acting prosecutor for Ash County?"

"No. He'd like to tell you that when you call him back on the Carver case."

~

WHEN I WAS twelve years old, my buddy Zach Stephenson got his hands on an M-80. His brother had driven across the state line to one of those fireworks shacks that magically opened along the border every summer and had purchased four of them at a Labor Day close out sale. He had given one to Zach who had run straight over to my house to present it to me, cupped in his hand like it was a blood diamond.

I don't know about you, but where I grew up, all the kids said that an M-80 was the equivalent of a quarter of a stick of dynamite and, although everyone seemed to have a story about a cousin or a friend or a kid one school over who'd lit one, very few had done it themselves, as was demonstrated by their full complement of fingers.

Of course, these stories didn't just involve loud booms and ringing ears. Invariably, they involved blowing something up. Zach and I weren't cruel, so there would be no frogs, and we weren't (totally) dumb, which meant a garbage can or other shrapnel-creating container was out, so we were stumped until we realized that it was September and there were pumpkins for sale.

Since Zach was supplying the munitions, it seemed fair that I supply the pumpkin, so I biked to Morsette's market, picked up the biggest pumpkin five bucks would buy (which was disappointingly small), and pedaled one-handed to the field behind Zach's house. We cut the top off jack-o-lantern style and scooped out most of the seed-mush to create some space but not all of it because you have to spatter something. After a brief debate, we agreed Zach would light the M-80, I would drop the pumpkin lid back on, and we'd both run like hell.

That's how it went and, being twelve, we were fast enough to get away but dumb enough (despite foregoing metal garbage cans) to stop and turn entirely too close to the small pumpkin when the M-80 exploded, unleashing a concussive boom, a cloud of smoke, and a glorious hail of pumpkin guts. Our ears ringing, we went back to look at the shallow depression and rind fragments that were all the oversized explosive had left of our undersized pumpkin.

On an unrelated note, Silas Winford was going to be prosecuting Logan Carver.

Silas Winford had been the Attorney General for the State of Michigan for years. He'd made his name as a young county prosecutor when he took down a cold case serial killer and a Fortune 100 CEO in the same year and had leveraged that national publicity into state office. As the State's chief prosecutor, he'd cracked down on organized crime, spearheaded an effort to eradicate public corruption, and fought the war on drugs.

That was just the administrative side of his office. What had kept him in the headlines was when he would leave the state capital in Lansing to handle prosecutions personally, usually when national counsel flew in to defend a case. A company that sold an adulterated drug, a mayor who'd accepted a series of payoffs, and a CEO who had hired out the death of his second wife before marrying his third all went down after Silas Winford decided their cases needed his personal attention.

I was pretty sure Winford had left office about a decade ago. I remembered that he'd chosen not to run again to pursue other interests, but I didn't remember what. He left, mind you—he wasn't defeated in an election—and now, if what Emily said was true, he was getting back in the game. In Ash County.

It appeared that I was being set up to be Nate Shepherd, Pumpkin at Law.

I dialed the number from Emily to find out. I spoke to a receptionist who forwarded me to a legal assistant who told me that Mr. Winford was out but had wanted to speak to me so if I'd wait just a moment, she'd patch me through.

A few seconds later, a baritone voice said, "Nate, Sye Winford. Thanks for calling me back so quickly."

"Hi, Sye. I had a message that you might be visiting our part of the state."

"Indeed, Nate, indeed. Hence the call."

"How can I help? Restaurant recommendation? Hotel?"

Winford chuckled. "This is a professional call, not a personal one, Nate, although I would be happy to hear your culinary suggestions when I'm down there. No, I'm going to be appointed to a special term as prosecutor by the Chief Judge down there, sort of a stop gap until someone can be elected a year from now."

"Are you running?"

He chuckled again in a deep rumble. "No, no, no grand plans here. As I understand it, Judge LaPlante's departure took the county off guard. I know a couple of the judges from my Attorney General days and when they offered a chance to step back into the courtroom for a time, well, I had to think about it, but I eventually succumbed to temptation."

"You couldn't have thought that long, Sye."

"A long time for me, I suppose then."

"Well, welcome back. What have you been up to?"

"Getting soft up here in Grosse Point. Oh, I've been doing some corporate litigation and served on some boards, more consulting than anything else, but it's not the same as entering the lists yourself now, is it?"

"I'll take your word for it, Sye."

The chuckling rumble. "I suppose you will. I understand you've been stepping into the arena quite a bit lately."

"Here and there. Nothing like you."

"And disarmingly modest too. This will be fun."

"I take it you're handling the Carver case then?"

"I am. There aren't many murders there in Ash County, so I wanted to contact you to let you know I'll be handling the case personally."

"I look forward to working with you."

"And I you, Nate. Now I understand that T. Marvin Stritch— do you know he goes by the whole thing? T. Marvin?"

"I do."

"How bad must the 'T.' be? Anyway, I understand T. Marvin gave you the basics before he was appointed to the bench— inventory from the scene, photos, potential witnesses, that kind of thing?"

"That's right."

"But no testing results yet—fingerprints, fibers, DNA, right?"

"Right, we haven't been given any of that."

"I'll send you everything we have right away."

"I appreciate that."

"Now, you'll have to excuse me, I'm just getting up to speed on all of this, but it seems to me that you would want Christopher Marsh's files from the *Torch* so you can see where he was and what he was doing before he died."

I was glad we were on the phone because I blinked. "Yes, I do. I've requested it, but they aren't interested in producing it."

"That's what I figured. I know the *Torch's* attorney, a guy named Fred Pressfield out of Lansing who handles all of the big media outlets in the state, so I gave him a call. He's a decent enough guy, but he's being sort of a pain in the ass on this, bent my ear about the First Amendment and confidential sources for I don't know how long, so I told him we'd cut right to it and take it to Judge Wesley. We'll have a hearing next week."

"It's scheduled?"

"My associate just got off the phone with the clerk, I'll send you the notice after we hang up."

"Thanks but, why would you do that?"

That rumbling chuckle. "Don't get me wrong, Nate, I'll probably move to keep all of it out at trial since it certainly looks like your client got caught red-handed—or red-batted, I should say. But we both should know everything there is to know going into trial, and then the judge can decide what to keep out."

"Which helps protect you on appeal."

That rumble again. "Just as sharp as I'd heard. I'll work out of my Detroit office for now, but I'll be in Ash County at least once a week to mind the store and then move there full time as the trial heats up."

"Makes sense."

"In the meantime, I'll forward you my contact information along with my secretary, legal assistants, and associates who will be on the case. If you ever can't reach me, one of them will be able to."

"I appreciate that."

"Pleasure meeting you by phone, Nate. I'll see you at the hearing if we don't talk before."

Silas Winford hung up and I swear not thirty seconds later, an email popped into my inbox with the address, office phone, cell, and email contact information for him, a legal assistant, two paralegals, and three associates whom I could reach out to any time I had a question.

I'd barely finished reading when Emily's head popped in the doorway.

"Was it him?"

"Yep."

"Is he handling the case?"

"Personally."

"Why?"

I shook my head. "He's homesick for the arena."

Emily waved a hand. "Maybe it'll take him a little while to shake the rust off."

As she spoke, a motion to compel the *Torch* to produce its files, calendars, emails, and stories for the sixty days prior to Christopher Marsh's death appeared in my inbox, along with a notice of hearing for the next week.

"Consider it shaken."

18

"What do you mean?" said Emily.

I explained that Winford had already put things in motion to get the *Torch* files. "So hold off on the *Torch* subpoena for now."

"That thing she worked on all weekend?" came Danny's voice from his office.

"Don't you have a stock to sell or an Inc. to corporate?" I looked back to Emily. "Sorry."

Emily waved. "Part of the job, Boss."

"How are you doing on the timeline after the break-in?"

Emily brightened. "I've got something! We already had the video of Logan at Second Chance Electronics. That was at 10:15 p.m."

"Right."

"You know how Logan told you that he went to McDonald's after he rob—after he may or may not have been at Marsh's house."

"I do."

"The manager at the McDonald's remembers Logan being in the drive-thru that night!"

"How in the world does he remember that?"

Emily grinned. "Turns out Logan ordered two shakes, dropped the second shake, then threw a stink that it was the cashier's fault. He was yelling the whole time they got him a replacement."

"I suppose that makes an impression."

"And, as part of their 'customer incident procedure,' the manager kept the video, just in case."

"'Customer incident procedure?'"

"Turns out people are assholes at drive-thrus more often than you think."

"So we have a time?"

"9:02 p.m."

"Alright, so that's a new time on the back end. Let's keep cobbling these things together—the narrower we can make the window where Logan could have committed the killing, the better. Good work."

Emily nodded. "What about the bat?"

"One thing at a time."

"Sure. But what about the bat?"

I sighed and sat down. "The bat's a problem. Winford said he'd get us DNA test results soon, but I don't have any doubts whose blood it was."

Emily nodded. "How could it have gotten in Logan's trunk if he didn't do it?"

"That is the question, isn't it? The simplest answer is either he did it or someone put it in there."

"I don't know that people will believe someone else it put in there."

"I agree. But that's the direction we may have to go. I suppose our first step is to figure out where it came from."

"We don't know?"

I shook my head. "Logan says it isn't his. That means

someone brought it to Marsh's house or it was already there. Find out if Marsh played softball. If he did, that might be our answer."

"Do you think that matters?"

"I don't know yet."

We were quiet for a few moments before Emily said, "Do you think he did it?"

I was quiet for a few moments more before I said, "I don't know. But I think there's enough floating around this that makes me doubt it."

"What if we get him off and it turns out he did?"

Now did not seem like the time to give Emily a description of just how incredibly shitty that makes you feel. Instead, I said, "We do our best to investigate the case, we always tell the truth, and we try the best case we can. What happens after that is out of our control."

"That seems like a cop-out, Nate."

"Maybe, but that's our life on this side of the line. Regret your choice?"

"Hell no. This was the experience I wanted."

Danny stuck his head into the office. "Hey Emily, do you have time to help me with some due diligence on my greenhouse transaction?"

"Sure," Emily said. "What's due diligence?"

I scooted out to refill my coffee before Danny could explain that he had just roped her into sitting in her office for days reviewing corporate documents.

When I heard her say, "How many?!" I figured I'd made the right choice.

rtisan Square sat on the northern fringe of downtown Carrefour. It was a section of old shops and warehouses that had thrived in the early 1900s, fallen into disrepair and blight in the late 1900s, and undergone a slow revitalization over the last ten years. The cheap, abandoned sites became the perfect incubators for budding artisans to build workshops, to practice their crafts, and to set up storefronts to display their art. There were traditional galleries and shared studios for painters and sculptors and jewelry makers, but there was also a section of craftspeople that you just don't see as often; potters had room for wheels and kilns, glassblowers had space for furnaces and grinders, and there was an honest-to-goodness blacksmith with a massive forge and room to swing his hammer.

Over the past few years, the resident artisans had taken to opening their doors on Friday nights to make it easy for people to wander in and out. Soon, food trucks had begun making their appearance and, before long, the more prosperous shop owners had gone in on obtaining a license to sell beer and wine from stands in the central square. Once the city saw that was successful, a couple of councilmen had jumped in and secured funding to renovate the decrepit fountain at the center of the square, which allowed them to unveil it with great ceremony and take credit for the surrounding revitalization.

In fairness, the fountain was a nice feature. It was also an easy place to meet up and that's where I found Josie Lacombe, sitting on the fountain's edge, watching the water.

She saw me, stood, and smiled.

"You look fantastic," I said.

Josie smiled, ducked her head, and tucked her blond hair behind one ear. "Thanks. And thanks for leaving work early. I have an early shift tomorrow."

"Easy choice. There's a good crowd already."

Josie nodded. "It'll fill up even more when the band plays."

We made our way over to one of the drink stands. "I didn't realize how busy it got. Have you been down here much?"

Josie nodded. "Peter helped some of the first artists secure financing. I always enjoyed walking around while they crunched the numb…" She stopped. "Nate, I'm sorry, when we were looking for a place to go on Friday afternoon, I just thought—"

I smiled. "Don't worry about it. This is way better than sitting inside somewhere. I've been cooped up all week."

"I just, I wasn't even thinking about that."

I waved her off. "Josie, we both lived in Carrefour with our spouses for a long time. If we eliminate the places we went with them, we won't have anywhere to go, including our own homes."

"Thanks." She smiled again and I have to say that I liked it.

Then we went to the stands where Josie picked a northern Michigan wine and I was handed a beer that had been crafted with far more care than that to which I was accustomed, before we toasted and I said, "Lead the way."

We started at a silversmith's shop where a huge man with a bushy black mustache that came down past his chin was hammering out tiny intricate pendants made of silver. We didn't say a word as we watched a strand of silver become a serpent eating its tail. By the time he finished, there were ten or eleven of us and when he held it up, we actually clapped.

As we walked away, I shook my head. "That's amazing."

"So is that." Josie pointed and we stopped at a glassblower's shop as a young man was working a molten swirl of blue and yellow and orange into, well, I had no idea at that point what it was going to be but judging from the items displayed in his window, it could be damn near anything.

As the molten ball lengthened, Josie pointed. "Oh, he does custom bottles. Hang on." She ducked in and took a card from his stand. The man winked and nodded as he continued his work.

Josie held it up. "Dad wants to do something special when his whiskey hits twelve years."

She had leaned into me to show me the card when a voice behind us said, "*Ma cousine!*"

We turned to see a smiling blond man walking toward us, arms extended.

"JP!" said Josie as the man engulfed her in a hug.

JP Lacombe grinned as he stepped back. "Marie-Josée! How's my favorite cousin?"

"Great. Not working tonight?"

JP smiled and looked around. "Well..."

Josie laughed. "I should've known better. JP, this is a friend of mine, Nate Shepherd."

JP Lacombe flashed me a bright smile and gave me the firm handshake of someone who did it hundreds of times a day. He was taller than I had realized from his ads and both a little wider and a little thinner if that makes sense.

"Nate Shepherd. Have we met? You seem familiar."

"I'm sorry, I don't think we have. I've certainly seen your ads but that's a one-way street."

"Are you a Michigan resident, Nate?"

"I am."

"All right, all right," said Josie. "No stump-speeching my date."

JP Lacombe put an innocent hand to his chest. "I'm crushed, dear cousin, crushed. I was not going to ask Nate here for his vote. I was simply going to ask if keeping dangerous vape pens out of the hands of children was a priority that Nate could get behind."

"JP." Josie's voice rose as she said it.

"Fine, fine. I'll just wander around and see if there are other people here who have an interest in saving our youth from corporate predation."

Josie smiled. "Good luck, JP. Give *Ma Tante* and your brother my love."

"Be sure to stop by. Mom misses you."

The two hugged, and JP shook my hand again, no doubt counting it as the second of seven touches.

Before he let go, JP Lacombe said, "Wait, are you related to David Shepherd?"

"Sure. He's my dad."

JP snapped his fingers. "That's it!"

"Do you know my dad?"

"No, I've just heard of him. From my mom."

"And who is your mom?"

JP tilted his head, glanced at Josie, then said, "Marie-Faye Lacombe."

"They know each other?"

"Back when, I think. Great to see you both." And with barely a pause, JP Lacombe was shaking another hand.

"So that's your famous representative cousin?

Josie smiled. "It is. He and his brother Maxime were the only ones my age at a lot of family gatherings, so we spent a lot of time together growing up."

"He seems like a nice guy."

"He is. Always working, but he is."

"I don't know that I ever met your aunt, though."

Josie glanced at me. "I doubt it."

"Why?"

"Because if you had met Marie-Faye Lacombe, you'd remember."

20

I took Roxie for an early walk Saturday morning so that I could go to the office, but when she saw me pick up my keys and head for the door, she gave me a look that said this Saturday morning stuff was bullshit and that I needed to rethink my priorities. I suppose it's possible that I was projecting, but she seemed pretty clear about it, so I arrived at another decision.

"Okay. Come on."

Roxie went right to the peg with the leash and sat. I smiled, hooked it up, and we left.

No one was there when we arrived, so I had time to take her off lead, show her around, and set up her spare bed behind my desk which she promptly curled into.

I checked my emails and was surprised to find that Emily had already drafted a motion to join the State in compelling the *Torch* to produce Christopher Marsh's files. I checked the time of her email. Ten-thirty on Friday night.

Judge Gallon had not been kidding about her.

I made a few edits and shot it back to her with a comment that it was well done.

I scrolled through other things that had come in after I had left early to see Josie. I had an email from Danny that we had received a pleasantly large first payment on the greenhouse deal he was working on and, sure enough, there was a check from Tri-State Landscaping and Nursery right on top of my in-tray.

"Good news, Roxie. Biscuits for another month."

At the word "biscuits," Roxie raised her head. She had me, so I gave her one.

There was also an email from Silas Winford or, I should say, from one of the three associates on behalf of Silas Winford, attaching electronic copies of the results of the prosecution's DNA and fiber testing.

The man was hitting the ground running.

I scanned the DNA test first. No surprise—the blood on the bat was Christopher Marsh's.

The fiber testing was next. That took a little more for me to sort through, but the test stated that a cloth fiber found in the TV stand at the scene matched the fibers of the "FU" sweatshirt Logan Carver had been wearing at the time he was arrested.

Shit.

The office door opened. I poked my head out and saw Emily blow in.

"What are you doing here?" I said.

"I got your revisions on our motion."

I blinked. "I didn't mean for you to come in now."

"I was planning on coming in this weekend if you got to it. Better to get it out of the way now. I want to file it first thing Monday."

"Emily, I don't expect you to come in when I send you an email on the weekend. I just do it so I don't lose track of things."

Emily sat down and docked her laptop. "I know. I just wanted to get it done so I could get back to the timeline. Something's bothering me."

As long as she was there, I sat down. "What?"

"The gap. Logan makes a scene at the McDonald's at 9:02 and sells the PlayStation at 10:15."

"Right."

"Where is he in between?"

I thought, then shook my head. "I don't know."

"And whatever he was doing in that time, why wouldn't he have gotten rid of the bat?"

"That's a good point. I'll have to ask Logan next time I meet with him. Speaking of the bat." I told her about the DNA match of the blood on the bat and the match of the "FU" sweatshirt fibers to those found at the scene.

She winced, then nodded. "I guess we expected that. I suppose they have matching blood on the sweatshirt, too."

I stared at Emily, then went, got my laptop, and came back. She scowled as I pulled up the test results and went through them all again.

"No," I said. "They don't."

"The blood doesn't match?"

"No. They don't mention any blood."

Emily's scowl deepened. "They have the sweatshirt."

"Uh-huh."

"And they don't mention any matching blood on it?"

"Nope."

Her eyes widened. "There isn't any?"

Both of our fingers clattered as we pulled up photos of the scene from our e-file.

"That's an awful lot of blood, Nate."

I nodded. "It's spattered everywhere."

"And the 'FU' fibers put Logan at the scene..."

I nodded. "But also prove what he was wearing."

"Meaning he'd have to kill Marsh without getting any blood on him."

I thought, then typed. "I wonder if we can prove that's not possible." I typed some more.

"How?" said Emily.

"First, we have to test everything he was wearing to see if there was any blood on it."

"Okay."

"And second, we need a spatter expert."

"A what?"

At that moment, Roxie sauntered in and flopped at my feet.

Emily did a double take, sprang from her chair, and made Roxie's acquaintance, which Roxie seemed equally happy to share.

"So we can bring pets in on Saturday?" she said.

"Um..."

"Good. I have a mini-horse."

"A what?"

"She's really no trouble."

"A horse?"

"A *mini*-horse. Barely three feet tall. You won't even notice her."

"Emily, I don't know if we can have—"

"It's a comfort animal. I have a prescription and everything."

"Um, I suppose we can try—"

Emily shook her head. "I'm kidding."

"Oh."

"Toughen up, Boss."

Then Emily finished our motion, and I spent a couple of hours lining up a forensics lab and a spatter expert.

21

On Monday afternoon, we went back to Christopher Marsh's house to meet our spatter expert. By we, I mean Emily and me, and by spatter expert, I mean Devon Payne, a guy who studies blood spatters and patterns.

Emily and I were standing in the driveway when Devon Payne pulled up in a dragonfly blue electric Kia vehicle. The quietness of the engine was offset by the pounding of the bass as he parked in the street out front. Emily looked at me. I shrugged. "He's the best around."

"With blood spatters?"

"Everybody needs a hobby."

The music continued for another few beats before Devon Payne emerged. His hair was a little long, his pants were a little short, and he wore glasses with wide white frames. He slung a canvas satchel type bag over his shoulder and was in no particular hurry to reach us, but when he did, he gave us a quick smile and pointed. "You Nate?"

"I am. This is Emily."

Devon Payne nodded without actually making eye contact, then stood there, thumb hooked in the strap of his satchel.

"Any trouble finding the place?"

He shook his head.

The silence stretched out until I said, "We're waiting on the Sheriff's deputy."

"Figured."

We stood there a little longer until I heard a rustling above us. The storm door on the tiny third-floor balcony opened and a man in khaki pants and a University of Michigan sweatshirt walked out and took a seat on a white plastic chair. He held up a small plastic cup to us in salute, or at least I thought it was a cup, until he pulled out a lighter, lit the front of it, and took a big inhale off the top. After he blew out a cloud of smoke, he said, "Who was playing the Lil Nas X?"

Devon Payne nodded upward.

The man raised his bong in salute.

An Ash County Sheriff's vehicle swerved into the driveway and Deputy Randy Pavlich got out, pulling his wide-brimmed hat over his short blond hair. He strode toward us, stopped, sniffed, then looked at us before looking up. The man on the balcony took his mouth off the top of the bong and blew an enormous cloud of smoke into the air before he smiled and said, "Welcome to my residence, Officer."

Deputy Pavlich stared at him, muttered something about "goddam legalization," then jerked a hand for us to follow him to the side door, which still had a broken windowpane in the bottom left corner.

"Don't take anything," said Deputy Pavlich as he opened it.

"Understood." I turned to Devon Payne. "They found him right back—"

"—Saw the pictures. Stay back." Then Devon Payne went into the kitchen, right to where Christopher Marsh had been found face down in front of his still open drawer, and squatted down.

I stayed back. Deputy Pavlich stood there, arms crossed, while Emily, who was in motion at the best of times, shifted her weight between her feet.

After five minutes of this, I decided to look around again.

I went into the family room where the TV stand door was still open, then over to the little desk and chair on the other side of the room that had some random papers, bills mostly, a docking station with monitor, and a small wireless printer.

The red light on the printer was blinking. I looked closer. It was out of paper.

I opened a drawer, then another, and found paper. I put it in and pressed the blinking red button.

It started to print.

Deputy Pavlich bolted into the room. "What are you doing?"

"Printing."

"Printing what?"

"I have no idea."

Deputy Pavlich came over then and the two of us watched the paper feed out slowly, one after another. Deputy Pavlich grabbed the first one, and then the second. He squinted, looking back and forth between the two, then shook his head. "Pesticides?"

I picked up the next three sheets off the printer. It looked like a running table on Michigan pesticide sales and use for the last five years.

"How do you want to do this?" I said to Deputy Pavlich.

"What do you mean?"

"I mean, I know you have to include this in your inventory, so we can either all go back to your office now and copy it or we can just take pictures of the papers right now."

Deputy Pavlich waved a hand. "Go ahead."

I motioned Emily over and the two of us scanned the documents with our phones. It kept printing. After about thirty pages, a new table started.

"Those aren't pesticides," said Emily.

"No, they're antibiotics."

The table was shorter, about twelve pages, and looked to be a listing of the sales of antibiotics in the state, broken down by region, brand name, medical use, and reimbursement rate.

The printer stopped and we scanned the last pages. I straightened them, set them back in the printer tray, and said, "They're over here when you need them, Deputy."

"Fine," he said from the other room, then to Devon, "Are you almost done?"

"Soon," said Devon Payne.

We rejoined them in the kitchen. Devon Payne was squatting at the base of the refrigerator, angling his camera up, taking pictures. His shutter snapped a few more times, then he stood. "Done."

"Alright, let's get out of here then." Deputy Pavlich waited until we went first, then shut the door behind us.

"Did you bring the papers from the printer for your inventory?" I asked.

Deputy Pavlich shot me a look, went back inside, and returned with a handful of papers. He waited again until we went first, so we walked down the driveway toward our cars.

"Farewell, fellow humans," came the voice from the deck. "And officer."

Deputy Pavlich stopped for a moment, apparently thought better of it, then got in his car and drove away. The man on the deck chuckled.

"What do you think?" I asked Devon Payne.

"Not done."

"What else do you need?"

"His clothes."

"We thought the same. I'll request access."

Devon Payne nodded once, then climbed into his metallic dragonfly blue car and silently drove away.

Emily and I were at the bottom of the driveway, but even from that distance could hear the distinctive watery gurgling of the bong on the third-floor deck.

Emily smiled. "I suppose we have to."

"It seems like the thorough thing to do."

Then the two of us walked back up the driveway to the smiling man sitting above us.

———

22

The man leaned back in his white plastic chair, one hand on the railing, and sent an impressive stream of smoke billowing into the air. Then he looked down, smiled, and said, "Greetings, cop-adjacent people."

"Mind if we talk to you for a minute?"

"Let's not set untrue arbitrary limits on our discourse."

I smiled, introduced ourselves, and said, "We're investigating the murder of your neighbor."

"Really? Our good officer didn't seem happy to be here with you." He took a hit from his bong.

"I represent the man accused of killing him."

"Did he?"

"I don't think so."

"And our good deputy's perception of that fact?"

"I don't believe our deputy has the requisite flexibility of mind to change it."

The man chuckled.

"Did you see anything that night?"

He shook his head. "Not a thing. I was filled with pizza pockets and a sense of peace."

"Did you hear anything like this glass here breaking?" I pointed at the door.

The man unscrewed the little metal bowl on the front of the plastic tube and tapped it upside down on the deck railing. "The window wasn't broken that night."

"No? When?"

He shrugged. "Some time before. Days for sure. Weeks maybe. And no, I don't know how." The man re-screwed the bowl onto the tube. "Was your guy here?"

"Possibly."

"What was he possibly doing?"

"The Sheriff thinks stealing."

"Hmm. What about murdering?"

"I don't think so."

"One can lead to the other."

"Not always."

"Not always, but if you feed the bad wolf long enough, he wants more to eat."

"True. But hummingbirds don't hunt fish."

The man chuckled at that. "I suppose it *is* a matter of weight ratios."

"Exactly."

As the man packed his metal bowl with absent-minded expertise, he said, "As much as I've enjoyed this not-murder related discussion, I have to eat. And get back to work."

"You work?" said Emily.

The man smiled. "I do, although I have to say I'm not thrilled with the tone of your stereotype-steeped inquiry."

"Can we get your name?"

"Cheech Lebowski."

"Really?"

"Of course not."

Emily laughed. "Please?"

"So much better. My name is Tommy Melton, I did not see or hear any intruders on the night of your client's not-murder, and you know where to find me if you need to hear more about that lack." Then Tommy Melton raised his bong in salute and went back into the house.

Emily looked at me. "Strange."

I smiled. "I suppose it's a matter of perception."

WHEN WE GOT BACK to the office, Wendy Carver was waiting for us. She wore a light coat over her black and white uniform, and she held a bottle of water that I assume was from Danny.

"Mrs. Carver, did we have an appointment today?"

"No, Mr. Shepherd, but I needed to see you."

I introduced her to Emily and told her that Emily would be part of the trial team.

Wendy Carver barely nodded. "I don't know if Logan will make it that far."

I gestured to the conference room and the three of us went in. "What's wrong?"

"Everything. I went up to see him, up at the jail in Dellville. It's..." She wrung the bottle top back and forth.

I nodded. "Jail is difficult."

"It's not that, it's...I don't know if Logan will make it."

"What do you mean?"

"My boy is...Logan is easily led, Mr. Shepherd."

"Nate, please. And what do you mean?"

Wendy Carver tightened the cap further. "Logan doesn't always see what's going on. It's how he gets in trouble. And sometimes it makes him an easy target."

I nodded.

"And I'm pretty sure he's already had a fight, and that's just in Dellville. If he has to go to Jackson…"

I nodded again, and I thought about how to give harsh news to a caring parent in a gentle way. "Wendy, we have two issues here, a short-term one and a long-term one."

Wendy Carver looked up.

"Logan is being held for murder and home invasion. That's as serious as it gets. You can get him out on bond, but…"

"I've checked. We can't afford it."

"You know you only need ten percent."

"We can't afford one percent."

"Then I'm afraid he will be staying in Dellville until trial."

"What if we win at trial?"

This was trickier. I told her why.

"You're not my client, Wendy, so the prosecutor can find out whatever I tell you about our case."

"But he's my son!"

"Who's an adult." I chose my words carefully. "Emily and I are finding ways to fight the murder charge. We just met with an expert and a witness this morning. It will be an uphill battle, but we could win that."

Wendy nodded, eyes intent.

"But the evidence is looking very bad on the charges that he broke into the home to steal something inside. And if he's convicted of that, he's going to go to prison even if we win the murder case."

Wendy Carver bit her lip. "How long?"

"Years. Not months."

Wendy Carver grasped the water bottle like a life rope, then folded into herself and said, "I don't know what to do."

"You've exhausted your financial resources, right?"

She nodded.

"You tried to help him before all this happened?"

"Every day." She wrung the bottle itself now, crunching the plastic. "My husband feels like there's nothing else we can do. I'm not so sure."

"May I offer a suggestion?"

"That's why I'm here."

"I'm going to do everything I can to defend your son because that's the only way I'll be able to sleep at night if we lose. Ultimately, at the end of this process, you'll want to know the same thing, that there was nothing else you could've done. Coming to me was a good step, to learn if you're missing something. You're not. Honestly, there aren't a lot of ways for you to help him right now. But if you think of something, do it. If that's a visit or a call or whatever you think would help him, do it. And then you'll know, however this ends, that you did all you could." I paused, then added. "It won't make the pain any less. But it will eliminate the doubt."

As quickly as she had folded in, Wendy Carver released the bottle and straightened up. "Thanks for seeing me. I'm sorry to barge in."

"Don't be."

She stood. "You said you saw some people today? Will they help Logan?"

"It's too soon to tell. I think my expert can. I don't think the witness will, but we'll keep working at it. I'm heading up to see Logan this week, too. I'll let you know how he is."

"Thank you."

"Of course."

We walked Wendy Carver out. When she was gone, I said to Emily, "I'll set up a meeting with Logan to talk about his clothes, and I'll let you know when we hear more from the experts. It'll be quiet for a couple of days, so this is probably a decent time to help Danny with his due diligence."

"Speaking of jail..."

"I heard that," came Danny's voice.

Emily raised her head and spoke louder, "I feel like I've been released from jail now that I can study purchase orders from 2012!" She smiled, stuck her finger down her throat, and went to her office.

"She made a face, didn't she?" said Danny.

"Just a smile." Then I went back to my office and made arrangements to see Logan Carver.

23

That night, I was awakened by a sharp bark. I opened my eyes to find myself face to face with boxer nose. Roxie blinked, licked my face twice and nuzzled my cheek, then pulled back and stared. I looked at the clock.

2:32 a.m.

Duty done, Roxie went back to her bed, curled up, and went to sleep. Jerk.

I resisted the urge to check the spare bathroom and instead flipped on the bedside lamp. Roxie shifted her head away from the light, but I didn't care because this was her fault anyway.

Roxie was a retired service dog. Her last owner had suffered from epilepsy, so part of Roxie's training had been to recognize seizures. When I first took her in, she'd been waking me up several times a week, always at the same time. This had caused me some concern until my sister-in-law Kate had offered that Roxie was probably sensitive to sleep disturbances in general. Once I put that together with the time Roxie was waking me up, it made sense. It didn't make me feel any better, but it made sense.

I grabbed the book I was reading off the nightstand and

returned to where one of the characters was explaining why he thought it was a good idea to send criminals back in time to a parallel universe. I tried to lose myself following the thread but since the story hinged on the death of a woman, it didn't help.

Roxie hadn't woken me in a while, and I wasn't sure why she had on this night until I remembered my conversation with Wendy Carver. It may have sounded trite, but I'd meant every word about exhausting every avenue for her son, so that if the worst ever happened, she could be certain that she had fulfilled her duties as a mother and done everything she could for her son.

I read the book as the main character was sent back in time himself, adrift somewhere unknown, until I journeyed far enough with him to turn off the light and go back to sleep.

24

The next day I went to the Ash County jail to see Logan Carver.

"I didn't kill him."

It was the first thing he said every time I met with him, so I moved on to why I was there. "Logan, were you wearing an FU sweatshirt the night you went to the house?"

Logan grinned. "It's a university, not the bad word."

"What is?"

"FU. It's not the bad word. It's a school."

I could see we weren't going any farther until I dealt with this. "What school?"

"Furman. Wait, Fordham. One of those. They are universities. Get it?"

"I get it."

"People think I'm swearing but I'm not."

"That is funny. Did you wear the FU sweatshirt in the house?"

He nodded.

"Anything over it?"

He shook his head.

"What else were you wearing?"

"Jeans. Black Nikes."

"Were those the same clothes you were arrested in?"

He nodded.

"You didn't change clothes? Even when you slept?"

"I fell asleep on the couch that night."

I thought, then said, "We're trying to put together the time-line for what you did that night. What were you doing before?"

"Gaming."

"What were you playing?"

"*Call of Duty*, I think."

"Were you playing with anybody?"

"I don't remember. Probably."

"Anybody you know?"

"I don't know. Probably not."

"When did you stop?"

"I don't know. It was dark."

"Why did you stop?"

Logan looked at me. "What do you mean?"

"Were you planning to go out and rob a place?"

Logan looked down and shrugged.

"What made you go out then?"

"It was dark. I was hungry. I needed money. All that stuff."

"Did you talk to anyone else about it?"

"I didn't talk to anybody."

"And you just randomly picked Marsh's house?"

"I told you, I could see the TV from the street."

"Had you done this before?"

Logan shrugged.

"You knew not to take your phone though."

Logan rocked back and forth. "You never take your phone."

"So you don't know what time it was when you left?"

"No, just that it was dark."

"Was McDonald's the first place you went after?"

"Yep. I was hungry."

"And Second Chance Electronics next?"

Logan nodded.

"It took a long time, Logan. Where did you go in-between?"

"Nowhere."

"It was more than an hour between the McDonald's and the electronics store, Logan. Where were you?"

"Driving."

"It doesn't take that long, Logan. Second Chance was only a few minutes away."

"Drinking my shakes then."

"For an hour?"

"I was driving and drinking my shakes."

"Did you stop somewhere when you were drinking your shakes?"

"Yes."

"Where?"

Logan rocked as he shook his head. "I was just driving."

"You need to tell me, Logan."

"I was just driving and drinking my shakes."

I was going to have to come back to this later, but I didn't think I was getting any farther with it today. "Did you go anywhere after the electronics store?"

"I got beer and snacks."

"What snacks?"

"Cheetos and cinnamon buns."

"Then went home?"

He nodded.

"Did you talk to anyone at all after you left Marsh's house?"

Logan kept rocking. "I didn't talk to nobody."

"Text? Email?"

Logan opened his mouth, closed it, then said, "I texted with my mom."

"When?"

"Probably about one."

"In the morning?"

Logan nodded.

"How do you know that?"

"She texts me when she gets home from her shift."

"Does she do that a lot?"

"Every night."

"What does she say?"

"She says good night." He hesitated.

"What else?"

Logan shrugged. "And that she loves me. She doesn't though."

"Why not?"

"Because she won't get me out."

"She can't, Logan. It costs too much money."

"She always says that."

"It's true."

"If she'd just give me money, I wouldn't be in here!"

There was no productive end to that conversation, so I said, "All right Logan, that's all I need for now."

"When will you be back?"

"I'm not sure. It depends on how the case goes."

I went to leave and when I looked back, Logan had stopped rocking. He had folded into himself, and I realized he looked just like Wendy Carver when she sat in my office the day before.

Some people want visits when they're inside, some don't want any contact to remind them of the outside world. There was only one way to know with Logan.

"Would you like your mom to visit?"
Logan nodded.
"I'll tell her."
Then I left.

25

L ate the following week, Emily and I went to the courtroom of Judge Wesley for the hearing on our joint motion to compel the *Torch* files. When we arrived, Silas Winford was already there.

He rose from the back row of the courtroom and extended a hand. "Nate, it's nice to finally meet you in person."

Silas Winford was in his mid-sixties with a full head of impeccably cut hair that was more salt than pepper. He was about my height, stood unbowed by age or a lifetime over law books, and had the faint facial lines and vigor of someone who still spent a great deal of time outside. He had a smile and a handshake that was as well practiced as JP Lacombe's but slightly more formal and reserved.

"Nice to meet you too, Sye."

I introduced Emily, and Silas immediately complimented her on the briefing in the case, then he pointed at the front row and said, "That's the *Torch* attorney, Fred Pressfield, over there. I talked to him on the way over and he's still going to oppose our motion."

"I'm not surprised. That's Ted Ringel sitting next to him, and he was pretty adamant about it."

Before we could say any more, Judge Wesley took the bench and we all took our seats. Ted Ringel was eyeing me, so I nodded to him, but he looked away.

Judge Wesley called our case and, after asking us all to identify ourselves for the record, said, "Mr. Winford, Mr. Shepherd, I've read your briefs and I'm not sure that I see the relevance of your request for the *Torch's* files."

Silas Winford went first. "Your Honor, Mr. Marsh was working on several stories at the time of his death, and his phone calendar indicates that he was actively meeting with different people in the week leading up to it. Both parties would like access to the information to have a full picture of Mr. Marsh's activities and contacts before he died."

Fred Pressfield, the *Torch* attorney, stood. "Your Honor, it is the *Torch's* understanding that its esteemed employee, Christopher Marsh, was bludgeoned to death in his own home by Mr. Shepherd's client, Logan Carver. We don't believe that Mr. Marsh's confidential work files will shed any new light on Mr. Carver's crime. Further, allowing access to Mr. Marsh's files could potentially expose confidential sources and interfere with the freedom of the press that our country holds constitutionally dear."

Judge Wesley looked at me. "Mr. Shepherd?"

"Your Honor, as I mentioned in our brief, we're willing to enter into a protective order that prohibits us from disclosing any of the information prior to trial and that requires us to seek the Court's approval prior to using any of that information in open court." I held out my hands. "As to the reason for the request, we need to have a full picture of what Mr. Marsh was doing leading up to his death so that we can present an accurate defense."

The *Torch* attorney shook his head. "Your Honor, what counsel is looking for is a red herring to distract from his client's conduct. The *Torch* should not be required to produce its confidential materials in response to a fishing expedition."

Judge Wesley frowned. "Mr. Winford, I'm a little surprised you joined in this motion."

"The State believes the defense is entitled to liberal discovery at this stage, Your Honor. I'd like a full picture of Mr. Marsh's activities as much as Mr. Shepherd. Now whether anything that's produced is actually admissible at trial? That's a battle for another day."

Judge Wesley tapped the point of her pen on her notepad. Her look was not promising.

"Your Honor," I said. "The *Torch* has already produced some materials to the State. It can't be selective now."

"What materials, Mr. Shepherd?"

"Mr. Marsh's work calendar."

"Mr. Pressfield?"

"A moment, Your Honor." Fred Pressfield leaned over the railing and whispered with Ted Ringel before straightening. "Your Honor, it's my understanding that the calendar was provided to law enforcement before Mr. Carver's involvement was known."

Judge Wesley's eyes narrowed. "To assist in the investigation?"

"That was before I became involved, Your Honor."

I raised a hand and Judge Wesley nodded. "Your Honor, the *Torch* has also published four stories about Mr. Marsh's death, his employment history, and popular stories that he published for the paper."

"That is news, Your Honor," said Fred Pressfield.

"Right, but since those stories have already been published, there have to be things in the background materials that aren't protected."

"I haven't reviewed those, so I can't say I agree at this stage, Your Honor."

Judge Wesley tapped her pen one, two, three times, then said, "The Court grants the parties' motion in part. The *Torch* will produce all of Mr. Marsh's notes, stories, or correspondence in its possession for the thirty days prior to Mr. Marsh's death. It will also provide limited access to Mr. Marsh's work computer, which can be cloned at defendant's expense so that access is only given for the requisite time and materials. Counsel for the *Torch* may review the items first and redact any confidential names and information and maintain a privilege log for any item they have redacted. I also expect the parties to work together to establish a protective order that will limit the parties' ability to disclose these items without Court approval. Does counsel have any questions?"

"I think that covers it, Your Honor," I said. "I'll submit a proposed order."

"May we have fourteen days to produce, Your Honor?" said Fred Pressfield.

When Winford and I nodded, Judge Wesley said, "Fourteen days is fine. And I expect counsel to work this disclosure process out. Understood?"

"Yes, Your Honor," we all said, and Judge Wesley dismissed us.

Silas Winford, Emily, and I made our way out to the hallway as the *Torch* attorney stayed behind whispering with Ted Ringel.

"I have a vendor who can clone the laptop unless you have a preference?" said Silas.

I shook my head. "If the *Torch* approves, it'll be fine with us. Oh, hey, I've been meaning to talk to you about something else

—I need access to my client's clothes, the ones he was arrested in."

Silas Winford nodded. "Your own testing, I assume?"

"Right."

"What are you looking for?" For the first time since I'd seen him, Winford looked overly casual.

"Whatever you were, I'm sure."

Winford smiled. "Of course. One of my associates will arrange it."

Fred Pressfield and Ted Ringel exited the courtroom. While Ted walked away toward the elevator, Pressfield came right over to us.

"There shouldn't be any problem getting you the materials in fourteen days."

"We were just discussing vendors for the computer," I said.

"That won't be necessary."

"Why?"

"Because the *Torch* doesn't have Marsh's laptop."

26

I raised an eyebrow. "Did it give him one?"

"Yes. But it's not at the *Torch* offices and Mr. Ringel hasn't seen it."

I looked at Winford. "Did the police take the laptop? I don't remember seeing one in the inventory."

Winford shook his head. "We don't have it." He cleared his throat. "Perhaps your client stole that too?"

"He didn't."

Fred Pressfield shrugged. "Not much of a leap from thief and to liar, but that's for you two to fight about."

I ignored the crack. "What about back-up files?"

The *Torch* attorney shook his head. "The publishing company has too many reporters in too many places like Carrefour to back them all up. When the reporter submits a final story, he sends in the story and background support. That's all that's saved."

Winford held out his hands. "What do you have then, Fred?"

"Without the laptop, all we'll be producing are emails and story materials that are currently in possession of other *Torch* employees. Most of Marsh's contact was with Ted Ringel so it shouldn't take too long."

The mention of emails triggered another source. "What about Marsh's phone? There should be emails on there."

Fred Pressfield shook his head. "Any communications with the *Torch* were through a secure app, which we assert an interest in since we issued him the phone."

I looked at Winford. "Do you have the phone?"

"We do."

"And?"

"We've respected the *Torch's* wishes and have not attempted to breach the app."

I had thoughts but decided this wasn't the place to share them. There was more talk about logistics and protective orders but eventually we broke up and left. Emily and I took the stairs so that we could talk on the way.

"So, Logan says he didn't steal the laptop?" she asked.

"He didn't mention it."

"Is he telling the truth?"

"He told me everything else he stole. I don't know why he'd leave that out."

"Then where is it?"

"That's the question, isn't it?"

Emily frowned. "We don't even know that the laptop was at the house. Marsh could have lost it or had it stolen before then and just hadn't told anyone yet."

"Do you believe that?"

"No."

"Me either."

～

EMILY and I were driving back to the office when she turned on me. "You're horrible by the way."

I blinked. "Is there a particular reason or just generally?"

"You knew exactly what due diligence was when you let Danny rope me into helping him."

"A well-rounded lawyer is an effective one."

"It's awful! Do you know how many purchase orders I've sorted through?"

"A lot?"

"Hundreds. And I'm only up to 2013!"

"Look at it as job security."

"I can't believe Danny's doing it voluntarily."

"Seems like he's good at it though."

"Was he good in trial too?"

"Very. He's just not a big fan of criminal work."

"What about on the civil side?"

It was a good question. At my former firm, we'd handled civil work together and he'd never shown the reluctance he had once we were on our own. I suppose murder is different. "I don't think that was as much of a problem."

"So there's hope for him?"

I smiled. "Maybe. I think he likes what he's doing though."

She shook her head. "I don't know how."

"How about you? Doing okay with the change? Are we giving you what you need?"

"So far so good. Thanks."

"We haven't taken on a new attorney since we started the place, so let me know if I missed something."

"Oh, you don't have to worry about that."

I smiled. "I suppose not."

"That's three."

"Three what?"

She pointed. "JP Lacombe billboards."

"To be fair, he does want to be *your* State Representative."

Emily shook her head. "Not mine. I live in our fair state to the south."

"I always forget. You seem like such a nice person."

"You're just bitter because my Buckeyes thrashed your Spartans last year."

"I wouldn't say thrashed. And yes, I am."

"Huh. You'd think you'd be used to it by now."

You almost didn't need the official border sign welcoming us back to Ohio as the JP Lacombe signs for the Michigan House switched to signs for a hot, newly redistricted Ohio Congressional seat.

THREE THINGS HAPPENED with the evidence in the case over the next week. First, Silas Winford was true to his word and made Logan Carver's clothes, including the FU sweatshirt, available for testing. There are all sorts of chain of custody protocols and spoliation rules involved in independently testing evidence from a crime scene, so I put Emily in touch with Winford's associate to coordinate getting our expert access to the materials so he could test for blood, among other things.

Second, Emily realized we'd been overlooking a piece of evidence that would help her create our timeline—Logan's video game system. He'd even told us he'd been playing the night of the robbery and the next day, but we hadn't thought of it. And by "we," I mean "I." So we texted Wendy Carver and made arrangements to get access to Logan's apartment that afternoon.

Third, we received the files from the *Torch*. I uploaded the thumb drive of materials into our electronic file system and dove in.

I went straight to the files labelled "Stories" and "Notes." The "Stories" looked like the final versions of any article that had been run in the *Torch*. Each article then had a "Note" file that documented Marsh's sources. It looked like a summary document Marsh had given the paper for its file in case someone ever questioned a story. For the most part, they were single line entries like "Carrefour Police Accident Report" or "City Council Meeting Minutes," followed by excerpts of the materials he'd used.

Two types of entries in the "Notes" files turned up repeatedly; one was "Full Interview notes—laptop" and the other "Full Sound File—laptop." It only took me a few minutes to figure out that Marsh gave the paper the direct quote in the article's "Note," but kept the full interview notes or the sound file on his laptop.

You know, the one that was missing.

I skimmed the list of stories—a protest against a ninety-nine-cent retailer coming to the county, a Dellville City Councilman with a DUI, and a missing toddler who was thankfully found hiding in her big brother's tree fort which no one thought she could climb up into in a million years. Toward the end of the list was the Lacombe Distillery profile, which I'd already read. Out of curiosity, I went to the "Note" document where Marsh had excerpted his interview with André Lacombe with the notation "Full Sound File—laptop" and quoted the ingredients of the Lacombe Classic Rye Whiskey with confirmation of the original recipe from "the Journal of Jean-Jacques Lacombe—laptop."

It was the last story, though, that caught my attention. It said, "Article 1: Withheld—Privilege." Sure enough, there was a corresponding "Note" item, which simply said, "Notes to Article 1: Withheld—Privilege."

I re-scanned the lists. No other story was being withheld. There were a couple of individual items in the Notes that had been redacted, but it was pretty clear that those were protecting the sources of a story, like whoever had given Marsh a heads-up to check on whether a certain councilman had been picked up for drinking and driving the night before. There were no instances where the entire story had been withheld. It took me a moment to realize the obvious reason—the story hadn't been published yet.

There was nothing on the log to indicate the time and date of the story that was being held back. But it was at the end of the list.

That led me to check the file labelled "Messages" to see if there were any messages about the story. What I found was a message string labelled "Messages related to Article 1: Withheld —Privilege."

Here, though, Fred Pressfield hadn't redacted everything. He told us that the messages were between Ted Ringel and Christopher Marsh. And he told us the dates.

The withheld messages ended on Friday, the day Christopher Marsh died.

Before I had time to consider it, my phone buzzed. Silas Winford.

"Hello, Sye."

"Did you get the *Torch* disclosures?"

"I'm looking at them right now."

"They're withholding messages and a story from the day he died."

"I noticed."

"We need to file another motion to compel them to produce it."

"I think so. I'm surprised you do."

"Why? I told you I have an interest in finding out all of the facts too."

"That hasn't been my experience with most prosecutors."

"Well, I'm not most...Goodness, that was going to sound arrogant, wasn't it?"

"Not at all."

"Liar. Look, I'll tell you exactly what I'm doing, Nate. I can't have you waving around a mystery file at trial. Knowing what it is eliminates the intrigue. If it's the latest dogcatcher article that the *Torch* is just withholding on principle, that's easy enough. And if it's something more, I need to be able to deal with it."

"What if it shows someone else could've been responsible?"

Winford chuckled. "I admire your optimism. Shall you take the first crack at this or shall I?"

"You took the lead on the last one. I'll do it."

"Grand. I'll join it when you file."

couple of hours later, I was leaving to meet Wendy Carver at Logan's apartment when Danny stuck his head in.

"Got a second, Nate?"

"A quick one. What's up?"

"I need to run a new matter by you. I'll be closing on that greenhouse sale in a couple of weeks. It's been a lot of work, but we should get our fees paid at closing."

"Great! Congratulations!"

"Thanks. The company wants to buy a second greenhouse business and wants me to handle it."

"Look at you. Lord of the Hothouse Tomatoes. What's the issue?"

"The first transaction was local here in Michigan. This second greenhouse is in central Ohio so it's a ways away."

"Are you checked out on Ohio law?"

Danny nodded. "Most of the way. I'll get there on the rest. This one's a little bigger though, so I would need more of Emily's time and might need to take at least one site visit down to see it."

"Neither is a problem. Just make sure that you take all that into account when you set your fee. What did you quote them?"

He told me.

I blinked. "What did they say?"

"They said they would pay it." Danny smiled. "Without blinking."

I smiled back. "Then it sounds to me like you have another transaction. Just make sure that you run a conflict check with the new entities."

"Already done."

"Then continue on your way to corporate moguldom."

Danny stood. "I might need to access that expense account."

I waved. "If you keep this up, I'll be asking you for access to the expense account."

I MET Wendy Carver at Logan's apartment, a small studio in need of ventilation and cleaning. She obviously hadn't been in it in some time and the concern on her face was wrenching. I looked around while she began collecting wrappers and cramming them into the already full trash.

It turned out Logan had an Xbox One, which I packed up. I thanked Wendy, but I don't think she heard me as she nodded and pulled a garbage bag out from under the sink.

I left to take the game system to a certain tattooed investigator.

"Noon?" said Olivia. "On a weekday? I better go buy lottery tickets."

She was standing behind the desk of the Brickhouse, a towel

over her shoulder. Because sweat poured off her shoulders and arms, I knew how this was going to go, but sometimes you just have to take your medicine.

I plopped the Xbox on the counter. She stared at it like a rattler had just coiled up in front of her. "What have you brought into my gym?"

"Work."

"Funny thing to call it."

"No, *work* work. I need you to check something."

"Well, get that thing down. Better yet," she reached under the counter and flipped a new towel at me. "Cover that thing up and let's take it back to my office."

I laughed, set the towel aside, and picked up the Xbox.

Olivia froze and stared at me.

"You're serious?"

I only saw myself reflected in her glasses.

"Fine." I put the towel over the Xbox and followed her back to her office.

When we arrived, Olivia ran the towel once over her forehead and spiked up her short white hair before slipping on a track jacket, sitting down, and saying, "So what have we here besides the reason for your broadening backside?"

"Staring at it, were you?"

"Hard to miss something that size."

"Logan Carver's game system."

"I doubt they'll let you take it to him in jail."

"We're trying to re-create the timeline for what he was doing the day of the murder. He told us he was playing at different times. Can we check?"

"Sure." Olivia began hooking cords to monitors.

"Can we get into it?"

"If he left it logged in, it'll be no problem."

"So it'll be a problem if he didn't?"

"I didn't say that at all, Shep. Do you have a controller?"

I handed it to her.

Olivia worked the buttons and joystick with surprising dexterity.

"You seem familiar with that."

"Part of the job." Screens opened and slid by faster than I could follow. She scanned and said, "He stayed logged in so that's a bonus. He's got all sorts of games in his account. *Call of Duty*, *Star Wars Battlefront*, *Halo*, they're all on here."

"Is there a way to see when he was playing?"

"We'll be able to see the time he saved games, but that requires me to actually go in to each one to check. I know this system tells you how long you've played something, but I'm not sure if it tells you exactly when—ah, wait, here's an easier way."

"What?"

"This." A few thumb waggles and a click later, a pane with another screen popped up. "Discord."

"And here I thought we were getting along just fine."

"Not when you're prancing around in my gym wearing a suit and holding a video game system we're not. But no," she tapped the side pane with a finger. "This is Discord."

"What's that?"

"It's an app that lets you talk, text, or share video with people."

"While you're playing video games?"

"That's where it started—people loved it because you could talk while you're playing. Now, people use it on its own or for work."

I peered closer. "Is it right in the game system?"

"You can get it in Xbox, but it can be in your phone or tablet too. What you do is set up a 'server'—that's a fancy name for a group—and invite the people you play with to join. Then they can see when you're playing online and join you or just talk while you're each playing something different."

"Does it save conversations?"

"It does unless you delete them, so let's go back...it looks like he was playing *Call of Duty*, well, every day for a couple of weeks until his arrest."

"What I'm seeing is a conversation?"

Olivia pointed to a column of text. "Right, so, for example, on Wednesday 'Buttmunch44' said 'Eat it noob!' to which 'Darkwing' replied, 'bust his ass.'"

"Are Buttmunch and Darkwing names?"

"It's Buttmunch44 and yes, it's this person's avatar that he goes by on here."

"Reminds me of the salons of Paris."

"Said geezers everywhere."

"I'm pretty sure using the word 'geezer' makes you one."

Olivia ignored me and stared at the screen, the characters scrolling down in reflection on her glasses. "It will take me some time to sift through this, but yeah, I can get you a timeline of when he was playing from this."

"Perfect. Thanks."

There was a ding, followed by another, and then another. Olivia smiled and tapped the screen. "See, this is what I was talking about. These three people saw Logan is online and are checking to see if he's playing."

There were more dings.

Olivia smiled. "Make that seven. See the messages?"

One after another, people named Darkwing and NastyBagginses and Slipstream Angel posted a series of messages that ranged from "He's back!" to "Where you been?" to "Let's raid!" As I watched, Peanutbutterfiend popped up with a "You out?" and the infamous Buttmunch44 chimed in with "He returns!"

"I'll pull together the timeline for you," said Olivia. "You can go do something constructive."

"I just did!"

She grinned. "No, *I* just did."

"Thanks, Liv."

Emily and I filed our motion to compel the *Torch* to produce Marsh's last article. Things ground forward on the case, moving at the glacial pace of law, so that, by the time Thanksgiving rolled around, Silas Winford had joined our motion, the *Torch* had opposed it, and the Court was still thinking about it.

THANKSGIVING

28

It was still dark when I pulled up in front of Josie's house on Thanksgiving morning. I went up to the door and tapped on it with my foot since I had a coffee in each hand.

The porch light winked out and Josie opened the door, holding a carrier with two thermal cups. She laughed. "I guess we'll have enough."

She took one out of my hand and gave me back one that she'd made.

I took a sip as she looked up. It was piping hot.

Josie giggled as we climbed into my Jeep.

"What?"

"I have to post a new meme—find someone who looks at you the way Nate sips his coffee."

I took another sip, and it's possible that I may have lingered over it more than was strictly necessary before I said, "Fortunately, you have."

"Have I now?"

"If getting up on a holiday at four-thirty in the morning isn't a sufficient demonstration of my affection for you and your coffee, I don't know what is." I took a sip. "Make that coffee, then you."

"If we didn't need your help, I wouldn't put up with these terrible insults."

I chuckled. "When you invited me over for Thanksgiving, you somehow didn't mention that we were making dinner for five hundred people."

"Closer to one thousand, I think."

"Does your family get together after?"

"No. We did Canadian Thanksgiving."

"When's that?"

"Early October."

"I don't recall getting an invitation."

Josie lifted her nose and looked away. "You and I weren't as serious then."

I smiled. "Serious enough to be kitchen staff? That's something. I guess."

"You'll be right there with my aunt and my cousins and my parents , so yes, it's a promotion."

"Cousins? Including our newly elected State Representative?"

Josie laughed. "At a Thanksgiving meal distributed by his family company? Especially our new State Representative."

I had finished my first coffee and was starting the second when we arrived at Lacombe Logistics.

It is one thing to say you're feeding one thousand people, but it is quite another to actually see it being done. We walked up to a high-ceilinged shipping bay with a line of open rolling doors that revealed rows of tables and chairs, a wall of mobile ovens, and lines of serving tables filled with empty trays and unlit burners. There was a tent outside with a number of official-looking cookers in black chefs' coats and ball caps putting rubs on turkeys and stacking them in the shelves of long smokers which, if my nose did not deceive me, were using apple wood.

Josie guided me by the hand into the bay where we were swept into a jetstream of chefs swirling about ovens. We finally stepped out of the culinary current next to JP Lacombe, who was taking serving trays off a mobile rack and lining them up in a row on the long table. He smiled as soon as he saw us and gave Josie a big hug. "*Ma cousine!* And you brought Nate," he shook my hand. "Mom hoped you would. We can never have enough hands here today."

"So, where are we stationed?" Josie asked.

"You two are on," JP Lacombe took out his phone, swiped a couple of times, then said, "Pickup station duty today, so head down to...that end and one of the chefs will get you started."

"How about you?"

He grinned. "I'll be manning a spoon."

"Is your brother here?"

"Somewhere. See you when the birds are gone." And he went back to putting down the trays.

Josie grabbed my hand again, which I didn't mind at all, and pulled me down to the end of the line where a chef showed us how a foil-covered turkey and containers of mashed potatoes, stuffing, gravy, and corn all fit in a carrying box before you placed a pumpkin pie on top and sealed the lid.

"The box is the perfect size," I said.

The chef nodded. "That's how we designed it. Make sure this lid clamps tight and none of the stuff will spill. I'll have two people helping you pack, but once we get going, it'll be coming pretty fast."

"How many do we do?"

Josie grinned. "As many as it takes."

THE NEXT THREE hours were a blur of boxes and plastic containers and pie tins, and I spent at least an hour of it lining up stacks of pumpkin pies that Josie assured me would all be necessary. At the end of it, she said that if I wanted to grab a coffee or use the restroom or do anything else, now was the time because I wasn't going to have another chance until we were done.

"Really?"

"Really."

She gave me directions and I found my way to the restroom, which was on the other side of the bay. On my way out, I almost hit a man with the door who caught it, nodded, and stepped aside.

"Oh, hey, so sorry."

The man shook his head and smiled. "It's nice to have you here, Nate."

I took in the man who I had almost run over. He was about my age, lean, with dark hair and startlingly light eyes. "I'm sorry, have we met?"

He smiled again. "No. Maxime Lacombe, Josie's cousin."

"Sure, JP's brother?"

Maxime Lacombe nodded. "It's good to finally meet you in person. We certainly appreciate you helping today."

"Glad to. This is quite the operation you have going here."

An old-time bell rang through the loading dock three times.

"Time to man our stations," Maxime said. "We'll catch up after."

I nodded and hustled back down the dock to Josie, who smiled, kissed my cheek, and said, "Ready?"

I nodded.

Then the bell rang one more time and the loading dock door directly in front of us rolled open.

WE PASSED out meals for the next few hours, surrounded by the permeating smell of turkey and gravy that I'd always associated with Thanksgiving, although not necessarily with a loading dock. We filled boxes non-stop, and I only spilled once when I squeezed a container of gravy too hard and popped the lid right off. Josie smiled, tossed me some paper towels, and before you knew it, we were rolling again.

Men, women, and the odd teenager picked up the boxed feast to take home. I saw a number of jackets with logos for Lacombe Logistics, Lacombe A&M, and Lacombe Capital. At one point, I said, "Are those your companies?

"Not mine," Josie smiled. "My aunt's."

"Are all of these people employees?"

"No." She smiled and said "Happy Thanksgiving" to a woman as she took the box.

"Who else is here?"

Her blue eyes stayed on me for a moment. "Anyone who needs it, Nate."

Once she said that, I noticed that the Lacombe jackets were only every third or fourth person. And I also noticed that Josie took extra care to answer any questions from those who weren't wearing them.

During a lull, I had a chance to see what was going on at the other end of the dock. Folks were going through the line manned by dark-coated chefs for individual servings of turkey and all the fixings. JP Lacombe and his brother Maxime stood at the end of the line, JP all smiles as he stacked heaps of white and dark meat on plates while Maxime quietly helped those who were having trouble find a seat.

Eventually, as things slowed and our line dwindled, I saw JP walking among the tables with a platter of turkey, insisting that folks take more.

Josie noticed. "He does enjoy that part."

"What's that?"

"Meeting people, helping them. It's why he's good at politics."

"I met his brother earlier."

"Maxime?"

"Yeah. Is he in politics too?"

"No, he was in the service. He works with my aunt on the business side now."

A couple of stragglers came in and Josie handed them boxes of Thanksgiving. The woman nodded and the man thanked Josie three times. She smiled and said it was our pleasure.

She was about to say something when Maxime walked up. He smiled and hugged Josie, nodded to me, and said, "When you're finished, my mom would like to say hello."

"Of course. Where is she?"

"In the office. I'd be happy to take you."

The line was gone and when one of the chefs said she could handle any stragglers, Josie turned to me and said, "Shall we?"

"Lead the way."

Josie nodded to Maxime, who led us through the loading dock into the building beyond to meet Marie-Faye Lacombe.

29

Marie-Faye Lacombe was striking. Not beautiful in the way magazines and influencers chase, although she was that, but striking, like a blow. Thick white hair that fell past her shoulders. High, carved cheek bones and a strong jaw. Pale blue eyes accentuated by dark eyebrows and fine lines at the corners. A black overcoat, black slacks, and black boots highlighted her height, her white hair, and her blue eyes, an effect that had to have been purposeful.

It's not fair to say that she smiled when we came in. I would say instead that she gave the impression that she was pleased.

"Thank you, Maxime," she said.

Maxime nodded and slipped out.

"Hello, *Ma Tante*." Josie walked up to her aunt and gave her an air kiss on one cheek.

"Hello, my dear girl. You have been well?"

"I have."

"André tells me that you've been helping him at the distillery?"

"When I don't have a shift, yes."

Marie-Faye Lacombe turned to me. "And I see you brought an assistant."

I stepped forward. "Good morning, Mrs. Lacombe. I'm—"

"—I know who you are, Nathan Shepherd." Again, I had the impression that she was smiling without smiling. She offered her hand, but as if she were presenting it to be kissed rather than shaken.

I can tell you that I had absolutely no idea what to do with that, so I took her hand gently with one of my own, then placed my other hand over top of them both and held them for a moment before I let go and said, "It's great to meet you, Mrs. Lacombe. This was an amazing event."

Her hand glided back into one of her overcoat pockets. "Thank you, Nathan. And I haven't been Mrs. Lacombe for some time, so please, Marie-Faye."

I smiled. "Sure. Thanks. And I mean it, what you all did was incredible."

"Everyone has a right to eat, Nathan. And we have more than enough." Marie-Faye Lacombe turned again. "And how about you, Marie-Josée? Did you enjoy this morning?"

"Very much."

"You could help a lot of people here with us."

"I'm helping people breathe every day, *Ma Tante*."

Marie-Faye Lacombe almost smiled. "Yes. But you must think of scale, dear."

Marie-Faye Lacombe trained her eyes back on me. "Speaking of scales, how is your practice going, Nathan?"

"Very well, thanks."

"Are you still doing criminal defense work?"

I cocked my head at her.

She gave the impression of a smile. "I pay attention to who my niece is dating."

"I am."

"I understand you're very good at it."

I shrugged.

"I have seen you in my social media feeds more than once."

"Don't believe what you read."

"What I read was quite flattering."

"I'll have to remember to pay the posters extra."

"The case with the farmer up this way, the one accused of trying to kill his brother's fiancé? That was most interesting."

"I was lucky."

"He was lucky to have you."

"I'm nothing special."

"Then you would be unlike any Shepherd I've met."

The weight of Marie-Faye's focus shifted back to Josie. "So do you have other plans today?"

"We do."

Marie-Faye Lacombe raised a black eyebrow and almost smiled. "We?"

"We're going to Nate's house this afternoon. His parents, I should say."

"Wonderful." She turned to me. "How is *mon loup*?"

"I'm sorry?"

"Your father. How is he?"

"Great. He's retired now and he and mom live on the lake full-time, so he spends most of his time fishing and taking grandkids out on the water."

"Sounds wonderful. And your mother? She is well?"

"Very much so. I think she was worried about having him around the house full time, but the lake seems to have done the trick."

"They sound very happy. Please give your mother my warmest regards."

"I sure will."

"Well, I won't keep you. Thank you for helping today."

Marie-Faye Lacombe gave Josie a brief hug and another air-kiss. "We should see more of you."

"I know, *Ma Tante.*"

Marie-Faye Lacombe motioned to me and, rather than offer her hand, took me by both shoulders and gave me the double air-kiss. "I enjoyed meeting you, Nathan."

"Thanks again for letting me help."

"We have plenty of projects here that need attention should you ever tire of murder."

I smiled as we stepped back and I realized that, with the boots, Marie-Faye Lacombe came very close to looking me straight in the eyes. She did, but only for a moment; then she turned her phone on and received a series of pings as we slipped out the door.

We were halfway down the stairs when Josie said, "She means it, you know."

"What's that?"

"That she would bury you in projects."

"She was being polite."

"My aunt is many things. Emptily polite is not one of them."

"She does make an impression."

"She'd probably hire you. They have a whole team of lawyers."

I stopped, turned. "I'm fine where I am, Josie." I smiled. "Or should I say Marie-Josée?"

She slipped a hand through my arm and said, "I prefer Josie. And I like where you are right now too." She looked up, we kissed, and I found that I agreed with her.

It wouldn't do to start making out in the hallway of the family shipping business, so Josie and I walked down the hall and back through the loading bays where the kitchen staff was breaking down the tables and chairs.

"Do we need to help?" I asked.

"No, the catering company will handle it. We need to get going if we're going to make it to your house in time anyway."

I checked my phone, saw that she was right, and we made our way to my car.

"Thanks for putting up with all this," said Josie as we buckled up.

"All what?"

"My family events can be a little much."

I smiled. "Hold that thought."

30

I don't know if you've ever experienced the potato-spatterings and gravy-spillings that come with boxing up hundreds of Thanksgiving meals, but trust me, you need to clean up and change clothes before you go anywhere else. Between that and some dog wrangling, we showed up a little late at my mom and dad's house.

Izzy answered the door. "Happy Thanksgiving." She gave Josie a hug, took the stuffing that was our contribution to the feast then, after giving Roxie a quick scratch, led us into my parents' great room which was already full.

Izzy leaned into Josie and pointed. "The slugs staring at the TV are Nate's brothers, Mark and Tom. The boys taking their unfortunate example are Justin, James, and Joe—all mine by the way, but you can only do so much."

"Love you too, honey," said Mark.

"They already kicked off, Uncle Nate," said Joe. "Uncle Tom said you're a turd."

"There's a Claw of Doom in your future, Joe."

"No way. Hey Page! Roxie's here!"

Joe came scampering over and Roxie sat and wagged when

he arrived. As a young girl joined him, Izzy said "That's Page, one of Tom and Kate's girls, ah, and here is Kate and her other girls Reed and Taylor. Girls, this is Josie."

Kate gave Josie a hug and the girls said hello and we all rolled in.

"Where's Mom and Dad?" I said to Izzy.

"Mom's finishing things up in the kitchen. Pop is minding the smoker."

I guided Josie out to the deck where my dad had the lid of the smoker open and was sticking a thermometer into an enormous bird.

"How's it coming, Dad?"

He peered a little closer. "Just about there." He pocketed the thermometer, shut the lid, and flashed a white smile. "And who is this?"

"Josie, this is my dad, David. Dad, Josie."

"Thanks for having me over today, Mr. Shepherd."

"Dave, please. And I'm glad you could come, Josie. We're going to need all the help we can get with this thing."

"I didn't know the pilgrims ate pterodactyl," I said.

My dad smiled. "Got tired of making two."

"How big is that one?"

"Forty-two pounds."

"Sweet Jesus."

My dad shook his head. "I know. Don't bring it up with your mother."

"Speaking of which, we'll go see her. How long should I tell her?"

"I think half an hour to cook and half an hour to rest. But I have also never cooked a dinosaur before."

"Got it."

"Welcome, Josie."

We popped over to the kitchen to find my mom and Kate

moving pans to find the proper place for food in the refrigerator, oven, and island.

"Was that stuffing already cooked, Josie?" asked Kate.

"Yes. Just needs to be warmed up."

"Let's keep that on the oven then," said my mom. "We can pop it in once the bird is resting. Did your father say how long, Nate?"

"He thinks about an hour."

She shook her head. "We could feed an army with that thing. Oh, look at me, I'm sorry, dear." My mom bustled over and gave Josie a quick hug. "Welcome. I'm so glad you could come."

"Mom, this is Josie."

"So nice to finally meet you, Josie."

"You too, Mrs. Shepherd."

"Monica, please. You know, you don't run into many 'Josies' anymore. Is that short for Josephine?"

"Marie-Josée."

My mom turned and moved a platter from the island to the stove top. "How beautiful. Is that a family name?"

Before Josie could respond, there was a ring at the doorbell and the clatter of activity as Olivia and Dr. Brad arrived.

There was a general melee as the two said hello and brought new dishes into the mix so that my mom, Kate, and Olivia were occupied with a great reshuffling.

Josie and I had gone out with Olivia and Dr. Brad, her rock-climbing cardiologist boyfriend, a couple of times, so the three of us escaped the kitchen whirlwind and traded small talk as we gravitated back out to the living room and the Detroit Lions. Reed and Taylor had been waiting to pounce on Josie and, before I knew it, the two of them had Josie talking about being a respiratory therapist, which led to a full blown discussion about shadowing programs at the hospital that seemed far more serious on the part of my nieces than I would've expected.

When Dr. Brad joined the mix, I decided to check back in with
Roxie.

I learned to my chagrin that, despite the fact that my nephew
Joe was laughing, Roxie did not approve of the Claw of Doom as
she gave me the ever so faintest growl. I stopped.

"What have you done to my dog, Joe?"

Joe, still laughing, sat up and hugged Roxie. "He's a mean old
man, isn't he, Roxie?"

"The Claw of Doom is not pleased."

"The Most-Best Boxer does not care." Joe kissed the top of
Roxie's head, and she flopped back down.

"Traitor," I said and went over to check the football game.

Olivia came out from the kitchen at the same time and
motioned me over.

I joined her, yawning. "Sorry."

Olivia smirked. "Up late?"

"No. Up early."

"What is that for a lawyer? Nine? Ten?"

"No, it was Olivia early." Olivia was notorious for eating
breakfast at four-thirty in the morning before starting pre-work
classes.

"I doubt it."

I told her about our morning.

"I stand corrected. How was it?"

"I couldn't believe how many they served."

"That's good work." Olivia and Cade had been coming to our
house for the holidays since high school. It's a complicated story
that doesn't play into Logan Carver's case, but I realized that she
would have a greater appreciation for what the Lacombes were
doing than most.

I was pulled back to the present when she said, "Has the
Judge ruled on the story the *Torch* is withholding yet?"

"Any day."

"Still think the article is about Paxton Plating?"

"No idea, but we know Marsh was talking to Ringel about Paxton during the same time period."

"Let me know if you need a crack investigator to do some exploring."

"Do you know one?"

She smiled. "Not that you can afford. Speaking of which, I've finished mapping out the times Carver was playing games on his Xbox."

"Anything interesting?"

"Nothing that will help your timeline. There's a pretty big gap when he wasn't playing."

"How big?"

"From 4 p.m. the day Marsh was murdered until 1 a.m. the next morning."

"Well, that's not helpful at all."

"No, it actually hurts since it shows he wasn't playing at the time of the murder."

I couldn't see Olivia's eyes behind her glasses, but her head snapped around as she said, "Good Lord, look at that thing!"

My dad was struggling to open the patio door while holding a forty-two-pound turkey on an enormous platter. We scrambled to open the door and steady the bird and make exclamations of amazement as we all chipped in on the final preparations for the feast.

It took my dad a little more time than usual to carve the dang thing, but eventually we were all set up at two long tables in my parents' great room. And yes, in a hideous display of ageism, we had a kiddy table. Reed loudly protested being included in this societal hinterland, which was overruled by my father, who pointed out that he was the oldest person in the room, and he was sitting there too.

My mom was at the end of the adult table closest to the kitchen with Mark and Izzy on one side, Tom and Kate on the other, while Olivia and Dr. Brad sat opposite Josie and me at the far end.

While the main dishes had passed in an orderly counter-clockwise fashion, we had reached the chaotic crisscross of condiments stage as gravy, salt, pepper, and butter were randomly exchanged, reached for, and grabbed when Izzy said, "This stuffing is delicious, Josie. Did you make it?"

Josie ducked her head. "I can't claim the credit for that."

"Well, I know Nate didn't do it. He's never made stuffing that didn't need to be drowned in gravy and this is delicious by itself."

"I'm afraid I picked it up."

Izzy waved a hand. "We've all been there. You have to tell me where though so I can get some myself the next time I'm up against it."

I wasn't sure how much she wanted to say but Josie smiled and said, "Carrefour Prime Catering."

"I thought they just did events?"

"My aunt's company had one this morning."

"Nate told me what you all do," said Olivia. "A thousand meals? That's incredible, Josie."

"It's not me," said Josie, eyes down.

"If you worked, you're a part of it," said Olivia, who looked over her shoulder. "Great bird, Mr. Shep."

"Thanks, Olivia," said my dad between mouthfuls.

"Did you work some extra spice into that rub?"

"Don't you go stirring up trouble." Then he winked and tossed her a spice shaker, which Olivia enthusiastically applied.

"Sounds like quite the event," said my mother.

"Your son slings a mean mashed potato, Mrs. Shepherd."

"Monica, dear." My mom put another scoop of corn on her plate. "You went too, Nate?"

I nodded. "Early this morning."

"Where was it again?"

"Lacombe Logistics. They opened up all the loading bays. It really was something."

"You didn't have any green beans, Tom." My mom passed him the bowl then said, "I imagine you had plenty of help. There are so many Lacombes in Carrefour."

Josie smiled. "Five generations of French-Canadian Catholics."

"So are you related to the new Speaker of the House?" said Dr. Brad.

Josie nodded "JP is my cousin."

Dr. Brad nodded. "I voted for him. He has some great ideas —cracking down on vaping, increased food safety regulations, expansion of insurance enrollment—all things that help my patients."

My mom put a roll on her already full plate. "How close a cousin?"

"First," said Josie. "His mother, Marie-Faye, is my dad's sister."

"I met her this morning, Mom. She said to give you her best. Do you know her?"

"I haven't seen her in some time." She smiled at Josie before looking at the kid's table. "Boys, is that broccoli-cheesy-rice bowl empty over there?"

"Yes!" said Justin, James, and Joe.

"Do you want some more?"

"Yes!"

My mother went over to the kids' table, and my dad handed her the empty cheesy rice bowl. "Do you want some help?"

"I can handle it, dear," she said and went to the kitchen. She was back a minute later and dished out a heaping spoonful of cheesy goodness to each of her grandsons, including little Charlie who hadn't even asked for it, before she sat back down with us and said, "So Olivia, Cade called to say he couldn't make it until later tonight. That was very sweet of him to let me know."

"You know he won't miss leftovers, Mrs. Shep."

"No, I don't suppose he would. He said he was going to that woman's house who came over with him on the Fourth of July. Kira, was it?"

Seven of the eight adults at my table paused. From the kiddy table, my niece Page said, "Kira is pretty."

Taylor elbowed Page in the side.

"And she only needs one ski," said Joe.

Josie smiled and said to me, "You and Cade both dated a girl named Kira?"

I smiled back. "No. Just me. Cade came over on the Fourth with Molly, who he's apparently with today."

My mother smiled. "Well, there you go. I knew it was one of those names. Who wants pie? Marie-Josée? We have pumpkin and apple."

"Who's Marie?" said Mark around a mouthful of turkey.

"Just Josie, Monica. And apple, please."

"Us too, Grandma!" said the boys.

My mom smiled. "It's on the way," she said, and went back to the kitchen.

"Clear your plates first," said Kate.

As the boys clattered into the kitchen, Kate glanced at me then looked down. I glanced at Izzy quickly, who mouthed, "What the?" and looked into the kitchen.

I looked at Josie, who smiled and said, "Which pie for you?"

"Coffee, probably."

She looked disappointed.

"With a little apple?"

"Perfect." Then she put her hand on my leg and squeezed.

I smiled back, kissed her cheek, then glanced at my dad who avoided my gaze and focused intently on little Charlie's description of a squirrel he'd seen out the window.

We finished dinner but with our pre-dawn start and an early shift for Josie the next day, we were running out of steam. Between the ruckus of the kids and the clatter of the dishes and the cheers from a last second rally during the game, I didn't have a chance to talk discreetly to my mom or dad. If truth be told, it seemed like both of them were avoiding me, although I suppose it was possible that it was just a coincidence that my dad finished cleaning the ashes out of the smoker and that my mom put the last dish away right as Josie and I said we were leaving. There were smiles and hugs as we left and I'm sure it was just my imagination that my mom and dad focused more on Roxie when we left than on Josie and me.

I dropped Josie off with thanks for sharing the day and a promise to call in a couple of days when she was off shift. Then I went home with Roxie to vegetate on the couch and wonder what the hell had just happened.

31

I decided to work from home the day after Thanksgiving. After a morning walk with Roxie, I checked my email and found a note from Judge Wesley's bailiff advising us that the judge had ruled on our motion to compel production of the *Torch's* file. I clicked on the decision and scrolled to the end.

She had granted it.

There were some limitations. The name of the confidential source would remain redacted, and we weren't allowed to use the contents of the file at trial without requesting permission from the Court, but we were allowed to see what the article was that Christopher Marsh was writing on the day he died.

The judge had attached the *Torch* file as it had been produced to her. I opened it. Each page had a watermark "Confidential-Protective Order" at the top. I ignored it and read the article first:

Paxton Plating Contaminates Ash County Forever

Some chemicals never go away. Once they get into the water, you can't get them out. Instead, they stay there forever before they find their way into the fish, into the animals, and into us, accumulating in our bloodstream with nowhere to go.

Paxton Plating dumped these forever chemicals into our river and then covered it up. Why? To make its earnings look good for a quarter. It poisoned our forever to buy three months.

Marsh reported that an anonymous source within Paxton Plating had warned it repeatedly that its wastewater treatment system wasn't working properly. Because it was a new system and because replacing it so soon would be a massive expense that would shut down the plant for weeks, management ignored the source's warnings for more than a year. Finally, the wastewater treatment system had broken down, resulting in a massive dump of PFAs, forever chemicals, into the river that ran through most of Ash County.

That's not where it ended, though. According to Marsh, the dump went on for days before it was stopped. Then Paxton cobbled together one questionably effective repair after another for more than a quarter in an effort to keep the plant churning along. Then, for reasons that weren't clear to the source, the company changed direction and replaced it all with a new state of the art system.

But Paxton covered it all up. It never revealed the dumping, not to the agencies that regulated it, and not to the people of Ash County.

Marsh concluded with a call for the state and federal government to intervene and shut Paxton down. He left a space blank at the end with a note to Ted saying, "*Ted, I'll insert Paxton's official response here but thought I should wait until just before the story runs. Let me know what you think.*"

The draft was dated on the day of Marsh's death.

Marsh had even submitted a proposed follow-up story,

giving more details on Paxton's history of prior incidents, its current production and wastewater containment system, and a detailed timeline of the system's failure and the company's cover-up.

I popped over to the related "Note" that had been withheld. Marsh had listed corporate filings for Paxton's business history, state and federal records for Paxton's prior dumping history, some descriptions of the chemicals involved and studies on their effects, and then direct quote after direct quote from the anonymous source.

Christopher Marsh provided a citation after each quote which said, "[Name Redacted]—Interview notes—laptop."

Finally, I checked the *Torch's* Messaging file that had been withheld which contained messages between Ted Ringel and Christopher Marsh. They started on the Tuesday before Marsh died:

Tuesday, 11:42 a.m.

Ringel: How's the Paxton draft coming?

Marsh:Good. I'll have it to you Friday.

Marsh:Do you have time for a call tomorrow? I need you to walk me through the last steps. Never handled one like this before.

Ringel:Of course. With this kind of story, we'll need to double-check the facts. How's 2:00?

Marsh: Perfect.

Wednesday, 3:37 p.m.

Marsh: Thanks again for the call today, Ted. I've arranged to meet the source at Muirfield Park tomorrow. Should still be able to get you a draft by Friday.

Ringel: You're doing great work, Chris. Keep it up.

Friday, 5:12 p.m.

Marsh: Here's the draft Paxton article and the notes, Ted.

Friday, 5:46 p.m.

Ringel: This is great, Chris! You're going to tack their nuts to the wall!! We need the source to confirm the quotes or agree to a recorded interview—corporate will need its own file when Paxton responds. Keep working! Great job!!!!

Marsh: Thanks! Going for a run. Will call later.

That was all. Christopher Marsh would be dead that night.

I let it all sink in for a moment, then I picked up the phone to do the only reasonable thing in that situation—I called Olivia.

"Hey, Shep."

"The Judge has released the *Torch* files."

"Talk to me."

"Paxton Plating dumped contaminated water into the river, then covered it up."

"Contaminated how?"

"Have you ever heard of PFAs?"

"Only that they exist. I don't know what they are."

"Let me make it simple. They're toxic chemicals that don't break down."

"That sounds bad."

"And since they don't break down, they build up in fish and animals and us."

"That's horrifying."

"Right. And Paxton covered it all up."

"Hang on a minute, let me go to my office."

"Are you out in the gym?"

"Stuffing doesn't work itself off."

I waited as I heard her pass pockets of clanking and rattles, then heard the clatter of a keyboard before she said, "That's what I thought. Remember I told you about the Paxton sale last month?"

"Four hundred million, right?"

"Right. In looking that up, I found a bunch of articles, which looked like regurgitated press releases, that showed Paxton had installed a new wastewater treatment system a few months before the sale 'as part of its commitment to supporting local environmental efforts.'"

"So not long before Marsh's murder. Sounding like a motive to you?"

"Sounds like something. Can you send me the files?"

"Doing it right now."

"I'll see what I can find. Just wait to make sure it goes through."

As I typed and she waited, Olivia said, "Hey, what was with your mom yesterday?"

"You noticed?"

"Hell yes, I noticed. Did Josie?"

"Not really. I mean, a little, it was hard to miss the Kira dig, but I think she wrote it off as typical in-law stuff."

"That was not typical."

"No, it wasn't. And I have no idea."

My mother was unfailingly courteous to anyone she met, and that was doubly true for someone in her house. Keep in mind that she had once scolded me for being slow to invite a killer—a man who had literally beaten another man into a bloody, unrecognizable mess—into her home and then patted him on the cheek in welcome. The way she had acted with Josie was the equivalent of a screaming fit.

"There, it just came in," Olivia said. "I'll see what else I can find out about Paxton Plating.

"And the source too, please."

"Do we have anything?"

"Only that he or she works at Paxton and was at Muirfield Park the day before Marsh died."

"I'm on it."

"Thanks, Liv."

"And look on the bright side."

"What's that?"

"Christmas should be fun."

"Let's stick to murder."

32

T he next morning, my father showed up at my door.
I invited him in and offered him coffee, but he
turned me down. "I can't stay long. I'm at the hardware store."

I raised an eyebrow. "Isn't there one two miles from your
house?"

"Sure, but they don't carry the type of submersible pump I've
been meaning to get. Have to come down to the big box store for
that."

"Gotcha."

"It wasn't your mom's fault yesterday."

"Okay."

"Josie just caught her by surprise is all."

"Josie didn't do anything, Dad."

"I don't mean that she did, son. It was her name."

"Josie?"

"Lacombe."

"I didn't know you had it in for French-Canadians."

"Not the name exactly."

"You're going to ruin your alibi, you know."

"What?"

"If you keep jerking around, you're going to be here a lot longer than it would take to pick out a submersible pump at a hardware store."

My dad ran a hand through that white hair, looked into the kitchen, and said, "Before I met your mother, I saw Marie-Faye Lacombe."

"In the grocery store or on a date?"

"On a bunch of dates. Two years' worth."

I had difficulty picturing the woman I had just met and my father together. "Was it serious?"

"Very."

"What happened?"

My dad gave me a look that was a little hard. "That's between me and her. What's important is that we broke it off, I met your mom a few months later, and we were married a year after that."

I smiled. "I didn't take Mom for the jealous type."

"It's not that exactly. You'd have to meet Marie-Faye to understand."

"I have, remember?"

"Oh, right. So, you know how she's..." He trailed off.

I didn't say anything.

Eventually, my dad shook his head. "Carrefour isn't that big a place, but for a couple of years there, while your mom and I were dating and just after we were married, we ran into Marie-Faye more than we should have. It was never rude but always...uncomfortable."

"I see." I didn't, of course, but that seemed like the thing to say.

"I really hadn't thought much about her until Josie came by and, like I said, it caught us off-guard."

"Is this going to be a problem, Dad?"

"Are you going to keep seeing her?"

I knew both of us were uncomfortable with this much talk about our relationships, but my dad had opened up with me, so I thought I would give him the same courtesy back. "I think so. We both lost our spouses so we're being pretty cautious, but it also means we understand each other more than most. And I would like to not worry about bringing her to family things."

"Does she work with her aunt?"

"She's a respiratory therapist, Dad. And she hands out turkeys at Thanksgiving."

My dad opened his mouth, shut it, then nodded his head. "Okay then. Did Josie notice yesterday?"

"It would be kind of hard not to. But I don't think she realized what Mom is normally like. Nothing to worry about. Or to apologize for later."

"All right."

"Besides, now I know that the next time I bring a new date around, I need to check with you to make sure it's not a daughter or niece or adoptive heir of a woman you had a fling with decades ago."

"It's not like that."

"Maybe not. But it was fun to say."

"I best get back."

I walked him back to the door. "Good luck with the submersible."

"I really am sorry, son."

"I know. Don't worry about it."

"And don't think twice about bringing Josie around."

"Thanks. I won't."

He started to speak, stopped, then said, "Right. Bye."

I watched that shaggy white hair go down my brick walk, thinking that we really don't know our parents at all. Then my phone buzzed.

"Emily! Did you have a good Thanksgiving?"

"If you consider five hours on the road for a three-hour dinner good, then yes."

"Five hours?"

"Round trip. My fiancé's family is in Columbus."

"I'm sorry about that."

"The traffic wasn't too bad."

"No, I meant about the family being from Columbus."

"It is a boring place, what with its teams always winning and winning and winning."

"So what's—"

"And winning."

I cleared my throat. "So what's going on?"

"I'm in the office. I just heard back from the lab on Logan Carver's clothes."

"Emily, you didn't have to work today."

"Maybe, but it's a good thing I did."

"Why's that?"

"Bad news first. The lab agrees that the fibers of Logan's sweatshirt match the fibers found at the scene."

"Is there good news?"

"Yep. There's not a speck of blood on it."

33

"Outstanding," I said. "What did the lab say, exactly?"

"There were fibers from the sweatshirt in the TV stand. You know that thingy on the inside that latches the door? He thinks the sleeve snagged on a jagged part of that."

"So he puts Logan there?"

"One hundred percent."

"I suppose we always knew that was the case, but it's not the most helpful."

"No, but here's what is. There is not a speck of blood on that glorious FU sweatshirt."

"How certain is he of that?"

"Also one hundred percent. If it's there, he didn't find it. And he thinks he would find it."

"He's willing to testify to that?"

"He is. And he'll testify that anyone who does say there is blood on the sweatshirt is full of shit."

"Is that the forensic term?"

"It's the legal one. You know what is on the sweatshirt, though?"

"What?"

She grinned. "A mixture of glucose syrup, whey powder, milk, cocoa powder, and a few unpronouncables on the left sleeve."

"Is that what I hope it is?"

"If you're hoping for a delicious chocolate shake, then yes."

I grinned. "Well."

"Exactly! So, what do we do next?"

I thought, then said, "I assume each restaurant chain has its own shake recipe. Have him test it to make sure it's from McDonald's."

"Way ahead of you. It's consistent."

"Excellent. Has the lab tested the jeans and shoes?"

"Yep. No blood there either."

"All right. Then I need to call Devon Payne and see how his spatter analysis is going."

"To see if you can beat someone to death with a baseball bat without getting blood on you?"

"You catch on fast."

"Can I sit in on the call?"

"I don't know if he'll be in but let's give it a try."

I texted Devon Payne and asked if he was working today and had time for a call. I got a text back to give him a few minutes.

"How does someone become a blood spatter expert anyway?" said Emily.

"I think you start with droplets, move up to smears, and eventually end up in spatters."

Emily suggested that my derriere should take a MENSA test.

While we waited, I said, "How's the due diligence with Danny coming?"

Emily sighed. "Purchase orders aren't blood spatters."

Devon Payne called then, and I conferenced us all in.

"What?" he said.

He didn't seem at all interested in pleasantries, so I went right to it. I explained the forensic testing results and said, "So my question is, could someone have clubbed Christopher Marsh in the back of the head with a baseball bat and caused the spatters you've seen without getting any on his clothes?"

"Best guess?" he said. "It's possible."

Emily cursed.

"But I don't think it's likely. And there will be a difference between the trajectory of the first blow and the second. I'm going to have to analyze it."

"Please do."

"Okay." Then he hung up.

"Charming," Emily said.

"He prefers genius. So we're making headway. Logan is in the house but has no blood on him and we have Devon Payne analyzing whether you can bludgeon someone without getting spattered."

"Right. And we have the 9:02 p.m. video at the drive-thru for a bracket on the back end but nothing of significance on the front end to narrow the window for the killing."

"That's right. Keep working that."

"I will."

"We still have time. It's a good start. Good work, Emily."

"But we still don't have any explanation for the bat."

"Actually, there's been a development there too." I told her about the Court's ruling and the Paxton article.

After complaining that she wasn't copied in by the Court, Emily said, "So you think it was Paxton Plating?"

"The question, Emily, is whether it *could have been* Paxton Plating. And whether we can get that possibility in."

"Seems like a stretch."

"It is right now. I've turned Olivia loose on it."

"So let me make sure I understand our strategy, Boss—we're

going to explain to the jury that while our client broke into the house and stole things, he didn't actually kill the victim."

"Right."

"Instead, our client was framed by an evil corporation who was trying to silence a report by a whistleblower about illegal dumping that might interfere with a multi-million-dollar sale."

"Hundreds of millions, yes."

"And our best evidence is the absence of blood and the presence of milkshake."

I grinned. "Exactly."

"Sounds fun."

I WAS GETTING ready to call it an afternoon and walk Roxie when Silas Winford called. "Oh good, I caught you," he said.

"Happy Thanksgiving, Sye."

"And you, Nate. I'm sorry to bother you on the holiday weekend, but something came up I wanted you to know about right away."

Here's a little legal insight for you—nothing good ever follows that sentence.

"What's up?" I said.

"Your client has been involved in a fight at the jail."

"How is he?"

"He's just a little banged up. The other guy was taken to the hospital."

"Are you serious?"

"I'm afraid I am. Your client jumped the victim from behind and smashed his face into the sink. Broke the guy's orbital bone, nose, a few teeth. The victim was out on his feet."

"Are charges going to be filed?"

"The Sheriff's office is investigating, but I don't think there's any doubt about that."

"I see."

"We will not be seeking to combine the cases. I think it would just muddy the waters."

"I agree."

"Although I expect the judge will take it into consideration at sentencing."

"Assuming you win, yes."

"Well, Nate, I think we can both assume that I'm at least going to win the home invasion case, which means your client is going to get convicted of something, which means that the judge will know about this attack when he is sentenced."

I couldn't argue with the logic of that, so I said, "I appreciate you letting me know so quickly, Sye. Since you're not seeking to combine the cases, we can brief up whether my client was at fault and whether the judge should consider this incident at sentencing after trial. If necessary, of course."

"No, Nate, that's not why I'm contacting you now. We still intend to introduce evidence of this attack at trial. I wanted to give you a heads-up."

"How is that relevant to the case? You just said yourself it would muddy the waters."

"A whole trial on whether your client's attack on a fellow inmate was justified or criminal would indeed muddy the waters, Nate. Limited evidence of the method of attack would not. Some might even call it a pattern."

"Seems like a stretch, Sye."

"Your client used a broken mop handle."

I didn't swear, kept my voice even, and said, "Still seems like a stretch. We'll move to exclude that evidence."

"I expect you would. I wanted to let you know now so that we could brief it up in advance. I'd really rather not do it over Christmas."

"That makes sense. Why don't we get more details about what happened next week, then I'll file our motion so that your response is due before the holiday."

"Perfect. Thanks, Nate."

"Thanks for letting me know, Sye."

"Of course. Happy Thanksgiving."

Silas Winford had a reputation for being courteous, a straight shooter, and very, very good. This call confirmed all those things.

It also confirmed that he believed he had just stuck an M-80 directly into my pumpkin. At that moment, I wasn't sure he was wrong.

34

There was no Shepherd lunch that Sunday since we'd all just been together for Thanksgiving. That freed up the afternoon to see Josie and allowed some time for the awkwardness with my parents to settle. I was glad for both.

Josie had just worked two twelves in a row and had another scheduled the next day, so she just felt like hanging out at my place which was fine with me. We took Roxie for a slow walk, then came back for a lunch of homemade dill pickle soup from me and fresh sourdough bread Josie had brought from the Stone Hearth Bakery.

Josie was cutting the bread, I was ladling out the soup, and Roxie had curled up in the corner so she could be in the same room with us when Josie said, "This was a good idea."

I smiled. "We'll have to plan not to make plans more often."

"I agree."

I tore off a piece of bread and took a bite, pretending not to watch as she blew on the spoon, then sipped. She started a bit, then looked over my shoulder at the pot on the stove. "You made this?"

"That depends."

"When you said dill pickle...this is really good." She ate another spoonful.

"Then, yes."

Josie ate a little more of the underestimated soup, then said, "Oh, my parents wanted me to make sure you're invited to the family New Year's Party."

I smiled. "Your parents are inviting me."

She leaned into me. "I am. But they wanted to be sure since they didn't get to see you at the Thanksgiving kitchen."

"Were they there?"

"They were in one of the delivery vans."

I raised my eyebrows. "You delivered too?"

She shrugged. "Just to a few people we know can't get out. Anyway, my mom wanted to meet you since the rest of the family did."

I debated with myself but only for a moment before I said, "Hey, speaking of parents, I'm sorry about my mom the other day."

Josie smiled. "I barely noticed." She gave me a look. "But if she mentions a new woman every time..."

I smiled. "Not a risk. She's usually not like that."

"No?"

"There was some history I wasn't aware of that she was reacting to."

"How could there be history with me?"

"No, with my father. And your Aunt Marie-Faye."

Josie put down her spoon. "You're kidding."

"I'm not."

"I would not have put them together."

"Me either. I didn't know about it. My dad apologized later and told me about it. Apparently, they were a fairly serious thing back in the day and the name caught my mom off guard."

"*Ma Tante*? And your dad?"

"So I've been told."

She shook her head. "That's a little weird. "

"Too weird?"

Josie smiled. "Not for me. You?"

"No."

"Good."

"I take it you didn't know about this either?"

Josie shook her head. "I only know about Uncle George, my cousins' dad. But gosh, I was pretty young when he died and after that, well, after that no one really brought up *Ma Tante's* relationships for obvious reasons."

"What happened?"

"He killed himself."

"I'm sorry."

She shook her head. "I was too young to know what was going on really. My dad told me at the time that he had an accident. I was a teenager before I questioned how a shotgun could go off in a study and in high school before I learned that a self-inflicted gunshot wound isn't really an accident."

"That must've been hard on your family."

"Like I said, I was pretty young. So was Maxime. But JP was a couple of years older and so it was a pretty rough go for him."

"I bet."

"Did you watch any of his speeches? Before he was elected?"

"I'm afraid not."

"Mental health is one of his big issues. Funding community support organizations, growing insurance coverage for counseling and access to medications, and veteran's support organizations...he's big on those since Maxime served. JP mentions his dad sometimes, not in an over-the-top 'this impacted my family' kind of way but in a 'someone you know needs support' kind of way. A lot of his philosophy stems from that."

"I mostly remember the vaping from talking to him."

Josie smiled. "That too. He's big on regulating the 'sin' industries. All part of that healthy body, healthy mind philosophy."

"Must make for interesting dinner table conversation."

"How so?"

"Since your dad is running a distillery."

"Farming is my dad's main business. The distillery is a hobby. But you're right, my dad does give JP some grief about taxes sometimes."

Josie's spoon clicked the bottom of the bowl, and she held it up with both hands, forlorn. "Please sir, may I have some more?"

"Whatever you want when you ask so nicely."

She smiled. "Is that all I have to do? Ask nicely?"

We ate more soup. Eventually.

35

First thing Monday morning, I was out at the Ash County jail to see Logan. He was seated at the table, hands folded, when I said, "Tell me about the fight, Logan."

"There wasn't a fight."

"The prosecutor called me. He told me you put a guy in the hospital."

Logan Carver shook his head. "But there wasn't a fight."

"Did you hit a guy in the head?"

Logan nodded. "But the guards didn't care; they didn't even do anything to me."

"The guards might not care, Logan, but the judge does. And putting a man in the hospital is a crime."

"But I'm already in jail!"

"That doesn't matter."

"I can't commit a crime in jail."

"Yes, you can."

"But I'm already in jail!"

"You'll be kept in jail longer if you hurt people while you're here."

Logan Carver's shoulders slumped as he considered it.

"Why did you do it, Logan?"

He straightened a little. "You can't let someone talk shit about your friend."

"Do you have friends here?"

"Yep."

"Did a friend tell you to attack the other man?"

Logan scowled. "Friends don't tell other people what they talk about."

"Did your friend tell you that?"

"Yes. I mean we don't talk about it."

"What if you hadn't beat the man up?"

"Friends help friends."

"And if you don't help?"

"Then you must not be friends."

I was caught in a different kind of friend circle here. "Logan, did your new friends tell you how to attack the man?"

"Friends don't tell other people what they talk about."

"Did your friends tell you about lawyers?"

"Yeah. They said most of them suck but that they can get you out sometimes, even if you did something."

"Did they tell you about lawyers and secrets?"

Logan frowned again. "No."

"Lawyers keep secrets. If you tell me something secret, I don't tell anyone else."

"Like I'm your only friend?"

"Yes."

"Like when I only had Peyton before?"

"Exactly like that. So did your friends in here tell you how to attack the man?"

"Friends help friends."

"I know. But did your friends tell you *how* to help them."

Logan scowled and he clenched his hands together and he didn't say anything.

"Let me explain what's going on, Logan. The prosecutor is going to say that you killed Christopher Marsh."

"I didn't kill anybody."

"I understand that. But he's going to say you hit Christopher Marsh in the head from behind with a bat."

"I didn't do that."

"I understand. But he's going to say that you did. And the prosecutor is going to say it's just like when you hit the man here in jail, when you waited 'til the man wasn't looking, and you hit him from behind with the mop handle."

"I did do that."

"Right. So, my question is, did someone tell you to do it that way?"

"I'm not big."

"No."

"It will be easier if I wait until he bends down over the sink."

"Right."

"If I'm behind him. I won't get hurt."

"Right."

There was silence then. It extended until I said, "Did someone give you the mop handle, Logan?"

He scowled until I thought his brow would break then his face relaxed and he straightened. "Friends don't talk about friends."

"Okay, Logan. I have to go."

"Will you come back?"

"When I can." I stood and knocked on the door.

"Tell my mom I have friends now."

"I will. And Logan, don't hurt anyone else, no matter what your friends say, or it might be a very long time before you see your mom again."

"Friends help each other," he said.

A thought occurred to me. "Do friends give each other money, Logan?"

Logan nodded. "If you bring them something. " He scowled. "Friends don't talk about friends."

I could see the "friends rules" stacking up on Logan as he sorted through them. "Logan."

He looked up.

"Friends don't ask you to do something that gets you in trouble. Ever."

Logan was working on that new rule as the guard let me out.

As soon as I made it to the parking lot, I called Olivia.

"What's up, Shep?"

"I need you to look for a man who specializes in the sale of stolen goods named Peyton."

36

There was a pause. "You're taking me for granted, Shep."

"Never."

"How about I snap my fingers and find a shoplifter named Mike."

"Liv–"

"Or, I know, I'll wave my magic wand and make all of the jaywalkers named John levitate so you can pick one out."

"Are you done?"

"It sounds like I'll never be done."

"I have more information."

"You couldn't lead with that?"

"I was trying."

"Go ahead."

"Thank you." I told her about my visit with Logan Carver. And about the attack.

"That's bad news," she said.

"Very. He slipped when he was talking to me, though, and mentioned that Peyton was his only friend before he was arrested."

"How do we get from there to stolen goods?"

I wasn't going to take Olivia through the circuitous track of Logan's "friend rules." "Something Logan said tripped me to it. Logan's been busted for robbery but never for moving stolen goods. He got fleeced when he sold Marsh's stuff to Second Chance Electronics." Another fact fell into place as I spoke. "And there's more than an hour between when he made a scene at the McDonald's and when he appeared at Second Chance Electronics."

"What?"

"I think Logan went to give what he'd stolen to his usual guy and when he couldn't find him, he tried to sell the PS5 and the Beats himself."

"I'll see what I can find, Shep, but it's going to be hard if he's never been caught."

"How many people can there be in Carrefour who move stolen goods?"

"You'd be surprised. Fortunately, you know an extraordinary investigator."

"I forget that sometimes."

"That's why I remind you. I'll get on this."

"Oh, hey, wait. I found out what the deal was at Thanksgiving."

I told her about Marie-Faye Lacombe and my dad.

"How did you learn that?"

"My dad told me. Said the name of the family threw my mom off."

"I'll say. Still, that was a long time ago."

"It apparently made an impact. It sounded like things were strange for a couple of years until Marie-Faye got married and had kids of her own."

"Huh. How are you and Josie doing?"

"Good. Cautious with the whole spouse thing, but I like spending time with her."

"Doe-eyed blonds do make that easy."

"Such a shallow opinion of me."

"No, admiration. You've always punched above your weight class."

"Speaking of which, it was good to see Dr. Brad."

"I assume you're implying that *he's* the one punching up?"

"Whatever lets you sleep at night."

"Hmph. He's great. We'll probably head west for some more climbing this winter."

"Keeping him around for most of the year *and* making plans a month in advance? Goodness."

"Now what are you saying?"

"Nothing but facts."

"I've had about enough of those. Let me get to work on this Peyton. Peace."

We hung up and as the miles rolled by, I thought about that hour gap and how Peyton might fill it. Judging from how Logan acted today, he wasn't going to tell me so we had to find Peyton ourselves. We didn't even know who Peyton was though. And we didn't figure it out over the next four weeks.

NEW YEAR'S

37

F our weeks of the holiday season passed without any developments so that, when I came to the office on the Monday after Christmas, I expected things to be fairly quiet. What I did not expect was to find Emily copying full-bore and Danny yelling into the phone.

"I don't give a rip what your current projections are, Bill. You're the one who put that provision in the purchase agreement...That's not my problem...No, I told you that this exact thing would happen, and you wanted to go ahead with it anyway...No, we're not pushing back the closing, you know it has to close by year-end. We're keeping the Wednesday date...Actually, it's less than 48 hours, so I would get cracking if I were you."

I heard his phone hang up and a "for Pete's sake" that would've been significantly saltier if I had uttered it. I stuck my head in.

"Awfully early to be kicking ass."

Danny rubbed his forehead with one hand and smiled. "I suppose it is."

"The Tri-State Nursery deal?"

"Is there another one?

"I take it you're closing Wednesday?"

Danny glanced at the phone and shook his head. "That's the plan. Looks like I'll be herding cats the whole way. Can you make sure that you get me the office bank account information today?"

"Sure. Why?"

"We're going to have our fees wired in at close."

"Really? I thought we'd get a check sometime next year."

"Welcome to the world of corporate business, my friend." Danny stared at some papers, then put one stack on top of another.

I smiled. "Not too late to return to murder."

"I'll stick with running around with my hair on fire. Are there any conflicts if Emily comes with me Wednesday?"

"I don't think so but check with her. And let me know if you need any help, with the grunt work or copies or anything. Things are slow this week."

"Thanks, Nate. I'm just finalizing the bank info today, but I may take you up on that tomorrow."

Danny was back into his computer before we had finished talking, so I slipped out, exchanged small talk with Emily about her holiday and then, when she answered without looking up from the copy machine, decided I best just get out of the way.

Courts tend to slow down between Christmas and New Year, so I was a little surprised to find that I had an email from Judge Wesley's secretary asking if I could be available for a pretrial on Wednesday at ten. I emailed right back that I could, then started in on the dozen little projects, responses, and messages that would be my morning.

I was halfway through when Olivia called.

"Hey, Liv."

"I figured out your problem."

"You'll have to be more specific."

"True. The Paxton source. I know who he is."

"You're kidding?" I said.

"That sounded suspiciously like disbelief."

"No, more like awed appreciation."

I could not swear that Olivia sniffed on the other end of the line, but she did say, "That's acceptable. His name is Ethan Ferris, he worked for fifteen years at the Paxton Plating plant, and his daughter was playing in the U10 soccer championship semifinals the Thursday night Christopher Marsh went to see his source at Muirfield Park."

"You're sure it's him?"

"I could waste your time and tell you about how I figured out what event was going on at the Park, found the rosters for all of the teams, and cross-referenced against the Paxton employment roll, or you could display the slightest bit of trust based on years of demonstrated competence."

"So you're sure it's him?"

"Yes. Because there's one other thing. He's gone."

"How gone? Like moved gone or left this earth gone?"

"Like up and moved, but I haven't found where he's landed yet."

"How can that be?"

"That's a good goddam question."

"What do we know?"

"We know that Ethan Ferris was working as a flow management engineer at Paxton at the time Marsh died but I can't find any trace of him since early October. He's never been much of a social media poster, but his wife and daughter are and there hasn't been anything from either of them since then either. We also know that a new flow management engineer is now working at Paxton."

"And how do we know that?"

"Because a brilliant investigator called Paxton, asked to

speak to Ferris, and was told that he no longer works there, but would I like to speak to Mr. Muckty-muck who now does."

"Where did you learn these advanced techniques?"

"Spy school."

"Would they give Ferris a message?"

"No. They said Mr. Muckty-muck would handle anything I was working on with Ferris. They also told me that they could not pass along any personal messages since that was against company policy."

"Okay."

"I also know that Ferris's house went up in mid-October and is still on the market."

"And do we know what the real estate agent knows?"

"Who do you think you're talking to?"

"My apologies. What does the real estate agent know?"

"That the family was transferred out-of-state, and that a company specializing in corporate relocations had bought it at a discount before putting it up."

"Was it Paxton's relocation company?"

"Nope."

"Interesting."

"Exactly."

"Did you make an offer on the house?"

"What does that have to do with anything?"

"Nothing. I just wondered how far you would go."

"Fair. In this case, I didn't have to go any further. The relocation company had already paid Ferris in full, so the agent was only dealing with the relocation company on price and didn't have any contact info for Ferris."

"What about Ferris's kids?"

"The school won't reveal whether they've withdrawn, so I didn't try. I can tell you, however, that our U10 soccer star left her team at the last-minute right before an October tournament in Cincinnati."

"And how do we know this?"

"Because the soccer coach was sending out panicked posts for a replacement striker the day before they left. And the young Ferris girl was not in the team photo holding the third-place trophy."

"And we have no idea where they've landed?"

"Not so far. And because I thought you might need to reveal some of this information in court, I've only used mechanisms that I could testify to if necessary or that you could represent as appropriate."

"Those are the only techniques you ever use for me, aren't they?"

"Right. Of course."

"Can you keep looking?"

"I view this as a personal challenge now."

"So personal you'd do it for free?"

"Never. Good try though."

"Thanks. I think another call to Ted Ringel might be in order."

"Why is that?"

"He hasn't wanted to cooperate because he's convinced Logan Carver killed his friend. I'm hoping that maybe this will change his mind."

I HAD JUST SENT the email to Ted Ringel when Emily came in. "Hey, Boss." She plopped down. "I thought I'd see if there's anything I should be doing on the Carver case."

"Not between now and your closing Wednesday. Sounds like you have your hands full."

Emily blew an errant lock of hair straight up. "And then some."

"You go to your closing, I'll go to the Carver pretrial, and we'll see where we are at the end of the week."

"Excuse me, Emily?" came Danny's voice.

Emily shook her head. "I don't think there's ever been a more polite tyrant."

"Probably not. Good luck."

She gave me a thumbs up, then called over her shoulder, "On the way."

As she walked out, I decided a field trip was in order.

38

I knocked on the door. After a minute or so, I knocked again, and this time leaned toward the doorbell camera. "I saw you pulling in right before me, Ted. Please give me a minute."

"You have no business being at my home," came Ted Ringel's voice over the speaker.

"You work from home. I didn't have a choice. Please."

"I already told you—I have no interest in helping your shit bag client."

"Ethan Ferris has disappeared, Ted."

No response.

"I thought you would want to know."

A moment later, Ted Ringel stepped out onto the porch, closing the door behind him. He was dressed in his usual loafers, khakis, and red polo shirt. His face was a little paler and his eyes a little more tired than the last time I had seen him.

He crossed his arms. "What do you know?"

"Ethan Ferris, the source for your story on Paxton Plating, disappeared last October. No one knows where they are."

"They?"

"His family is gone too." I told him about what Olivia had learned.

"How did you find all that out?"

"You should appreciate confidential sources, Ted. Especially since yours is gone. I will say it's nothing you can't verify for yourself. With a little legwork."

Ted Ringel stood there, arms still crossed, but now he was rubbing his chin. "None of this is news, Shepherd."

"What do you mean?"

"I've been after him for weeks. First, he wouldn't talk to me, then he was gone."

"His family's gone, and the house is for sale. That makes it unlikely that it was foul play."

Ted Ringel pulled a battered notepad out of his back pocket and a pen out of the spirals but didn't say anything.

I tried again. "Sounds too competent for a government whistleblower relocation. So, is he running for Paxton or from Paxton?"

Ted Ringel muttered and scrawled.

"Why haven't you run the story?"

He kept scrawling. "That's not the way it works."

"Enlighten me."

"Chris was the one who had contact with Ferris. With Chris dead, we can't run the story unless I can confirm Ferris's information. Once Chris died, Ferris would have nothing to do with me, wouldn't return calls, avoided me when I tried to see him. To publish, I need to find him or get another source."

"You can't just publish it based on Christopher's notes?"

"Not something like this. It needs to be confirmed by someone who can testify to what was said. I don't know what Ferris actually said to Christopher."

"There are no recordings?"

Ted Ringel shook his head. "No source, especially one who's

scared and wants to stay anonymous, is going to want a recording of his voice out there blowing the whistle. If there were, we could run the story. Since there's not..." Ted Ringel shrugged.

"So Christopher's death effectively killed the story?"

"Christopher's death and Ferris's disappearance."

"And that doesn't bother you?"

Ted Ringel's face went beet red as he stepped forward and punched his finger into my chest.

I let him.

"You bet your ass it bothers me, Shepherd, and I'm gonna figure this out for Chris and for me. But don't you think for a minute that this gets your client off the hook. You come traipsing over here to my house dangling bait to get me to do your dirty work, but you know what you're not saying? Maybe Paxton is behind it *and* your client did it. Maybe Paxton hired your guy to do the deed and then left him swinging once he was stupid enough to get caught."

He punched his finger into my chest a second time. I let him again. I had shown up on his porch, after all.

Ted kept going. "I've covered enough of your cases to know how you work. Your plan is to go in and start flinging conspiracies around, maybe putting another person at the scene, all to get your client off. Well, I'm not going to be a part of that. I owe it to Chris to figure out this story, his *last* story, and see that it's published with all the credit going to him so that people know what a great goddam kid, what a great goddam *reporter*, he was. But I don't give two shits about your thieving murderer of a client and my only regret is that Michigan doesn't have the death penalty so that I can watch him fry."

"And I intend to publish a story about the trial every day once it starts to make sure everyone knows what a scumbag your client is. Got it?"

Ted Ringel punctuated that last with another poke at my chest. This time, I caught it. He pushed two more times, but his hand didn't move. I let go right as he yanked back, and he stumbled a step before catching his balance.

Not my proudest moment, but I did let him poke me twice.

"I've got it, Ted. But it seems to me that you should be interested in the truth of what Christopher was doing, not its impact."

"Get off my porch."

"Somebody killed Christopher to kill his story."

"Leave."

"A friend would want to know who it was."

"Do I have to get my gun?"

"A friend who was a reporter would actually figure it out."

I did not make Ted get his gun and went to my Jeep. I kept an eye on him to make sure he didn't dip into his house, but Ted stood on his porch until I backed out and drove away.

hat night, I met Josie for dinner at her place. We hadn't seen each other since the day before Christmas Eve—we each had family obligations and she had worked a shift the day after Christmas—and she gave me a hug that was warm and soft and the slightest bit fierce.

"Hey."

"It's good to see you," she said, then gave me a kiss that pretty much proved it.

I smiled. "You too."

She pulled me along to her large kitchen where dinner was already laid out. I had been there before, but I know you haven't, so I should say that it was bigger and nicer than I expected when I first saw it—the back wall was two stories worth of windows and there were granite countertops and an eight-burner stove with porcelain handles and an honest-to-God butler pantry off to the side so that one wouldn't have to see the byproducts of cooking when one ate one's meal.

It wasn't the house of a person living alone. It was the house a well-off couple bought when they were starting a family.

I understood.

We sat down next to each other with what looked like a pie sitting in the middle of the table.

"That smells delicious."

Josie smiled. "That's because it is." She cut a generous slice and put it on my plate. I caught the smell of onions, sage, and cloves as the steam rose. "Wow. Is that meat?"

"It is."

"It smells amazing. What are the spices?"

"A special blend."

"Come on."

"I will not reveal the secrets of the family *tourtière*."

"The what?"

"A *tourtière*. It's a traditional Christmas Eve meal with our family. I thought I would make one for you."

Once things were ready, I took a bite that was as delicious as it smelled. After complimenting her again, I said, "What did you wind up doing Christmas Eve?"

"The entire Lacombe clan gathers at *Ma Tante's*."

"That would be a big party?"

Josie smiled. "My aunt doesn't throw any other kind. She's made it a point to bring the whole family in ever since Uncle George died. If your last name is Lacombe, you're invited."

"Where does she live?"

"Remember where the distillery is? That's part of a property that is a little over eight hundred acres. Her house is on the far north side."

"Was it fun?"

"I have more distant cousins than I can count, so it's nice to see them all. I grew up with JP and Maxime though, so I mostly hang out with them and their families."

"How about Christmas Day?"

"Christmas Day is when we would go to Peter's over in Grand

Rapids. This year I went to my parents in the morning and picked up a shift in the afternoon."

"It used to be Christmas Eve at Sarah's parents' in Carrefour for us."

"What did you do this year?"

"It was Friday, so I worked until about six or so then Roxie and I wrapped presents and drank beer."

"Oh? And what is she better at?"

"To be fair, she needs quite a bit of help with both."

After a moment, Josie said, "Thanks for understanding. About doing New Year's Eve instead, I mean."

"No, thank you. It was nice not to have to explain it."

There were a couple of tings of forks on plates before she said, "Do you see Sarah's family at the holidays?"

"I did at first. It would be different if there were grandkids but..." I trailed off.

Josie nodded. "Same. I went the first two years, but it's all day to GR and back and I honestly don't think I could take another conversation about what kind of grandkids we would have made." She bit her lip. "That's a terrible thing to say."

I shrugged. "But true. I usually stop by and drop something off a couple of weeks before. Let them know I'm thinking of them, of her, without spending the whole holiday *in it*."

"I may have to steal that. Maybe combine it with a holiday shopping trip."

"There you go."

She looked at me, suddenly intent. "Sarah's was sudden, right?"

I looked down. "Yes."

Josie grabbed my hand. "I'm sorry. I meant to say, what I meant to ask was, it was a surprise? Because that's what it was for us, his parents and me, with Peter. One minute he's calling me from work asking if I need anything from the store and an hour later, Sheriff Dushane is standing on my front porch telling me that there's been an accident and that he's so, so sorry. And then I have to tell Peter's parents and I have to do it over the phone because they are two and a half hours away and—" When Josie stopped, her blue eyes filled not with grief but intensity. "We just didn't have any warning. He was there and he was gone."

I remembered our first date. "You said it was a car accident?"

She nodded. "He took a curve too fast and rolled it. I'm sorry to have asked you, Nate. It's just that the suddenness made it that much harder for his parents. And for me, of course, but especially for his parents."

I nodded. "Same here. None of us had any idea that Sarah was struggling. And then one morning at 2:32 a.m., I wake up and she's not there and I go to the spare bathroom and there she was. And none of us could believe it."

I thought, then said, "You're right, the suddenness made all of it worse. Especially the guilt."

Josie nodded. "Why for you?"

"Because I didn't even know there was a problem. It had been going on for months and I didn't see it happening. You?"

"Peter was doing it because of me."

"Hurrying home?"

Josie nodded, a few times, before saying, "Right."

She smiled, then gave my hand another squeeze, and said in a maniacally cheerful voice, "And that is why our no Christmas plan was a good idea!"

I smiled. "It was."

"Maybe next year will be different?"

I smiled. "I hope so."

It's hard to explain, but that discussion, which probably seemed pretty morose to you, lightened and comforted us both, as did the shared hope that the next Christmas would be better.

40

W hen I arrived for the pretrial in Judge Wesley's court on Wednesday morning, Silas Winford was already there. "Good to see you, Nate."

"You too, Sye. Any idea what this is for?"

He shook his head. "The judge's secretary just asked that I be here. I assume she's ready to rule on your motion related to Mr. Carver's attack in jail. Nice work, by the way. My team had missed that unreported case."

I shrugged. "We'll see, I suppose. How was the drive from Detroit?"

"I'm getting used to it. My wife likes it more than I do."

"To get you out of the house?"

"You've talked to her, I see. It does give me time to catch up on my reading, though."

"While you're driving?"

"Audiobooks. The best thing ever. I am re-listening to *Seabiscuit* right now. The narrator's fantastic. Makes the miles fly by."

"How's the travel been?"

"Honestly, not bad. It's easier knowing it's only for a year before they send me back out to pasture."

I smiled. "With Seabiscuit?"

Silas Winford laughed, and it was an easy, pleasant sound that I was certain a jury would find charming.

Judge Wesley's bailiff came out of her office. "Mr. Shepherd, Mr. Winford, the Judge will see you now. She'd like to see you in chambers rather than have an on the record pretrial."

"Perfect," said Silas Winford and put his camel hair overcoat over his arm and strode in. I followed.

Judge Eliza Jane Wesley stood as we entered and shook both of our hands. She was not wearing her robes but was just as formidable in her black suit, piled high hair, and silver-tipped, black hair sticks.

There was a mutual exchange of holiday stories that both Winford and Judge Wesley punctuated with tales of the lengths to which they would go to spoil their grandchildren before Judge Wesley said, "Thank you both for coming up today. We're a little over a month out from trial, and I figured that your preparations would begin in earnest after the new year."

Silas Winford nodded. "We've already been going for a couple of weeks, Your Honor. In part responding to Mr. Shepherd's motion, but you're right, it will likely ramp up even more after next week."

"Yes, I have reviewed Mr. Shepherd's motion to exclude evidence of Logan Carver's attack on another inmate in the Ash County jail. I have also reviewed Mr. Winford's response asserting that the attack was carried out in a manner similar to the way in which Christopher Marsh was murdered and establishes evidence of a pattern when considered with the Marsh attack."

"Your Honor," I said, "we believe that evidence of this attack is unfairly prejudicial and not linked—"

Judge Wesley raised her hand. "I've read your briefs, Mr. Shepherd. Both of you have done a fine job of directing the

Court to the appropriate decisions and have laid out the arguments, very clearly I might add, for and against my allowing this evidence in. It's a close call. It seems to me that allowing evidence of a separate crime and incident into this trial has the potential to be prejudicial on many levels, both in showing that Mr. Carver has committed other crimes and leading to an improper inference as to whether he committed this one. On the other hand, Mr. Winford raises a very good point that the method of attack is virtually identical to the Marsh murder with the only difference being that Mr. Carver used a mop handle instead of a bat."

Judge Wesley shook her head then continued.

"I can see myself going either way on this. I have much of the opinion written, but I have not yet decided definitively which way I'm going to go. And of course, this is a motion *in limine,* so any decision I make is preliminary and can be changed based on the way the evidence is presented at trial. And we all know that can take unexpected turns."

"It certainly can, Your Honor," said Silas Winford.

"Sure," I said.

"So, it was my thought, before you start revving up your trial engines and before I finish my opinion, that the two of you might have a discussion about whether this case should plead out. Am I correct that the two of you have not dealt with each other before?"

"Not before this case, no, Your Honor," said Silas Winford.

"That's right." I said.

"Well, I have presided over trials with both of you and I can tell you that it's not at all clear to me which way this one will go. I think it's very possible that my ruling could tip it in either direction. So it's my thought that the two of you should have a discussion this morning, without me of course, and see if there is a plea agreement that will satisfy both of your obligations."

"I'm always happy to talk with defense counsel," said Silas Winford.

"We'll always listen, Your Honor."

"Excellent." Judge Wesley gave her desk a light tap with the point of her pen. "Why don't the two of you grab a coffee downstairs and see what you can do. I don't need to hear from you today. But I would like to know the results of your discussions by Friday."

"Absolutely, Your Honor," said Silas Winford.

"We'll be sure to let you know," I said.

"Then I hope you both have a Happy New Year with less work for us all."

We stood, took turns shaking Judge Wesley's hand, and left.

THE ASH COUNTY Courthouse had the industrial look of an institution built in the 1960s or 70s and its cafeteria was a similar no-nonsense affair, with high windows, painted cinderblock walls, and circular tables surrounded by egg-shaped chairs. It offered a limited selection of food choices in venues ranging from the four vending machines in one corner to Cindy McLaren's coffee cart in the other.

It being the week between Christmas and New Year, Cindy McLaren had red and green lights wound around the cart frame. "Mr. Winford," she said. "This is a surprise on Wednesday."

"Here to see Judge Wesley, Cindy," he said.

"And Mr. Shepherd, word is I'll be brewing your daily usual soon?"

"It's looking that way, Cindy. Good Christmas?"

"Well, Mr. McLaren outdid himself this year. I thought I was being a little too direct, leaving little catalogs about and search windows open and whatnot, but do you know he not only got me the boots I was angling for but bought me this smartwatch I didn't even know I wanted." She jangled one wrist as she put a second cup under one of her coffee pump pots.

Winford and I gave the appropriate chorus of "Ooo's."

Cindy McLaren grinned. "That's right, it's pretty and it's useful, but I'll tell you right now, if it asks me one more time if I want to take another step just to close some damn ring, I'm going to smash it on that wall right over there. And there we go, that's two creams one sugar for you, Mr. Winford, and black for you, Mr. Shepherd."

"Thank you, Cindy," we both said.

"Let me get this one," said Silas Winford, and handed her a twenty with a wave.

"Thanks."

We made our way over to the farthest corner and took a seat. We each took a sip before Silas Winford put his coffee down and leaned back. "I thought this might be what Judge Wesley would ask us to do, so I've given this some thought. Mind if I just get right at it?"

"Not at all."

"I won't go through the evidence. You know it. I'm going to have your client breaking into the home and committing a theft offense once he's in there, so I really don't feel the need to be flexible with any of that."

He paused. When I didn't respond, he continued, "I suppose you could argue that your client didn't come into the house with a deadly weapon. So from my perspective, the best argument you can make is to say that Marsh surprised your client when he came home, Marsh jumped him, and your client defended himself. Of course, since he was in the process of committing a crime, your client can't claim self-defense, so that doesn't help much, but I suppose it could make the jury a little more sympathetic. I can offer voluntary manslaughter on the death."

"That's still up to fifteen years."

"I wouldn't object if the judge makes it concurrent with the home invasion charge."

"That's a lot for a plea deal."

Winford shrugged. "It's not a lot for killing someone. And it's better than life for first degree murder."

"Does that include the jail assault?"

Silas Winford shook his head. "We haven't made a charging decision on that yet. Jail cases are always so murky. You never know who started what."

"But those may be coming later?"

He shrugged. "You never know."

"It seems to me that if we win at trial, Logan will serve a lot less time."

Silas Winford tightened the lid on his coffee cup. "The jury's going to want an explanation, you know."

"For what?"

"If your client didn't kill Christopher Marsh, the jury's going to want to know who did. Do you have a theory?"

"I don't have to prove who did it. I just have to show reasonable doubt that my client did."

Silas Winford smiled. "You know better than that, Nate. You can sow doubt, sure, but you have to give them something, something that explains how a promising young reporter got his head bashed in."

"Nothing that I care to share right now."

The lines at the corner of Winford's eyes crinkled. "Nate, I believe that if you had something, you would be standing on this table shouting to the rooftops."

"I think if I did that, Sye, Cindy would knock me right back down."

He chuckled. "She would at that. Especially if it closed her activity circle for the day."

Silas Winford tapped the table lightly. "My daughter is in town for the week, so I'm going to head back to Grosse Pointe. The offer is open through Friday, like the judge said. Let me know."

"Can I get you a coffee for the ride back?"

"That would be very nice, thank you."

Cindy would not have eavesdropped, but she did have the ESP developed over long years with lawyers so that by the time I got back to the cart, she was holding out two more coffees with a smile. I paid and wished her a Happy New Year before I took the coffees and handed the one with the red stopper to Winford.

"Safe travels."

"It's a fair offer, Nate."

"I'm not saying it's not, Sye. But I don't know that I can take it. I'll let you know."

He pulled on his camel hair coat, and we walked out together before he turned right for his return trip to Grosse Point and I turned left toward the Ash County jail.

41

Logan Carver stared at me from across the table. "Manslaughter? That's still killing someone, right?"

"Yes."

"But I didn't kill him."

"They have a good chance of proving you did."

"How can that be when I didn't kill him?"

"They're going to put you in the house with the stolen property and the sweatshirt fibers. And they're going to link you to the killing with the bat."

"But it's not my bat."

"No, it was Marsh's."

"Marsh?"

"The guy they say you killed."

"See, it's not my bat. How can that be proof if it's not my bat?"

"Because they found it in your car with Christopher Marsh's blood on it."

"But I didn't put it there."

"How did it get there then?"

"I don't know, but it wasn't me. Why don't you prove it wasn't me?"

"How am I going to do that, Logan?"

"How should I know? I'm not a lawyer."

"Did you see anyone put it in your car?"

"No."

"Did you see any evidence that someone broke into your car?"

"Yeah, there was a bat in it!"

"Besides that. Scratches on the trunk? A dent from prying it open? Anything like that."

"No, but I didn't put it in there."

I took a breath, then said, "Let me put it this way. The prosecutor is going to prove that you broke into Christopher Marsh's house, that you stole his game system, that you sold his game system, and that you were found with a bat that had his blood on it. A jury could decide, just based on those facts, that you killed him."

"But I didn't!"

"I'm not saying that you did. I'm saying that the jury could decide that you did."

"So prove to them that I didn't!"

"I'll try. But they might not believe me."

Logan shook his head. "I thought you were a good lawyer."

"I am."

"You can't be very good if I go to jail for something I didn't do."

"You're going to be going to prison for something you did do, for breaking into the house and stealing things. If you take this deal, you'll get out in about the same time as that."

"Except that I'd be saying I'm a murderer."

"Technically, a manslaughterer, but yes."

"I'm not."

"If we go to trial and lose, Logan, you will be in prison a lot longer. For most of your life."

"I didn't kill anybody." He hit the table with a fist and yelled. "Explain to them that I didn't kill anybody."

"So help me do that."

He immediately calmed down. "How?"

"Answer some things for me that will help me prove it."

Logan nodded.

"Where did you go after McDonald's that night?"

"To the electronics store."

"No, after McDonald's and before the electronics store."

Logan looked away. "Nowhere."

"It was more than an hour before you got to the electronics store, Logan. It's not that far away."

Logan shrugged.

"Did you see Peyton?"

Logan looked at me, wary. "No."

"Peyton was a friend of yours, right? You mentioned Peyton before when I was here."

Logan nodded.

"Did you ever give Peyton things?"

Logan smiled. "Peanut butter."

"Yeah? Did Peyton ever give you money for things?"

Logan opened his mouth, closed it, then looked down.

"Did you try to give Peyton the PlayStation that night?"

"Friends don't talk about friends."

"Did Peyton tell you what houses to break into?"

"Friends don't tell other people what they talk about."

"Logan, it could help your trial. It could help us win if I could talk to Peyton. Can you tell me how to talk to Peyton?"

Logan shook his head.

"Friends help friends, Logan."

Logan's struggle played out right there on his face as competing "friend rules" clashed. Finally, he shook his head. "Friends don't talk about friends."

I tried a little longer, but I'd gone too far—Logan was done talking about Peyton and all I got was a circular recitation of Logan's "friend rules."

I left with a clear understanding of my answer to the plea offer. As I walked out, I tried to let go of the frustration that came from speaking with Logan, from trying to get past his repeated tracks of "friend rules" and innocence, tracks that made him unable to even consider a deal or to point me in Peyton's direction.

Another thing was clear to me too—Logan wasn't a good liar. Which meant that if I lost, I was probably letting an innocent man go to jail. A burglar, yes. A murderer? I didn't think so.

The weight of that realization was new. I was still working through it when my phone buzzed. "What's up, Danny?"

"You need to check your bank account," Danny said. "Now."

42

"I'm not in the office," I said.

"Why am I not surprised?" said Danny.

"Hang on." I shifted my phone to speaker and thumbed my way around to the banking app. "Okay, what am I looking for—holy crap!"

Danny chuckled. "So the wire came through?"

"It sure did. How much of that is ours?"

"All of it."

"You're kidding."

"I'm not."

"It appears I'm going to have to be nicer to you."

"You certainly are."

"Has it wrapped up then?"

"We're just confirming the final details. The bank told me it went through, but I was paranoid with that amount."

"I don't blame you. Do you have someone from Tri-State there?"

"A representative, yeah."

"Take them out for lunch on us."

"I was planning on it."

"Good. As nice a place as you can find. Your expense allowance just went up."

"Way ahead of you."

"Clearly. Danny, this is great work. Well done!"

"Thanks, Nate. All right, people are starting to head back in."

"Hey, is Emily there?"

"Yeah, she's right here."

"Tell her that Winford offered a plea deal."

Emily's voice came over the phone. "We're not taking it, are we?"

I smiled. "Our client doesn't want to."

"Good."

"I'll see you both tomorrow. Safe travels. And great job."

We hung up, but I couldn't resist staring at the banking screen a little longer. I was going to text Danny a suggestion of where to take the client to lunch when something Logan said hit me. I texted Olivia instead.

Peyton loves peanut butter.

Then I drove straight to the Brickhouse.

"So what do you have?" I said as I walked into Olivia's office. Logan Carver's Xbox was sitting on her desk, hooked up to one of her monitors. She waved me around and I stood behind her so I could see the screen.

Olivia pointed. "This is what a typical Discord conversation looks like. There's an alert that shows one of the members of the group is online, then others join. So in this one, NastyBagginses came on first, then Darkwing, then Buttmunch44, then Slipstream Angel joins and asks if they want to play *Call of Duty*, and they dive in."

I squinted. "That's what that says?"

"I figured you'd rather have the translation than the actual text."

Olivia pointed again and scrolled at the same time. "See all of this back and forth are things related to gameplay—tactics, yelling, celebrating, swearing."

"That I can follow."

"Sometimes it's about other things, but usually, the conversation is 'hey, let's play,' followed by a couple of hours of banter."

"Got it."

Olivia pointed farther up. "That's what's in this particular server. Logan has a few other servers on here but Peanutbutterfiend was only in one and it's unusual." She pointed.

"The server that says, '*League of Legends*?'"

"Yes."

"What's *League of Legends*?"

"One of the most popular video games in the world. Take a break from your cave painting sometime."

I ignored her. "What's unusual about it?"

"A couple of things. During the summer before Marsh was murdered, *League of Legends* wasn't available on the Xbox, so Logan couldn't have been playing it on this game system. Now plenty of people watch the esport professional league, so it's possible that he just liked to talk about *League of Legends*. But then, look here when you go into the server, look at this conversation."

I read:

> *Peanutbutterfiend: Do you want to play?*
> *Turkeywood: Sure, sure.*
> *Peanutbutterfiend: 11*

"Who's Turkeywood?"

"That's Logan." Olivia shook her head. "Don't try to under-stand it, just read the next one from the following week."

> *Peanutbutterfiend: Do you want to play at 12?*
> *Turkeywood: Sure, sure.*

"Okay," I said.

Olivia pointed at a series of exchanges like that. "So what do you notice about this?"

I leaned closer. "That Logan plays *League of Legends* with Peanutbutterfiend every week or so."

Olivia shook her head. "Except *League of Legends* wasn't available on the Xbox, so he couldn't have been playing the game on that. Does Logan have a computer or tablet?"

"Let's find out." I texted Wendy Carver asking if she knew whether Logan had either before he was arrested, then said, "Was there something else?"

Olivia nodded. "What do you notice about their conversa-tion while they're playing?"

"There isn't any." Then I understood. "Which isn't like any other server when he plays on Discord."

Olivia nodded. "Exactly. And if you weren't sure, check out the last entry on this server."

I read:

> *Peanutbutterfiend: Want to play at 7?*
> *Turkeywood: Sure, sure.*

"Got it. Same as the others."

"Look at the date."

I did. "That's the day Christopher Marsh was killed."

"Yep."

My phone buzzed. A return text from Wendy Carver.

"He doesn't have a computer or tablet, right?" said Olivia.

"You got it." I processed the new information. "This Peyton was telling Logan which houses to rob."

"Yep."

"Then moving the goods for him after."

"Yep."

I pointed at the screen. "So what's next?"

"Now that I know Peyton is Peanutbutterfiend, I'll see if I can find him."

"You can do that?"

"Who are you talking to?"

"I know, but it doesn't seem like Peanutbutterfiend is going to be on his credit report."

"No, but you'd be surprised how much people carry over their gaming nicknames into traceable places. Just give me some time."

I thanked her, she accepted her due as a genius, and I made my way out to head back to the office.

Cade was waiting by the gym door, a box of supplies under one arm. Although it was freezing cold, he wore a black T-shirt that fit him like a second skin. "You coming Friday night?"

"For sure. Josie and I have to stop by her family's party first, but we'll be here."

"You're welcome."

"I think you'd throw the party without me."

"No. For setting you up with someone so far beyond you."

"Yes, Cade, thank you for pushing your nose into my business when it was totally unnecessary."

"And yet here you are, once again better off for knowing me."

"Isn't that always the way?" I pointed at the box. "Are those more dietary supplements?"

He scowled and looked down. "No, why?"

"I was going to say they're working. How much weight have you lost?

"I haven't—" Then Cade told me to consider self-fornication.

We both started to go our separate ways when I caught myself. "Hey, what do you know about who's in the Ash County jail?"

Cade turned back. "I know generally. I can find out specifics. What do you need?"

"I have a client, Carver, who's in there making friends. He's already assaulted one inmate for them. I was wondering how much trouble he can get in, who he could be tying himself to."

Cade twisted, cracking his back. "Ash County is a short-term facility. Anyone locked up for more than a year is sent somewhere else, usually Jackson. There's no long-term internal inmate structure there, the whole vibe of the facility can shift from week to week depending on who gets shipped out and who gets brought in. Do you want me to check?"

"Could you find out if any group is running the place right now?"

"Easy."

"Would you?"

"Yep. I'll let you know by Friday night."

"I appreciate it," I said and went back out into the cold.

43

T he next morning Danny and Emily rolled in late and, between the holiday weekend and the way they had been grinding on the Tri-State closing, I was glad they did.

They were still buzzing from the deal and spent an hour telling me about it and another half hour after that discussing the celebratory lunch.

"It turns out Tri-State Nursery is part of a larger holding company," said Danny. "They handle the landscaping business from cradle-to-grave, from property ownership to husbandry to greenhouse growing to wholesale distribution. They liked our work so much that they're going to use us for about as much work as we can handle."

"Danny, that's fantastic," I said.

Danny grinned. "They think we could have two more deals in the first half of next year alone."

"Really? Then the two of you better spend this now. It sounds like you won't have much time later."

I handed each of them an envelope. They both looked at me questioningly, then in surprise after they opened them.

"Nate, what...?" said Danny.

"Bonuses. We had a great year, and it's because of you two. You've been amazing."

Danny shook his head. "It's too much."

"I hope you didn't negotiate like that during the closing."

Danny scowled as he said, "Of course I didn't..." then smiled. "Thanks, Nate."

"I don't know," said Emily. "Mine seems a little light."

I looked at her and Emily had a stone serious look on her face. Then she turned to Danny, slapped him in the chest with her envelope, and said, "That's how you do it."

As she walked to her office, she waved the envelope over her head. "Thanks, Boss."

"You're welcome."

"She did do a great job," said Danny. "But I don't think this is her cup of tea."

"Yeah, we will have to figure out staffing when those other deals start coming through."

Danny nodded and started to go, but I waved him over toward the coffee machine and said, "You've done a great job transitioning to a new practice, Danny. Do you like it?"

He smiled. "A lot."

"You know, with a growing business practice, you'll have a lot of options."

"Sure."

"You may want to explore them."

Danny started. "What do you mean?"

"I'd like you to consider going into partnership with me, but you should know whether that's a good deal for you before you do."

Danny may stumble when he's nervous, but his mind is as agile as a big cat. His options flashed across his face as he went from surprise to consideration to a big grin. "I'm sure we can figure it out."

"I'm sure we can. Do you know a good corporate lawyer?"

"For me. I'm not sure what you're going to do. When are you thinking?"

"As soon as we get back from the holiday, so that it captures the whole new year. I'd like to get it set up in principle before the Carver trial. We can finalize the paperwork after."

"I would like that." He held out his hand and I shook it.

"Talk to Jenny over the weekend and make sure."

"I will. But you know what her answer will be. Nate, thanks."

"Don't thank me, Danny. We've been in this together since we moved over here. I'm glad it's finally paying off. Let's talk next week."

The two of us went back to our offices and I was glad to hear Danny call Jenny before he closed his door. I was still smiling when Emily walked in.

"Please don't make me do that again."

"Don't you like working with Danny?"

"I love working with Danny. But being locked in a room squinting at documents for a month is being locked in a room squinting at documents for a month, no matter how nice the jailkeeper is."

"That seems strong."

"Listen Boss, you could lock me in a warehouse with these documents and Harry Styles and it would still be torture."

"That seems like an exaggeration."

"Barely."

"He told me you did a good job."

Emily waved. "He just wants me to do it again. You have to promise me that you'll get him help for these other deals."

"I don't know. It sounds like he has some big deals cooking. Could be lucrative."

"What good is money if you waste away from grief? Now tell me about this plea deal."

I told her about Winford's plea offer and Logan's refusal to consider it.

"Why?"

"Because he says he didn't do it."

"Shocking."

"Right. He told me something important, though."

"What?"

"That Peyton loves peanut butter."

"And that matters because?"

I told her about my meeting with Olivia and the Discord conversations with Peanutbutterfiend.

"You think it's Peyton?" she said.

"I'm almost certain."

"Can we find him?"

"Olivia's working on it."

Emily swore. "I know better. I should've figured it out."

"You use Discord?"

"Who doesn't?"

"Do you game?"

"My fiancé does. I mostly use it during the Oscars and Buckeye games."

"During Buckeye games?"

"I could explain to you how much more convenient it is to have a pane open during a game rather than being glued to typing with your thumbs on a two-inch screen, or we can talk about how this affects the case."

I nodded. "What's always been the hardest part of the case to explain?"

"The bat."

"Let's live in a world where Logan is telling the truth and he didn't kill Christopher Marsh."

"Okay."

"If that were the case, how does the bat get there?"

"It gets there because someone planted it."

"And why would someone plant it?"

"Because they killed Christopher Marsh and wanted to throw suspicion onto someone else."

"And of all the people in the world, why would they want to throw suspicion on Logan Carver?"

She grinned. "Because they knew he had broken in that night."

"And to know that, they either had the great good fortune to see him do it or..."

"Or they told him about the job in the first place." Emily shook her head. "That theory always seemed too far out there but now..."

"I agree."

"We need to find this Peanutbutterfiend Peyton."

"I agree with that too."

"Then what?"

"Then we talk to Logan and tell him that his friend on the outside is no friend at all."

The two of us sat there for a moment, both thinking through the angles, when Emily said, "So, what do you want me to do next?"

"Next, you take New Year's Eve off."

"Come on, I haven't done anything fun all week."

"That's your assignment, Emily."

"What am I supposed to do?"

"Find something personally enjoyable between now and next Monday."

"You're a pain."

"So I've been told. Don't come back until Monday."

Emily stood. "Thanks for the bonus."

"Thanks for your work."

As Emily left, I kept thinking. Peyton really was the linchpin to our theory that there was a conspiracy to frame Logan for killing Christopher Marsh. We had to find him.

Then, I caught myself in the lawyer's trap. I was pursuing our theory so hard that I was making an important assumption.

I was assuming that Logan didn't do it.

I pulled back, just enough to see that both things could be true, this Peyton could have guided Logan to the Marsh job *and* Logan could have killed Marsh. Then I went back to work.

44

T he next day, the morning of New Year's Eve, I took my time going into the office since the courts were slow and Danny and Emily would not be in. I took a slow extra walk with Roxie then spent a little time with her on the couch, me drinking coffee and reading the *Torch*, her chasing dream squirrels with her eyes closed next to me.

If you have a local paper, you know what the New Year's Eve issue of the *Torch* looked like—a listing on the front page of the events of the year, a column trailing along the side with some mustached man's view of why the past year was the best (or worst) year ever with a hope (or fear) that the coming year would be even better (or worse). The *Torch* was no different, although it included an insert of the year in pictures including renovations to the Dellville firehouse, a picture of the Carrefour North girls' softball team winning its first league championship in eighteen years, and a picture of JP Lacombe giving his victory speech on the way to being the next Speaker of the Michigan House.

I was skimming through without paying much attention

when I came to the page of "Those We Have Lost." There was a list of notables, including the oldest woman in South Central Michigan and a former mayor of Dellville, along with an entire section devoted to the *Torch's* own Christopher Marsh. The article recited all the same things from his obituary that made him the well-loved hometown boy made good and revealed that the *Torch* was honoring his legacy by setting up the Christopher Marsh Memorial Scholarship that would give a small amount each year to an Ash County high school student pursuing a degree in journalism.

I stared at the article for a moment then, though it was slightly earlier than acceptable, made a phone call.

Ted Ringel did not pick up, so I left him a message.

"Ted, Nate Shepherd. I just read the Christopher Marsh tribute in your paper today. It seems to me that if you really wanted to honor his legacy, you'd source the last article he gave you and print that. Happy New Year."

I hung up. That really wasn't the most festive thing to do, but sometimes you just have to do your work, even on the holidays. I gave Roxie a pat and got ready to head to the office.

I was on my front step when I got a text from Olivia.

Since you're going out tonight, you're going to work out at noon, right?

I swore before texting, *Of course.*

Good.

I waited and her three dots were blinking but nothing came. I sighed and typed, *Why?*

The answer was instant.

Because I figured out who Peyton is.

I went back inside and packed my bag.

~

"How'd you do it?" I said.

Olivia sat in her rolling chair like it was a throne. "I've told you how people tend to overlap their nicknames. Like you can find Logan Carver on a bunch of social media accounts under variations of Turkeywood."

"Okay."

"So I could give you the whole daisy-chain but basically I searched a bunch of platforms for Peanutbutterfiend then cross-referenced big CONs in the Detroit and Chicago and—"

"—CONs?"

"Conferences where people go to gaming and cosplay events and then looked for people from the Carrefour area and eventually, by tracking VPNs and metadata in a way that you neither know nor care about, I arrived at this social media page and picture."

I stared. "Peyton is a woman?"

Olivia nodded. "Peyton is a woman."

"And that's her?"

"Yep. Peyton Rush is her name."

"Any pictures where she's not in costume?"

"Not that I've found yet."

"I assume her hair is not purple, green, blue, or yellow?"

"You never know."

"I guess you don't. What's next?"

"I'll figure out where Peyton lives, and we'll go from there."

As I went back to the other side of the desk and grabbed my gym bag. "Peyton is the best lead I have to go up the chain to Paxton Plating. She's not going to just admit it, though."

"You never know what tips people leave behind. I'll see what I can find."

"How?"

Olivia stared at me.

"Right," I said.

She waved. "See you tonight."

I waved back and, since she was watching, put the gym bag to good use and left about an hour later to finish up the day.

45

When I picked Josie up that night, she was wearing a long, formal black coat and diamond pendant earrings that had me concerned that my sport coat, white shirt, and dark jeans were underdressed for her family gathering. She assured me it was fine and that we would only be there for a little while which of course didn't reassure me at all but that's what happens when you try to balance the Lacombe New Year's Gala with the Bricksons' No Mercy Eve.

We drove through northern Carrefour out into the country and Josie guided me to the other side of the massive eight-hundred-acre parcel that was the Lacombe family land to a private drive that I might very well have missed in broad daylight, let alone the dark. We followed a tree-lined lane lit with regular gas lamps but, even though it was winter, the view was still obstructed by thick pines on both sides. It wasn't until we drove another hundred yards or so that the way opened into a massive clearing with an old three-story colonial house that seemed more manor than residence. It was red brick with white shutters and sported candle-shaped lights in each of its numerous windows. Strategically placed spotlights highlighted a number of wreaths and an enormous tree was visible in the foyer through the second-story window above the front door. We were only halfway up the drive when we had to slow down as cars lined up to drop folks off at the front door.

"I'll let you out then park," I said.

"They'll valet it for us."

"Sorry. How could I forget the valet at the family holiday party?"

"Be nice."

"I will. I wouldn't want the butler to throw me out."

Josie hit my leg.

We waited our turn until we were next to the pedestals that supported the three-story tall gable roof protecting the entryway and I hustled around to help Josie out of the car as a young man climbed in the driver's seat and drove my Jeep away.

Josie took my arm as we walked through the oversized double doors into the foyer that featured a sweeping staircase with a twenty-five-foot tree tucked in beside it.

"Why didn't you tell me about your humble upbringing?"

"Because I grew up in a farmhouse." She grinned at me. "But *Ma Tante's* was always a fun place to visit. Let's check my coat."

"The coat check. I should've thought of that."

Josie squeezed my arm with only the slightest dig of nails as she giggled.

We walked over to one of the front rooms where a young woman handed Josie a ticket as a young man took her coat and I would be critical of the young man for standing there staring except for the fact that Josie's sleeveless glittering silver dress had the exact same effect on me. Josie thanked the young lady, smiled at the young man, and took my arm again, which prodded me out of my stupor enough to say, "You look fantastic."

She leaned into my arm and said, "Why thank you." She squeezed. "I'm glad you came."

"Me too. I've resolved to spend more time with the common folk this year."

"It's not that bad."

"Champagne, sir?" said a waitress, complete with the black pants, white shirt, and black tie.

"No, thanks," I said and gestured at the tray to Josie. "Dear?"

Josie smiled, took one, sipped, and whispered, "You're terrible," around the edge of the glass.

I kissed her cheek and smiled.

"*Ma cousine!*" came a joyful voice and JP Lacombe swept Josie in for a hug. The tall blond man embraced Josie, then held her back at arm's length. "My God, look at you! And that dress! Amelia will not let you rest until she finds out where you got it."

JP turned to me. "And Nate, great to see you again."

"Congratulations on the win, Mr. Speaker."

"Now I haven't been formally voted in by my colleagues yet, but for the general seat, I thank you and thank you for your vote. Of course, I don't know if you voted for me, but no one minds saying they backed the winning side, right?"

I smiled. "I suppose that's true."

"So are you ready to fight tonight?"

"I hadn't planned on it."

"Well, I don't know how you're going to avoid it with my cousin looking like that."

"Hardly, JP," said Josie. "It looks like more of an over sixty crowd tonight."

"Bah, Josie, you know those are the worst kind. Always chasing, whether it's the favors of my cousin or a favor from their Speaker." JP smiled and swept the room with the quick assessment of a practiced politician before he eyed me. "You seem to have one locked up, Nate. How about the other? What concerns do you have for your representative?"

"Whether there is a beer option besides champagne."

JP laughed. "You need to bring him more often," he said to Josie. "Seriously, Nate, you might be the only one here tonight who isn't working an angle. What's something that concerns you?"

"A health and safety issue?"

"That's my sweet spot—we already have the votes lined up for a new food safety initiative increasing inspection standards for dairy livestock--but any issue really, what matters to you?"

"I've heard more about groundwater contamination lately. It sounds like some of the stuff companies have dumped into our water supply lasts forever. It's scary."

JP snapped his fingers. "No, it's terrifying. Do you know there are spots in the Lower Peninsula where you can't eat the deer or fish because of the PFA build-up? It's an outrage and it will be my priority as Speaker to encourage our corporate partners to be better stewards of our land."

"That's good to know, JP."

"Now if you'll excuse me, I see that Commissioner Perry has arrived and I promised I would introduce her to Senator Helmuth. Delighted to see you both." Then, with a handshake for me and a hug for his cousin, JP Lacombe spun off to greet the Commissioner.

"The man is a whirlwind," I said to Josie.

"Always has been. Here, let's go this way."

Josie guided me across the foyer to a set of open double doors. As we went through, I stopped in true, one hundred percent rube fashion. "You have a ballroom?"

"No. My aunt does."

"A ballroom?"

Josie went back to taking my arm, this time so she could lead me out of the doorway to the side. The room was filled with people, so I absorbed more of a general sense of the room than the fine details, but I can tell you that it was two-stories tall, with a wood-paneled ceiling and a parquet floor. A bar ran half the length of one side and tables of appetizers ran along another, while slightly raised stage for a band who'd set up their instruments but not yet appeared ran along a third.

I started to laugh. "You could've warned me."

Josie shrugged but her blue eyes sparkled. "Where's the fun in that?"

"Honestly, a ballroom?"

"My great-grandfather Jacques built this house in 1925 and 1926. There were different standards of entertainment then."

"Apparently."

She gestured at the bar. "I think you might be able to find something you like there."

"Seems like. Want something?"

"Wine. I'm going to say hi to my dad." She pointed across the room to where André stood in the corner.

"I'll meet you."

I made my way to the bar where I ordered a beer and made a judgment call on one of five chardonnays. My hands were filled before I knew it, and I turned straight into Silas Winford.

"Nate! Toiling away on our case, I see." He looked over my shoulder at the bartender. "Special Reserve Rye, neat and an olive martini, please."

"You seem to be working with the same diligence, Sye."

He smiled. "The prosecutor's life is a hard one."

"What brings you all the way down here?"

"I could tell you that I felt it was my duty as the local prosecutor to make sure I made an appearance at the premier Ash County event of the season, but the truth is that once my wife found out we were invited, I had no choice."

"Why's that?"

Winford laughed. "Have you looked around?"

"True."

He shook his head. "I made the mistake of bringing my wife to this shindig some years ago, back when I was running for State Attorney General, so now any time we get the invitation, it's off to Carrefour."

Winford took his drinks, thanked the bartender, then said, "Not to talk shop, Nate, but I received your message today, thank you. Are you sure you want to reject this plea deal?"

"I am, Sye. Thanks for making it."

"You know if we convict, I'll have to ask for the max."

"I understand."

"Your client will never get out of prison."

"I understand that too."

Winford nodded, then wiggled both hands. "Look at us, two-fisted cogs in the wheels of justice."

"Good to see you, Sye."

"Glad to hear it because it sounds like it's going to be happening a lot more."

We separated and I went to find Josie.

I suppose I should mention that the far end of the ballroom was a two-story wall of glass formed by a series of ten-foot-high glass double doors that ran the length of the room, topped by windows that went all the way to the ceiling. I figured the windows made it hell to heat in the winter, but you know what they say—if you're worried about heating the ballroom, you probably can't afford the ballroom. I didn't see her at first, but then Josie waved from a group of three men and two women. As I approached, she ducked behind one of the women's shoulders and mouthed "Help."

"Here you go, Josie," I said, handing her the wine.

"Thank you. Nate, these are some of my husband Peter's

partners." She introduced me and I no more remember their names than you would if I told you.

"Josie tells us that you're a lawyer," said one guy. "Court must be rougher than it looks..." And he made a motion to his ear.

"Why's that?"

The accountant grinned. "You know, with the ear."

I leaned closer. "No, I don't. What do you mean?"

The man stepped back. "You know, your ear."

I stared.

The accountant's smile faded as he glanced at his friends. "What, what happened to it?"

I smiled. "It filled with blood after a punch, then hardened."

"I've never heard of that."

"Hard to believe. Josie, sorry to pull you away, but your dad is looking for you."

Josie appeared to be biting the inside of both cheeks. "Have a great time, everyone."

I gave her my arm and we walked away. "Friends?"

"Not really, no. They've been angling to work for my aunt's companies for years. They were always haranguing Peter to dig into the books and 'find an opportunity' for them."

"Did Peter work for your aunt?"

"No, Peter asked *Ma Tante* to get involved a few times, but she was pretty direct in her refusals. Said the Lacombe companies were perfectly happy with the team they'd been with since her grandfather's time."

"So, what's the accountant contingent doing here tonight, then?"

"This place is dripping with business, so I'm not surprised they wrangled invitations. Probably by making a donation to some charity in their beloved former partner Peter's name."

"They sound like a delight."

"If I ever hear about another commercial 1031 exchange, it

will be too soon." She looked over her shoulder and giggled. "I think you might've made Terry piss his pants."

Just then, André Lacombe found us. He gave Josie a hug and shook my hand before saying, "I'm sorry to bother you, Jos, but your mom is having a problem with her dress and asked if I could find you to help. Would you mind?"

"Of course not."

"Great! I'd do it, but I need to run over and get another case of Reserve from the distillery. Well, I'm not getting it, I'm just showing Marie-Faye's staff which bottles to grab, but you know what I mean. Your mom's in the bathroom." Then André gave me a smile and a nod and hustled off.

Josie looked at me.

"Go, go." I pointed at the bar. "I'll make do."

Josie gave me a kiss and I grabbed a beer from the bar. As I walked back, the only group I knew were the accountants, so I tried a gold handled patio door. It was unlocked, so I counted myself a party-lottery winner and slipped out.

The air was cold but still and it was snowing lightly in a way that was more effect than accumulation. I was standing not so much on a porch or a patio but in a covered breezeway that seemed to extend along the side of the house. There were gas fire pits set at regular intervals, which led me to believe my escape was anticipated. I walked out to the edge of the breezeway, then took a breath of crisp air and a sip of cold beer.

"Your father could never stand these things either," said a voice.

46

M arie-Faye Lacombe stood on the other side of a fire pit.

"The party's wonderful, Mrs. Lacombe," I said. "Thanks for the invitation."

Her lips twitched. "You do lie better than him though."

Marie-Faye Lacombe wore a jet-black fur wrap that descended all the way to her feet. The glitter of a full-length black dress winked out from beneath it, as did a diamond pendant necklace at her throat. Her white hair fell about her shoulders in stark contrast to the black fur and the flames of the pit cast shadows across the angles of her face.

She drifted over, unmindful of the snow.

"He came to this?"

She nodded and gave me that impression of a smile. "More than once. And I often found him out here."

"I wasn't aware of your history the last time we spoke."

"No?"

"I didn't appreciate being used to stir a pot with my parents."

"That certainly wasn't my intent, Nathan. I assumed you knew."

"No. Neither of my parents had ever mentioned it."

"Interesting. Still, I thought the topic would have come up once you started seeing my niece. It didn't cause you any trouble, I hope?"

"No."

"Good. And how are you and my niece?"

"Josie is wonderful," I said before I realized it and I felt heat on my face that wasn't from the fire.

Marie-Faye Lacombe almost smiled. "It seems she's finally opening up again. Losing a spouse...but I guess you understand."

"You too."

She nodded slowly and I found that the shared experience dissolved my irritation.

I pointed with the top of the bottle. "Your property is beautiful. Especially with the snow."

"It is."

"What are those lights?"

"That's the pump house for one of our wells."

"Does it still work?"

"No one's ever told you about our wells?"

"Who would?"

"Marie-Josée. Her father."

"Ah. No."

"My family struck nine artesian wells on this property. It's one of the reasons the place appealed to us. That one there has always been a special one. My grandfather, Jean-Jacques, said the water from that well was what made our rye unique."

"Why the Christmas lights?"

"To keep the guardian happy."

"Guardian?"

"A terrible beast, half-human, half-serpent that we were not to disturb. He even had us listen at the door to hear her thump about. The sound was the pump from the well, of course, and the story one he stole from a traditional French folktale, but it did keep us from going where we didn't belong."

She almost smiled.

"The lights remind me of him. And of the water our family enjoys."

There didn't seem to be much to say to that.

Marie-Faye Lacombe turned her ice-blue eyes on me. "My son tells me you have an interest in water too?"

I shrugged. "He asked me if I have any issues for his health and safety agenda. I told him I was concerned about companies dumping into our water supply."

"Have you always had that concern?"

"I only learned about the worst of it recently."

She nodded. "I trust he'll act on it right away then. You can't let a threat like that take hold."

"You can't replace water."

She looked back at the well. "No, you can't."

One of the patio doors opened and a man with black hair in a black suit stuck his head out. "Pardon me, Mother, but you wanted me to let you know when the Congresswoman arrived." He nodded to me. "Nate."

"Thank you, Maxime," she said. "I'll be right there."

Maxime Lacombe nodded and closed the door.

Marie-Faye Lacombe straightened and faced me. "My niece tells me that we only have you for a little while tonight?"

"Yes, ma'am."

"And whose party is better than mine?"

"I'm sure no one's, ma'am, but we're going to meet some old friends."

"And who are these old friends?"

"The Bricksons."

"The famous Cade and Olivia. Well, we shan't keep you. I

may be with the Congresswoman when you leave, so give my niece my love."

"Yes, ma'am."

"And Nathan Shepherd, if you call me ma'am again, you will never leave this party because I will have you buried in my backyard."

I smiled. "I'm sorry. Happy New Year, Marie-Faye."

I won't say she started because I don't think that was possible for her. But she blinked and she tilted her head, and said, "*Bonne Année, mon jeune loup.*" Then she patted my chest once and swept back inside.

I stood there for a moment before Josie popped out the same door. "There you are! Ready to go?"

"I am."

WE WERE on our way to Cade's when Josie said, "Thanks for going with me."

I waved. "No problem. It's very important during this holiday season to spend time with those less fortunate."

"It wasn't that bad."

"To remember those who are barely scraping by."

"It wasn't like that."

"No?"

"It certainly was not. There was so little staff there I had to bring my own flunky to get my drink."

"How did your flunky do?"

"I kept my drink order simple, so he managed. A little slow though."

"In fairness, your humble staff was not brought up in such surroundings."

Josie smiled. "Neither was I."

"No?"

"No. Don't get me wrong, *Ma Tante* is very generous with Dad and me—she paid for my school and she invested in the distillery even though I don't think she wanted to. And I think there's a family trust floating around that sends us a little money and gave Peter fits when he had to account for it at tax time. But my dad is a farmer and I'm a respiratory therapist and we both enjoy going to my rich aunt's house for outrageous holiday parties."

"Your staff apologizes for his mischaracterizations and for losing his way in the dazzling manor, which is definitively not yours."

Josie patted my leg. "I'm sure my bewildered man is doing the best he can."

I smiled. "Just point me in the right direction next time."

Josie smiled. "I will. Turn here."

We were still out in the country and there was no light to mark the lane tucked behind the hill that she was pointing to. "There?"

"Yes."

I turned, which took us onto a one lane paved road with trees close on either side. "Are you sure?"

"It's a shortcut."

We drove a little ways and I saw two other drives branch off but eventually the road we were on went from asphalt to a two track to a grassy dead-end turnaround that ended in woods.

I looked at Josie.

She shrugged. "Oops." She reached over and turned off the car.

47

The parking lot was full outside the Railcar, but we found a spot for my Jeep on the edge in the grass. I came around to help Josie out and she took my arm and gave me a kiss. As we started walking, she said, "I thought we were going to the Railcar?"

"We are. Eventually."

"Wait, you're taking me to the Brickhouse?"

"Only for," I looked at my phone, "about five minutes."

"What are we doing there?"

"We're going to bear witness to mass psychosis."

She looked at me.

"Bear witness to. Not participate in."

I opened the door. A wave of sound blasted out.

The place was packed.

Josie looked at me again.

"I know," I said in her ear to be heard over the bass. "It's a cult."

Every inch of space in the Brickhouse was being used. Every weight was being lifted, every heavy bag was being smacked, every battle rope was being waggled, every, well, you get the picture. Olivia was running a class in the back that looked like some sort of weight-based cardio torture while Cade was running some sort of group drilling session on the mat.

"What are they doing?"

"Starting out the new year." I pulled a bottle of beer and a tiny wine out of my coat and placed them on the front desk but did not open them.

Cade motioned to someone who took over the drills and loomed his way up to the front desk.

"Not yet," he said as he approached.

"Wouldn't think of it."

As Cade fiddled with something under the counter, Josie said, "I'm overdressed."

"No more than I was underdressed at your place."

"Unfair."

Suddenly all of the closed-circuit TVs in the place went to a countdown. Rather than stop, all of the activity in the place increased until, by the time it hit "10," there was nothing but a riot of clanks and grunts and encouragement. The frenzy peaked at "3-2-1" until, with a "Happy New Year!" there was a great racking of weights, dropping of ropes, and clapping of hands.

"Happy New Year," I said to Josie and gave her a kiss.

She returned it before saying, "I think that's the weirdest thing I've ever seen."

"It is. But it's a great party afterward." Then I made a show of opening her wine and cracking my beer and we toasted the new year.

As things quieted down, Olivia gave a fiery speech about starting the year right that climaxed with a pledge of drinks on the Bricksons at the Railcar while Cade went around individually clapping shoulders and shaking hands.

"All right, we can head over now."

"What about...?"

"They'll be there. You're about to see a land speed record for showers."

As we made our way across the parking lot, Josie said, "Would you have done that if you hadn't gone out with me?"

"Not anymore."

"No?"

"There was a time, right after Sarah, where Olivia and Cade were a big part of getting me back on track. I think that included one of these parties, but I really wasn't paying attention at the time."

"They're good friends?"

"The best. How about you?"

"I always had people checking in on me. My parents, a couple of friends, even JP made an appearance." She looked up. "I'm glad to spend this one with you, though."

"Me too."

THERE WAS nobody at the Railcar at first but within fifteen minutes, Olivia and Dr. Brad came in on the front end of a wave. There were hugs, hellos, and a mutual admiration between Josie and Olivia of their short sparkly dresses before Olivia said, "Josie, would you mind if you and Brad found a table while Nate and I get the drinks? I promise I'll be done with work talk by the time we get back."

Josie's eyes sparkled and she winked at me. "Don't get lost."

"I know who to ask for directions."

As we headed for the bar, Olivia said, "Three things."

"Shoot."

"First, Peyton Rush. She lived right here in Carrefour,

appears to have spent far beyond her means, and frequented resale shops."

"Any indication she knows Logan?"

"Other than what Logan has told you and the Discord group, no. No other common contacts or friends on social media or anything like that, but I'm pretty sure we had the right person."

I had a bad feeling. "Is there a reason you're talking about her in the past tense?"

Olivia nodded. "That brings us to the second thing. I'm pretty sure she's gone."

"What do you mean?"

"I mean that she hasn't shown up at work since October and her landlord evicted her for non-payment last month."

"And no forwarding?"

"None. And no posts or conventions or anything else that she was known for. In fact, the last thing I've been able to find is when you and I fired up Logan's Xbox and Peanutbutterfiend popped into Discord and said, 'You out?'"

I nodded. "Knowing he was in jail."

"Right. And that either spooked her enough to take off—"

"Or led her to ask questions up the chain that someone didn't want to hear."

Olivia nodded. "I'll keep an eye out to see if she turns up, but I doubt she will. And if she doesn't, then we know your conspiracy theory isn't a theory, it's a fact."

"Because our link to it has disappeared?"

"Exactly."

"Which makes it significantly harder to prove, by the way."

Olivia shrugged and smiled. "I just find the facts. Hotshot lawyers have to prove them."

We paused to get our drinks and were about to head back when I stopped. "Oh, what's the third thing?"

"Right. The third thing is that your shirt is mis-buttoned."

I resisted the urge to look down. "You don't say."

"Not all of them, just starting from about halfway there." She pointed around her drinks.

"I'll have to fix that. Thanks."

"Seems like you would have had plenty of time to get ready since you got here so late."

"We were at her family party."

"Is that what the kids call it these days?"

The two of us went over to a standing table that Brad and Josie had staked out. Olivia took a place next to Josie, set her drinks on the table and said, "Oh, Josie, the clasp above your zipper came undone. Let me get that."

"Thanks!"

Josie turned her back slightly toward Olivia who fastened the clasp then tapped Josie's shoulder. "There you go."

Olivia eyes were unreadable behind her glasses, but her smirk was not as she picked up her glass. "To the New Year."

Brad, Josie, and I joined her in touching glasses. "To the New Year!"

I waited until the next round to go fix my shirt.

HAVE you ever been to a party after a 10K or maybe a Spartan race or something like it? The Brickson No Mercy Eve party was a lot like that. People rolled into the Railcar in waves tied to their level of done-upness—athletic clothes followed by work casual followed by full-boat New Year's Eve ensemble—but no one took long and all of them were in a festive mood from feeling like they'd earned it.

Besides the drinks, Cade and Olivia laid out a massive amount of food. Everyone has their own rationalizations for what is acceptable to eat when, especially with a crowd like this, but it appeared to be a universal truth that anything eaten or drunk after a workout at midnight on New Year's Eve simply does not count.

At one point, I went to fill a plate when I found Cade standing at a table wearing a sleeveless tuxedo and combat boots and you just have to trust me when I say that in some way, beyond all comprehension, it worked for him.

He saw me, excused himself from his conversation with several patrons, and came over to give me a hug.

"Josie having a good time?"

"She is."

"Maybe you all can join the fun part next year."

I smiled. "This is about all the fun we can handle."

Cade shrugged. "You have to push these things. Hey, I found out about your boy Carver in the jail."

"What's up?"

"He has made friends with a couple of guys that don't have any obvious local affiliations."

"How about out of town?"

Cade shook his head. "They don't appear to be connected to Detroit, Chicago, or Toledo. And none of the rural mid-Michigan groups you run into now and then. Seems to be just a couple of local boys from up around Dellville, one serving a few months for a bar fight that went bad and the other accidentally spilled a load of fertilizer on the highway and caused a non-fatal accident. I don't think either of them will be serving more than a few months."

"So neither have an affiliation? They're just helping Logan?"

"Looks that way. Sounds like the guy Logan cracked was bothering everyone but was going after Logan in particular. These guys helped Logan stand up for himself."

"I guess that's good."

Cade shrugged. "Could be worse. Sticking around for a bit?"

"I am."

"I'm going to get back then," he said, pointing at the table where it did indeed appear that several people were acutely aware of his presence. "I'll catch you later."

I returned to Josie with a couple of plates of savory and tasty things just as she returned with another round of drinks, and we welcomed a year of new possibilities.

D ogs don't care what time you got in. If it's time to go out, it's time to go out, and if you aren't ready, well, then you just should have made better life choices.

I slipped out of bed as quietly as I could and ignored Roxie's look of impatience and judgment as I slowly eased a drawer open to grab a shirt. My soft steps were offset by the clack of claws on hardwood as we found our way to the sliding door, and I let her out.

As she did her business, I filled the coffee maker, thought, then programmed it to brew in a couple of hours instead of right then.

Roxie scratched at the back door and when I let her in, she went to her bed in the family room, determined to get about her day.

"Knock yourself out," I said, and went back upstairs. I slipped back into bed and scooched closer to the center. Josie backed into me and pulled my arm around her.

"We're not getting up," she said.

"No."

"Good."

She pulled my arm closer, and we went back to sleep.

A FEW HOURS LATER, I snuck back downstairs and was pulling eggs and the related fixings out of the refrigerator when Olivia called.

"You'll never guess who showed up in Indonesia."

"Liv, that's the truest statement you could ever utter."

"Ethan Ferris."

That collection of words took a moment to bubble through my brain before I said, "Ethan Ferris is in Indonesia?"

"Yes."

"How the hell did you figure that out?"

"His daughter couldn't resist posting. A Merry Christmas message from the Church of the Birth of Our Lady along with a sad face and missing her friends."

"The church of the birth of our who?"

"That would be the oldest Catholic church in the city of Surabaya in the province of East Java in the country of Indonesia."

"I have to imagine there's a story about your genius lurking in that?"

"You mean discovering one of the Ferris girls posting a picture inside a church with the comment 'selamat hari natal,' which gave me all the info I needed to find the city on the other side of the world, which I confirmed with the metadata on the picture, which had not been scrubbed? No, nothing to speak of."

"What in the world would she be doing in Indonesia?"

"You know what's big in Indonesia?"

"What?"

"Electroplating."

"Long way to go for a new job." I grabbed my laptop.

"Is that the clack of your fingers on keys or the rattling of a hamster wheel?"

"Both. Just a second. Here we go. Extradition from Indonesia is possible but difficult because the U.S. has relations with it but no treaty, and that's assuming the person has committed a crime, which Ethan Ferris has not, which means if you're just trying to get process on him to testify as a witness, it's an incredibly high bar."

"English please."

"No one's hauling Ethan Ferris back here to be a witness to anything anytime soon. This is incredible, Liv. Not sure it helps, but incredible."

"I agree with both."

"How are you coming with finding Peyton Rush?"

There was silence at the other end of the line before she said, "That's a little like saying 'Gee, these loaves and fish are great, but we were really hoping to feed *ten* thousand.'"

I chuckled. "True enough. Let me know if you come up with anything."

"I'll check again later today. I have to raise some dead first."

After we hung up, I thought about what Ethan Ferris being halfway around the world meant. He wasn't suspected of a crime so there was no basis to try to bring him back using any of those procedures. At most he was a potential witness in a homicide case, and not even to the act itself but to the motive of an organization I suspected. A little more research confirmed that getting process on him and forcing a deposition or even an interview would be incredibly difficult, and even if it were possible, there was no way it was going to get done before our February trial. Ethan Ferris might have information, but I wasn't going to be getting it.

I started to call Ted Ringel and realized it was New Year's morning, so I emailed him instead. I told him that I had information that Ethan Ferris had been located in Surabaya, East Java, Indonesia if that mattered to him.

"That had better not be work on New Year's Day," said Josie as she walked in.

I shut the laptop and raised my hands. "Not anymore."

"Good. Because I have the day off, I found some comfy clothes," she lifted her arms to reveal one of my Henley shirts and sweatpants, which looked delightfully baggy and soft on her, "and I propose doing nothing, all day, right here." Then she flopped down on the couch and reached down to put a hand on Roxie's head, who sighed.

"Done. Breakfast?"

"Coffee and whatever you got."

I went back to cooking.

WE HAD FINISHED our lunchtime breakfast and were curled up on the couch with a blanket and a delightful lack of purpose flipping back and forth between a holiday movie and a meaningless bowl game when my phone buzzed.

I stood, mouthed "work" to Josie, and answered as I reached my sliding door.

"What the hell do you expect me to do with this?!" yelled Ted Ringel as I stepped outside and closed the door.

"I don't expect you to do anything, Ted. I just know you're sitting on a story that needs verification from its source."

"You know I have watched you from the outside and always thought you were a pretty upfront guy, but this is really sleazy."

"How so?"

"You're going to truck out some bullshit conspiracy theory at trial and you're trying to inoculate me against it by saying you provided me with the source material."

"All I'm doing is telling you the location of someone you said you were interested in."

"And hoping that I will report it. I'm not doing your job for you, Shepherd."

"No, it appears *I'm* doing your job for *you*."

"Oh, fuck off. How very convenient that the person who could verify the bullshit you're about to sling around the courtroom is now on the other side of the world."

"That's actually very inconvenient."

"Well, you know what Ethan Ferris turning up in Indonesia doesn't change?"

"What?"

"That Logan Carver broke into Chris's house and beat him to death with a bat."

"I haven't forgotten the *Torch's* position on this."

"No, and you're not going to because I'm going to keep reminding you of it in twenty-point print."

Ted Ringel hung up then, and I made my barefoot way back into the house.

"Don't you dare think about getting under this blanket until you warm up."

"How am I supposed to warm up if I don't get under the blanket?"

"Such a lawyer." She raised the blanket, and I hopped under.

"What was that?"

"A development on a case."

"Today?"

Just so you know, it's always tricky as a lawyer deciding what you can tell a significant other. You can never tell them a client confidence, of course, and a lot of times you can't even tell them that you've met with someone at all. On the other hand, they need to be comfortable with the people that you have working relationships with because you're going to be talking to them all the time. So I said, "Olivia called earlier about some research on a case she's doing for me. I passed it along and that was someone getting back to me."

"Which case?"

"The Carver case."

"The one where your client killed the reporter?"

I winced. "The one where my client is accused of killing the reporter, yes."

"If your client didn't do it, then who did?"

"Well, that answers that question."

"What question?"

"Whether the jury is going to want an explanation for who did do it."

"Seems like a logical question."

"It does."

"So who was it?"

"I'm sorry, I can't get into that right now."

"Because you don't know or because you can't tell me?"

I smiled. "I can't answer that question either."

She looked at me, intent. "This is a different side of you."

"It is. I imagine you have a different side with doctors and patients too."

"Don't shift the examination to me, Counselor."

"Did I?"

Josie smacked my arm. Roxie looked up but sustained the objection by putting her head back on her bed.

We had settled back in and flipped over to the movie, where a series of misunderstandings led the heroine to believe that the hero did not want to be with her at Christmas at all but in fact he was busily out trying to make something of himself so that he would be worthy of her, when Josie looked back.

"It's strange to think that one of his last articles was about the Distillery."

"I bet."

"My dad texted me when it was in the paper. It was so nice."

"I enjoyed it."

"You know my dad never did get my great-grandfather's journal back from him."

"No?"

"No, apparently it's in evidence. The Sheriff said he'd give it back after your trial." She smiled. "So hurry up."

"I'm working on it."

She snuggled back in and finally, when the game was almost over, I realized it was dark and suggested dinner. Josie sighed, sat up, and said, "I really should get home."

"Working tomorrow?"

She nodded. "Early." Then she bent her arms above her head, stretched in the most delightful way, and leaned into me. "I haven't had a day like this in a long time."

"Me either."

She kissed me. "Thank you."

"Thank you."

She stood and looked down. "Can I wear these home?"

"Thief."

"I might return them. If you're nice."

Then she gathered her things, we said goodbye, and she left.

When I turned back from the door, Roxie was standing there, waiting.

"I suppose you're overdue at that." Then I bundled up and took her for a walk.

49

W hen the New Year holiday was over, we hit the ground running and spent the next month in frenetic preparation for trial. Emily and I batted it around for a couple of days, but in the end, we decided that our only credible strategy was to admit that Logan Carver was in the house but say he had left before Marsh came home. I was going to have to soft play the part about whether Logan actually broke in because the difference between breaking in and walking in was measured in years.

We were going to argue, based on the timeline and the lack of blood, that it was practically impossible for Logan to have killed Marsh. "Practically" being the operative word.

The question of who killed Christopher Marsh if it wasn't Logan Carver was trickier. I'd been pretty sure that we needed to give the jury an alternative explanation and Josie's reaction on New Year's Day had convinced me. Our evidence on that score was still incredibly light. I'd had Emily combing Marsh's past stories and notes, but she thought the only one that was explosive enough was Paxton Plating and I agreed. Of course, that story was unpublished, so the jury wouldn't know about it unless I told them, and I wasn't sure if I was going to be able to get it into evidence.

The month of January passed and the *Torch* still didn't post the Paxton Plating article, I assumed because neither Ted nor anyone else had been able to confirm Marsh's reporting. I assumed it because none of them were talking to me.

I also couldn't put on evidence that Peyton Rush had been working with someone else when she guided Logan to Christopher Marsh's house. Why? Because Peyton Rush was gone and by gone, I mean she was good and vanished. There was no trace of her physically in Carrefour and no trace of her electronically anywhere to such an extent that Olivia believed that Peyton had either gone off-grid completely or that she had been killed. Both seemed improbable for a dealer in stolen goods in Carrefour, but the fact was that she was gone and with it, my only upstream link from Logan Carver to whomever at Paxton had orchestrated Christopher Marsh's death.

That was all assuming, of course, that my client hadn't killed Christopher Marsh himself. I found myself asking the same question the jury would—was it more likely that Logan Carver was interrupted while robbing Christopher Marsh and killed him with a bat or that some murky conspiracy had guided Logan Carver to Christopher Marsh's house then used Logan as cover to come in and kill Christopher to spike a story the conspirators didn't want published?

Right. I wasn't crazy about my odds either.

So Emily and I kept preparing—I lined up our spatter expert and prepared our cross-examinations, and Emily prepared a timeline of the evening's events which, if it didn't eliminate the possibility of Logan Carver murdering Christopher Marsh, narrowed the window considerably. Emily was a treat; she was enthusiastic, soaked up everything, and was usually onto a task before I mentioned it. She wasn't as skilled as Danny, not yet, but

that was only because she hadn't done it as long. Her enthusiasm would carry her past him shortly.

Which was just fine with Danny. He helped us here and
there, but for the most part, he was focused on another business
deal for Tri-State Nursery that would close in early March just
after our trial. Given all the legwork he and Emily had done
with the earlier closing, he thought he could handle this one
himself, but if this corporate work kept up, he thought we might
need someone new, and I tended to agree with him.

Between all that, Danny and I became partners. Danny drew
up the paperwork, I tweaked it, and we had an agreement in less
than a week. Figuring out a fair way to split the money took
about five minutes, which convinced me I had made the right
choice. The only issue was the name. I suggested Shepherd &
Reddy, but Danny insisted that we continue to call it the Shepherd Firm for the eminently practical reason that he hoped that
we would continue to grow, and he was not going to waste all
that money creating new letterhead every time we took on a
partner. I thought that was both practical and generous and the
Shepherd Firm we remained.

Personally, I saw Josie a couple of more times before the trial
but then between her schedule and my prep it became impossible. The week before trial she offered to take Roxie, but Justin,
James, and Joe had called dibs, so I dropped Roxie off at Mark
and Izzy's house to the delight of my nephews, with the promise
that I would return for her in two weeks. Judging from the ball
of boys and boxer on the living room floor when I left, I figured
they would all think that was too soon.

Then February hit, and with it, the last sprint from the crack
of dawn to midnight. I was spending prep time at the jail with
Logan and reporting to Wendy Carver and confirming Devon
Payne's spatter analysis while tweaking Emily's timeline and
drafting my opening statement and confirming Peyton Rush was

still gone and checking the last exhibits and making sure our presentation system worked and running through the logistics of how Emily and I would work at trial and responding to Silas Winford's constant motions to admit evidence and filing my own to keep it out and before you knew it, it was the Sunday night before trial and we were out of time.

The trial of Logan Carver for the murder of Christopher Marsh began the next day.

VALENTINE'S DAY

50

Wendy Carver sat in the first row of the courtroom. Her waitress uniform, black skirt and tights, white shirt, and black tie topped by a black coat, actually blended right in.

"Will we be done by five?" she asked.

"Four-thirty most days."

"I need to be to the Open Grill by six."

"You can always leave early. You just have to be quiet."

Wendy Carver gave me a look that indicated that wasn't happening. "Where's Logan?"

"The deputies are bringing him over from the jail. He'll get here a little bit before we start."

"Will I be able to talk to him?"

"I don't think that's a good idea right before trial. There will be a chance during some of the breaks."

Wendy Carver gave me a look that indicated what she thought of this second piece of advice, but this time nodded.

"Nate?" Silas Winford said from the other counsel table. He gestured and I came over.

Winford's salt-and-pepper hair had been newly trimmed,

and he wore a well cut, dark blue suit that was more expensive than it appeared. He looked every bit the former state attorney charged with putting away Michigan's worst criminals.

We shook hands and he said, "You know, Judge Wesley is going to ask us if we've had a discussion this morning about a plea deal."

"For sure."

"I'll offer the same one this morning that I did at the new year—manslaughter on the killing served concurrently with the theft-related charges."

"My client isn't here yet, but it's going to be the same response as before."

Winford nodded. "That's what I expected, but we need to do the dance."

"I'll confirm after he gets here."

Winford went back to his associate and paralegal to put the finishing touches on their trial set-up while I joined Emily to do the same.

She scowled. "You're not settling this on me, are you?"

"Only if it's in our client's best interest."

Her scowl deepened.

"But it's not today so we'll be going."

She smiled and went back to work.

A couple of minutes later, the deputies brought in Logan Carver. He wore a blue suit that hung off his shoulders and billowed at the waist with a shirt that was a little too tight at the neck. I buttoned his coat for him, pulled back the shoulders and said, "Are you ready?"

He nodded.

"What do we do?"

"Keep quiet and don't make faces."

"What if you have a question?"

"I write it down on that paper."

"Good man. Once the judge comes in, we'll pick a jury and do opening statements."

Logan nodded. "My friends told me what would happen first."

"No one in there is your friend, Logan, not until this is over."

Logan shrugged.

"Logan, people snitch from jail all the time to get their sentences reduced. Don't tell them anything about the trial when you go back, understand?"

He looked at me.

"Not a word, Logan. If someone comes in from jail and testifies at this trial, we're sunk."

"I got it, I got it."

I didn't know that he did, but I moved on. I told him about the plea offer.

"I didn't kill him."

"This might be our last chance to get a plea deal."

"I won't say I killed him. I didn't do it."

"That's what I figured. I'll let them know. Have a seat with Emily."

Logan and Emily spoke as I went over and told Winford that there was no deal.

Silas Winford smiled. "So we'll have some fun this week after all."

"Looks like."

A moment later, Judge Wesley's bailiff let us know that we were about to begin and a moment later, Judge Wesley herself took the bench. She sat down, her dark hair piled high, and motioned for us to approach.

"Good morning, gentlemen."

"Good morning, Your Honor," we said.

"Have the two of you discussed a plea resolution?"

"We have, Your Honor," said Silas.

"And?"

"We are proceeding to trial, Your Honor," I said.

Judge Wesley nodded. "This is normally the time when I pull the two of you into my office and twist some arms, but I know you both well enough to believe that Mr. Winford made a reasonable offer, but that Mr. Shepherd's client will not admit that he killed anyone. Would that be about right, Mr. Shepherd?"

I smiled. "From our perspective, it's not reasonable to admit killing someone when you didn't, Your Honor."

"Your client knows that I'm going to allow the evidence of the prison assault to come in?"

"He does, Your Honor. He believes the incidents are unrelated because he was involved in one but not the other."

"Very well. Let's pick a jury."

IN A TRIAL in Michigan where the defendant is facing life in prison, each party gets twelve peremptory challenges when picking the jury. That basically means we can remove a person from the jury without giving a reason in hopes of getting jurors who are most likely to see things our way. Of course, the other side is doing the same thing, so the theory is that it eventually evens out.

Logan, Emily, and I were huddled together in the judge's office discussing whether we wanted to exclude anyone from the first batch of potential jurors.

"Number Fourteen has to go for sure," said Emily.

I did not even have to look at my grid to remember this mother of four, grandmother of nine, and general enforcer of rules for three generations in her home who let it be known that if you go astray in the little things, the big things will follow. "Agreed. She's out. Number Six has to go too."

"The retired Marine? For sure. Any others?"

I looked at the grid. The mother of two boys who were Christopher Marsh's age and the science teacher from Marsh's high school stood out. "I think Number Two and Number Nine."

"Me too," said Emily.

We looked at Logan.

"Whatever you think."

"Counsel?" said Judge Wesley.

Silas Winford said, "We do not have any peremptory challenges at this time, Your Honor."

"Very well. Mr. Shepherd?"

"Your Honor, we thank and exclude Juror Number Fourteen."

Judge Wesley made a note on her sheet. "Mr. Winford?"

"We are fine with this panel, Your Honor."

"Mr. Shepherd?"

"Your Honor, we thank and exclude Juror Number Six."

Judge Wesley ticked a box. "Mr. Winford?"

"Your Honor, we will not have any peremptories of anyone on this section of the panel."

Judge Wesley looked at me. "Your Honor, we would exclude Jurors Two and Nine." I had a last-minute thought. "And Five."

Judge Wesley made three ticks on her sheet and said, "That does not give us enough yet for our jury. I'll excuse those jurors and bring in the next group."

WHEN WE WERE BACK in the office, I said, "Your Honor, we believe that Jurors Twenty-Two, Thirty-One, and Thirty-Four should be dismissed for cause. All of them knew Christopher Marsh personally."

"They all said they could be fair and impartial, Your Honor," said Winford.

"I know what they said, Mr. Winford, but I agree with Mr. Shepherd. Those jurors will be excused." She ticked the boxes.

"We also ask that Jurors Twenty-Three, Twenty-Six, Thirty-Seven, and Forty-One be excused as they were regular readers of his articles."

"That's way too far afield, Your Honor," said Winford. "And those jurors also said they could be fair and impartial."

Judge Wesley nodded. "I agree. Reading an article does not prejudice a juror without evidence of more. Mr. Shepherd, if you want any of those jurors excused, you will have to use your peremptories."

"Very well, Your Honor, we thank and excuse juror number Twenty-Three."

I stopped and looked at Winford.

He smiled. "Just to move things along, Your Honor, we're fine with all of the jurors in this batch too. We will not be exercising any peremptories."

"Very well. Mr. Shepherd?"

"We'll excuse those we mentioned then, Your Honor."

Judge Wesley ticked her chart. "Twenty-Six, Thirty-Seven, Forty-One. Any others?"

I looked over. Emily pointed at my grid, and I nodded. "And Juror Thirty-Eight, Your Honor."

Judge Wesley did a quick count. "Between that and our challenges for cause, we still do not have enough jurors."

"Goodness," said Winford. "Do we have any more people out there, Judge?"

"Fortunately, we have one more group of thirty and Mr. Shepherd only has two peremptory challenges so, unless they're all part of Christopher Marsh's family, this should be the last group."

As we went back out into the courtroom, Winford held the door open and smiled. "Maybe this will be the fair and impartial group you're looking for."

As we stared at the grid, I saw the problem you always risk when you go through multiple pools—the next five people to go on the jury were going to be worse than a few we'd already kicked off. We were down to our last spot. We either left a pastor's wife on the jury, or we kicked her off and a mechanic took her place.

"I think the pastor's wife is worse," I said.

The side of Emily's mouth curled in before she shook her head. "I think it's the mechanic."

"Why?"

"That story about having the wrench stolen at work? He was way too mad about something that happened ten years ago."

"I do not know. The pastor's wife was practically dabbing her eyes when Winford was describing what this case was about."

We both stared.

"Logan?" I said finally.

Logan was concentrating. Hard. He whispered, "I've seen people who are really mad about getting their stuff taken. I think this guy will be mad at me."

I thought, then said, "You're right."

"Well, Counsel?" said Judge Wesley.

"We continue to be fine with everyone on this panel," said Winford.

"Mr. Shepherd?"

"We will not exercise any further challenges, Your Honor."

Judge Wesley nodded. "Very well, we have our jury. Let's go swear them in and then we'll break and do openings after lunch.

As we walked out, Winford said, "So you left the pastor's wife on. Interesting."

I smiled. "Not as interesting as leaving them all on."

Silas Winford smiled and shrugged. "To be fair, I have an advantage."

"What's that?"

"The truth."

51

I looked back at the gallery while Judge Wesley swore in the jury. Wendy Carver sat immediately behind me, but there were four people who were noticeable for their absence.

The first was Ted Ringel. The *Torch* had been running stories nonstop in the days leading up to the trial. Nothing new, just small updates that were excuses to remind people of the case and run Logan's FU mugshot. I assumed somebody was there from the *Torch* but I didn't recognize them, and I was a little shocked that Ted would delegate that to someone else.

The other three were Christopher Marsh's family. His mom, dad, and sister had been featured prominently in the *Torch* stories, but I did not see them, which surprised me more than Ted's absence.

When the jury was situated, Judge Wesley said, "Mr. Winford, is the State ready to proceed?"

"We are, Your Honor." Winford strode over to the projector that would put his presentation up on the screen. "If you will give me just a moment to turn this on?"

"Of course."

He fumbled at the projector for a moment before smiling at the pastor's wife. "These darn things."

She smiled back.

At that precise moment, the swinging doors to the court-room opened. Winford straightened and looked and damn me if I didn't too.

So I saw the Marsh family walk down the aisle.

Mr. Marsh was a burly man with wide shoulders and a broad belly who walked with his shoulders stooped, as if he were carrying an invisible backpack. His wife was a thin woman with feathered brown hair who stood taller than him, although I couldn't tell if that was from height or posture. Christopher Marsh's sister, a college-aged woman with long brown hair, walked behind them with her arms folded and her eyes down.

I looked at the jury as the Marshes took their seat in the front row behind the prosecutor's table. They were all watching.

Winford stood there, hands crossed in front of him, until the Marshes were settled. Then he turned to the jury, his seeming trouble with the projector now forgotten, and said, "Your Honor?"

"You may proceed, Mr. Winford."

Silas Winford faced the jury. "We talked a little while ago, during the jury selection process, about what this case is about and your role in it. This part is where I tell you what the evidence is going to show, what I'm going to prove to you beyond a reasonable doubt."

Winford waited, but he didn't need to. He had the jury's full attention.

"The evidence is going to show that the defendant, the man sitting right over there, Logan Carver, murdered Christopher Marsh. Logan Carver broke into Christopher Marsh's home and then beat him to death with an aluminum bat. This was a horrific, brutal killing and at the end of this trial, we're going to ask you to convict Logan Carver of murder."

"Now there are a lot of rules we have to follow for how we present evidence to you, and it's easy to get lost in all the back and forth between the attorneys and the judge, so let me give you a roadmap so that you know the big picture."

"First, Logan Carver broke into Christopher Marsh's house. How will you know this? We're going to show you evidence that the fibers from the sweatshirt Logan Carver wore that night were found in the TV stand in Christopher's house."

"Second, Logan Carver stole from Christopher's house. He stole Christopher's PlayStation 5, his Beats headphones and his prescription drugs. And how will you know this? We're going to provide you with evidence that Logan Carver went to a store called Second Chance Electronics to sell the PlayStation and the Beats, and we're going to provide you with evidence that a prescription bottle made out to Christopher was found in the garbage of Logan Carver's apartment."

"Third, and tragically, Logan Carver beat Christopher to death in that house. And I'm sorry to tell you about how you're going to know this. We'll provide you with evidence from Christopher's father, Jerry, of finding his son's bloody and beaten body the next day. We'll provide you with evidence of the Sheriff's investigation and all of the physical evidence linking Logan Carver to that crime. And you'll also hear from the arresting officers who found the aluminum bat used to kill Christopher Marsh, a bat covered in Christopher's blood, in the trunk of Logan Carver's car."

"That's the big picture. That's how we know that on a night last fall, Logan Carver crept into Christopher Marsh's house, stole his things, and beat him to death with a metal bat."

"Now, you may wonder if it's that clear why we're even here? Well, that brings us to the second part of the big picture. You're also going to hear from Mr. Shepherd, the very fine attorney who is representing Logan Carver, and he's going to present you with evidence too. Based on what I know, I believe Mr. Shepherd is going to admit to you that Logan Carver was in Christopher Marsh's house that night and stole Christopher's things. I believe he's also going to say that, even though Logan Carver broke into the house and stole Christopher Marsh's things, he didn't kill Christopher. I don't know exactly how he's going to argue that because he doesn't have to tell me before trial, but I encourage you to listen closely to everything he says and to all of the evidence he can muster, and weigh it against what we will show you—that Logan Carver invaded Christopher's house, stole Christopher's possessions, and beat Christopher to death, all so he could sell Christopher's things for a couple of bucks."

"At the end of this trial, when we've provided you with our evidence and Mr. Shepherd has had an opportunity to present you with whatever evidence he has, we will ask you to find Logan Carver guilty of home invasion and murder. Because he is."

Silas Winford turned and went back to his chair without ever using the damn projector.

"Mr. Shepherd?" said Judge Wesley.

"Thank you, Your Honor."

When you've tried enough cases, you get used to the looks of skepticism and anger on jurors' faces after a prosecutor has just described how he thinks your client killed someone. That's why, as I approached the jury now, the anger and skepticism I saw on half of their faces didn't overly trouble me. What troubled me was that half of them were still staring at the Marsh family when I began.

"Logan Carver did not kill Christopher Marsh. In fact, we're going to prove to you that it would've been almost impossible for things to have happened the way Mr. Winford just described."

I had all of their attention now and there was anger aplenty.

"Now Mr. Winford and the State have to prove that what they say is true, they have to prove beyond a reasonable doubt that Logan Carver killed Christopher Marsh. Mr. Winford can talk all he wants about the evidence that we may or may not put on, but the fact is we aren't obliged to put on any evidence, not a single bit. Instead, it's up to the State to prove to you that what it claims is true. We don't think their case stands up to that kind of scrutiny."

"Mr. Winford talked an awful lot about evidence that puts Logan Carver in the house and at the electronics shop. Those facts don't prove that Logan Carver killed Christopher Marsh, though. They don't prove that at all."

"In fact, you're not going to hear any direct evidence that Logan Carver attacked Christopher Marsh. They're not going to present you with any evidence that shows Logan Carver was there during or after the murder occurred. By that I mean, you're not going to see any evidence of footprints in the blood or swipes along the walls. You're not going to hear any evidence from witnesses who saw or heard a fight. You're not going to be given a video or a picture or even an eyewitness who puts Logan Carver at the house after Christopher Marsh arrived home. You're not going to be given any evidence like that because it doesn't exist."

"No, what the State will lean on is the bat. We expect that you're going to hear testimony from the sheriff's department that they conveniently found a bat in the trunk of my client's car. What you will also hear is that the bat is not my client's bat, that my client's fingerprints weren't on the bat, and that he was shocked that the bat was even there. In fact, you'll hear that he gave the detective permission to open the trunk of his car where they found it, which would be awfully strange if he knew a murder weapon was inside, so I'll be just as interested as you to hear how the deputies say the bat got there."

"Now, as I mentioned, we don't have to put on any evidence at all since it's up the State to prove its case. But we're going to anyway. And you're going to see that it's virtually impossible for the murder to have happened the way the State claims. And we're going to present you with evidence that shows why."

"First, we're going to show you that there wasn't time for Logan Carver to have killed Christopher Marsh. We're going to present you with direct tangible evidence of where Logan Carver and Christopher Marsh were at different times during that evening, evidence shows the window of time in which Logan Carver could have killed Christopher Marsh was so small that it would have been practically impossible.

"Second, you're going to hear that this was a bloody crime scene, so bloody that our expert will show you that the killer had to have blood on him afterwards. And you're going to hear evidence from multiple sources, including eyewitnesses and the State's own forensic team, that Logan didn't have any blood on him that night. Not a single drop."

"When you see all of this evidence, combined with the evidence the State lacks, we think you'll see that the killing of Christopher Marsh couldn't have happened how the State claims."

"For that reason, we ask that you listen carefully to the prosecution's case and examine it closely for evidence, not that Logan Carver took something or sold something, but actual evidence that Logan Carver killed Christopher Marsh. We don't think you're going to hear it. What you're going to hear is just how unlikely the State's whole scenario is. And when we come back here after the evidence is done, we will ask you to find Logan Carver not guilty of murder. Thank you."

As I sat down, I saw that most of the jurors' faces had lost their anger but still carried an awful lot of skepticism. As I sat down, Emily passed me a note.

The bat is a problem.

I kept my face straight, folded the note, and put it in my pocket, which is the only thing you can do when you agree.

"Thank you, Mr. Shepherd," said Judge Wesley. "Mr. Winford, you may call your first witness."

"Thank you, Your Honor. The State calls Deputy Randy Pavlich."

52

D eputy Randy Pavlich wore his full uniform—long-sleeved brown shirt, tan tie, and tan pants. He removed his hat as he walked through the swinging gate and ran one hand over his blond buzz cut to stand it straight. He was in his early thirties and when I had last seen him testify in the Colton Daniels trial, he had seemed stiff and green. This time, Deputy Pavlich seemed more assured as he nodded to the judge, then the jury, and took his seat.

After running through Deputy Pavlich's nine-year history as an Ash County Sheriff's Deputy, Winford asked, "Deputy Pavlich, how did you become involved in the investigation of Christopher Marsh's death?"

"I was told by dispatch that a 911 call had been placed regarding the body of a man who had been beaten to death in the north section of Carrefour under our jurisdiction."

"Did you have an understanding who made that call?"

"I was told by dispatch that the call came from the victim's father."

"And what did you do?"

"I went immediately to the scene. Because it was a murder,

all hands were on deck so to speak, but I was the first to arrive because I was in the area."

"And what did you do?"

"I entered the premises and found Mr. Marsh holding the body of his son, Christopher."

"Could you describe that for the jury, please?"

"Yes sir. I had been told by dispatch that it was not an active scene, but I was somewhat cautious anyway. I noted two cars in the driveway and a side-door to the house that was open. I exited my vehicle, approached the door, and called out identifying myself as law enforcement. I received a response consenting to my entrance and asking me to hurry."

Deputy Pavlich faced the jury. "Then I went through a small entryway to the kitchen where I found Mr. Marsh holding Christopher."

"What did you do next?"

"I asked if there was anyone else in the house and Mr. Marsh said 'no.' I asked him to identify himself and he said he was the victim's father and he also identified the victim, Christopher Marsh."

"What were your first impressions of the scene, Deputy Pavlich?"

Deputy Pavlich paused for a moment, then said, "Mr. Marsh was sitting on the kitchen floor with his son face up in his lap. Mr. Marsh was holding Christopher by the upper torso. There was a moderate amount of blood on the victim and on the surroundings. Although it was apparent, I checked the victim for a pulse and confirmed that he was deceased. In doing so, I saw that the back of the victim's head was bloody and misshapen, although my view was obstructed by Mr. Marsh's arm. I then stepped out of the kitchen, alerted dispatch that there was no ongoing threat, and requested the investigative unit and the coroner. Then I came back into the kitchen to secure the scene for investigation."

"What does that mean?"

Deputy Pavlich looked at the jury again. "It means that I had to convince Mr. Marsh to lay his son back down."

"Why did you do that Deputy Pavlich?"

"Because we had an active murder scene and we needed to preserve as much evidence as possible."

"I see. Were you able to do that, Deputy Pavlich? Were you able to convince Mr. Marsh to lay his son down on the kitchen floor?"

"Eventually."

"He did not want to?"

"No, sir, he did not."

"How did you convince him?"

"I told him it was necessary to help us find out who did it."

"And what did he say?"

"He asked if he could hold his son until the investigative team arrived."

"And what did you say?"

Deputy Pavlich cleared his throat. "I told him that would be fine."

Silas Winford nodded and just stood there. He didn't even pretend to check his notes and he didn't repeat what Deputy Pavlich said. He just stood there and let the scene hang in the air.

Eventually, Winford said, "And did the investigative team arrive, Deputy Pavlich?"

"It did."

"What did you do?"

"I encouraged Mr. Marsh to lay his son on the floor and helped him outside."

"Helped him?"

"Yes, sir."

"Please describe what you mean."

"As we left the house, Mr. Marsh's legs collapsed, so I held him up and helped him to the rear of his car so that he could lean against the trunk."

"And then what did you do?"

Deputy Pavlich shifted in his seat and looked down.

Silas Winford said, "Deputy Pavlich? What did you do next?"

"I hugged him, sir." Deputy Pavlich looked up. "I know that's not within protocol and technically it gave him access to my weapon and it's not a mistake I will ever make again but—"

Winford raised a hand. "No one in this courtroom is going to criticize you for being a human being, Deputy Pavlich. What happened next?"

"Eventually, Mr. Marsh was able to give me his statement."

"Now Deputy Pavlich, we are going to call Mr. Marsh to testify later and get his statement directly from him, but what information did he give you that affected your investigation?"

"Mr. Marsh told me that his son had been having car trouble and so they had arranged for Mr. Marsh to come over on Saturday morning, take a look, then follow Christopher to an auto shop. When Mr. Marsh arrived, the side door was open. Then he went in, found Christopher, and called 911."

"After taking his statement, what did you do next, Deputy Pavlich?"

"I coordinated the arrival of other law enforcement officers and the ambulance for removal of the victim's body."

"Did you do anything else?"

"I assessed Mr. Marsh. I determined that he seemed capable of driving, then allowed him to go."

"Were you involved in the examination of the house itself?"

"Other than my initial entrance, no. Detective Durbin handles the forensics."

"Very good. Deputy Pavlich, did you receive any other information related to this investigation?"

"I did."

"Tell us about that."

"In the late afternoon of that same day, Saturday, a call came in to the general number. I was in the office because I was preparing to go home for the day, so it was forwarded to me."

"And what was that call?"

"A man identifying himself as Sam Perkins, the owner of Second Chance Electronics, called to say that he may have information related to the killing of Christopher Marsh."

"And what did you do?"

"I took his contact information and forwarded it to Sheriff Dushane."

"That's all I have at this time, Deputy Pavlich, thank you. Mr. Shepherd may have some questions for you."

"Mr. Shepherd?" said Judge Wesley.

I stood. "Good afternoon, Deputy Pavlich."

Deputy Pavlich nodded, his eyes wary.

"Deputy Pavlich, you were not the first person on the scene, were you?"

"I was the first law enforcement officer."

"Correct, but you were not the first person to find Christopher Marsh, right?"

"I was not. As I already testified, Mr. Marsh was there before me."

"Deputy Pavlich, you testified that there was blood at the scene when you arrived, right?"

"I did."

"You described it as a moderate amount, do I have that right?"

"Yes."

"There was some on the floor?"

"There was."

"It was on the walls and appliances too, wasn't it?"

"I believe so. I can't say for sure because it was more spatters than large amounts."

"You mentioned that Mr. Marsh was holding his son when you arrived?"

"He was."

"Mr. Marsh had altered the scene by the time you arrived, hadn't he?"

"He was holding his son."

"Which is completely understandable, but the fact is the scene had been altered by Mr. Marsh when you arrived, true?"

"That's true."

"So the best understanding we have of the original scene is Mr. Marsh's description, is that right?"

"That and the physical evidence, yes."

"The best description we have of the original scene is from Mr. Marsh though, right? Because he's the only one who saw it before it was disturbed."

"Do you expect him to just leave his son there?"

"Of course not, Deputy Pavlich, but I do expect you as a law enforcement officer to answer a basic question about a crime scene. I know this is difficult, so I'll ask it another way. Mr. Marsh's description is the best evidence we have of the way in which Christopher Marsh's body was found, is that right?"

Deputy Pavlich stared. "That's right."

"And by that, I mean the way Christopher's body was positioned in the kitchen. Mr. Marsh's description is the best evidence of that, right?"

"His description of that terrible scene is the best evidence of it, yes."

"Mr. Marsh had blood on his clothes when he left the house, didn't he?"

"From holding his son's broken head, yes."

"And his hands too?"

"For the same reason, yes."

"You observed Mr. Marsh step in blood, is that right?"

"It was unavoidable."

"Unavoidable, I see. So Mr. Marsh had blood on his clothes, his hands, and his shoes when he left the kitchen?"

"Yes."

"You had blood on you as well didn't you, Deputy Pavlich?"

He thought, then said, "I did."

"And you did not touch the victim other than to check his pulse, true?"

"That's true."

"And that's because you did not want to contaminate the scene further?"

"I don't know that I like your word 'contaminate.'"

I raised a hand. "I don't mean that in a judgmental way, Deputy. How about this—you did not want to introduce any physical evidence into the scene that would not have been there when Christopher Marsh was killed, right?"

"That's right. We tried to alter the scene as little as possible."

"You had blood on your hands, right?"

"A little."

"Blood on your shoes?"

Deputy Pavlich hesitated.

"On the soles?"

"Yes."

"Blood on your shirt?"

"I did. But that was from hugging Mr. Marsh, not from the scene itself."

"Fair enough. You mentioned you took a statement from Mr. Marsh?"

"I did."

"That's how you learned about the car issue?"

"That's right."

"It's how you learned when the window in the door was broken, right?"

"I observed the broken window in the door when I arrived. I don't know anything about the timing."

"Well, in Mr. Marsh's statement, the statement you took, Mr. Marsh mentioned that his son had told him about the broken window in his door. You believed Mr. Marsh, right?"

"Of course I did."

"And when you observed the door when you arrived, it was open, right?"

"That's right. Mr. Marsh was already inside."

"That's all I have, Deputy Pavlich. Thank you."

Silas Winford stood. "Deputy Pavlich, are you surprised that Mr. Marsh was holding his son?"

"Not at all."

"Were you concerned in any way that the crime scene was being contaminated by his presence?"

"Absolutely not. Like I said, it was understandable."

"Do you believe that it affected the investigation in any way?"

"Not that I am aware of, no."

"And you were careful when you came into the kitchen to disturb the scene as little as possible?"

"I was."

"Thank you, Deputy Pavlich."

I stood. "Deputy Pavlich, as careful as you were, you had blood on you when you left the kitchen, right?"

"That's right."

"On your hands?"

"Yes."

"On your shoes?"

"Yes."

"Thank you." I sat.

"Thank you, Mr. Shepherd," said Judge Wesley. "Members of the jury, that concludes our proceedings for today. We will start tomorrow at eight-thirty. Please do not discuss this with each other or anyone else, and I remind you that you should not research the matters presented to you here in the trial independently. Instead, your deliberations will ultimately be limited to the evidence presented by the parties."

Judge Wesley was about to dismiss them but then I saw her reconsider as she said, "You will hear throughout this trial that Christopher Marsh worked for the Ash County *Torch*. You may also know that the *Torch* has been running stories related to this case. I remind you that those stories are not evidence and encourage you not to read them at all during the course of this trial."

I saw a few nods and a few stony faces. I figured there was no way they were going to listen to the judge, but I appreciated her effort.

With that, we rose and Judge Wesley dismissed the jury. We waited until they were gone and then Judge Wesley left herself.

As I gathered my things, one of the deputies who would be escorting Logan raised a hand to me.

I nodded to him, then said, "Do you have any questions, Logan?"

"I didn't kill him."

"I know."

"Is that all they're going to talk about?"

"That's what the trial's about."

"But I didn't do it."

"That's what we're going to show them."

He nodded as if that were enough. "Okay."

I nodded to the deputy.

"Goodbye, Logan," said Mrs. Carver.

"Bye, Mom," he said, and they led him away.

I was gathering my things when I noticed Emily staring. I followed her gaze to where Mr. Marsh sat in the front row slightly hunched, hands clenched in his lap, shaking. His wife held one arm and was whispering to him in one ear, while Silas Winford bent over the rail, one arm on Mr. Marsh's shoulder, and whispered in the other. Mr. Marsh nodded, then nodded again, then eventually waved them both off. Silas Winford patted his shoulder as he stood while Mrs. Marsh held onto his arm. Mr. Marsh wiped his eyes once, took a deep breath, then walked out, hunched over, his wife on his arm.

I turned back to my things and packed up my laptop. "You okay?" I said without looking at Emily.

"I'm fine, Boss. Just the first time on this side of it is all."

I nodded. "Let's get back to the office."

53

I
f you have spent any time with me at all, then you know
that Daniel Reddy is an exceedingly good man. He
confirmed that once again when Emily and I arrived back
at the office to find three Black Boar Cuban sandwiches already
in the conference room.

"Bless you," I said as we unloaded.

"I figured it would be one less thing," said Danny. "How'd
it go?"

Emily and I told him about the jury selection and the fact
that we didn't feel like we had a lot of choices at the end.

"How did they react to the openings?"

I pointed to Emily, who appeared to choose her words carefully. "I think we have some work to do."

Daniel looked at me.

I nodded. "A lot."

"You're going to have to hit the other explanation for the
murder harder."

"I can throw some doubt around, but I'm a little light on
proof at the moment."

Danny nodded and took a bite. "Any witnesses today?"

We told him about Deputy Pavlich.

Danny chewed and thought before he said, "Not a lot you can do with that, but you laid the groundwork for the blood evidence."

"I think it was more damaging than we anticipated."

"How so?"

"Ask Emily."

Danny looked at her.

"Mr. Marsh was pretty compelling."

"Did the jury notice?"

Emily nodded.

Danny shrugged. "The prosecutor's case is never better than on the first day."

Emily pulled at a string of cheese until it separated. "Yeah. But I'm used to being the one delivering that blow."

Danny grinned. "Welcome to the world of counter punching." He stood and grabbed the rest of his sandwich. "Need anything?"

"No, thanks. How about you? Head above water?"

He nodded. "The next deal isn't going to heat up for a while yet. I'm just looking at the letters of intent to line up what I'll need to do."

I lifted the sandwich. "Thanks for these."

He smiled and left with nary a stumble.

"What do we have tomorrow?" said Emily.

"The electronics store owner, the investigative detective, and, if there's time, the lab guy."

"Are you sure I can't take one?"

"I'd like you and I to get through a trial together first."

"I've handled dozens of witnesses, you know."

"I do. But the angle's a little different."

"But—"

"—And it's murder."

Emily wasn't mad, but she didn't stop either.

"I can do it."

"You will. Just not tomorrow."

She took that as an answer and the two of us went back to work.

SILAS WINFORD STARTED the next day by calling Sam Perkins, the owner of Second Chance Electronics. Mr. Perkins had ditched the My Chemical Romance t-shirt for a black button-down long sleeve and black jeans, but his longish thinning hair remained unruly with one strand in particular falling repeatedly below his eyebrows.

"What do you do at the Second Chance Electronics store, Mr. Perkins?" said Winford.

"Pretty much what it says. I buy electronic appliances and equipment from people and then resell it."

"TVs?"

"Yes."

"Smart phones?"

"Yes. Along with tablets and computers and just about anything else you can plug in."

"Are game systems one of the things you buy and sell?"

Sam Perkins nodded. "All kinds."

"Have you ever purchased electronics from the defendant, Logan Carver?"

"One time, last fall."

"Tell me about that."

"Well, he came in—"

"—By he, you mean?"

"That man right over there, Logan Carver."

"I'm sorry to interrupt you. Go ahead."

"He came in carrying a PS5—"

"—What's a PS5?"

"A PlayStation 5, a gaming console made by Sony."

"Was that unusual?"

"Very."

"Why is that?"

"Because at that time they were hard to come by. It's a lot easier to get them now but back then, if people had one, they held onto them. So that man over there comes in holding one and says he wants to sell it, along with a pair of Beats."

"Beats?"

"A set of headphones, Beats by Dr. Dre. So I give him a price on the Beats but tell him I'm going to need to check out the PS5."

"What do you mean check it out?"

"I told him to make sure it was operational, but I run a clean shop, so I also wanted to check to make sure it was his."

"How did Mr. Carver respond?"

"He told me he was in a hurry. I said I understood, but I needed to check the PS5 out. He showed me that it turned on and I told him I understood but that I still needed to check it out." Sam Perkins looked at Judge Wesley. "I run a clean shop."

"So what did you do?" said Winford.

"Carver over there started to get irritated then and said he really needed to go. So I offered him a compromise—I offered him a standard trade-in price on the Beats and told him that I would give him a deposit of fifty dollars on the PS5 and, if he wanted to come back the next day and the system worked, I would give them the rest. He was mad so we talked it out some and finally settled on a seventy-five-dollar deposit and my promise that he could come back the next day to get the rest."

"Then what happened?"

"I asked him what his name was and he seemed distracted and he pulls out a prescription bottle and was looking at it so I asked him again what his name was so I could write down who to give the money to."

"And what did he do?"

"He put the bottle back in his pocket and said his name was Christopher Marsh."

Silas Winford nodded. "Then what happened?"

"Then I bought the Beats and paid him the deposit on the PS5, and he left."

"What time was that, Mr. Perkins?"

"I'd say the whole thing took about ten minutes and he came in at maybe ten fifteen."

"What happened next?"

"I had customers the rest of the night like usual and closed up around midnight. Then, I went home and I was pretty hungry so I made—"

"—I'm sorry Mr. Perkins, what happened next in relation to Christopher Marsh?"

"Oh, right, so I came back the next morning, took the PS5 back into my workshop in the back of the store, and hooked it up. I turned it on, saw it worked and saw that the user was logged in."

"Did you notice the name?"

"I did. It said MarshRules."

"Did that mean anything to you?"

"It seemed to me that the account name matched the name of the man who sold it to me."

"Then what happened?"

"I was excited because I hadn't had a chance to sell one of these and I knew it would go right away."

"So what did you do?"

"I put the PS5 up for sale online and sure enough it goes in minutes. I box it up for shipping and set it aside to wait until the money clears my account before I send it out. Now I always have

TVs on in the shop—it shows they work and makes the hi-def sets look even better—and that afternoon there's a newsbreak and I see a report that a guy named Christopher Marsh has been found murdered. Except it's not Christopher Marsh."

"What do you mean?"

"I mean, I turned on the sound and I hear them talk about a young man who was killed the night before not too far from my shop and they have his picture up because he was a reporter or something and they say he was Christopher Marsh only he's not the Christopher Marsh that I saw the night before. Then the report says that he was killed during a break-in and I about shit my—excuse me—I freak out a little and then call the police."

"Why did you call the police?"

"Because I was worried that I had just bought stolen property from a murderer."

Emily jerked her head at me in a way that showed she wanted to jump up and object but that was not the time to explain that jumping up and objecting would just emphasize Perkins' words, would make it look like we were worried we looked guilty, and would just get overruled in any event because it was actually the reason why Perkins had called the police. Instead, I shook my head slightly and listened.

"And what happened next?" said Winford.

"The police came and I told them what had happened and gave them the PS5 and the Beats. I answered their questions, and they seemed real interested with what time this had all happened. Then I downloaded some video footage for them and they left."

"What video footage?"

"I have a security camera outside the store. They used that to get a picture of Carver as he came in."

"What happened next?"

"I had customers but mostly I was freaking out. I run a clean shop."

"I understand. Did you hear from the police again?"

"Oh, right. Later that night. They asked me to come up to the sheriff's station. That's all the way up in Dellville so I convinced them to let me come up the next morning. I did and they asked me if I could identify the man who sold me the PS5. They had me look at a line of guys and I said right away that was him."

"By 'him' you're identifying Logan Carver, the defendant sitting right over there?"

"Yeah. It wasn't hard. He was still wearing the same clothes."

"Thank you, Mr. Perkins. Mr. Shepherd may have some questions for you now."

I stood. "Good morning, Mr. Perkins."

He nodded and pushed the stray hair above his eyebrows. "Morning."

"Mr. Carver was wearing a sweatshirt when he came into your store, wasn't he?"

"He was. It was gray with a big purple 'FU' on it."

"That's why you remember it, right?"

"A capital 'FU' gets your attention. I asked him about it and he laughed and said it was for Furman University."

"Mr. Perkins, you didn't see any blood on Mr. Carver's light gray sweatshirt, did you?"

He scowled. "No."

"And when you were exchanging the electronics and the money you didn't see any blood on his hands, right?"

"Of course not."

"And you didn't see any on his face or clothes or shoes or anywhere at all, did you?"

"No way."

"I'd bet that if you had seen blood on Mr. Carver, any blood at all, you would not have done business with him, would you?"

"No, I would not."

"Because you run a clean shop."

"That's right."

"And by that, you mean you don't deal in stolen goods, right?"

"Never."

"And we know you had a chance to observe his sweatshirt that night because you testified a little bit ago that Mr. Carver was wearing the same clothes when you saw him at the police station the next day, right?"

"That's right."

"A light gray sweatshirt with the purple 'FU' on it?"

"Unless he has more than one, it was the same."

"Mr. Perkins, you mentioned that you bought a set of Beats and a PS5 from Mr. Carver that night, right?"

Sam Perkins slowly said, "I bought a set of Beats and put a deposit on a PS5, yes."

"Your store buys and sells computers, doesn't it?"

"We do."

"You didn't buy a laptop from Logan Carver, did you?"

"What?"

"Logan Carver did not try to sell you a laptop, did he?"

"No."

"Just the Beats and the PS5, right?"

"That's what I said."

"There was no laptop?"

"There was no laptop."

"One of the things that's missing from Christopher Marsh's possessions is his work laptop computer. I understand that the Sheriff's department has never found it. You don't have it, do you?"

Sam Perkins eyes got bigger. "No way. If I did, I would have given it to the police."

"Because you run a clean shop."

"That's right."

"Mr. Perkins, are you worried about the police charging you for dealing in stolen property in this case?"

Sam Perkins jerked his head. "Are they?"

Winford stood. "Objection, Your Honor. No such charges have ever been suggested until this moment by Mr. Shepherd."

"We've just seen that the witness is clearly worried about it, Your Honor. Goes to bias and his state of mind."

Judge Wesley did not look up from whatever she was working on. "Overruled."

"Mr. Perkins, are you worried about being charged with dealing in stolen property in this case?"

Sam Perkins looked from me to Silas Winford and back. "They aren't, are they?"

I shrugged. "Mr. Winford says they aren't. But you did buy stolen property that night, didn't you?"

"I didn't know! And I called right away!"

"Actually, you called after you resold the game system, didn't you?"

"I didn't go through with it! I cancelled it as soon as I knew."

"So back to my original question—were you worried about being charged before you testified today?"

"I don't want any trouble."

"So that's a 'yes?' You were worried?"

"Who wouldn't be?"

I nodded. "I understand. One last thing, have you ever bought goods from Peyton Rush?"

Out of the corner of my eye, I saw Silas Winford twitch but stay seated.

Sam Perkins sat back in his chair. "Never heard of her."

"I see." I walked back to my chair. "And how did you know Peyton Rush is a her?"

He shifted. "It's a girl's name."

"Peyton Manning would disagree."

His mouth opened, then closed as he pushed the stray hair over to the side. "Lucky guess."

"Sure. No further questions, Your Honor."

Silas Winford stood. "Mr. Perkins, the Ash County Sheriff never threatened to arrest you for dealing in stolen goods, did they?"

"No."

"I never threatened to charge you with the crime before you testified today, did I?"

"No."

"You called the Sheriff's Department yourself once you realized you had information related to Christopher Marsh's murder, didn't you?"

"Yes, sir. It was my duty as a citizen."

"And you identified Mr. Carver as the man who sold you Christopher Marsh's PlayStation and Beats, right?"

"Yes sir, I did."

"No further questions."

I stood. "Mr. Perkins, you didn't see any blood on Mr. Carver when he sold you the PlayStation, did you?"

"No."

"You didn't see any sign at all that he'd been involved in a violent altercation, did you?"

"No."

"Because if you had seen any sign, the smallest sign whatsoever that Mr. Carver had been involved in a violent altercation, you would not have dealt with him, would you?"

"That's right."

"And according to your security video, he was in your shop at 10:15 that night, right?"

"That's right."

"No further questions."

Judge Wesley took a look and when we both shook our heads, said, "You may step down, Mr. Perkins. We will take a short break and then return. Mr. Winford is your next witness here?"

Silas stood. "Yes, Your Honor. We will be calling Detective Lee Durbin."

"Very well, then we will...Yes, Mr. Perkins?"

Sam Perkins was standing in the middle of the courtroom floor with his hand raised. "When do I get the PS5 back, Judge?"

"Excuse me?"

"I bought it, but the Sheriff took it. When do I get it back? Or at least my money."

Silas Winford sprang to his feet. "Perhaps this is something that can be handled on a break, Your Honor?"

Judge Wesley nodded. "I would think so. We'll see you all back here in fifteen minutes."

The jury left with Perkins standing at Silas Winford's side, waiting.

54

D uring the break, Emily looked over my shoulder. "He's not here."

"Who?"

"Mr. Marsh."

I kept working on my notes. "There's a lot of crime scene evidence today."

"Mrs. Marsh is though."

"Emily."

"Right. The slides are loaded."

"Thanks."

~

AFTER THE MORNING BREAK, Ash County Detective Lee Durbin took the stand. Although he was a detective, he still wore his dress uniform and, as he sat down, he removed his hat, placed it on the rail, and rotated it until the insignia on the front faced squarely out. He was a broad man and tall with black hair cut short and tight to the sides. He sat straight, folded his hands, and measured out a single nod to Silas Winford to indicate that he was ready.

"Could you introduce yourself to the jury, please?" said Winford.

His voice was deep. "Detective Lee Durbin of the Investigative Unit of the Ash County Sheriff's Department."

They ran through Detective Durbin's credentials which included twenty years with the department, sixteen of those being spent in the Investigative Unit handling homicides, robberies, and complex crimes.

"Detective Durbin, were you involved in the investigation of Christopher Marsh's death?"

"I was."

"How?"

"I received a call from Deputy Randy Pavlich indicating that a victim had been found in a house in the north section of Carrefour. I arrived shortly thereafter to investigate the scene."

"And what did you find?"

"I found the victim, Christopher Marsh, dead in his kitchen."

"Could you tell what had happened?"

"Mr. Marsh had been struck in the back of the head with a blunt instrument."

"And how did you know that?"

"Because the back of his skull was crushed and there was blood on the floor and on the surrounding walls."

"And did you take pictures of the scene?"

"I did."

Winford led Detective Durbin through twelve pictures of the blood-spattered kitchen. The final one was of Christopher Marsh's body laid out, the back of his head a bloodied mass.

I heard at least two gasps from the jury.

"What else did you do?"

"I investigated the scene and collected evidence."

"Such as?"

"I took the photos you saw. I took samples of blood to be tested by the lab. I also checked for additional physical evidence such as fingerprints and fibers. Finally, I took an inventory of items of potential significance and directed officers in taking those items into custody as potential evidence."

"Did you find anything of interest to you?"

"I did. I found cloth fibers on the jagged edge of the inner latch of the entertainment console. I collected them and sent them to the lab for examination."

"What else did you do?"

"I canvassed the surrounding houses and the other tenant of Christopher Marsh's residence who lives on the third floor. None of them reported hearing any signs of a struggle or seeing an intruder."

"Detective Durbin, what was your conclusion after investigating the scene?"

"The entertainment console was open and disorganized with loose wires indicating that something had likely been taken. The bathroom medicine cabinet was open and appeared to have been disturbed. In general, things were disorganized in a way that typically means someone was searching quickly. And of course, Christopher Marsh was dead in his kitchen. This indicated to me that items had likely been stolen from the house and that Christopher Marsh had been killed during the robbery."

"Did you find a murder weapon at the scene?"

Detective Durbin shook his head. "I did not. It was clear to me that a blunt instrument had been used, but I did not find anything at the time which I suspected of being the weapon."

"Were you able to draw any conclusions about the killing itself based upon the evidence that you observed?"

"I would defer to the coroner, but I did not see any signs of struggle on Christopher Marsh."

"What do you mean by that?"

"We did not find any tissue or DNA under his fingernails. We did not find bruising anywhere else on his body. We did not find abrasions or bruising on his knuckles."

"What did that lead you to conclude?"

"That he was struck by surprise from behind with the blunt instrument and the perpetrator then struck one or more additional blows to make sure he was dead."

"What did you do next?"

"We examined the scene for some time, taking the pictures you've shown, marking evidence, and taking samples. Deputy Pavlich had interviewed Mr. Marsh so, given what he had been through, I did not interview him again at that time."

"Then what?"

"I had returned to our office to write out my preliminary findings when we received a call related to the case."

"What was that call?"

"It was from Sam Perkins, the owner of Second Chance Electronics, who indicated he may have evidence connected to the murder of Christopher Marsh."

"What was that evidence?"

"A gaming console owned by a Christopher Marsh had been sold to him the night before."

"What did you do?"

"I immediately went and interviewed Mr. Perkins, took possession of the game console and Beats headphones, and downloaded video footage of the person who had sold the items to Mr. Perkins."

"What did you do next?"

"I circulated the photo within the department and used specialty software to compare it to our files. Within an hour, I had a match in the software to the photo of a person...familiar to our department and a confirmation from an officer who recognized the person."

"And who was that person?"

Detective Durbin indicated with his head. "The defendant, Logan Carver."

"What did you do next?"

"I went to Logan Carver's house to speak with him."

I stood. "Your Honor, may we approach?"

Judge Wesley waved me up. Silas Winford joined us.

"Your Honor, for the reasons we cited in our pretrial motion, we request that the Court exclude any evidence of Detective Durbin's conversation with Mr. Carver."

Judge Wesley looked at Winford.

"And for the reasons set forth in our response, Judge, Mr. Carver was in the comfort of his own home when he volunteered information to Detective Durbin and consented to the search of his car."

Judge Wesley nodded. "And for the reasons I set forth in our preliminary ruling, that evidence is admissible and is coming in, Mr. Shepherd. You have made your record."

I nodded and we returned to our places.

"What did you say when you met with Logan Carver?"

"I identified myself as a deputy with the Ash County Sheriff's Department and asked whether he had been at Second Chance Electronics the night before."

"And how did Logan Carver reply?"

"He said that he had not."

"What was your reaction to that?"

"I knew he was lying, so I said we had video of him being there and asked if I could come in."

"How did he reply?"

"He said I could not."

"What did you do?"

"I said there was an issue with merchandise he had sold at the store and asked if he would mind if I looked in his car."

"What did he say?"

"He said, 'Yes, but just my car.'"

"What happened next?"

"I asked him to unlock it for me and he did. I examined the front and back compartments and did not find anything of note. Then I asked him to open the trunk. He did, and that is when I found the aluminum bat."

"Was that significant to you?"

"Yes."

"Why?"

"Because it had blood on it."

"Did Mr. Carver have an explanation?"

"Yes. He said it wasn't his."

"What did you do?"

"I arrested Mr. Carver on suspicion of murder."

"What did Mr. Carver say?"

"After reading him his rights, Mr. Carver asked who he had killed. I told him Christopher Marsh."

"How did he react?"

"He said 'I didn't kill anyone, I only took'—and then he stopped."

"Did he say anything else?"

"No."

"Did you obtain any further evidence in your investigation?"

"After his arrest, we searched his residence. We found a prescription bottle of Adderall made out to Christopher Marsh in the trash and a box of latex surgical gloves in the kitchen."

"What was the significance of those?"

"The Adderall bottle was further evidence that Mr. Carver

had been in Christopher Marsh's residence and surgical gloves are often used—"

I stood. "Objection, speculation, Your Honor, unless we're also going to have an extended discussion of cleaning toilets or handling raw meat or unclogging pipes or—"

"I get the point, Mr. Shepherd. Sustained."

"What other evidence did you obtain, Detective Durbin?"

"Our lab tests found—"

I stood. "Objection, Your Honor. Detective Durbin did not perform any tests."

Winford smiled and raised a hand. "I'll rephrase, Your Honor. Detective Durbin, did you subsequently receive any reports that affected your investigation?"

"Yes. I received a report from our lab that fibers found at the scene matched the clothes worn by Mr. Carver and that the blood on the bat matched that of Christopher Marsh. Any further details can be obtained from them. At that point, however, I turned our materials over to the prosecutor's office."

"Very good. Thank you, Detective Durbin. Mr. Shepherd may wish to speak to you now."

I stood. "Detective Durbin, the crime scene had been disturbed by the time that you arrived, hadn't it?"

"I don't know that I would use the word disturbed."

"Christopher Marsh's body had been moved, right?"

"I understand that Christopher Marsh's body was being held by his father when law enforcement arrived, yes."

"So it had been moved, right?

"It's understandable when one has found their son murdered."

"It is. But I didn't ask if it was understandable. I asked if he had moved Christopher's body and the answer is 'yes,' isn't it?"

Detective Durbin's gaze was stony. "Yes."

"And Deputy Pavlich moved Christopher's body too, didn't he?"

"I understand that Deputy Pavlich put the body back in the position in which Mr. Marsh described finding it."

"Right, but Deputy Pavlich never saw where the body was lying, did he?"

"I don't see how he could have."

"Well, he could have if the body hadn't been moved."

"I think it is outrageous, Mr. Shepherd, to suggest that a parent should not hold his child in that situation."

"Then I don't know why you're suggesting it, Detective Durbin. What I am suggesting is that your office staged the positioning of Christopher Marsh's body for the photos you've just shown the jury."

"That's not true at all."

"No? But Christopher's body had been moved and then your office re-staged the scene before you took photos, didn't you?"

"We didn't stage anything."

"Okay, you don't like the word 'stage.' But you'll agree that your officers positioned Christopher Marsh's body before you took your pictures, won't you?"

Detective Durbin thought for a time before he said, "Yes. Based on the best information that we had."

"Sure. And the reason I'm asking this is because there are experts who are going to testify later about certain aspects of this scene and it is important for the jury to know that those photos you showed them don't represent the exact way Christopher Marsh was found. And they don't, do they?"

"They represent our best estimation based on the information that we received from Mr. Marsh."

"Exactly. It was your best guess."

"Our best estimation, yes."

"Detective Durbin, you saw Mr. Marsh at the scene, didn't you?"

"I did."

"He had blood on him, didn't he?"

"That was understandable since he had held his son."

"Again, Detective Durbin, I didn't ask if it was understandable. You saw that Mr. Marsh had blood on his arms and hands, right?"

"I did."

"You found Mr. Marsh's footprints in the blood, didn't you?"

"I did."

"You found Deputy Pavlich's footprints in the blood too, didn't you?"

"Yes."

"You did not find any footprints that matched my client's shoes at the scene, did you?"

"I did not."

"Detective Durbin, you were the one who went to Logan Carver's house to interview him, aren't you?"

"I am."

"He was wearing a gray Furman University sweatshirt when you arrested him, right?

"It was a gray sweatshirt that said 'FU' on it."

"Yes, that's a marketing program for Furman University. Were you aware of that?"

"Not at the time."

"Well, the marketing programs of small southern universities are not really important here, Detective Durbin. What is important is that you did not see any blood on Mr. Carver's sweatshirt when you spoke to him, did you?"

"I don't know that I looked that close."

"Let's try this again, Detective Durbin. You did not see any blood on Mr. Carver's gray Furman sweatshirt, did you?"

"It was almost a day later when I saw Mr. Carver. He could've washed it."

"Really? Because your lab is going to testify that it found chocolate shake on his sweatshirt sleeve from the night before. Is your lab wrong?"

"No. But the lab report didn't say the shake was from the night before."

"No, Detective Durbin, the drive-thru video shows it was spilled the night before. The video this jury is going to watch isn't wrong, is it?"

"I haven't seen that video."

"Well I have, and Mr. Winford has, and the jury will. So, Mr. Carver didn't wash his sweatshirt, did he?"

"Apparently not."

"You just made that up, didn't you?"

Detective Durbin looked at the jury before he stared at me. "I offered a theory that was mistaken."

"You made something up to fit your theory, right here in front of the jury."

"I was mistaken." He bit off each word. "I apologize. I was wrong."

"Gosh, I hope that's the only thing."

"Your Honor," said Winford.

"Mr. Shepherd, limit yourself to questions, not comments," said Judge Wesley.

"Yes, Your Honor. Let's get back to the original question, Detective Durbin. You did not see any blood on Mr. Carver's Furman sweatshirt, did you?"

"Not that I recall."

"If you had seen blood on his sweatshirt, you would've noted it in your report, wouldn't you?"

"Probably."

"And you would've told the jury about it in your testimony a moment ago, wouldn't you?"

"I don't know.

"You don't know if you would've told the jury that you had found blood on the suspect's clothes? Are they really supposed to believe that?"

"It didn't happen, so I don't know."

"Right. It didn't happen. You didn't find any blood on Mr. Carver's shoes either, did you?"

"I don't recall any."

"You're a careful detective, aren't you, Detective Durbin?"

"I am."

"The public can count on you to give your full attention to the details of a murder investigation, can't they?"

"They can."

"So as part of your careful, detailed investigation of a murder, you would note in your report if you found blood on the suspect's clothes or shoes, wouldn't you?"

"I would."

"And you did not make such a note in this case, did you?"

"I did not note any blood on Logan Carver's shirt or shoes in my report."

"Detective Durbin, you mentioned that Christopher Marsh's home looked as if it had been quickly searched, true?"

"That's true. The TV stand was disturbed and the medicine cabinet and there was a general disorder as if things had been moved around."

"You also mentioned that you inventoried items at the scene?"

"I did."

"I noticed that Christopher Marsh was wearing a smart watch when he was found?"

"Yes."

"That's easier to take than a game console, isn't it?"

"I couldn't say."

"A money clip was found on the counter next to his car keys, wasn't it?"

"Yes."

"It still had cash in it, right?"

"Yes."

"Cash is certainly easier to take than electronics you have to resell, isn't it?"

Detective Durbin shrugged. "I'm not surprised that Mr. Carver fled after the attack without searching further."

"Speaking of searching further, Christopher Marsh had a laptop computer for work. You did not find the laptop in his house, did you?"

"We did not."

"And you did not find a laptop in my client's possession, did you?"

"We did not."

"And you found no evidence that Mr. Carver ever tried to sell a laptop, did you?"

"We did not."

"So this reporter's laptop just mysteriously vanished?"

Silas Winford stood. "Objection to that implication, Your Honor."

I turned to Winford. "I thought we agreed that Christopher Marsh was a reporter?"

"That's not what I mean."

"His laptop has vanished. I can rephrase to 'disappeared' if you like."

Winford caught himself. "May we approach, Your Honor?"

Judge Wesley waved us up.

Winford started speaking as soon as we got there. "Your Honor, we object because Mr. Shepherd appears to be implying that there is some sort of conspiracy here for which there is no basis."

"Your Honor, my question did no such thing. Mr. Marsh was a reporter, he had a laptop which he used for work, and it has vanished. All of these things are true and demonstrated by the prosecution's own witnesses and inventory."

"But 'mysteriously?'" said Winford.

I shrugged. "Do you know where it is?"

Judge Wesley raised a hand. "I am going to allow this question, and only this question, as it is supported by the evidence currently admitted in the case. You will not go any farther afield, Mr. Shepherd, unless you have evidence to back it up. Evidence that is allowed by this Court. Understood?"

I nodded and we returned to our places.

"Detective Durbin, you testified that Christopher Marsh's laptop was never found by your office. The question pending to you is 'So this reporter's laptop just mysteriously vanished?'"

Detective Durbin looked at Silas Winford who gave him a slight nod. "We were never able to locate it."

"Were you ever looking for it?"

"Not really."

"Detective Durbin, the lower windowpane on the side door was broken, right?"

"It was."

"And we can agree that the windowpane was broken before the night Christopher Marsh was killed, can't we?"

"That is what I understand from both Mr. Marsh and Christopher's upstairs neighbor."

"You can't say for certain as we sit here whether that door was opened or closed on the night Christopher Marsh was killed, can you?"

"I think it's overwhelmingly likely that—"

"—I didn't say overwhelmingly likely, Detective. I said certain."

"It's overwhelmingly likely the door was closed."

"But not certain."

Detective Durbin stared. "We don't have a photo if that's what you mean."

"Or testimony or evidence one way or the other."

"No, we don't have evidence of whether your client opened the door before he robbed the place."

"I wish your evidence were as clear as your opinions, Detective. Speaking of opinions, when you first spoke to my client, you did not tell him that he was a murder suspect, did you?"

"I'm not obligated to do that."

"I didn't ask if you're obligated to do it, I asked if you did it. You did not tell my client that he was a suspect in a murder investigation, did you?"

"My first priority was to gain information about the killing of Christopher Marsh."

"Then you shouldn't have any trouble at all answering my question. You, Detective Durbin, did not tell Logan Carver that he was a suspect in a murder case when you first spoke to him, did you?"

"I did not."

"You told him that there was an issue with Second Chance Electronics, didn't you?"

"I did. And he denied it."

"When he denied it, you told him that you had video of him there, right?"

"That's right."

"And you then asked to come into his house, right?"

"I did."

"And he said no?"

"He did."

"But when you asked to search his car, you say he consented, true?"

"He in fact consented to that search, yes."

"And you did not find anything of note in the front or back seat, correct?"

"That's right."

"Incidentally, you did find two McDonald's shake cups, didn't you?"

"There were a few food wrappers and cups. I don't recall if there were shake cups."

"But you found a bloody bat, the murder weapon, in his trunk. True?"

"I did."

"He acted surprised, didn't he?"

"They all do."

"Let's focus on Logan Carver instead of 'they,' Detective. Logan Carver immediately denied the bat was his, right?"

"Of course, he did."

"It turns out that was true though, wasn't it?"

Detective Durbin cocked his head. "How do you mean?"

"The bat was Christopher Marsh's, right?"

"That's true. So what?"

"So, it was not my client's."

"It was in his car."

"But it was not his."

Detective Durbin shrugged. "So he stole it the same as he stole the PS5 and the Beats and the Adderall."

"Logan Carver's car was parked in the street when you searched it, wasn't it?"

"It was."

"So the car was out in the open all night?"

Detective Durbin scoffed. "Nobody popped the trunk and planted the bat."

"I never said they did but you raise an interesting theory. Did you investigate whether anybody popped the trunk and planted the bat?"

Winford stood. "Your Honor, objection to this line of inquiry."

"I'm just following up on the theory that Detective Durbin has put forth and ruled out, Your Honor."

Judge Wesley looked at me, eyes narrow. "Keep it concise, Mr. Shepherd."

"Yes, Your Honor. Detective Durbin, did you investigate whether anyone had popped the trunk on Logan Carver's car and planted the bat?"

Detective Durbin looked at Winford and then the judge and then me. I waited.

"No," he said finally.

"Did you check the trunk or its lock for damage consistent with a break in?"

"No."

"Did you canvas the neighbors around Mr. Carver's house to find out if they saw anyone suspicious lurking around his car?"

"No."

"Did you canvas neighbors to see if anyone had a doorbell camera that would have captured people breaking into Mr. Carver's car?"

"No."

"So you have no idea whether somebody, and I quote, 'popped the trunk and planted the bat,' do you?"

"There's no way someone did that."

"You don't know though, do you?"

"That doesn't make any sense."

"No, what doesn't make any sense is that my client would let you search his car knowing there was a murder weapon in it."

"Objection, Your Honor," said Winford.

"Withdrawn," I said. "No further questions."

Winford stood. "Detective you have not found any evidence that someone else planted the bat in Logan Carver's trunk, have you?"

"I have not."

"However, you did find evidence that Logan Carver broke into Christopher Marsh's house, didn't you?"

"With the fibers, yes."

"And you did find evidence that Mr. Carver sold Mr. Marsh's possessions on the night Christopher Marsh was killed?"

"I did."

"And you found an empty prescription bottle made out to Christopher Marsh in Logan Carver's trash?"

"We did."

"Mr. Shepherd made a point of saying that you did not find the footprints of Logan Carver in Christopher Marsh's blood, do you remember that?"

"I do."

"In fact, you did not find any footprints in the blood that you could not identify, is that right?"

"That's right. The only footprints belonged to Deputy Pavlich and Mr. Marsh."

"Neither Deputy Pavlich nor Mr. Marsh killed Christopher Marsh that day, did they?"

"No sir."

"So the fact is, whoever killed Christopher Marsh did not leave any footprints at the scene, did they?"

"No sir, they did not."

"No further questions."

I stood. "There was a significant amount of blood at the scene, wasn't there, Detective Durbin?"

"There was."

"You'd have to be skilled and careful to avoid leaving foot-prints there, wouldn't you?"

"I'm not sure what you mean."

"I mean with all of that blood you would have to be very, very careful about what you were doing to avoid leaving foot-prints or smears, wouldn't you?"

I felt Winford tense behind me but kept my eyes on Detective Durbin. Eventually he said, "I don't know."

"No further questions, Your Honor."

"Thank you, Detective Durbin," said Judge Wesley. "Let's take a break for lunch."

55

The afternoon was spent with the Ash County lab guy, and I'll spare you the details. Silas Winford took him, with exacting and precise detail, through the way in which the lab matched the fibers from Logan's FU sweatshirt to the fibers found on the scene, confirming Logan had left fibers from the sweatshirt in the latch of the TV stand.

He also showed that the blood found on the aluminum baseball bat was indisputably Christopher Marsh's. Besides the initial test for type, he'd subsequently done a DNA test which conclusively established that the bat found in Logan's car was covered in Christopher Marsh's blood.

I got three important admissions out of him. He admitted that he had done a complete forensic examination of the FU sweatshirt and that there was not a single drop of blood on it. He also admitted that the left sleeve of the sweatshirt was smeared with the delicious mixture of ingredients that comprised a McDonald's chocolate shake, which let me bang on Detective Durbin again for making up his sweatshirt-washing theory. Finally, he confirmed that there were no fingerprints on the aluminum bat—not Logan Carver's, not Christopher

Marsh's, and not anyone else's. In assessing the jury, they seemed mildly interested in the fact that there was no blood on the sweatshirt and frowned at the mention of Detective Durbin and the shake, but gave me stony faces on the lack of finger-prints on the bat.

Winford then finished the day with some chain of custody evidence, showing how the fibers and the blood samples traveled from the crime scene to the Sheriff's office to the lab and back to the Sheriff's office before arriving here at trial without any deviation or detours. There was really nothing much to say about that; I would've expected nothing less from Sheriff Dushane.

When the last chain of custody witness was finished, Judge Wesley dismissed the jury and said, "Counsel, please see me in my office."

Judge Wesley was already on her way by the time I looked up. I caught Winford's eye, who shrugged before heading in. Emily and I followed.

We had not even sat down before Judge Wesley said, "What's this laptop business?"

Winford shrugged. "I'd love to know."

I crossed my legs and sat back. "Christopher Marsh was a reporter. I understand he had notes and files on his laptop. That laptop was not found in his house, in his car, or at the *Torch* offices. It's missing."

"That's interesting," said Judge Wesley.

"I agree."

"But I don't see how it has anything to do with this particular trial."

I shrugged. "If the prosecution is sloppy with one piece of evidence, it could be sloppy with others."

"Nate, that's not what you're doing, and you know it," said Winford. "Your Honor, he's trying to imply that there is a conspiracy and that someone else might have been involved in Christopher's killing."

I shrugged again. "I'm not the one who suggested someone planted the bat in Logan Carver's trunk. That was Detective Durbin."

"In response to your question!"

Judge Wesley's voice was serene. "I was there too, Mr. Winford. Mr. Shepherd, it is perfectly acceptable for you to call into question the handling of evidence, but you have done that. I expect that you will not bring up conspiracies or the presence of another person unless you have actual proof. Do you have evidence of a conspiracy you'd like to present to the Court?"

"Not at this time, Your Honor."

"Then you will not do so. And you won't say anything in front of the jury unless you obtain the Court's permission first."

"I understand, Your Honor. I assume I can respond if any of Mr. Winford's witnesses open those doors?"

"As long as they are the ones who open them." Judge Wesley turned to Winford. "Am I understood?"

"Yes, Your Honor."

"Very well. What do we have tomorrow, Mr. Winford?"

"Sheriff Dushane and Mr. Marsh."

"Will that wrap up your case?"

"Pretty near, Your Honor."

"Very well. Mr. Shepherd, plan on starting your case Thursday. Let's see if we can get this wrapped up by the end of the week."

"Yes, Your Honor," we all said and left.

As we walked back to our tables, Silas Winford smiled. "Is there anything you want to tell me about?"

"Not right now."

Winford nodded. "That's what I thought."

Then we packed up and left.

∼

EMILY and I were driving back to the office when she said, "There's just too much with Paxton for it not to be related."

I didn't rehash all the Paxton details with her; she knew them as well as I did. Instead, I just said, "If we can't prove it, it doesn't matter."

"But the timing! He turned the story in that day!"

"That's not enough, Emily. Not for Judge Wesley. Not for any judge really."

We let a few miles roll by as we each turned the evidence over.

"At least we got the thought out there and, if any of State's witnesses slip up, we'll do it again. I think we're going to be stuck relying on the blood and the timeline. How was the jury reacting to it all today?"

"They were interested by the blood, but the fibers and the bat still seem like problems."

"I agree."

"Do I get any witnesses tomorrow?"

"The Sheriff and Mr. Marsh? I'm sorry, Emily, I don't think so."

She nodded and stared ahead. "I saw what you meant, with Detective Durbin? There are some angles I might not have picked up on the fly."

"You will. It just takes time."

"Maybe the McDonald's witness?"

"Maybe. Let's see how things are going."

"Okay."

∼

DANNY HAD TAKEN time out from his business deals to pick up some West of Philly cheesesteaks, for which I was eternally grateful. When Emily proclaimed that next time she wanted hers 'Provolone wit,' I decided I had an outstanding office.

I had eaten my sandwich and was working on my cross-examination of Sheriff Dushane when Josie called. "Sorry to bother you."

"No bother at all."

"Are you still at the office? I can call later."

"No, I'll be here for a while yet. How are you?"

"Good. I have the day off tomorrow, so I grabbed dinner with a couple of friends."

"Great! Did you have fun?"

"I did. I can think of someone I'd rather spend time with, but it was a good second."

"Excellent."

"I won't keep you, but I was talking to Lana, she works in the NICU, and she said she and her husband loved the food at the Lakeside Public House but that reservations can be tough to come by. I wondered if you might be interested in going on Valentine's Day? I'd make all the arrangements."

I smiled. "I'd love to."

"Great! I just wanted to check with you because of the trial."

Reality returned. "I promise you I'm not normally that guy but...what day is Valentine's Day?"

Josie laughed. "Monday. That's why I thought I should check."

I looked at my calendar and ticked off our potential witnesses. "We should be done Friday or Monday at the latest. If I'm done with witnesses and closings, I should be able to go regardless."

"Is that a yes?"

"I think so. Would you be okay with canceling at the last minute if something unexpected happens with the trial?"

"So long as we still go later in the week."

"Done."

"How's the trial going?"

"About as expected."

"What did you expect?"

I thought about how to say it without saying too much. It took me a moment because I was a little out of practice. "It's an uphill battle, but we're making some progress. If a couple of rulings on the evidence go our way, we'll be in business."

"Good luck."

"Thanks."

We exchanged a couple of things that couples say, which, along with making Valentine's Day plans, felt a little strange. Nice, exciting even, but strange.

It took me about ten minutes after we hung up to transition back to Sheriff Dushane but, eventually, I did and finished up for the night.

56

The next day, Silas Winford put Sheriff Dushane on first thing. His graying hair and mustache were both neatly trimmed, and he hitched his gun belt for just a moment before sitting and nodding to Winford that he was ready to go.

"Could you introduce yourself to the jury please, sir?"

"I'm Warren Dushane, the Sheriff of Ash County."

"What is your jurisdiction, Sheriff Dushane?"

"I oversee law enforcement for all of Ash County."

"So the jury is clear, although the murder of Christopher Marsh happened in Carrefour, it was on the Michigan side of the line and so fell under your jurisdiction?"

"That's right."

"What departments are under your supervision, Sheriff Dushane?"

"There are a number of them, Mr. Winford, but I believe the two you'd like me to speak about today are my role overseeing the investigative unit and my role overseeing the Ash County jail."

"Let's start with the investigative unit. Was it involved in this case?"

"Yes. Because it involved a murder, this case was given to our most senior detective, Detective Durbin."

"What role did you play in the investigation?"

"Detective Durbin reported his findings and the status of the investigation to me, but he handled the nuts and bolts of it all."

"The jurors have already heard from Detective Durbin about the details of that investigation, so I won't ask you to repeat any of those. Were you involved in any firsthand investigation in this case?"

"A little, yes."

"What was that?"

"I helped determine where Christopher Marsh was before he came home on the evening he was killed and helped determine an estimate of the time he would've arrived home."

"What did you do?"

"Detective Durbin advised me that there was a bag from a Quick Carry store in the front seat of Mr. Marsh's car. There's a Quick Carry a couple of miles from Mr. Marsh's house, so I volunteered to go over there and see if anyone recalled seeing Mr. Marsh that night."

"What did you find?"

"There was a cashier who recalled seeing Mr. Marsh, but she was unable to give an exact time."

"Did she recall anything else?"

"She did. She remembered that he used the ATM before purchasing food."

"So what did you do?"

"We obtained a warrant and obtained the photos and time records from the ATM."

"Is that what's been marked as State's Exhibits 72 and 73?"

"That's correct. Exhibit 72 is the photo of Christopher Marsh taken by the ATM that evening. Exhibit 73 is the time record showing he withdrew two hundred dollars at 8:09 p.m."

Winford blew up Christopher Marsh's picture so that it filled the video screen for the jury to see. He looked young, he looked intent as he stared down at the screen, and most importantly, his skull was not bashed in the way it was in every other picture the jury had seen.

And did I mention? He looked very, very young.

"What did you do with that information, Sheriff Dushane?"

"I passed it along to Detective Durbin for use in his investigation."

"Did you play any other role?"

"Only as a supervisor and consultant to Detective Durbin."

"Very good. Sheriff Dushane, I understand you are also ultimately in charge of the management of the Ash County Jail?"

"That's correct."

"In that capacity, does the administrator of the jail report directly to you?"

"He does."

"And are you involved in assessing the conduct of both the guards and the inmates of that institution?"

"I am."

I stood. "Your Honor, may we approach?"

"You may, Mr. Shepherd."

When we arrived, I said, "Your Honor, I assume Mr. Winford is about to question Sheriff Dushane about the incident involving my client in the jail?"

Winford nodded. "I am, Your Honor."

"Your Honor, we again object as this is both irrelevant and highly prejudicial."

Winford said, "As we addressed in our brief, Your Honor, we believe the act of attacking an inmate with a blunt instrument from behind shows a pattern to Mr. Carver's attacks."

Judge Wesley nodded. "You have a very narrow window here, Mr. Winford. The Court overrules Mr. Shepherd's objection to the extent it elicits testimony regarding the way in which the attack was carried out. You will limit yourself to the facts in the incident report. Understood?"

He nodded and we returned our seats.

Winford continued, "Sheriff Dushane, in your role as supervisor of the Ash County Jail, do you receive reports related to attacks involving inmates?"

"I do."

"Did Mr. Carver await trial in the Ash County Jail?"

"He did."

"Now we should not imply any guilt or innocence in this trial because he was in jail, that was simply the place where he was being held because he was unable to post bond, is that correct?"

"That's my understanding, yes."

"While Mr. Carver was in the Ash County Jail, was he involved in a physical altercation with another inmate?"

"He was."

"Could you describe that for us, please?"

"An inmate with whom Logan Carver was having difficulties was bent over a sink in the bathroom. Mr. Carver came up from behind and struck him in the back of the head with a broken mop handle, causing the other inmate serious injury."

"When you say came up from behind, what do you mean?"

"It appeared that Mr. Carver waited in a stall until the other inmate bent over the sink to wash his face and, when he wasn't looking, Mr. Carver struck him repeatedly with the mop handle."

"And when you say the other inmate sustained serious injury, what do you mean?"

"Besides the impact blows to the back of the head, the other inmate's face was driven into the sink itself and the faucet, causing multiple fractures to his nose and teeth."

"Was that inmate hospitalized?"

"Yes."

"Did he survive the attack?"

"Yes."

"Now Sheriff Dushane, why, in your opinion, was that attack relevant to this case?"

"Because, to me, the method of attack seemed to be the same as the way in which Christopher Marsh was killed."

"What do you mean?"

"Christopher Marsh was a tall, fit man. Not overly large, but bigger than Mr. Carver. Christopher appeared to have been attacked from behind when he was bending over a kitchen drawer and was struck in the back of the skull until dead. This seemed to me to be a similar method of attack to that used by Mr. Carver against the inmate in the Ash County Jail."

"Meaning that the attack was carried out by stealth, from behind, using a blunt instrument when the victim was bending over and not looking?"

"Exactly, Mr. Winford."

Silas Winford nodded. "Thank you, Sheriff Dushane. Mr. Shepherd may have some questions for you now."

Sheriff Dushane was a friend and a good one, but the look he gave me now was the even, assessing stare he used as a coach on the football field when he was trying to beat the pants off an opposing defensive coordinator.

I nodded and he nodded and then I said, "Let's start with this fight in your jail, Sheriff Dushane."

"The attack? Certainly."

"You're charged with keeping inmates safe in your jail, aren't you?"

"I am. We unfortunately are not always successful, but we do our best with the resources we have."

"You are aware that this inmate threatened to—pardon my language—'beat the shit' out of my client?"

"I don't know that for certain."

"It's in your incident report, isn't it?"

"It is."

"My client told you that at the time, didn't he?"

"Yes, but it is typical for an inmate to blame the other person for an attack."

"My client had been pushed repeatedly by this inmate, hadn't he?"

Winford stood. "Objection, Your Honor. This is getting a little far field."

"Sustained."

"This inmate told my client he would 'stomp his bitch-ass guts,' didn't he?"

"Objection, Your Honor."

"Sustained."

I pointed at Wendy Carver. "This inmate told my client he would 'track down his mother and—'"

"Your Honor!"

"Mr. Shepherd! That is enough."

I nodded. "Withdrawn, Your Honor. Sheriff Dushane, you have other fights in your jail, don't you?"

"As I mentioned, that unfortunately happens on occasion."

"How many of them involve an inmate pushing or hitting someone from behind?"

"Objection, Your Honor."

"Sustained."

"It happens dozens of times a year, doesn't it?"

"Objection, Your Honor."

"Sustained."

"I mean, this supposed pattern of yours isn't like the Zodiac Killer or anything, is it?"

"Your Honor. Please."

"Your Honor," I said. "Mr. Winford is trying to make an everyday fight involving a blow from behind seem like some sort of complex criminal pattern when we both know that half the fights in his jail probably start that way."

Judge Wesley thought. "Overruled as to this question only. And then you will move on, Mr. Shepherd."

"Sheriff Dushane, hitting someone from behind happens all the time in fights, both in your jail and elsewhere, doesn't it?"

"It does. But using a blunt instrument is rarer."

"But still happens?"

"Rarely. But yes."

I shifted gears. "Sheriff Dushane, when my client attacked the inmate in jail, he had blood on his hands afterward, didn't he?"

Winford stood. "Objection, Your Honor. Irrelevant."

I sighed. "Then why did the State bring this whole jail business up, Your Honor?"

"Overruled."

"My client had blood on his hands after the fight, didn't he, Sheriff Dushane?"

"He did."

"He had blood on his face, yes?"

"He did."

"He had blood on his shirt and pants?"

"Yes."

"Sheriff Dushane, there wasn't any blood on Logan Carver's gray Furman University sweatshirt when he was arrested, was there?"

"No."

"There was no blood on his hands or face or skin?"

"No. But the attack on the inmate in the jail was an exceptionally bloody scene."

"I see. Emily, please put up State Exhibits 12, 15, and 16."

Pictures of blood on the walls and floor of Christopher Marsh's kitchen popped up. "Sheriff Dushane, these are pictures that your own office took of Christopher Marsh's kitchen. That's an exceptionally bloody scene too, isn't it?"

"There is blood there, true."

"It's an exceptional amount, isn't it?"

"I don't know that I'd use that term."

"What term would you use? A significant amount? A substantial amount? A lot?"

Sheriff Dushane's face remained passive as he stared at the screen. "It is a significant amount."

"Finally, Sheriff, you said that you were able to find a photo of Christopher Marsh using the ATM at the Quick Carry store?"

"I was."

"You said it was a couple of miles from Christopher Marsh's house, right?"

"That's right."

"Is it fair to say that's a five to ten-minute drive depending on traffic?"

"Closer to five, but five to ten is fair."

"And just so the jury is clear, Christopher's withdrawal occurred at 8:09 p.m. on the night he was killed, right?"

"That's what the ATM records indicate."

"And Mr. Marsh withdrew two hundred dollars?"

"He did."

"Your department found Mr. Marsh's money clip on his kitchen counter, right?"

"We did."

"It had two hundred and eight dollars in it, right?"

"Yes, but I would not be surprised if someone—"

I raised a hand. "Sheriff Dushane, I didn't ask for your theories as to *why* more than two hundred dollars in cash was lying on the kitchen counter. I asked *if* your deputies found two hundred and eight dollars lying on the counter. And the answer is 'yes,' correct?"

"Yes."

"No further questions, Your Honor."

Winford stood. "Sheriff Dushane, what did you want to say before Mr. Shepherd cut you off?"

"That I would not be surprised if an attacker fled once he had killed someone without checking around for more money."

"I see. Is it possible that a killer might not want to get blood or other evidence on them by staying on the scene?"

"That's very possible, yes."

"No further questions."

I stood. "Another possible explanation is that Logan Carver was not there when Christopher Marsh put his money clip on the counter, isn't it, Sheriff Dushane?"

"I don't think that's likely."

"And it's also possible that the person who killed Christopher Marsh wasn't interested in stealing things for money, isn't it?"

Winford stood. "Objection, Your Honor."

"Sustained."

"No further questions."

Judge Wesley nodded. "Sheriff Dushane, you are excused. Let's take a break and then the prosecution will call its next witness. Who's that Mr. Winford?"

"Mr. Marsh, Your Honor."

After the jury filed out and the judge had left, Logan Carver turned to me and said, "Why were they talking about Perry?"

"Perry?"

"The guy I cracked in jail."

"Because they're saying you attacked him in the same way that you attacked Christopher Marsh."

"But I didn't attack Christopher Marsh."

Logan was nothing if not consistent. I put a hand on his shoulder. "That's what I'm trying to show them."

Logan looked over his shoulder at the gallery, which was mostly empty.

"So, Marsh's dad is going to talk next?"

I nodded.

"He thinks I killed his son?"

"He does."

"I didn't though."

My phone buzzed with an unknown number. Without thinking, I turfed it, then said, "I know. Logan, this is going to be really hard. He's going to be very upset. You're going to disagree with a lot of what he says. I need you to keep a straight face, write on a notepad if you have to, but don't react to what he says, okay?"

"But if I didn't do it and he says I did—"

"That's what I'm here for. If the jury sees you getting angry, it's not going to help. Can you do that?"

My phone buzzed again. I had a text. *Pick up your goddam phone. It's Ringel.*

"Logan," Wendy Carver was saying at the railing. "Do what Nate says."

"I'll try," said Logan.

My phone buzzed from the same unknown number. I motioned to the Carvers, then answered. "Ted? I didn't recognize your number."

"Of course not. I'm calling from Indonesia."

I walked out of the courtroom.

"What are you doing in Indonesia?" I said quietly.

"What the hell do you think I'm doing in Indonesia?"

"Right."

I found an isolated corner of the hall as Ted said, "The time difference has me all screwed up. What time is it there?"

"We're on a break in trial so I just have a minute. Did you actually go out there to find Ethan Ferris?"

"It wasn't to vacation on Papuma Beach!"

Ted Ringel took a deep breath. "Listen Shepherd, it's true. All of Christopher's story is true. Paxton dumped PFAs into our river and covered it up. Ferris confirmed the whole thing."

I had a million questions. "Did Ferris go to Indonesia voluntarily?"

"If by voluntarily you mean, did he accept a job for three times his former salary including stock options, then yes."

"So why the secrecy?"

"He was going to a competitor, but mostly, he was scared to death after Marsh died."

"Does Ferris think it was Paxton who went after Marsh?"

"The man just moved his family to the other side of the world. What do you think?"

"How did he get his family to play along?"

"Money and fear will do that."

I nodded. "We had testimony from the investigating detective today. He confirmed that they never found Christopher's laptop."

"Well, unfortunately for those Paxton bastards, Chris had already emailed me the story. Now that I've confirmed it, we'll run it when I get back."

"Would you be willing to testify at trial?"

"About what?"

"That Christopher had a laptop and that it's missing. About what his final story turned out to be."

"You know, I'm still not sure if your client did it."

"I know. But what if I could show you that someone guided my client to the Marsh job?"

"What?!"

"And now that person has disappeared too."

"You can prove that?"

"Not in court. Maybe not enough to publish. But I think I can prove it to you."

Ted was quiet. "I'm flying seven hours to Korea, then the better part of the day to Detroit. I'll arrive twenty-five, maybe twenty-seven hours from now. I'll think about it on the way."

"Ted, if there's any chance Paxton was involved in this, we have to get it out there."

"I have to get Christopher's last story out there, Shepherd. I don't have to do anything for the guy who robbed him."

"Unless he's taking the fall for the guy who killed him."

"I said, I'll think about it."

Ted Ringel hung up. Before I could process what it meant, Emily stuck her head out of the courtroom door. "They're ready for Mr. Marsh."

57

When Jerry Marsh entered the courtroom, he looked worse than he had two days before. He hunched his shoulders so that his blue suit fell crooked around his waist, and he touched the rails and tables he passed as if keeping his balance with the wood. His whitish gray hair hid his eyes until he sat in the witness chair and was able to finally straighten. When he did, he took a deep breath, exhaled, then nodded.

"Could you state your name please?" said Winford.

"Jerry Marsh."

Winford smiled. "I'm sorry, Jerry. You're going to have to speak up just a little."

"Jerry Marsh," he said into the microphone.

"That's it. I know you're nervous, but we'll get through this, okay?"

Jerry Marsh nodded.

"You are Christopher Marsh's father?"

"I am."

"Jerry, I'm going to ask you a couple of things about the day Chris died. If you need to take a break, just let me know, okay?"

Jerry Marsh nodded.

"Jerry, did you hear from Chris the day he passed?"

Jerry Marsh nodded.

"I'm sorry, Jerry, you have to answer out loud."

"Oh, right. Yes, yes I did."

"Tell us about that call."

"It was that Friday and I had just gotten off work, so it must've been about five-thirty when Chris called me. He said he had been having trouble with his car and asked if I could take a look at it. I said I would swing by the next morning and if I couldn't fix it, the two of us could drive to a shop together."

"What was wrong with it?"

"It was rattling and squealing pretty bad. Christopher thought it was the muffler, but he was having a hard time describing it, so I thought it was worth a try to see if it was just a loose belt or something that I could fix."

"Did Chris know cars?"

Jerry Marsh smiled. "No. Chris loved running and writing. Cars are my thing."

"Are you good with cars?"

"Pretty fair, yes. It's harder with all the computers now, but there's a lot of things I can do, that my dad taught me."

"So what did Chris say?"

"He said that sounded good and that he would see me tomorrow."

Then Mr. Marsh started to cry. Not loud. In fact, he made no noise at all. He just held his hand over his mouth and shook.

Winford waited a few seconds. "Jerry?"

Jerry Marsh waved a hand. "That was the last time I talked to him."

"Do you want to—"

He waved again. "No. Let's finish, please."

"Sure. So that's when you made arrangements to see him the next day?"

"Yes. I went over there about nine on Saturday morning."

"So what happened Saturday morning?"

"I saw his car in the drive so I knew he was home. I went to the side door and knocked but no one answered. I knocked again and when he still didn't come, I pushed the door open and went in."

"What happened next?"

"I called to him, but I didn't hear anything. You come into the kitchen pretty quick from the side door there so that was the first place I went and when I got there, I really didn't understand what I was seeing."

"And what was that?"

"A body." Jerry's voice broke. "A body that was face down on the floor. But I didn't realize...the back of the head was all mushed up and it wasn't the right shape and the blood changed the color of the hair."

"What did you do?"

Jerry's voice continued to break, and he spoke faster. "I called for Chris again because I just didn't understand what I was looking at and then I...Chris had these New Balance Trail Runners that he just loved, he'd wear them any time he ran. He'd been buying them for years, ever since he was in cross-country. I must've bought him nine, ten pairs in high school and he just kept getting them after he went away to college. These were blue and they had the white N and...and then I realized it was him."

"What did you do?"

"I yelled his name...and I dropped to the floor...and I turned him over...and I think I called his name some more and I was cradling his head because I knew he was hurt so I pulled him into my lap and I tried to press under his solar plexus because I read that can help revive somebody and so I kept doing it and I called his name...and I was trying not to feel the back of his head against my arm...and then...and then I realized that his skin was cold and that he was gone."

Silas Winford started to speak but Jerry Marsh raised his hand and continued. "I stayed there for a while because I knew that once I called they were going to take him away. So I waited and I didn't call and I'm sorry if that messed things up but I didn't want him to go and I didn't want to leave him."

"Do not apologize, Jerry," said Winford.

"Eventually, I called. I had a phone in my pocket so I called 911 even though I knew it was too late because I didn't know what else to do...and I waited...and they came...and they took me away...and he was all by himself with strangers."

"What happened next, Jerry?"

"One of the deputies asked me what happened and I told him what I just told you. The deputy wanted to talk some more but I told him that I had to tell his mother."

"Your wife?

Jerry Marsh nodded. "I couldn't let her find out over the phone so I told him I had to go. The deputy wanted to drive me but I couldn't have her see me pull up in a squad car but I also didn't want to leave Chris there by himself but that deputy, Deputy Pavlich, I'll always remember his name, he promised me that he would take care of Chris and he told me where they would be going so I left and I went home and I told my wife that Chris was dead."

Winford waited for a moment. When Jerry nodded, Winford said, "I'm sorry, Jerry, but as far as we know, you're the first person to see Chris after he died—"

"Other than the killer—"

"—that's right, other than the killer, so I need to ask you a couple of questions about where Chris's body was."

"I understand."

"As best as you can, please describe to the jury exactly where you found him."

"Where I was coming from, from the side door, he was sort of diagonal with his feet facing the far hallway and his head near one of the kitchen drawers. One of them, I think the second one from the bottom, was part way open, like he was bending over to open it."

"Was there blood on the walls and counter when you arrived?"

"I remember blood. I don't remember exactly where it was."

"You said you turned Christopher over and held him?"

Jerry Marsh nodded.

"You have to answer out loud, Jerry."

"I'm sorry. Yes, I did."

"Did you move him across the room at all?"

"No. I just rolled him over."

"So you were holding him pretty close to the original spot where you found him?"

"Yes. Give or take a few feet."

"Thank you, Mr. Marsh. As part of his job, Mr. Shepherd has to ask you a few questions too."

"I understand."

I stood. I have been on the receiving end of angry and venomous looks from witnesses when I have questioned them on things far less than the death of their son. All I received from Mr. Marsh was raw pain.

"Would you like to take a break, Mr. Marsh?"

"No. Thank you. Let's get through this."

"Mr. Marsh, the lower left window on Christopher's door was broken. Had you seen it broken before that day?"

Jerry Marsh nodded. "I had. Christopher locked himself out

a month or so earlier and had broken it himself. He hadn't gotten around to fixing it."

"You mentioned that you pushed open the side door? Did you have to reach in the window?"

He shook his head. "No, the door popped open all the time too. It was an old house. I was after him to fix it."

"I understand you eventually went back to Christopher's house and had to organize his possessions?"

"His mom and I did."

"His keys and money clip were in a bowl on the counter?"

"They were."

"There was money in his money clip?"

"There was. I don't know how much."

"That's fine. Did Christopher use a laptop for work?"

"He did. When he started at the *Torch,* his mom and I wanted to buy him one, but he said that the paper would give him one."

"And after the paper gave him one, you saw him working on it, the laptop?"

"I did."

"When you were going through Christopher's possessions, did you ever come across the laptop?"

"No. I assumed the paper had it."

"If the paper doesn't have it, is it fair to say that you don't know where it is?"

"It is."

"Did Christopher ever discuss his stories with you while he was working on them?"

"No. He was always real serious about that. Mostly, I would just read the articles when they appeared in the paper and then ask questions later."

"Finally, Mr. Marsh you said that Christopher had called you to work on his car?"

"That's right?"

"What did it wind up being?"

"What do you mean?"

"The problem with the car."

"It was the muffler. So I took it in before we sold it."

"That's all I have. Thank you, Mr. Marsh."

I thought that Silas Winford might ask some follow-up questions just because Mr. Marsh was so effective, but Winford saw the same thing I did—Mr. Marsh's testimony had been compelling and devastating and all he could do was screw it up.

Winford thanked Mr. Marsh, and the judge excused all of us for the day.

As the jury left, I saw more jurors than I was comfortable with, four at least, pulling tissues out of purses and pockets. I didn't feel any better when I saw Wendy Carver in the front row, doing the same.

"Jesus," whispered Emily.

"I know."

"What do we do now?"

I packed away Mr. Marsh's pain for another day. "We're going to interview a witness, but we'll need to stop for an extra sandwich first."

Emily scowled.

"And probably some cookies."

58

The next morning, Silas Winford wrapped up his case. He put on another couple of brief witnesses who confirmed Logan Carver had been in possession of property that had been stolen from Christopher Marsh's house. By the end, while there might have been the smallest sliver of doubt about whether Logan had actually forced his way in— since the door with the broken window might have already popped open—there was no doubt that Logan had robbed the place.

After that, Judge Wesley gave the jury an early lunch break while we argued our motion for directed verdict of acquittal, which was basically an attempt to dismiss the case or reduce the charges. I'll give you the short version: Judge Wesley wasn't buying what I was selling and ruled that all charges would continue for the jury's deliberation.

"We expected that, right?" said Emily.

"We did."

"So we focus on the timing and the blood?"

"Exactly. And hope that Ted gets here in time to help us with the bat."

After the jury was seated for the afternoon, Judge Wesley said, "Mr. Shepherd, are you ready to proceed?"

"We are, Your Honor. The defense calls Benjamin Fischer."

A man just a little younger than me came forward. He wore black glasses and an earnest look as he took a seat and leaned forward.

"Could you state your name please, sir?"

"My name is Benjamin Fischer."

"What do you do, Mr. Fischer?"

"I'm the night manager at the North Carrefour McDonald's."

"In your capacity as the night manager at the North Carrefour McDonald's, have you ever had an encounter with my client, Logan Carver?"

"That man right over there?"

"Yes, sir."

"Yes, I have."

"Could you tell us about it, please?"

"Sure. I was on duty one Friday night when one of our employees told me that there was a disturbance at the drive-thru window. I hurried over and found that customer yelling at our drive-thru cashier."

"By 'that customer,' you're indicating my client, Logan Carver?"

"Right."

"Did you hear what he was yelling about?"

"He was yelling that he wanted another shake and that he wasn't going to pay for it."

"What did you do?"

"I asked the cashier what had happened, and she told me that when she was handing the shakes to the customer, he dropped one of them and it fell to the ground. The customer heard her say that and started screaming that she had dropped it and he wasn't going to pay for it."

"What did you do next?"

"We were slammed that night, the line was wrapped around both speakers, so I asked him to pull over into one of our designated waiting spots and I would bring him another shake right away."

"What did he say?"

"He yelled again that he wasn't going to pay for it. I assured him that he wasn't and that if he would just pull over, I would bring it to him personally."

"Did he pull over to the side?"

"He did. I wanted to get him out of there as soon as possible so I left my team to manage the line and filled the shake order myself and took it out to him."

"What happened next?"

"I took him a shake, apologized about his wait, and told him to have a good night."

"How was he acting then?"

"Once he realized we weren't going to charge him, he was calm. Almost cheerful."

"Mr. Fischer, you know this is a murder trial?"

"I do."

"That's why I'm asking you this—did you see any blood on Mr. Carver?"

"No sir, I did not."

"Did you see any blood on his hands or shirt or face?"

"No, sir."

"Do you remember what kind of shirt he was wearing?"

Benjamin Fischer smiled. "I do. It was a gray sweatshirt with a big purple 'FU' on it. I wouldn't normally remember that, but it seemed appropriate given what was going on."

"Did you see any blood on that sweatshirt?"

"No, I didn't."

"Did you see anything on it?"

"I did. There was chocolate shake on his left sleeve. He was complaining that our cashier spilled it on him when she spilled the shake."

"Now Mr. Fischer, as part of your operations, do you maintain video of your drive-thru window?"

"We do."

"Did you save the video of your interaction with Logan Carver?"

"We don't have video of when he pulled over to the side. We do have video of when he was at the drive-thru window. I saved this one in case Mr. Carver ever came back and made a claim against us."

"A claim over a shake?"

Benjamin Fischer shook his head. "People make claims over all kinds of things. Our company policy is to keep the video if we think something could come of it."

I motioned to Emily and she loaded a video so that it appeared on the screen. Before we played it, I said, "Mr. Fischer, my associate has just put the beginning of the video up on the screen. Can you identify it for the jury?"

"Yes, sir. That's a copy of the security video I was just mentioning."

"That shows an internal view of your drive-thru window?"

"That's right."

"And that is at the North Carrefour McDonald's located on Eighth Street?"

"That's right."

"And I see that there is a date and time in the bottom right corner of the screen. What is it and how does it get there?"

"That's our timestamp of when the video is taken, and it's added automatically by our computer."

"So that's showing that this video started at 9:02 p.m.?"

"That's right."

"Emily, would you run it just a little bit, please? There you go, stop. Mr. Fischer that's Logan Carver visible right there in the window, isn't it?

"That's right."

"At 9:02 p.m.?"

"Yes."

"And you said you were slammed that night?"

"We were."

"How long was the wait for him to get to the window?"

"We were running between nine and twelve minutes that night, which is very unusual for us. We pride ourselves in getting our customers through in less than five."

"I'm sure. Thank you, Mr. Fischer. That's all I have."

Silas Winford stood. "Pardon me, Mr. Shepherd, do you mind if we have Ms. Lake play the video? I have my own copy, but it might be easier if she just hit play."

"Certainly." I nodded to Emily.

"Could you turn the volume up please, Ms. Lake," said Winford. "We're having a little trouble hearing it."

I nodded, Emily took it off mute, and Logan's voice was now audible as the video showed him squeeze his second shake so that the lid popped off and overflowed over his hand before he dropped it.

"A little louder please, Ms. Lake, if you don't mind."

I nodded and Logan's voice sent MF'ers echoing through the courtroom as he cursed the "clumsy bitch who spilled my goddam shake."

Winford didn't say anything. He just let the video run as the girl, who could not have been more than seventeen, apologized while Logan ranted at her, holding up his hand to show that she had gotten chocolate shake all over him and ruined his goddam sweatshirt. When she apologized again and said she would get him another one, he told her that if she thought he was going to pay "one fucking cent for another fucking shake, she was sadly fucking mistaken."

Benjamin Fischer then made an appearance. His voice was less audible but eventually he seemed to appease Logan and got him to pull over but not before a final yell that he wasn't going to pay for what his "sorry ass employee" had dropped.

You could see the girl was a little shaken as Benjamin Fischer put a hand on her shoulder and talked to her before he pointed out the window and up at the line and went off-camera.

The video stopped.

"Thank you, Ms. Lake. Mr. Fischer, is that a true and accurate representation of your encounter with Logan Carver?"

"It is."

"Was he angry?"

"Yes."

"Vulgar?"

"Yes."

"He cursed out you and your staff?"

"Yes."

"Was he violent?"

"Not directly, no. I was worried he could be."

"Why is that?"

"Because he was so angry."

"Was it dark when you went out to his car?"

"Yes. We have lighting out there, but it was night."

"You did not take the time to inspect his clothes, did you?"

"No. I just wanted to give him a shake and get him out of there."

"Thank you, Mr. Fischer."

I stood. "Mr. Fischer, Logan Carver was never physically violent with you, was he?"

"No, sir."

"He was angry but he never threatened physical violence to anyone?"

"No sir, he did not."

"And there is no doubt in your mind that he was at the drive-thru window at 9:02 p.m.?"

"No, no doubt at all. It's on the video, but I remember it too."

"And he had likely been there nine to twelve minutes before then?"

"That's my best estimate, yes."

"Thank you, Mr. Fischer. That's all I have."

As the judge dismissed Benjamin Fischer, Winford sat there, a faint smile on his face. I couldn't blame him. When your opposing counsel leads with evidence that shows his client is an angry asshole, he's doing your work for you. I was banking on the fact that the jury would eventually realize that the time was more important than the attitude, but man, that was an unpleasant way to get there.

"Mr. Shepherd, are you ready with your next witness?"

I looked into the gallery. My witness wasn't there.

59

"I believe so, Judge. Can we check to see if he's outside?"

"Of course."

Emily hustled out to the hall. We waited a minute then two then three. I sat there as if I meant it and Winford sat there with that same little smile.

Judge Wesley said, "Do we need to take a recess, Mr. Shepherd?"

At that moment, Emily stuck her head in and nodded to me.

"No, Your Honor. The defense calls Thomas Melton."

Tommy Melton, the man who lived on the third floor of Christopher Marsh's house, strolled in. He wore dark cotton pants and a dark blue, three-quarter zip pullover with a small yellow 'M" which, judging from the slightly frizzy static of his hair, he had just pulled on. As Tommy Melton made his way to the front, Silas Winford said, "Your Honor, may we approach?"

Judge Wesley waved us up. When we arrived, Winford said, "Judge, this witness was not disclosed by the defense. They shouldn't be allowed to call him."

"Mr. Shepherd?"

"He's not on our witness list, Your Honor, but he is on the prosecution's."

"He is?" said Winford.

"Yes, Your Honor," said Emily, who had come up with me. "The State disclosed 'Any and all neighbors who may have witnessed anything relevant to the death of Christopher Marsh.'"

"He's a neighbor?" said Judge Wesley.

"Yes. He lives on the third floor of Christopher Marsh's house."

Winford scowled. "It's my understanding that none of the neighbors heard the attack or the commotion."

"That's true. But Mr. Marsh opened the door to another line of inquiry yesterday."

"What line of inquiry is that?"

I shrugged.

Judge Wesley tapped her pen once. "Mr. Shepherd, you may not have to disclose the testimony that you are going to elicit to counsel ahead of time but in this circumstance, you do need to give me the topic."

"Yes, Your Honor. Mr. Melton has information related to Christopher Marsh's car."

"Very well. You may proceed."

"But Your Honor, we don't know—" said Winford.

"—Mr. Winford, would you like to put the State's lack of investigation of a witness it disclosed on the record as part of its argument?"

"No, Your Honor."

"I didn't think so. The defense has met the threshold for calling this witness. If you find something objectionable to his testimony, you may object, Mr. Winford."

Judge Wesley dismissed us, and we returned to our places.

I came around to the lectern and said, "Could you state your name, please?"

"Tommy Melton. Thomas Melton I suppose my mom would say."

"Thank you for coming today, Mr. Melton."

"Sure."

"Did you know Christopher Marsh?"

"Chris and I shared the same space sometimes."

"How did you share the same space?"

"We lived in the same house. I rented out the third floor and he rented the first."

"You are aware that someone killed Christopher?"

"I am."

"When did you learn that?"

"When the police showed up and the ambulance took away his body."

"The night before the police showed up, did you hear anything?"

"I heard Chris's car. That was about it."

"How did you know it was his car?"

"Because it was loud as hell. I think Chris thought the muffler was coming loose, but the engine had a big vroom and rattle to it every time he hit the gas."

"So you heard Christopher's car in the driveway that night?"

"I did."

"What time was it?"

"8:27 p.m."

"How do you know that? That it was 8:27 p.m.?"

"I saved the game I was playing and got something to eat."

"What do you mean?"

"The car was so loud it broke my flow. Then I got distracted by the thought of pizza pockets and made some."

"And you're sure that it was Christopher's car you heard?"

Tommy Melton smiled. "Seems to me that was borne out by the presence of Chris's car in the driveway."

"I have to ask like that since we're in Court."

Tommy Melton raised a hand. "Right, sorry. Yes, I'm sure it was his car. It had a squeak and a rumble that was pretty distinct."

"And so the jury understands, how do you know that it was exactly 8:27 p.m.?"

He looked up. "Well, when you came to see me last night, you asked if I had heard Chris's car the night he was killed, and I said I had, and you asked if I knew what time I heard it, and I said I did, then I went and checked my saved games and saw that I saved my game at 8:27 p.m. so that's how I knew what time I heard it."

"How did you know which saved game it was?"

"This game lets you save with a title so that you know what you're looking for if you go back, you know like 'killed Dragon' or 'found map.' I saved this game under 'Rattle and pizza roll,' then made my food."

I was about to sit down when what Tommy Melton had said about food made me think of something else.

"Do you ever go to the McDonald's on Eighth Street from your house?"

"All the time."

"How long does it take?"

"In time or distance?"

I smiled. "However you would measure it."

"Ten minutes by bike."

"Thanks, Mr. Melton." I sat.

Tommy Melton started to stand when Silas Winford said, "Excuse me, Mr. Melton, I have a couple of questions too."

Tommy Melton nodded and sat back down. Winford stood, leafing through a series of papers. "Mr. Melton, I'm looking through some police reports here. It appears that you were interviewed by a sheriff's deputy?"

"Does it?"

Winford looked up. "Are you denying that?"

"No, you said it appears I was interviewed by a sheriff's deputy. I have no idea what appears on that report."

Winford smiled. "Fair enough. Were you interviewed by a sheriff's deputy?"

"I was."

"You told him that you didn't hear anything that night, didn't you?"

"There's no way I would've said that."

"Why is that?"

"Because I heard all sorts of things that night—music, my microwave going off, the sound of a Balrog falling off a bridge."

"A what?"

"That one was on my screen."

"I see. I should've said you told the deputy that you didn't hear anything related to Christopher Marsh's death, didn't you?"

Tommy Melton shook his head. "I wouldn't know what's related to Chris's death and what's not. I know I was asked whether I heard a commotion or fighting or screaming to indicate Christopher was being killed. I certainly didn't hear anything like that."

"You didn't tell the deputy that you heard Christopher's car?"

"No, I did not."

"But you told Mr. Shepherd last night?"

"There's a simple reason for that."

"What is that?"

"Mr. Shepherd asked me if I heard Chris's car the night he died. Your deputy didn't."

"Shouldn't you tell a deputy investigating a murder anything that's important?"

"Seems to me that the deputy should investigate what's important and then ask about it."

Winford flipped the page. "The deputy indicates in his notes that you smelled of marijuana."

Tommy Melton sat there, waiting.

Finally, Winford asked, "Do you use marijuana, Mr. Melton?"

"Only when I want to."

"Were you using marijuana the night you heard Christopher Marsh's car?"

"I'm pretty sure that was the impetus of the pizza pocket plan."

"And did you legally obtain the substance you used on that night, Mr. Melton?"

Tommy Melton gave him a cool look. "Things have changed since you waged your war on drugs, Mr. State Attorney General. I purchased a legal amount of marijuana at a legal dispensary and partook in my private residence in a manner legally allowed by our state."

"Legality aside, your use of marijuana would have impacted your ability to perceive what was occurring, wouldn't it?"

"I don't see how weed is going to change the time stamp on my saved game that was prompted by the noise of Chris's car and my concurrent hunger."

"But it could alter your perception of the time that passed between when you saved the game and when you heard the car, couldn't it?"

"Since I persistently perceive time through that lens, no."

Winford pressed his lips together. "Mr. Melton, did you smoke today?"

"Yes."

"Did you drive here?"

"That would be irresponsible. I Ubered."

"And you expect the jury to believe that as you sit here, high, that you can tell them the exact time Christopher Marsh's car came into your driveway all the way back last fall on a night when you were also high?"

"It seems like you're projecting your expectations onto them." Tommy Melton pointed at the jury, then shrugged. "I'm not so arrogant that I'm going to speak for any other person's beliefs. If you're asking me if *I* believe, in my current state of existence, whether *I* can remember when Chris's car came into our driveway, my answer is 'yes.'"

Winford's face was calm, but he flipped back and forth among his papers before flopping them down on the table. "You said it takes you ten minutes to bike from your house to the Eighth Street McDonald's?"

"Approximately."

"So someone could get there even faster by car?"

"You mean in less time? Not usually."

"A car isn't faster than a bike?"

"In the abstract, a car can achieve greater speeds than a bike. In reality, a car will not get you to the Eighth Street McDonald's from my house in less time."

"How can that be, Mr. Melton?"

"I can't tell you how that can be, Mr. Winford. I can tell you that in-town traffic, unsynchronized red lights, and ample bike lanes lead to my perception of that reality."

"So ten minutes by bike or by car?"

"That's *my* expectation."

Winford looked at another note, but he'd had enough.

"No further questions."

I stood. "Mr. Melton, do you work at home?"

"I do."

"What do you do?"

"I'm a mechanical engineer for the auto industry."

"As a mechanical engineer for the auto industry, what do you do on a daily basis?"

Tommy Melton smiled. "I make calculations regarding the stress that differing materials can withstand while maintaining structural integrity and then work with a team matching my findings with weight and aerodynamic considerations to determine the most efficient design from both a performance and fuel consumption basis."

I smiled. "Do you smoke when you do that?"

"Daily."

"Any doubt in your mind when you heard Christopher's car?"

"None in mine. I would meet anyone else's perception with my saved game at 8:27 p.m."

"Thanks for your time, Mr. Melton."

60

A s Tommy Melton sauntered out, Judge Wesley
dismissed the jurors for the night, then said, "Mr.
Shepherd, will you be wrapping up tomorrow?"

"Probably, Your Honor, but it could easily take most of the day."

"I thought as much. I will tell the jury that they should plan on being here Monday, too."

As Judge Wesley left, I caught Wendy Carver's voice saying, "How could you treat her like that?!"

"I'm sorry, Mom," said Logan Carver.

"She was just trying to do her job, and you were yelling and swearing at her."

"But she spilled my shake!"

"Logan Carver, *you* spilled your shake. Anyone could see that you squeezed the cup too hard."

"Sorry," he said again. Then the deputy came to take the accused murderer away.

"I love you, son," Wendy Carver said quickly.

Logan nodded on the way out.

Wendy Carver watched him go, then took a deep breath. "That video made him look terrible."

I nodded. "Rude, certainly."

"Why would you show that? I saw the jury's faces. They can't stand him."

"The time on the video."

"Is it the same time as the murder?"

"Not exactly. But it would've been hard for Logan to wash a bunch of blood off him and still get there in time to make a scene about his chocolate shakes."

Wendy Carver stared at me, her face full of doubt.

"We're lucky Logan made such a scene. Otherwise, they wouldn't have saved the video."

"I don't feel lucky."

"No. I suppose not."

"It's not going well, Nate."

"We build cases brick by brick, Wendy. Not all at once."

"But if they hate Logan, they're going to convict him no matter what."

"Not necessarily. Hang in there, Wendy."

Wendy Carver stared at me. "My boy is a thief and can be a brat. But he's not a murderer."

She waited until I nodded before she took her coat and left.

Emily and I packed up and did the same.

I WAS STILL at the office that night when Ted Ringel called me.

"Ted, where are you?"

"Just getting home."

"Just now?"

"You'd be shocked at what missing your connector in Korea,

a hurricane in the Philippines, and leaving your headlights on in a parking garage does to your travel schedule."

"I would think so."

"Listen, I know my phone says that it's Thursday at 9 p.m. but is that right?"

"Yes."

"Yeah, I'm all screwed up then."

"Welcome back."

"Fortunately for you, long layovers in Korea provide time for introspection. The trial is still going on?"

"Yes. We have at least another couple of days."

"I don't know how all this fits in, but the jury deserves a complete picture of Christopher, including what he was working on at the time he was killed."

"That's all I ask."

"This Paxton story, the dumping, it's bad. It affects all of us. Now that I've been able to confirm the source material, we're running it Sunday."

"Not tomorrow?"

"Jesus Christ, Shepherd. I just returned from Indo-fucking-nesia to confirm the story."

"Sorry. Would you be willing to appear in court tomorrow without a subpoena?"

"I'm not giving up any sources."

"I won't ask you to. All I would ask you about is the story Christopher was working on at the time he died and the messages you received from him."

There was silence on the other end of the line.

"Seems like it would be quite the promo for the Sunday edition."

"Don't patronize me, Shepherd. Testifying is appropriate for me to do or it's not."

I let the silence hang there again.

Finally, Ringel said, "Is there really a chance that your client didn't do it? And no lawyer bullshit."

"We put on video and eyewitness testimony that the timing would be almost impossible. I'm putting a witness on tomorrow that says the killer should have been spattered with blood. There's been no explanation for the missing laptop. Yes, I really think there is a chance Logan Carver didn't do it. Because it doesn't make any sense that he did."

"So you say. You said you had more information for me? About someone steering your client to the job?"

"Peyton Rush." I told Ted about the woman who had been steering Logan toward burglary jobs through Discord using the avatar Peanutbutterfiend. "Discord is—"

"I know what Discord is, I'm a journalist, not a neanderthal!"

I didn't feel good about my own caveman status as I said, "I think she was helping him move the goods afterward, at least until this job, but I have no proof of that at all."

"What does she say?"

"She's gone." I told him about our investigation.

"That's an important part of the story."

"It is."

"It screams conspiracy."

"It does."

"Send me the Discord information."

"Done. I need anonymous sourcing if it's included in your story."

"You have it. I'll send you my confirmation of Christopher's notes." He paused. "And I'll appear tomorrow."

"Thank you."

"But not before noon. My sleep is nine different kinds of screwed up."

"Make it one o'clock. We'll put you on after lunch."

"And no mention of confidential sources."

"I have my own obligations, Ted, but I promise that I'll give you a chance to shield your source with the Court before I mention anything about him in particular."

"Good enough. I'll send you the notes in a few minutes."

"I'll do the same with the Discord."

We both hung up, and I got to work.

TWENTY MINUTES LATER, I had an email, not from Ted Ringel, but from the *Torch's* lawyer, Fred Pressfield. I about shat myself because with all that was going on, I'd forgotten that Fred Pressfield had been involved in the original disclosure of materials months ago. His email put my fears to rest, saying he understood that Ted had reached out directly to me, that here were the materials we discussed, and that I should direct future communications to him. I breathed a sigh of relief and forwarded the Discord materials to him with a request that he send them along to Ted.

That ethical crisis averted, I opened the file from Ted Ringel. It was another copy of the original Paxton article and of Christopher's notes, but now Ted had highlighted and footnoted all of the factual statements he had confirmed. He didn't reveal in the document that he'd confirmed it all with Ferris, but of course I knew that was the source.

In that light, I re-read Christopher's last article—how Paxton had ignored warnings its system was failing, dumped chemicals that would never go away into our river, and hid the whole thing while it lined up a sale.

I dug into the nitty-gritty, outlining two different paths I might be able to go down with Ted Ringel depending on what the Judge let me do. The whole thing was attenuated, and the Judge would probably limit me significantly, but I had to try because it gave us our best shot to explain the bat.

And because I now believed it was true.

61

"Help me plan my day, Mr. Shepherd," said Judge Wesley.

"Your Honor, we'll call our crime scene expert Devon Payne first. I imagine that will take the morning. Then this afternoon, we'll call Ted Ringel of the *Torch*."

Winford started. "Really? We were going to call him during the victim impact portion of the trial."

"Assuming you have one."

Winford shrugged modestly. "You have to plan for everything."

"What are you going to call Ringel about?" said Judge Wesley.

"Communications to and from Christopher Marsh in the days leading up to his death."

Judge Wesley tapped her pen on her papers. "Interesting, Mr. Shepherd. Perhaps you'd like to tell me more?"

"Those communications would include the last story Christopher Marsh filed with Mr. Ringel."

Judge Wesley's eyes narrowed.

"And what would that story be, Mr. Shepherd?"

"I think that story is best heard from Mr. Ringel when he testifies, Your Honor."

"I think a summary of it is best delivered by you to me right now."

I chose my words carefully. "It is my understanding that Christopher Marsh uncovered a story that a local company engaged in acts that are detrimental to our community."

Winford started to speak, but Judge Wesley raised her hand. "What kind of acts and detrimental in what way?"

"I'm not the one who investigated it, Your Honor."

"No, but you are the one who knows what type of testimony you are going to elicit or you are not the prepared attorney I think you are. Specifics, please."

I thought again, then said, "It's my understanding that Christopher Marsh's story involves long-term chemicals and a local body of water."

Judge Wesley stared at me. "And how is this story related to our murder case?"

"It was what the victim was working on when he died."

"And how is this story related to our murder case?" she repeated.

"It seems to me that a victim working on explosive investigation is directly relevant, Your Honor."

Winford shook his head. "Your Honor, this is exactly the kind of conspiracy nonsense you kept out of this trial in the first place. Mr. Ringel should not be allowed to testify."

Judge Wesley tapped the pen once, then set it down. "We'll hear from Mr. Payne first while I consider Mr. Ringel's testimony. My inclination is to allow him to testify regarding the timing and nature of his contacts with Mr. Marsh before his death but not allow a discussion of the content of his story without more evidence of a direct link to this case. Mr. Shepherd, let's proceed with your expert witness."

We went back to our tables and remained standing as the jury was escorted in.

"Will she let it in?" whispered Emily.

"It doesn't sound like it."

Then we started the testimony of Devon Payne.

DEVON PAYNE WALKED in wearing a dark suit that was more purple than blue with pants that were just short enough to show flashes of skin above his light shoes. His hair was still a little long but now had product in it that kept it up and out of his wide white glasses. He sat down, slung the white leather satchel he carried over the corner of the chair, then nodded.

"Could you state your name, please?"

"Devon Payne."

"Mr. Payne, I've called you as an expert in this case to talk about the blood spatters found at the site of Christopher Marsh's home. Are you prepared to do that today?"

"Yes."

"Before I do that, we have to go through some of your qualifications."

"Shoot."

"Tell me about your education."

"I have undergrad degrees from the University of Michigan in mathematics and art."

"That's kind of unusual. What led you to do that?"

"I started out studying art theory, but then when I learned about the Golden Ratio and other mathematical concepts that the masters incorporated into their work, I dove into the math side to round things out."

"What did you do next?"

"I went to New York University and obtained an MFA in painting and art theory."

"Is that your choice of artistic expression, painting?"

Devon Payne nodded. "I've been painting since middle school and have sold to studios since high school."

"Did you pursue any educational training after NYU?"

"I did. My love of art continued to feed my interest in mathematics, so I picked up a masters in physics from NYU studying the mathematics of motion."

"What did you do next?"

"While I was going to school in New York, I was able to establish myself artistically. I spent another four years there before I returned to Detroit to be part of the scene back here."

"Could you explain that a little more for me?"

Devon Payne thought and pushed his white rimmed glasses up a little farther before he said, "I established a market for myself with galleries and private buyers in New York. Once I did that, it didn't matter where I lived and worked anymore. I liked what was happening back home in Detroit and wanted to be part of that, so I moved back here. That allows me to sell both here and there."

"You know, as I listen to you, Mr. Payne, the one thing I'm not hearing is any education in criminal justice or investigation."

"That's true."

"How did you come to participate in that?"

He smiled faintly. "By dating a New York police detective."

"Could you explain that?"

"Sure. I was seeing a woman who had just become a homicide detective. She was having trouble interpreting a messy crime scene and told me about it. I looked at the pictures, helped her interpret the splash patterns, which in turn led her to the murder weapon and an arrest."

"Splash patterns?"

"Of the blood."

"I see. And have you done that to assist other investigations?"

"Yes. A few in New York and some more since I came home to Detroit."

"I think you're being modest, Mr. Payne. Isn't it more than a dozen in New York and another fifteen here in Michigan?

"I suppose. It's all listed on that form I put together for you."

"Mr. Payne, at my request, did you look at some information in this case?"

"I did."

"What did you examine?"

"I looked at photos of the scene of Christopher Marsh's murder and inspected the scene personally. I also made some calculations and prepared a simulation based upon those factors."

"Based upon your inspection and assessment, were you able to reach any opinions in this case?"

"I was."

"What is that opinion?"

"That whoever struck Mr. Marsh in the head had blood on him."

"What's the basis for that conclusion?"

"The first is the radial jet of blood that was scattered as a result of the strikes. You can see the overlapping pattern distribution, how it goes in most directions and has covered the walls and counters in a surprisingly uniform way. Anyone within that radius would've been sprayed with blood."

"Is there a second basis?"

"Yes. I was able to find blood spatters on the surrounding walls and countertops in a complete three-hundred-and-sixty-degree radius from Christopher Marsh's body except for approximately fifteen degrees between one hundred eighty-five and two hundred degrees from where the body was found where spatters were virtually non-existent."

"What is the significance of that?"

"It's my opinion that is the area where the body of the attacker blocked the spray of blood."

"Meaning it got on him or her instead of the wall?"

"Exactly. I've prepared a simulation to show you an example of how this works if you'd like to see it."

"I would."

Winford stood. "Objection, Your Honor. There's no basis to conclude that this simulation is scientifically accurate."

"Your Honor, this simulation was previously provided to counsel and the Court and is derived from the photos marked as State's Exhibits 13 through 18, which the State itself took. Further, this simulation is just being used as demonstrative evidence to show the jury what Mr. Payne was just talking about."

"I will allow it," said Judge Wesley. "But it will not go back to the jury during deliberations."

"Understood, Your Honor."

I nodded to Emily. She clicked a couple of buttons and a side-by-side animation popped up. Devon Payne took us through the first one, which showed a uniform pattern with nothing blocking the way of the splash, and then a second when a man was standing within the splash radius, getting liquid on himself and leaving the area behind him relatively unspattered.

Devon Payne concluded. "A similar splash pattern was found here."

"Because the killer blocked the blood?"

"Yes. Because he blocked the blood, it never reached the walls behind him. It would have been on his clothes instead."

"Or shoes or skin or face?"

"Yes."

"Mr. Payne, I think it's apparent from your statement, but let me make sure and ask this another way. Do you have an opinion to a reasonable degree of scientific probability as to whether the killer had Christopher Marsh's blood on him?"

"I do."

"What is that opinion?"

"The killer had to have had the victim's blood on him. There was no way to avoid it, and the evidence at the scene shows the killer blocked it."

"Thank you, Mr. Payne."

I sat.

Silas Winford stood. "Ms. Lake, if you could hang on just a moment before you turn that off." He waved his hand at the animation. "Mr. Payne, you made all that up, didn't you?"

"Excuse me?"

"The simulation. You created it."

"Based on the photos your officers took of the scene, yes."

"And you interpreted those photos as you saw fit, right?"

"No. The radius of the area without blood spatters was measured precisely. It was an angle of exactly—"

"I'm sure you have an angle all set to go, Mr. Payne. You conducted your inspection after you were hired by Mr. Shepherd, didn't you?"

"That's how I became involved in the case, yes."

"And he hired you to do this so-called spatter analysis, right?"

"To evaluate the scene using my expertise, yes."

"Let's talk about your expertise. What's it called? Spatterology? Are you a spatterologist?"

"I don't know if there is a formal term. I tend to use blood spatter analysis."

"That's right, there's no formal term for what you do, is there?"

"I believe I just gave you one."

"There's no formal degree program for blood spatter analysis, is there?"

"Not that I'm aware of."

"There is no national governing body of spatterologists, is there?"

"I don't believe so."

"There is no license or certification for blood spatter analysis, is there?"

"There are more general cert—"

"—I didn't ask if there were more general forensic certifications. I asked if there was one for blood spatter analysis."

"Not that I'm aware of."

"So, anyone can run around and call themselves a spatterologist?"

"I don't know what anyone else can do. I know I have advanced degrees in art and physics that allow me to analyze how droplets fall. I'm sure other people could develop skills in a different way that lets them do the same thing."

"Your so-called expertise is limited to how these drops fall, correct?"

"That's right."

"You can't say how many blows Christopher Marsh was struck with, can you?"

"No, I would leave that to a medical examiner."

"You can't tell what type of weapon was used to kill Christopher Marsh, can you?"

"No, again I would leave that to a medical examiner."

"You have no reason to doubt that an aluminum bat was used to kill Christopher Marsh, do you?"

"I do not. That's not my expertise."

"You would agree with me that an aluminum bat used to kill

Christopher Marsh would have Christopher Marsh's blood on it, wouldn't you?"

"I would."

"Now you said it was your opinion based on your analysis of the scene that the killer would have blood on him, true?"

"Yes."

"And you believe that to a reasonable degree of scientific probability?"

"I do."

"Is it possible that the killer did not get blood on him?"

"It is extremely unlikely."

"That's not what I asked. I asked if it was possible that the killer did not get blood on him."

"He almost certainly did."

"You're avoiding my question, Mr. Payne. By the way, it is Mr. Payne, not Dr. Payne, right?"

"That's right."

"So let's ask my question another way—can you tell the jury with one hundred percent certainty that the killer had blood on him?"

"I wasn't aware that was the standard for scientific testimony in Michigan."

"It's not. I'm asking you if you are one hundred percent certain that the killer had blood on him."

Devon Payne thought before saying, "I am 99.9% certain."

"So it's possible that he did not."

"It's possible, but so unlikely that it's not worth considering."

"It's also possible the killer had blood on him which wasn't noticed by others, right?"

"It's my understanding that Logan Carver's sweatshirt was examined microscopically and that no blood was found."

"See, now I was just asking a hypothetical question about the killer, I wasn't talking about Logan Carver specifically. So, hypothetically Mr. Payne, it is possible that the killer had blood on him that would not be observed by others, true?"

"Possible but unlikely."

"It's possible that the killer could have changed clothes or washed himself before being seen by others?"

"I'm not aware of that hypothetical being based in the reality of the facts of this case."

"Humor me. Please assume that they are true."

"Hypothetically, given time, I assume the killer could have at some point washed *herself* and changed clothes before anyone saw *her*. I also assume, *hypothetically*, that if an alien killed Christopher Marsh, he could have returned to his spaceship and flown away before anyone saw him."

"This isn't funny, Mr. Payne."

"No, it's not. That's why I think your question should have a basis in fact."

"Mr. Payne," said Judge Wesley. "Please just answer the questions."

Devon Payne nodded.

"It's possible that people at the scene, Jerry Marsh, first responders, could have smeared blood or wiped it off in the vector you're talking about, isn't it?"

"The areas where smears had occurred, such as where Mr. Marsh and first responders worked, were apparent. I did not see any indication of cleaning or wiping in the empty vector."

"Well, you wouldn't if they did a good job, would you?"

"I believe I would have."

"Because you're an expert in spatters?"

"Yes."

"Such an expert that Mr. Shepherd has paid you more than ten thousand dollars to support his case today, right?"

"No."

"Mr. Shepherd has paid you more than ten thousand dollars in this case, hasn't he?"

"Mr. Shepherd paid me to provide him with my analysis of the scene. He didn't know what my opinion would be any more than I did before I looked."

"Your uncertified, unlicensed spatter opinion?"

"The opinion of my particular expertise."

"I suppose that's one way to feed a starving artist."

"Excuse me?"

Winford waved. "No further questions, Your Honor."

I stood. "Mr. Payne, I don't think Mr. Winford allowed you to fully answer some of his questions, so let's get a few things out of the way. I have paid you more than ten thousand dollars to examine the scene and for you to come testify to the jury about what you found, is that right?"

"It is."

I smiled. "How is your art career going, Mr. Payne?"

"I'm selling more in Detroit and New York than I ever have."

"What do you do with the money from your expert witness work?"

"I donate it to a program supporting arts education in Detroit area schools."

"All of it?"

"Every cent."

"Mr. Winford spent some time asking you about your qualifications and seemed focused on whether there were any degrees or licenses certifying your expertise."

"I remember."

"He appeared to be questioning your competency as an expert."

Devon Payne looked at Winford. "I had the same impression."

"Did you know that Mr. Winford was the Attorney General for the State of Michigan?"

"I did not."

"Mr. Payne, have you ever provided expert testimony for the Attorney General of the State of Michigan?"

Winford stood. "Objection. I've never hired this man on any of my cases."

"Your Honor, the Office of the Attorney General is no individual man or woman. It is the office charged with supervising prosecutions for our entire state. The position that office has taken regarding reliable evidence in criminal prosecutions is certainly relevant."

I saw his face. Winford knew it was a mistake as soon as he said it, so when Judge Wesley said, "Overruled," he sat down.

"Mr. Payne, again, have you ever provided expert testimony for the Office of the Attorney General of the State of Michigan?"

"I have. As recently as last year."

"To be fair to Mr. Winford, and so the jury understands, Mr. Winford never hired you when he was the Attorney General, did he?"

"How long ago was that?"

"A decade and a half."

Devon Payne smiled. "I was still in college. Things have changed a lot since then."

"They certainly have. You've testified for defendants too, right?"

"I have."

"In fact, in at least one instance, your testimony led to the reversal of a conviction obtained by Mr. Winford's office years lat—"

Winford stood. "Objection, Your Honor."

"Sustained. Mr. Shepherd, that is a bit far afield."

"Your Honor, Mr. Winford has questioned my client's

credentials. Unless Mr. Winford stipulates that Mr. Payne is an expert on blood spatter analysis, I believe I should be entitled to question the witness on matters that demonstrate his qualifications, especially in relation to Mr. Winford's prior office."

Judge Wesley shook her head. "The State does not seek to bar Mr. Payne from testifying. Is that right, Mr. Winford?"

"That's correct, Your Honor."

"Your point has been made, Mr. Shepherd. Please move on."

As Winford sat, I said, "Mr. Payne, let's cut to the chase then. Do you think Christopher Marsh's killer had blood on him?"

"Yes. Based on my expert knowledge of the trajectory of liquids in motion, yes. The killer would've had blood on him."

"Thank you, Mr. Payne."

All eyes went to Silas Winford, who shook his head.

"Thank you, Mr. Payne. Members of the jury, we'll take a break for lunch and pick up again after."

As the jury filed out, Devon Payne came over and shook my hand. "You ever need anything, you call."

"Thank you."

Silas Winford came over to shake his hand and say something. Devon Payne put both hands on the strap of his satchel and walked out.

62

L ogan could hardly contain himself. "There, they can see, there's no way I did it!"

"It was helpful," I said.

"I didn't have any blood on me! We win, right?"

"The State will argue around it."

"But the guy just said the killer had to have blood on him!"

"The prosecutor will argue that people didn't see the blood or that you changed. Or that it was possible you just didn't get any on you."

"But I didn't have blood on me! How—"

"Emily, why don't you go with Logan and the deputy and Mrs. Carver for some lunch."

We had some leeway at lunchtime, but the deputy was always with us, so Emily had to make sure Logan didn't say anything in front of him that was related to our defense. She saw the point of her presence, but that didn't prevent her from giving me the sunniest possible smile as she said, "Sure thing, Boss."

I returned her sunshine in equal measure and grabbed my bag lunch, water, and trial notebook to head up to a quiet corner on the fourth floor to gather my thoughts for Ted Ringel.

Silas Winford caught me on the way, smiling.

"Did you have to make me seem so old?"

I smiled back. "What's a couple of decades between friends?"

"Indeed. Those darn whippersnapper experts in emerging areas of science." He looked around the room. "Are we going to have Ringel this afternoon?"

I nodded. "He should be here about one."

"Nice job this morning."

I nodded as I walked away. And if you haven't picked up on it yet, a compliment from the ever-courteous Silas Winford was a sure sign of his fury.

I found that quiet corner and thought about Ted Ringel as I munched a turkey sandwich and peeled an orange.

TED RINGEL POPPED into the courtroom just before one. He wore his khaki pants but had added a blue blazer and a thick striped tie. His face was redder than normal, and he had new black circles under his eyes.

Fred Pressfield, the *Torch* attorney, came in right after him.

I went right over to Ted Ringel. "Glad you made it."

"It wasn't easy. When am I on?"

"A couple of minutes."

"Brought reinforcements, I see?" I shook Pressfield's hand.

"Just in case," Pressfield said.

"What is Judge Wesley going to let me say?" said Ted Ringel.

"I don't know for sure. I think she's going to let in the times of your communications with Christopher right before he died, but after that it gets tricky. I'll just start asking and we'll see where it goes."

"I looked at the Discord file you sent me. This was a set up."

"I agree."

"Christopher nailed these Paxton shitbirds. We have to—"

Ted Ringel was looking over my shoulder. His face fell.

"What?"

"Mr. and Mrs. Marsh. I didn't realize they'd be here. I should have but—"

"Ted. The truth is the truth. Their son deserves it."

"But if your client did it—"

"If my client did it, then your testimony isn't going to get him off. And if he didn't, it could help get the person who did. Or the company."

The bailiff came out of the judge's office. "The judge will be out in just a moment, counsel."

I nodded to Ted, and we took our seats.

"STATE YOUR NAME for the record, please."

"Theoden Arthur Ringel. One of the perils of having an English literature professor for a father. Everyone calls me Ted."

"What do you do for a living, Ted?"

"I am the chief reporter and editor of the *Ash County Torch*."

"How long have you worked at the *Torch*?"

"Thirty-two years. I was born and raised here in Ash County, went away to school, then returned here and have been reporting for the *Torch* ever since."

"I understand the *Torch* was sold some years ago?"

Ted nodded. "It was. We are now part of a network of small papers across the country that share national resources but still report local."

"Is that important? In journalism?"

"It is. People don't realize how many stories break locally.

Good local reporters find stories that are then picked up and expanded by national news media. Without local reporters on the ground, some of the most important stories of the day are never broken."

"Did you know Christopher Marsh?"

"Very well."

"How?"

"I first met Chris when he was still in high school, reporting on the cross-country state championships. Sometime later when he was considering journalism school, he reached out to me and we spoke about it as a career path. To be honest, I tried to dissuade him against it because of how difficult it's become to get a decent job, but he was pretty persistent and went to one of the best schools there is at Northwestern University. After he graduated, he reached out to me for an internship, which turned into a job. He wanted to work for a couple years closer to home before getting a graduate degree and heading out into the wider world."

"Were you Christopher's immediate supervisor at the *Torch*?"

"I was."

"Tell me how that worked."

"I would monitor what stories Christopher was working on. Sometimes I would assign them to him and sometimes he would come to me with suggestions. Once he was working on the story, I would review and edit his final draft, double-check any needed sources, and then publish the work."

"Ted, did you communicate with Christopher in the week before his death?"

"I did."

"When?"

"I touched base with Christopher just about every day. Email, text, phone, whatever was necessary."

"How about on the day he died? When was last time you had contact with him?"

"It was a little after 5 p.m. He messaged me through the secure app our company uses to send me the draft of a story he had been working on and his notes. I read the story and messaged him back about half an hour later to tell him that it was great and that I needed some additional source materials. He replied right away that he was going to go for a run and would call me later."

"What time was that last message from him?"

"5:47 p.m."

"Did Christopher call you later that night?"

"No."

"Did that concern you?"

"No. Christopher was twenty-four and it was a Friday night. I wish...no, it did not concern me."

"When did you learn something was wrong?"

"I keep the police scanner on at my house so that I know if anything happens. I heard the dispatch to Christopher's house on Saturday morning."

"You mentioned your last communication with Christopher was through a messaging app?"

"That's right."

"As his employer, did the *Torch* give Christopher a laptop?"

"We did. It had a variety of software preloaded onto it for security and to make our job easier, including the app."

"Was that laptop ever returned to you?"

"No, it was not."

"To your knowledge did the police ever recover it?"

"Not to my knowledge."

"Was Christopher using the laptop to message you at 5:47 p.m. on the day he died?"

"I believe so. He attached his draft story and notes to the message, so I assume he was using his laptop. That would've been very difficult to do from his phone."

"Mr. Ringel, what was the last story Christopher submitted to you?"

Winford stood. "Your Honor, may we approach?"

She nodded and Winford, Emily, and I all went up to the bench. An argument you've heard several times now ensued—Winford objected to any questioning regarding the Paxton story, I argued that what Christopher was doing hours before he was killed was relevant, and Winford accused me of trying to distract the jury with a "fantastic conspiracy cut from whole cloth." When I told him he could put the whole thing to bed if he just told us where the missing laptop was, Judge Wesley had heard enough.

She raised a hand. We fell silent.

"It's difficult for me to make a ruling without knowing what Mr. Ringel is going to say. At the same time, what he says could corrupt the jury so significantly that a curative instruction will do no good. We're going to give the jury a break and I'm going to conduct an *in camera* examination before I make my decision."

As both Winford and I started to speak, Judge Wesley said, "Thank you, counsel."

The two of us returned to our seats.

"Members of the jury," said Judge Wesley. "A matter has arisen that requires me to make a ruling on some evidence in this case. As a result, I'm going to give you a break for about an hour while I take care of this. This is a normal part of the judicial process and you're not to make any assumptions that it means one thing or another or anything at all. I also remind you that you're not to discuss the case amongst yourselves until all of the evidence is in. At this time, you are excused to the jury room until we call you back."

We all stood as the jury left.

Judge Wesley thought for a moment then said, "I think, given the nature of this, we will do it in my office."

"I need you to stay with Logan," I said to Emily.

Her eyes flashed. "Why?"

"He can't be left alone, Emily, not out here in court. He'll say something to someone."

"I didn't go to law school to be a babysitter."

"No, but you did go to win cases."

She looked disgusted. "Fine."

Within five minutes, we were set up in Judge Wesley's office. Judge Wesley sat behind her desk, while the court reporter and Ted Ringel sat in two plush chairs in front of it. Winford, the bailiff, Pressfield, and I took seats around the periphery.

Judge Wesley set a pen on a small pad of paper, folded her hands, and said, "Mr. Ringel, I'm going to ask you some questions about what you know and what you would testify to at trial so that I can decide whether it is relevant to this case. The court reporter is going to continue to transcribe what we say, and you are still under oath. Do you understand?"

"Yes, Your Honor."

"I will then decide whether I'm going to permit Mr. Shepherd and Mr. Winford to examine you on these topics, okay?"

"Sure."

"What was the story that Christopher Marsh sent to you the day he died?"

"Chris had learned that a local company had been dumping PFAs into our river."

"PFAs?"

"Forever chemicals. I don't even know how he came on the idea originally; I think an obscure water quality report led him to an even more obscure EPA assessment that found excess levels in the parts per billion of some multi-syllable chemicals. I know he was checking all sorts of pollutants which then led him to check companies that might produce them. I'm not sure exactly how all that led him to Paxton, but it did, I think about six months ago."

Judge Wesley motioned for him to continue. The court reporter kept typing.

"When he dug into Paxton's history, he found that it had two prior incidents of dumping in the last ten years, not too bad but bad enough, and that it had been placed under a monitoring order. That's when he made contact with a confidential source in the company. Chris just wanted more background on the earlier incidents but what the source told him was that Paxton had accidentally dumped again and had covered it up."

"Mr. Marsh confirmed this?"

Ted Ringel nodded. "Yes. He learned Paxton had put off installing a new wastewater treatment system to save money, so of course the old system failed and dumped PFAs into the water for weeks."

"Is the dumping still going on?"

"No, Judge. Paxton replaced the system the next quarter, which we believe worked. But they kept operating the whole time, never announced what happened and, to our knowledge, never tried to remediate the river or the surrounding area."

Judge Wesley began to tap her pen. "Paxton let the chemical sit there?"

"It did, Your Honor."

"Mr. Marsh verified all of this?"

"A confidential source within the organization confirmed it all."

Judge Wesley made a note on her pad. "So Mr. Marsh delivered this story to you on the day he was killed?"

"Yes, fortunately just hours before."

"If Mr. Marsh had not been killed, when would you have run the story?"

"I had to confirm the source material. This was a large story so normally I would've said one week but given the explosive nature of what we were reporting, it probably would've been two to three."

The pen kept tapping.

"There was another fact that developed after Chris's death that I believe is relevant, Your Honor," said Ted Ringel.

"What's that?"

"Paxton was sold two months later for four hundred million dollars."

The pen stopped.

Judge Wesley's face revealed nothing as she asked, "To your knowledge Mr. Ringel, was Christopher Marsh ever threatened by anyone in relation to this story?"

"Not that I know of, Your Honor."

"Did he ever express any concern for his safety?"

"Not to me. He knew this was a big story though."

"How big, in your opinion?"

"Enough to carry hundreds of millions of dollars in exposure and potential criminal penalties for all involved, including the company. The actions are pretty purposeful."

"Why hasn't the story run? Christopher's death?"

Ringel nodded. "In part. Since Christopher was killed, I had to confirm his anonymous source material personally. Unfortunately, the source disappeared too."

Judge Wesley's eyes narrowed but only for a moment. "Really?"

"Yes, Your Honor. It took months to find him."

The pen started tapping again. "Tell me about that."

"I can't reveal the identity of the source, Judge."

"Tell me what you can."

Ted Ringel looked at the ceiling for a moment before saying, "The source disappeared a couple of weeks after Chris died. After months of investigating, the source was found on the other side of the world."

"Indiana?"

Ted Ringel smiled. "The other side of the Pacific Rim, Your Honor."

"Where exactly?"

"I'm not comfortable disclosing that, Your Honor, but I can tell you that it borders the Indian Ocean."

"You spoke to him?"

"I met with her or him personally."

Judge Wesley raised an eyebrow. "Impressive. And as a result of that meeting?"

"We will be running the story."

"When?"

"Given what's happened, Your Honor, I'd rather not say."

"I could order you not to publish it."

Pressfield spoke for the first time. "Respectfully, Your Honor, I don't think you can. The *Torch* is not, at this point, going to report any connection between Mr. Marsh's death and the story. It will only report that it was the last story Mr. Marsh ever turned in. We don't believe you can restrict that exercise of the free press."

Judge Wesley pursed her lips. "I suppose not." She tapped the pen a few times before looking at me. "Is that all?"

I shook my head. "Your Honor, Christopher Marsh sent this story and his notes to Mr. Ringel at 5:12 p.m., just hours before he died. His laptop contained additional materials, including extensive notes from interviews with the source. That laptop is nowhere to be found."

Judge Wesley pursed her lips. "You mentioned that, Mr. Shepherd." She looked at Ringel. "Did that matter?"

"It did. It delayed the story significantly. Also, Your Honor?"

"Go ahead."

"We often interview sources and keep the recording on our computers. Whoever took the laptop wouldn't know whether we did so here."

Winford leaned forward in his seat. "Your Honor, this is—"

"You're not in front of a jury, Mr. Winford. I'm sifting through all of this just fine."

He smiled. "Yes, Your Honor."

She turned to me. "Mr. Shepherd, this is all an interesting coincidence, but I'm not sure that it's relevant to a tragic killing that appears to have happened when your client was interrupted robbing a house."

"It wasn't a coincidence, Your Honor. Logan Carver was guided to that house."

All eyes turned to me.

"What do you mean, Mr. Shepherd?"

"A connection of Mr. Carver's suggested that he rob Christopher Marsh's house."

"Go on."

I had hoped to spring this in the courtroom, but the fact was that I was never going to get it into the courtroom if I didn't convince the judge first, so I said, "Are you familiar with Discord, Your Honor?"

"Pretend that I am not."

I explained what it was and how people used it to communicate during work or video games. "Your Honor, we have evidence of a conversation between Logan Carver and a woman named Peyton Rush in which she—"

"—Your Honor, this is ridiculous," said Winford. "There is absolutely no foundation for this. Mr. Shepherd just produced this 'Discord' evidence, whatever that even is, out of nowhere and claims a conspiracy—"

"Your Honor, the state has had this evidence the entire time."

"We most certainly have not."

"Yes, you have. Your Honor, I obtained access to the Discord conversation between Peyton Rush and Logan Carver through Mr. Carver's Xbox. However, the same conversation is on the Discord app in Mr. Carver's phone, which has been in the possession of the police and the prosecutor's office since Mr. Carver was arrested. Based on the disclosures provided to us, the state was successful in opening Mr. Carver's phone and had full access to all of the contents therein. There can be no argument of surprise."

"Come on," said Winford. "That's a video game app."

"That is how it's often used, yes."

"How would we know to check that?"

I shrugged. "We did."

"You have another issue, Mr. Shepherd," said Judge Wesley. "You need to establish a foundation that this communication actually occurred between Ms. Rush and Mr. Carver."

"We can forensically establish that this Discord conversation occurred and was present in Logan Carver's Xbox on the day of the alleged murder."

"I don't know that that's enough." Judge Wesley tapped her pen. "I assume you're not calling Mr. Carver to the stand to testify to this?"

"That's correct, Your Honor."

"So are you going to call this Peyton Rush?"

"I would subpoena her, Your Honor. But she has disappeared too."

"What do you mean?"

"I mean I have had an investigator looking for Peyton Rush since I discovered this Discord conversation and she has disappeared."

"What are you suggesting, Mr. Shepherd?"

"I'm not suggesting anything. I'm telling you that Peyton Rush's car is still at her apartment, her lease has been terminated for non-payment, and her sister had to come get all of her possessions, including her cat who had not been fed in weeks, because Peyton Rush is gone."

Silas Winford broke in. "Your Honor, none of this tapestry Mr. Shepherd has woven is relevant to this trial. If you let him lead the jury down this rabbit hole, then I need to be able to put on evidence of chemical dumping and cross world travel and video game forensics—none of which has anything to do with the fact that Logan Carver broke into Christopher Marsh's home and killed him."

I shook my head. "Just because it's messy, doesn't mean it's not true."

"Your Honor, Mr. Shepherd's conspiracy theory is ridiculous."

"It's convoluted." Judge Wesley nodded. "But I don't know that it's ridiculous."

"Respectfully, it is. And it has a major flaw."

"What's that?"

"The laptop wasn't that important. Christopher Marsh had already sent the materials to Mr. Ringel here so there was no reason to take and destroy the laptop."

"They wouldn't know that," said Ted Ringel.

The three of us turned to him. "Whoever did this would not have known that Chris had already sent me the story a couple of hours before. And up until the story was finalized, all I had was a rough outline—I didn't have any background or source information. The story could've died with Chris. It almost did."

Winford was having none of it. "So you're saying a huge corporation plotted to kill a small-town local reporter to stop a story about dumping in a backwater river in Michigan?"

"Maybe," I said. "Or maybe it just planned to steal the laptop to see what he had, and it went awry just like you say it did with Logan Carver. That's up to the jury to decide."

"You can't possibly think that all this should go in front of the jury."

"Why not? It happened."

Judge Wesley raised her hand and we both fell silent. "I would've appreciated some notice of this, Mr. Shepherd."

"Mr. Ringel has literally stepped off a flight from—"

Ted's head jerked around.

"—the other side of the world last night."

Judge Wesley shook her head. "We have issues of scope and foundation here. I have a lot to sort out and, even if I let any of this in, there would have to be parameters. That's not going to get done in the time we have left on a Friday afternoon. I'm going to send the jury home for the weekend and tell them we'll be finishing on Monday. I will send you an email Sunday night that lets you know generally how I'm going to rule, and you'll have the formal written opinion Monday morning. Mr. Ringel, I ask that you return Monday morning. If there's anything to finish up with your testimony, we'll do it then."

"Yes, Your Honor."

With that, we returned to the courtroom. The judge dismissed the jury early for the weekend with a promise that we would finish on Monday. Judge Wesley returned to her office. As Silas Winford and his associates gathered their things, I explained to Logan and Wendy Carver what was going on before the deputy took Logan away.

Ted Ringel nodded to me then made to leave before stopping in front of Mr. and Mrs. Marsh. They spoke for a moment before Jerry Marsh and Ted Ringel embraced as the two men began to weep. Mrs. Marsh stared at me over her husband's shaking shoulder.

I met her gaze, which was neither angry nor sad but piercing, before collecting my own things.

"What happened?" said Emily.

"You had to keep Logan from talking, didn't you?"

"Yes, yes, yes, all-knowing Boss, you were right, I kept him from blabbing three times. What happened in there?"

"A lot. I'll tell you on the way back."

63

I filled Emily in on Ted Ringel's questioning on the way back to the office. Then, when we found Danny waiting for us, I repeated it again. Both of them thought that when you heard all the facts strung together, it seemed like something. Emily was certain that Judge Wesley would allow most of it to come in. Danny was more cautious and put the odds at fifty-fifty. I was pretty sure Judge Wesley wasn't going to let us expand the case into a sideshow of conspiracies without more.

It was getting late, so I didn't argue with them. Instead, I encouraged them both to go home. It took a little arm-twisting and an assurance to Emily that there would be plenty of time for briefing over the weekend, but eventually, they left.

As soon as they did, I called Olivia.

"Hey, Shep. I assume you didn't get to the jury today?"

"No." I told her what happened with the Ted Ringel.

"How can I help?"

"I need you to check one more time to see if you can find anything, anything at all, on Peyton Rush."

"I haven't stopped looking, Shep. She's gone."

"What do you think?

"When people go on the run, they take stuff with them. All of hers was still there. The only thing that saved her cat was an anonymous tip to her landlord."

"I wonder who the soft-hearted investigator was who did that?"

"No idea."

There was a pause on the other end of the line before Olivia said, "She also hasn't used any credit cards."

"How would you know that?"

"By knowing that she hasn't used any credit cards."

"Sorry. Long week at trial."

"Forgiven. I'll keep looking though. And I'll poke around in some other places to see if anyone's seen her."

"Thanks. The judge is going to issue a preliminary ruling Sunday night."

"I'll let you know before then."

"You're the best."

"Get some rest, Shep."

It's a strange sort of break on a Friday night in the middle of trial. You're still in full trial mode but since you don't have to appear in court the next day, it feels like a vacation if you can go home at eight. After I hung up with Olivia, I locked up and was considering making another dinner at home when Josie called.

"Hey," she said. "You almost done for the day?"

"Actually, I am."

"I just got off shift. Feel like a quick dinner?"

"I would love to. I can't stay out though."

"Me either. I'm on shift again tomorrow."

"Then I am on my way."

We went to a place that served home-style food in a fast casual environment, or at least that's what the sign said, and after we placed our order at the counter, we took a seat in a booth with our drinks and a cardholder sign with a plastic number "43" flying like a flag at the top. We talked as we waited, and she told me about a particularly trying day she'd had splitting her time between a man in a COPD crisis and a young woman with cystic fibrosis.

"Neither of them sound too good," I said.

"They're both having a tough time, but I think we can get them through it."

"You seem pretty positive."

Josie gave me a sweet smile I'd grown quite fond of. "That's the only way to be if I'm going to help."

A server came with a plate of beef stroganoff for her and a grilled ham and cheese with tomato soup for me.

"How about you? How's the trial going?"

"Most everything's coming in as expected. I can't tell how the jury is taking it though."

She covered her mouth as she finished a noodle before saying, "Really?"

I nodded around a spoonful of soup.

"That must be infuriating. And nerve-racking."

I shrugged. "Not as much as an intubation."

Josie shook her head. "You're not going to find me talking in front of a group of people."

"No more than you'd find me snaking a tube down someone's throat."

She smiled again and the corners of her blue eyes crinkled in a way that I found charming. "Is the trial almost done?"

"Almost. We might have one witness to testify yet."

"You don't know?"

I shook my head. "He started today, but we're waiting for the judge to rule on whether he can testify on some other subjects related to Marsh's death."

"So can you tell which way the judge is going to rule?"

"No idea."

"We are on for Monday night though?"

It took me a moment to shift out of trial mode into normal human mode and remember 1) that Monday was Valentine's Day; and 2) that I had a date scheduled with the beautiful woman who was literally sitting right in front of me.

"Absolutely. Even if the jury still has the case, the heavy lifting will be done. Seven-thirty, right?"

"Right."

We talked then, about everything and nothing, enjoying being together after most of a week apart. She was in scrubs she'd worn through a twelve-hour shift while I was in a suit that was rolling into hour number fifteen while we ate counter service family-style food, and it was the most pleasant, warm, comfortable dinner I'd had in days.

We lingered a little longer than necessary but eventually her next shift and my next day of trial prep wormed their way between us, and we left. I walked her to her car, pulled her in, and enjoyed the yielding warmth of her embrace for what seemed in retrospect like a very short time.

Then we got into our cars and I waited until she was on her way before going home.

64

When I arrived at the office Saturday morning, Wendy Carver was waiting by the door.

"Good morning, Wendy," I said as I unlocked it. "You're up early after a late shift, aren't you?"

"I'm sorry to bother you, Nate, but I had to leave for work yesterday before you came out from your meeting with the judge. I couldn't sleep."

"Coffee?"

"Please."

I set up the coffee, then said, "It'll take a second, why don't we wait in the conference room?"

I turned on some lights and the two of us took a seat. She fidgeted for a moment, then said, "What was that all about?"

"There are some things that I want to ask Ted about and the judge is deciding whether to let me."

"About Paxton framing my son and planting the bat?"

"We don't have evidence of that, Wendy. We have evidence that Marsh's last story was about Paxton and that his laptop is missing."

"Why can you not say Paxton framed him?"

"Because I can't prove it. I'm hoping to be able to imply it."

"So what did the judge say?"

"She's thinking about it. "

"What are our chances if she doesn't let it in?"

"These things are always hard to estimate."

"Please try."

I thought. "Since they can prove Logan was in the house, I think slightly against us."

Wendy nodded. "That's what I thought too."

The coffee maker beeped, and I poured a couple for us, mine black, hers with sugar, no cream. We each took a sip, and I took a little more time answering her questions. I hadn't been expecting to talk to her, but it wasn't a waste for me either—it was always helpful to get a lay person's opinion of the testimony and how they thought the jury was reacting. For example, she thought the jury reacted pretty well to Tommy Melton where I had been a little more neutral. She also thought that Devon Payne's testimony was confusing—she got the gist but some of the vector analysis went past her, which meant I needed to explain it more in my closing.

We'd just about finished our coffee when the door opened and a "Hi, Boss!" announced that Emily had arrived.

Wendy Carver stood. "I've taken enough of your time. Thank you, Nate."

"Of course, Wendy. Call me if you have questions."

"I'm sure I won't. I'll see you Monday."

I stood and said goodbye, then heard her exchange greetings with Emily on the way out. A moment later, Emily came in and said, "Did you read the *Torch* this morning?"

"No."

"He ran it. He ran the whole thing."

"The Paxton story?"

"Yep. With a helpful kicker at the end."

I pulled out my phone and found the *Torch* website. It wasn't hard to find the article. "Paxton Contaminates River Forever" was the lead headline. I skimmed it and read what was essentially Christopher's article about Paxton dumping PFAs in the river and then covering it up for months before the sale of the company. "I don't see anything new in—"

"—No," said Emily. "In the next article."

"Murdered Reporter Files Last Story" was the headline right below. The *Torch* reporter, whose name I did not recognize, explained that the Paxton story was the last story Christopher Marsh had ever filed. She said that although he had died some months ago, there had been a delay in publication while his sources had been verified. The story concluded:

> *"Christopher filed the Paxton story with me just hours before his death," said Ted Ringel, chief editor of the Torch. "This story is indicative of what a fine young reporter Christopher Marsh was, and shows that no matter how big you are, no matter how great your reach, a smart, insightful, dogged reporter can bring the truth to light no matter how deeply it's buried. It was an honor to work with him."*
>
> *When asked to confirm rumors that the judge was considering whether to allow him to testify regarding whether the Paxton story played a role in Christopher Marsh's death, Mr. Ringel stated that, "I am not permitted to comment on that at this time." It should be noted, however, that Mr. Ringel was in the judge's chambers for a good part of Friday afternoon.*

I looked at Emily. "We couldn't ask for more than that. I don't know if it will help us, but it certainly doesn't hurt."

Emily nodded. "This might not help Logan. But it's going to have some other people shitting bricks."

65

I worked until mid-afternoon. By then, I had Ted Ringel's direct examination ready, and the base of my closing argument prepared but then I found that I really couldn't do any more on those until the judge let us know how she was going to rule, so I decided to take a quick trip out to my brother Mark's house to check on Roxie.

Now I know what you're thinking and you're probably right —I should've waited until the trial was over Monday night so that I didn't confuse her. But in my defense, she'd always managed the transfers back and forth between Kira and me pretty well and, of course, she'd handled the original transition from Theo Plutides to Kira to me without a hitch. I think it was her service training. I'm not going to lie though, when I walked into Mark and Izzy's house, and she trotted right over to me and rested her head in my hand so I could scratch her jaw, I felt pretty good.

"How's she doing?" I said to Izzy.

"Honestly? She's exhausted."

"Yeah?"

"The boys won't stop petting her and calling her name. Oh, she's also an expert at *Final Fantasy VII* now."

"You don't say."

Izzy shook her head. "Justin has been playing and Roxie has been sitting right on his bed watching the whole thing."

"So she hasn't been too much trouble?"

"Compared to the four animals I normally look after? She's a dream."

"Four?"

"Have you forgotten about your brother?"

"Fair enough."

"Stay for dinner? Mark will have Justin and James back from practice soon and in the meantime..."

"Uncle Nate!" Little Joe came running around the corner and attacked my leg. I picked him up and gave him the Chin of Doom to the middle of his chest as he cackled.

"It seems like you need to put in some bigger squirrel traps, Iz."

"I'm not a squirrel!" said Joe.

"No?" The Chin of Doom elicited more cackles. "You sound like one."

I hung out with Joe and Roxie as Izzy put the finishing touches on a pot of chili until Mark, Justin, and James came home. We ate and I heard about Justin's latest basketball game and James's wrestling practice and Mark's first attempt at a late season goose hunt—unsuccessful but a new experience in case you're wondering. They asked me a little about the trial, more in a hey how's it going kind of way than a specific interest kind of way.

The one thing the boys were interested in was when the trial would be over because they thought Monday was far too early to let Roxie go home. I recalled my Monday night date with Josie and grudgingly agreed to let Roxie stay with them until Tuesday, which was enough of a victory to distract them.

Yes, I am a master strategist at outwitting middle schoolers and elementary children.

It was a little after seven by the time we had eaten and cleaned up. Mark offered a beer and a game on TV, but I passed since I had to be at work the next day. I gave my nephews a hug, thanked Izzy, and told Roxie to go back to her bed which, after a moderately long stare, she did. I told them all good night and left.

I live a decent ways away from my brother—we're both out in the suburban country to the north of Carrefour but he lives on the east part of the district, and I live on the west. The drive was no hardship—about fifteen minutes on County Road 393 with nothing but a hanging light or a stop sign at an intersection every mile.

Even though it was a Saturday night, there wasn't much traffic. A car passed me going in the opposite direction and it was another couple of miles before a pair of headlights shown behind me. They were coming up kind of fast and there was a curve just ahead, so I inched over to let him by since all was clear the other way. The car came alongside me and I let off the gas to make it easier to pass.

The next thing I knew, I was headed for the ditch.

Michigan ditches on county roads are deep—six to eight feet at least to allow for drainage from all those farm fields. The winter is the worst time. That's when they're full.

I hit my brakes and jerked the wheel left, but something blocked me and I kept going straight, right through the curve. Then I crashed and the airbag deployed and I was a little disoriented for a bit.

～

IT TURNS out there's an element of relief when you realize that the white you see isn't clouds but the remains of a deployed airbag. I felt like my bell was rung, like I had just filled the gap against a two-hundred-and-twenty-pound fullback. I heard some dinging and felt some broken glass and I eventually was able to unbuckle and open my door. I climbed out and found myself calf deep in freezing cold ditch water.

I swore and scrambled up the slope to the road. I had been lucky—the ditch around the curve was shallow, the banks weren't steep, and my Jeep hadn't rolled over. One look told me my car wasn't going anywhere though.

I looked for the other car to see if they were all right.

No one was there.

Not a headlight coming in either direction. Not a taillight of a car that had passed. Nothing.

I took another look at my Jeep and sighed as I realized I'd have to make an insurance claim. So I pulled out my phone to call for a tow, for the police, and for a ride.

THE POLICE CAME FIRST. In what some would call irony and others karma, Deputy Pavlich was the responding officer to my call. He was polite as he checked me, checked my Jeep, and checked the scene.

"Single car accident?" he asked.

"No. I was forced off the road at the curve."

Deputy Pavlich did a double take then walked over to the driver's side of my Jeep and shined his flashlight over it. "Were these scrapes here before?" He circled the light over some scratches in the driver's side door and a dent on the front left quarter panel.

"No."

Deputy Pavlich took my statement then, and I found that I had very little to offer him. He knew what he was doing and asked me questions that made me realize that the lights were a little high and a little wide so that it might have been a truck, but I didn't have much else because it was utterly dark on that section of the road and I hadn't noticed a thing until I was on my way into the ditch. No make, no model; no color, no license plate; no driver, no clue.

Deputy Pavlich was giving me a basic sobriety test when Olivia and Cade pulled up in separate cars.

"What the hell?" said Olivia.

I raised my hand. "It's all right."

"That'll do it, Mr. Shepherd." He glanced at Olivia. "I just needed to confirm your sobriety so that some clever defense lawyer doesn't get the jerk who did this off."

"I understand, Deputy. Thanks."

He handed me his card. "Let me know where you take it for repairs. We'll want to a look at it in the light."

"I will."

"You have a tow coming?"

"I do. Thanks, Deputy."

He nodded to me, nodded to Olivia, glanced at Cade who was standing arms crossed on the side of the road looking in both directions, then left.

Olivia looked at the car, looked at me, and said, "Someone ran you in there?"

I nodded. "I didn't get a look at them."

She stared at the Jeep. "The ditch is shallow here. Another fifty yards either way and you'd have been in deep shit."

I glanced at the beginning of the curve where the ditch, and the water, were significantly deeper.

"Come on," she said. "Cade can wait for the tow truck."

"I can do that."

"No. You're shivering and you're coming with me."

"That's not necessary."

"You don't have a car, so you don't have a lot to say about it."

I admitted defeat, yanked a door open on my Jeep, and grabbed my laptop and a file folder that had thankfully survived. Then we went to Olivia's car with a short detour to thank Cade, who gave me a quick shoulder hug without taking his eyes off the road. Then we left.

"What happened?" Olivia said on the way.

I told her with the same lack of detail I'd given the deputy.

"The driver didn't stop?"

I shook my head. "Saturday night. He'd probably been drinking."

Olivia glanced at me. "Did you try to stay on the road?"

"Of course."

"Did the car let you?"

"No. It forced me straight off the curve."

"And you still think it was an accident?"

"Why wouldn't it be?"

"Do you pay any attention at all to the cases you're working on?"

The answer, of course, is that I spend every bit of my attention on the case I'm trying—so much so that I fail to see anything outside it, even if it runs me off the road.

"But the article let the cat out of the bag, didn't it?" I said. "Everyone knows about the dumping."

"The article let one cat out of the bag. It also implied pretty clearly that more cats are getting released on Monday. And conspiracy to murder is different than dumping."

"We don't even know if the judge is going to allow the testimony."

"Will there be testimony on Monday if the defense attorney is dead?"

"Not right away, but eventually."

Olivia shook her head. "Eventually, a new lawyer handles the case. Eventually, time passes, evidence gets stale, pleas change."

"That's a little out there, Liv."

"Where's Christopher Marsh, Shep?"

"Come on."

"Where's Peyton Rush?"

I didn't say anything.

"Why did Ethan Farris run to the other side of the world?"

I stayed quiet, thinking.

We pulled into my driveway.

"I'm coming in with you," she said. "You shower up and then the two of us will wait for Cade to take care of your car. Then he's going to come over and spend the night."

"That seems excessive."

"Maybe. But that's what we're going to do."

She stared at me, those reflective glasses giving me nothing.

"Okay," I said finally.

"Good boy." She put one arm around my neck and kissed my cheek. Then we went inside and did exactly what she said.

IN THE MIDDLE of the night, at a time that was not 2:32 a.m., I started awake without a dog to prompt me. I was alone so you only have my version of what happened, but I can tell you that there was no sudden nausea or shaking, and certainly no pacing or sweats after. Not a bit. I was a rock.

Eventually, I went back to sleep.

66

I was a little late getting to the office on Sunday. Cade had spent the night which, in the bright sunlight of the next morning, seemed like overkill, but it was helpful to have a ride to the car rental agency. I picked up another Jeep—I'm nothing if not predictable—thanked Cade, and headed to the office.

Emily was already there so I filled her in on what had happened. I hesitated to tell her Olivia's theory, which I was coming to discount in the light of day, but since Emily was involved in the case too, I figured she should know.

She listened, then bobbed her head from side to side in the universal "maybe" nod. "I suppose it's possible, but it doesn't seem likely, does it?"

"I don't think so. I'm not going to lie, it seemed like it last night, but now I don't see the angle."

"I suppose it could be something from the article, that they were worried about some new disclosure, but Ted Ringel would have access to whatever you had. Probably more."

"True."

Emily kept thinking, then nodded. "I hear what Olivia is

saying. Your death would screw up the case and prevent the disclosures in open court at least for a little while, but there's nothing to prevent Ted from just printing whatever he knows."

"No, you're right, it doesn't make sense. I'm sorry to scare you."

Emily grinned. "Scare me? Beats the hell out of document review!"

We went back to work, me on my closing and Emily preparing two versions of slides for our closing, one if the judge let the additional testimony from Ted in and the other if she kept it out.

At four o'clock, I received an email from Judge Wesley's bailiff:

Dear Counsel,

Attached is Judge Wesley's opinion denying the admission of testimony from Theoden Arthur Ringel regarding the contents of the story Christopher Marsh filed the day he died, the relocation of the Torch source, the disappearance of Peyton Rush, and any Discord conversations between Logan Carver and Peyton Rush unless Mr. Carver or Ms. Rush testify directly. Argument will be permitted regarding the fact that Christopher Marsh's laptop is missing but only to the extent that this fact has already been placed in evidence for the limited purpose of showing that the item itself is missing. The judge will address any questions regarding implementation before the jury is seated. Thank you.

And that was that. Emily and I opened the opinion, which said the same thing with more words and strings of case citations.

When we were done, Emily said, "She's keeping it all out. The whole thing."

"So we'll argue the lack of blood and the timing."

"But we have no explanation for the bat."

I smiled. "Implications it is."

Emily nodded and we got to work. Once the court decided to keep all mention of Paxton out, I found that whatever small worry I had that Paxton was trying to kill me was now gone and I didn't think any more about it, except to text Olivia and Cade to tell them what had happened so that they didn't stop by again that night. Then Emily and I worked the rest of the afternoon.

MONDAY MORNING BEFORE WE STARTED, I pulled Logan and Wendy aside and explained the court's ruling. Wendy understood the problem, hung her head, and nodded.

"It doesn't matter, Mom," he said. "I didn't do it."

"I know, Logan. But it doesn't give us an explanation for the bat."

"But I didn't use a bat. I didn't use anything."

"I know. I know."

Silas Winford came into the courtroom, and I drifted over to speak with him.

He shook my hand. "I thought she was going to let it in."

I shrugged. "You never know with these things."

"Gives you something to argue about on appeal, I suppose."

"If necessary."

"Of course. So we just finish up with Ringel and close?"

"Yeah, I don't have much left now with him."

"Me either. Shall we tell the Court we can close this morning?"

"Sounds good."

We let the bailiff know where things stood, then spent a few minutes with the judge doing the same. She sent us back out and we recalled Ted Ringel to the stand.

Before we resumed, Judge Wesley said, "Members of the jury, over the weekend the Court has been considering and ruling on different matters relating to the case. Part of that was determining the things Mr. Ringel is permitted to testify about. This is a normal part of the trial process and should not be considered by you one way or the other. Mr. Shepherd, do you have any remaining questions?"

I had called Ted after the ruling came in so that he knew we weren't going to be allowed to get into the whole Paxton plot. It took a while to calm him down and a little longer to convince him that nothing could be done about it. All we could do was leave a trail for the jury.

"Thanks, Your Honor. Mr. Ringel, just to remind the jury where we were last Friday, Christopher Marsh turned in a story to you at 5:12 p.m. on the day he was killed, is that right?"

"It is, yes."

"And that included his notes of source materials related to the story?"

"It did. Chris would turn in his notes once the story was finalized."

"And those notes referenced additional source materials that were contained on Christopher's laptop?"

"Yes. He was going to download those materials to a drive and send it to me later."

"Download those materials from his laptop?"

"Yes, exactly."

"And you said that you believe Christopher sent you that story and his notes to you from his laptop?"

"I believe so, yes."

"And to your knowledge, that laptop has never been recovered."

"That's right."

"It's not been found in the possession of the sheriff's department, the prosecutor's office, my client, Second Chance Electronics, the *Torch*, or his family?"

"That is my understanding, yes. It is *Torch* property and has valuable information on it, which we would like to have returned."

"Thank you, Mr. Ringel."

Silas Winford stood, and I waited to pounce on anything Winford said at all, anything that would open the door for me to talk about Paxton or the missing laptop or Peyton Rush or a conspiracy.

Silas Winford was way too smart for that. He didn't go near any of it. Instead, he spent twenty minutes having Ted Ringel testify about what a wonderful man Christopher Marsh had been, as a young teenager running cross-country, as an enthusiastic college student anxious to dive into a journalism career, as a conscientious young reporter at a small regional newspaper.

"You know, Mr. Ringel," said Winford. "One thing struck me about that. Northwestern is one of the best journalism schools in the country, isn't it?"

"It is."

"I assume its graduates can go to some of the most prestigious news institutions there are?"

"Yes, they can."

"And yet Christopher Marsh wanted to come back here, is that right?"

"He did."

"Do you know why?"

"I do."

"Could you tell the jury, please?"

Ted Ringel looked at the first row of the gallery, right behind the prosecutor's table. "Because his dad Jerry was going to be receiving chemotherapy and radiation treatments that would last most of a year. He wanted to help."

"I see. And did he give you a timeframe when he took the job?"

"He did. Chris committed to two years. He figured that employers would understand that length of time for an internship and that he could put together some good stories for his application package in the meantime."

"I see." Winford wandered to the center of the courtroom, right in front of the jury, so that he stood at an equal distance between Ringel and Mr. and Mrs. Marsh. "That was the professional component. There was also a personal component to that two-year time frame, wasn't there?"

Ted Ringel glanced at the Marshes. "There was."

When Ted didn't say anything more, Winford said, "What was that?"

Ringel stared at the Marshes a moment more before he broke off and looked at Winford. "His dad's treatment was supposed to end last year. After that, they would know."

"Know what?"

"Whether Mr. Marsh's treatment was successful."

"Whether he would survive?"

"Yes."

"Mr. Marsh's treatment was successful, wasn't it?"

"My understanding is that it was, yes."

"The Marshes received that good news last summer, didn't they?"

"That timing sounds about right."

"About a month before Christopher was killed?"

Ringel looked at the Marshes. "Yes."

"Shortly after that, once he knew his father was in the clear, he applied to grad school?"

"I believe so."

"That's all I have, Mr. Ringel. Thank you."

The judge looked at me. Rather than say, "No, Your Honor, I have no further questions for this witness which Silas Winford has just shoved squarely and completely up my ass," I shook my head.

Judge Wesley dismissed Ted Ringel then said, "Mr. Shepherd, you may call your next witness."

I had nothing else. No Ethan Ferris, no Discord, no Peyton Rush, no evidence that someone else had killed Christopher Marsh. I had a timeline and a lack of blood.

"The defense has no further witnesses at this time, Your Honor."

"Very good. Members of the jury, we will take a short break while we handle a few housekeeping details and when you return, we will have closing arguments."

The jury left. We entered our exhibits into evidence and rested. Winford declared he had no further rebuttal witnesses, and the two of us made our close of evidence motions which the Court denied, sending the case to the jury. Then Judge Wesley told us we had five minutes more to get our things together and we would close.

67

S ilas Winford stood in front of the jury.

"You've been listening to the evidence for a week now and I'm sure Mr. Shepherd will join me in thanking you for your patience and attention. It's always interesting as we put together our last argument to you, where we summarize everything you've heard because sometimes it's hard to decide what evidence to talk about and what to leave out. Not in this case, though. No, in this case, the evidence of how Christopher Marsh died is clear."

This time, Winford used the projector. He put each heading on the screen in a huge yellow font.

"Number one—Logan Carver broke into Christopher Marsh's house. There's no argument there. You heard testimony from our forensic experts matching the material from Logan Carver's sweatshirt to fibers found inside the home in the TV console. So we know, from the evidence, that Logan Carver was in the house that night."

"Number two—Logan Carver stole from Christopher Marsh. We know that Logan Carver sold Chris's PlayStation game system and his Beats headphones to Second Chance Electronics.

We also know that Chris's Adderall prescription bottle was found in Logan Carver's garbage. So we know, from the evidence, that Logan Carver stole from the house that night."

"Number three—Logan Carver killed Christopher Marsh. We know that Chris was killed by being struck repeatedly in the back of the head. You've seen the pictures. You've heard Mr. Marsh's description of his son's body as he held it in his arms."

"We know the killer used a blunt instrument to kill Chris. And we found that blunt instrument, an aluminum bat, in the trunk of Logan Carver's car. "

"Further, we know that Logan Carver has attacked other people using the exact same method that he used to kill Chris. You heard testimony from the Sheriff that Logan jumped a fellow inmate at the Ash County jail in the same way, hitting the inmate from behind in the back of the head with a mop handle, putting him in the hospital. The only difference was that the inmate was more fortunate than Chris. Probably because the mop handle was lighter than an aluminum bat."

"So we know, from the evidence, that Logan Carver killed Chris in the house that night."

Silas Winford stepped closer. "It's clear what happened. Logan Carver broke into Christopher Marsh's house to steal. Chris interrupted him. So Logan Carver took the bat, hid, then bludgeoned him from behind. It's simple."

Winford pointed at me. "Mr. Shepherd talks next. He's going to make it complicated. He's going to talk about time-lines and blood and experts and talk about things that confuse the issue. I suspect, though, that there are some things that Mr. Shepherd isn't going to talk about, so you listen closely to him and see if I'm right. I don't think he's going to talk much about the fact that his client broke into Christopher Marsh's home. To rob Chris. To steal Chris's things for a little bit of money."

"I don't think he's going to talk much about his client selling Christopher Marsh's things at a secondhand shop."

"And I don't think he's going to talk at all about that aluminum bat. The bat that was in his client's car. The bat with Chris's blood on it."

Silas Winford stepped back and shrugged. "Maybe he has an explanation for why the fibers of his client's clothes were in Christopher Marsh's house. Maybe he has an explanation for why his client sold Christopher Marsh's things. Maybe he has an explanation for how the bloody bat got in his client's car and, boy, let me tell you, that's the one I'd sure like to hear. But I don't think you're going to hear much from Mr. Shepherd on those topics. We'll see."

"After he's done, I'll tell you what you will hear. You will hear the State ask you to convict Logan Carver of the murder of Christopher Marsh. He invaded Christopher's home, he stole his things, and when Christopher Marsh interrupted him in his theft, Logan Carver beat Christopher Marsh to death with a bat in the same way that he beat an inmate in the Ash County jail, in cowardly stealth, from behind."

"Logan Carver is a thief and a killer. Convict him for it."

I waited until Silas Winford sat before I stood. The jury's eyes followed me as I took my place in front of them and said, "As the judge is about to explain to you, it's up to the State to prove every element of its case beyond a reasonable doubt. Every single one."

"So it's interesting, what prosecutors tend to do when their evidence on one of those elements is weak is they blow by it and focus on the elements where their evidence is strong. But that's not how the law works. The law requires the State to prove on every element, not just the strong ones."

"Let me give you an example from this case. Mr. Winford has brought charges for first degree home invasion. One of the elements of this crime is that the accused *entered* the dwelling with a weapon. However, we know that the weapon that was used to kill Christopher Marsh was Christopher Marsh's bat so *the bat was already in the house.* So the State has not offered you any evidence, at all, that any person entered the house with a weapon that night."

"The State can harp all it wants about evidence that puts Logan in the house that night. That's not enough for first degree home invasion. It still has to prove that he entered the house with a weapon. And it hasn't. The only evidence of any weapon they've given you was already in the house."

"Now you may be thinking, why are we talking about this? This is a murder case, and that's true. But you know the saying, what we do in little things, we do with big things."

"And the State has done the same thing with its murder charge. It wants you to assume that because there was evidence that Logan Carver was in the house that night, that he must've been the one who killed Christopher. Yet they have given you no proof that he committed that particular act. Instead, they want you to extrapolate proof from one act to impose guilt for another."

"There is certainly proof that Logan was in Christopher's house that night and there is certainly proof that he sold things from the house later on. That's all relevant evidence to consider when determining whether Logan Carver stole something from the house that night. It is not, however, evidence that Logan Carver killed Christopher Marsh. In fact, when you look at the actual evidence, not assumptions, you'll see that it was virtually impossible for Logan Carver to have done it."

"Let's start with the timing."

Emily put a timeline on the screen.

"On the front end, we know from his ATM picture that Christopher Marsh was at the Quick Carry Store at 8:09 p.m."

The time and description popped up. "We also know that the Quick Carry store is a five to ten-minute drive from Christopher's house."

"Along with that, we have the testimony of Tommy Melton and Mr. Marsh, who told us that Christopher's car had a rattling muffler that needed repair. Tommy Melton told us that he heard that rattle when Christopher's car came home that night at 8:27 p.m."

"Now maybe some of you don't want to believe Tommy Melton. Maybe some of you find him unreliable because he had been legally smoking marijuana in his home. But remember, his recollection is completely consistent with the evidence—the ATM photo at 8:09 and the video game he saved at 8:27. All of that evidence puts Christopher Marsh in his house no earlier than 8:27 p.m."

Emily populated the timeline with those times.

"Now let's take the backend. We know that Logan Carver was at the Eighth Street McDonald's no later than at 9:02 p.m. that night. We know because we have the drive-thru video, a video which Mr. Winford himself played for you. That video he played certainly showed my client was rude to the drive-thru staff. But it also showed he was there at 9:02 p.m."

Emily put the time up.

"You also heard the testimony of manager, Benjamin Fischer, who told you that the lines were unusually long that night, that it took nine to twelve minutes from the time the customers got in line to the time they were served. Let's use nine minutes. That means Logan had to have been in line by 8:53 p.m."

Emily put the time up.

"Finally, we heard from Tommy Melton that it takes approximately ten minutes to get to the McDonald's. You heard Mr. Winford's skepticism that it was the same time by car or bike, but Mr. Winford also didn't put in any evidence to dispute that time. So the *evidence* in the case is that it would have taken ten minutes for Logan to drive from Christopher's house to the McDonald's. That means he would have had to leave by 8:43 p.m. to arrive at 8:53 p.m."

Emily put up the time.

"Where does that leave us? According to the video and eyewitness evidence, Christopher Marsh arrived home no earlier than 8:27 p.m. that night. And according to the video and eyewitness evidence, Logan Carver, if he were there, had to have left the house by 8:43 p.m. that night."

Emily highlighted the gap in yellow and added, "16 minutes."

"That leaves sixteen minutes if the State is to be believed. Sixteen minutes for Christopher Marsh to enter his house, sixteen minutes for Logan Carver to find a bat and hide and catch Christopher Marsh unawares, sixteen minutes for Logan Carver to beat Christopher Marsh to death, for Logan Carver to grab the items he supposedly stole and a bloody bat and hop into his car. And most importantly, sixteen minutes to find somewhere to remove all traces of blood from his hands and face and clothes before heading to McDonald's while still carrying the murder weapon."

"The timing of that theory makes no sense, especially when you consider the second thing—the complete and utter lack of blood found on Logan Carver. You saw what he was wearing that night—you couldn't miss it—a gray sweatshirt with a big purple 'FU' on it. I have to say I wasn't aware of Furman University's marketing plan until I became involved in this case, but it's a good one because it grabs your attention. The McDonald's workers, the Second Chance store owner, the sheriff's deputies and detective, all of them noticed the 'FU' sweatshirt. And when they took that sweatshirt and microscopically examined it— what did they find? Not a single, solitary drop of blood."

"You all saw the photographs of the scene, of the blood that was spattered all around that kitchen. Mr. Winford posted them time and again for you. You heard the testimony that Mr. Marsh was covered in blood, that Deputy Pavlich had blood on his shirt and on his arms and on his shoes just from being at the scene after the fact."

"And what evidence did you hear about Logan Carver? The McDonald's staff didn't see any blood on him. The store owner didn't see any blood on him. The arresting deputies didn't see any blood on him. And the sheriff's forensics department didn't find any blood on him or on his sweatshirt or on his shoes or his pants. Not one drop. Not a single speck or spatter."

"Now the State has presented you with evidence that Logan was wearing the FU sweatshirt at the scene so they can't have it both ways—if you believe Logan was wearing that sweatshirt in the house, then he didn't get a drop of blood on it while he was there. Mr. Winford knows this; it's why he hasn't argued that Logan changed clothes before his arrest. So the State is stuck asking you to believe that Logan Carver wore the FU sweatshirt when he killed Christopher Marsh and miraculously didn't get a drop of blood on him."

"You heard from our expert, though, Devon Payne, who analyzed the scene and the way in which the blood was spattered. I know there was a lot of science and trajectory analysis in it, but he also told you the conclusion—that the person who killed Christopher Marsh almost certainly got blood on him or herself in the process. It was virtually unavoidable. And we know, based on numerous eyewitnesses and the sheriff's own lab, that Logan Carver did not have any blood on him. Why? Because he wasn't there when Christopher Marsh was killed."

"Mr. Winford has tried to shift the burden to us. Just a few minutes ago he said, 'What about the bat, Mr. Shepherd? How do you explain the bat?' And I would point out to you, again, that I don't have the burden of explaining anything under the law. Because there are a lot of things about that bat that don't make sense. Why weren't there any fingerprints on the bat? Why would someone wipe off the fingerprints but not blood? And why in the world would someone put a bloody murder weapon in the trunk of their car and then let the police search it? Detective Durbin was willing to throw some 'theories' around for you, but he certainly didn't have any answers."

"And the bat's not the only question in this case either. Where did Christopher Marsh's laptop go? Who has it? And, if Logan Carver had it, why would he sell the PS5 and the headphones but throw away a laptop that was worth just as much? No, there are a bunch of things that don't make sense in this case because the State hasn't given you a good explanation for any of it."

"The State has presented you with evidence that Logan Carver was at Christopher Marsh's house that night and later sold some of Christopher Marsh's things. The State has not presented you with evidence that my client killed Christopher Marsh. In fact, their theory is impossible. We know, from the evidence, what time Christopher Marsh came home, and we know, from the evidence, that Logan Carver did not have time to hide, find a bat, and beat Christopher Marsh to death before running off to McDonald's after. We also know, from the evidence, that Logan Carver could not have beaten Christopher Marsh to death and avoided all of his blood, blood that stained every other person who came into that room. Blood that no one ever saw or found on Logan Carver."

"The State would have you ignore all of those things, but if you are going to hold my client accountable under the law, you must hold Mr. Winford accountable to prove it. For these reasons, we submit that Logan Carver is not guilty of first degree home invasion and unequivocally is not guilty of murdering Christopher Marsh. Thank you."

As soon as I sat, Winford hit me back in his rebuttal, like he had to. He pounded on the fibers and said that I had practically admitted that Logan had looted the house. He emphasized that Logan had been caught red-handed with Christopher Marsh's things and that the only way he could have gotten them was if he'd stolen them. He blasted me for the bat, expressing incredulity that it might have just magically appeared in Logan's car. He buried me on all of those things.

And then he made a mistake, or at least I hoped it was. He focused on my timeline, trying to get a few minutes on either side, arguing that Tommy Melton was an unreliable witness, that we couldn't really know how long it took Christopher Marsh to drive from the store to his home or for Logan to drive to the McDonald's, that we couldn't be sure how long the drive-thru line was. Winford, I'm sure, thought he was expanding the window by another fifteen minutes. To me, he was just emphasizing how short that window was.

Especially when he didn't explain the lack of blood. He didn't even try. Winford just hammered what he had on the murder again and again and again.

When he was done, I felt like each side's theory had a high peak and a deep valley. The question was which one the jury would believe.

Judge Wesley instructed the jury and sent it back to decide.

68

Because Logan was still in custody, our options for where to wait out the jury verdict were limited. Eventually, Emily and I, Logan and Wendy, and the deputy assigned to watch Logan made our way down to the beige cinderblock cafeteria and staked out a table in one corner. Emily and I made our way over to Cindy McLaren's coffee cart, which was now strung with heart-shaped lights of red and pink and silver.

"Mr. Shepherd, it's good to see you in the flesh. Now, I know you'll want coffee regardless of the hour. How about the rest of you? Ms. Lake?"

"Coffee for me please, Cindy."

"And your client, Mr. Shepherd?"

"Could I please have one Pepsi, one diet and one of whatever the deputy would like."

"Deputy Duncan gets by on coffee with extra cream, but he enjoys splurging on caramel lattes."

I smiled. "One of those then."

"I'll be just a moment." Her hands flew from carafe to fountain to fridge. "The jury is deliberating then?"

"They are. What's the word?"

"Oh, I don't know as *I* would know."

I smiled. "I believe that you are the only one who would know, Cindy."

"Flatterer. The word around the stand is that the murder is too close to call," she leaned forward and lowered her voice as she pumped the carafe, "but that the home invasion is a lock for Mr. Winford."

"First or second degree?"

Cindy McLaren's eyes twinkled. "Apparently, a certain counselor made a late run at an argument that has made that a tossup."

I nodded at the cart. "Do you have lights for every season?"

"That I do. I tend to make a big show of it when I leave the house with the new set. I do believe I saved Mr. McLaren's bacon this morning when I left with these." She tapped a glowing heart with one finger. "Our credit card app showed a purchase of flowers this morning, bless his heart. And you, Mr. Shepherd? Any plans this evening?"

"Dinner, if the jury is back."

"I don't believe they'll go more than the day."

"Really? Why?"

"Let's just call it a coffee cart premonition. And here you are —one large black coffee, one medium coffee with cream, two sodas, one regular one diet, and one caramel latte with some extra heart shaped sprinkles."

"Happy Valentine's Day, Cindy."

"And to you Mr. Shepherd and Ms. Lake."

"Do you think she's right?" said Emily on our way back.

"No idea. But I'd bet she has a better sense of it than us."

∾

WE SPENT the better part of the afternoon at that table. Folks came in and out all day but the presence of Deputy Duncan, and probably Logan, kept people away. Emily and I talked quietly about the evidence while Wendy spoke with Logan, asking about the food and when he had exercise and whether people were leaving him alone. Logan told her about it all, with no detail too small, and Wendy took it all in.

She knew, even if things worked out for the absolute best, this type of proximity would be rare in the years ahead.

At four twenty-five, my phone buzzed. It was a text from the bailiff. The jury was back. I told the others, and we gathered our things.

As we left, I held out my phone to Cindy McLaren. "You called it."

She gave me the slightest bow, then said, "Have a nice dinner."

"WHAT WE DO NOW?" said Logan on our way back.

"We'll go in, stand up, and the jury will tell us their verdict."

"I didn't kill him."

"I know, Logan. But the jury is the one who decides that."

"But I didn't."

"I understand."

"So how could they say that I did?"

"They might believe all the things Mr. Winford said."

"But he's wrong."

"I understand."

"How can they say I did it if he's wrong?"

We stopped. I motioned for Wendy and Emily and the deputy to give us a little space. They did, the deputy a little less than the others.

I put my hand on Logan's shoulder. "We have to go in there, we have to stand straight, and we have to be quiet no matter what, okay?"

"Yeah, Nate, sure."

"No matter what, Logan."

"Okay."

"The jury is going to find you guilty of going into Christopher's house and stealing something."

Logan nodded. "Okay."

"What we don't know is the exact charge they're going to find you guilty of. We have to listen real closely because it could make a difference of five, or even ten years, okay?"

"Okay. You'll tell me which one?"

"I will. I don't know what they're going to find on the murder. That's the most important thing and so we have to listen really carefully. No questions until the end, all right?"

"All right, Nate."

"I'll make sure the judge gives us time to talk afterward and I'll explain it all to you then, okay?"

"Okay."

"Are you ready?"

Logan nodded.

"Then let's go."

WE WERE all standing at our table, with Wendy Carver seated behind us. Silas Winford stood at his. Mr. Marsh had not been in the courtroom for closing arguments, but he had joined his wife now, sitting in the first row behind Winford, holding hands. Ted Ringel sat a few rows back, on the prosecutor's side.

"Have you reached a verdict?" said Judge Wesley.

The foreperson stood, holding the papers.

It was the pastor's wife, the last person we had left on the jury. "We have, Your Honor."

The bailiff took the papers from her and delivered them to Judge Wesley who scanned them one by one.

"What are they doing?" whispered Logan.

"They are reading it and then they will tell us."

He started to talk, and I put a finger to my lips.

"Right, right."

I made a show of crossing my hands in front of me and he did the same.

I looked up as Judge Wesley handed the verdict back to the bailiff who delivered it back to the pastor's wife.

Once she had the papers in order, Judge Wesley said, "Members of the jury, in the matter of State versus Logan Carver on the charge of murder in the first degree, how say you?"

The pastor's wife stood straight and looked at the judge. "Not guilty."

"In the matter of home invasion in the first degree, how say you?"

"Not guilty."

"In the matter of home invasion in the second degree, how say you?"

"Guilty."

"In the matter of breaking and entering or entering without breaking with intent to commit a felony or larceny, how say you?"

"Guilty."

Logan had questions, but I held them off while Silas and I checked the verdict forms and made sure everything was square before the judge dismissed the jury. It was and as Judge Wesley thanked the jury and gave them their final instructions, I came back to Logan who said, "They found I didn't kill him?"

"That's right."

Logan didn't seem excited. Instead, he just said, "Good. Because I didn't."

That didn't seem like a road to go down again just then, but I didn't have to because Logan had moved on. "They found I stole from his house?"

"Yes. But that you didn't have a weapon with you when you went in."

Wendy Carver leaned over the rail. "What happens next?"

"They'll take Logan back into custody and sentence him in a couple of weeks."

"How long will he get?"

"I don't know yet. Less than it could have been."

"Don't worry, Mom. I told you: I have friends."

She bit her lip. "I know, son."

Once the jury was gone, Judge Wesley conferred with the bailiff and set a date for sentencing. Then she remanded Logan back into custody and the deputy came to take him away. Before he went, Logan stopped, came back, and shook my hand. "Thank you." He glanced at his mom, who nodded.

"You're welcome, Logan. I'll see you in a couple weeks."

Logan Carver nodded, and the deputy took him away.

"Counselors?"

Judge Wesley waved us all up. "You too, Ms. Lake."

When we arrived, she reached over the bench and shook our hands. "Always a pleasure dealing with professionals."

"The same, Judge," said Winford.

"Thanks, Your Honor," I said.

"A moment, Ms. Lake?" Judge Wesley said.

As Judge Wesley talked to Emily, Winford and I gravitated away and shook hands. "Congratulations on the acquittal," he said.

"Congratulations on the conviction."

"I got the bare minimum and you know it. This one went to you."

I shrugged.

"I thought I had you when we kept the Paxton evidence out, but you did a nice job piecing together that timeline."

"Thanks. So will I be seeing you around yet this year?"

He smiled. "I hope to stick to supervising for the rest of my term. Unless something interesting comes along again."

We were about to separate when Mr. Marsh came through the swinging gate and headed straight for me. He walked as fast as I'd seen him.

Winford stepped forward. "Jerry, I don't think—"

"Did you believe what you said? Do you really think your client didn't do it?"

"Jerry," said Winford. "This isn't—"

"—It's okay, Sye," I said. "I really don't, Mr. Marsh." Because I really didn't.

"Do you know who did?"

"I do not. I'm sorry."

"Is what was in the paper true, the article Saturday about Paxton?"

"I understand that it is."

"Could it have been them?"

I looked at Winford who, now that it was clear Marsh wasn't a danger, had stepped back.

"I don't know, Mr. Marsh. It seemed like there was an awful lot there."

Jerry Marsh nodded once, twice, then said, "Thank you for being respectful of my son."

I blinked. "Of course."

He turned to Silas Winford. "And thank you for the support you've given my family."

Winford nodded. "I will be in touch this week."

Then Jerry Marsh walked away, took his wife's arm, and left.

I was overwhelmed by his grace. By the look of it, so was Winford.

The two of us exchanged a nod and went back to our tables to clear up. Emily joined me a moment later.

"What was that about?" I asked.

"She wanted to make sure I knew about some informal women's bar functions. Then she mentioned some nonsense about making sure I learned from you."

I looked up. "Why the grin?"

"Because she also said that I could call her EJ. But that you shouldn't think you could."

"Wouldn't dream of it." Then we gathered our things and left.

69

Danny was waiting for us when Emily and I got back to the office. As he congratulated us, he seemed genuinely happy that we'd won and grateful that he hadn't been involved.

Emily was giving him a play-by-play of the closing when Olivia called. I made a motion that I had to take it and Emily nodded and continued.

"Hey, Liv. You were my next call. We won."

"So I hear. Congratulations."

"Thanks. And thanks for your help."

"Always."

"And thanks again for your help on Saturday."

"Someone has to bring the shepherd in from the cold."

"In retrospect, I think it was a coincidence."

"Probably. But I'm more paranoid than you—"

"—Indisputably—"

"—so if you see anything suspicious, at all, let me or Cade know right away."

"I'm sure I won't."

Olivia sighed. "It's probably nothing. But Marsh, Rush, and

Ferris say there's a chance it was something. Just don't be stupid."

"You're right."

"The more you say that, the better off you'll be. Oh, and the trial's over so I expect your droopy ass over here tomorrow."

"Isn't a cooldown period in order?"

"You just had one for a week and a half. No excuses."

"Thanks again, Liv."

"Bye."

As I rejoined Emily and Danny, I caught her saying "that's what makes them both so effective; they make sure what they say is true."

Danny shook his head. "You didn't actually tell him that, did you? He's insufferable enough as it is."

Emily grinned. "I think that's why she invited me to a county bar outing and not him."

"Betrayed at every turn," I said. "I have to get to a dinner tonight. Go out tomorrow to celebrate?"

"I'm going to be traveling to Columbus tomorrow," said Danny. "How about Thursday?"

"Works for me. What's going on?"

"Meetings on the next Tri-State Nursery deal."

Emily rolled her eyes.

"It's not closing for a few weeks yet."

She sighed. "I suppose it's bad form to hope someone gets murdered between now and then."

Danny and I blinked.

"I don't want anyone to die, obviously. But if a defendant walked in here...I mean, that would be good for business, right?"

I looked at Danny. "I'd check your brake lines."

He kept his eyes on Emily. "Every day."

It turned out I wasn't the only one with Valentine's Day

plans. Emily and Danny left while I closed up the office, still humming with adrenaline from the win.

AFTER A QUICK SHOWER AND CHANGE, I picked Josie up at her place. She wore a silk shirt as blue as her eyes and I had to say that her smile when she saw me made me feel better than the win. "You look amazing," I said.

"Thanks." She gave me a warm hug and a better kiss. "You seem cheerful."

"We won."

"Congratulations! I want to hear all about it."

As we walked out, she said, "Where's your car?"

"In the shop. This is a loaner."

She nodded as I opened the door for her. "So tell me about the trial."

"Are you sure?"

"Of course."

"What do you want to know?"

"All of it."

I closed her door, went around to my side, and told her about it on the way to the Lakeside Public House.

JOSIE SEEMED LEGITIMATELY INTERESTED, so I told her all about it. I apologized at one point for going on, but she said, "Nonsense!" and instead asked me what made me think to ask Tommy Melton about the car. That led us down a whole other rabbit hole so that by the time we were seated at the Lakeside and the server had brought our drinks, I was telling her about Ted Ringel's testimony and about the fight over the Paxton story.

"That seems important," she said. "Why wouldn't the judge let it in?"

"Because she thought it would confuse the jury more than establish what actually happened to Christopher."

"But this Peyton Rush person actually disappeared?"

I nodded.

"And she had been in touch with Logan? To tell him to rob Marsh?"

"Yes."

"How in the world can that not be relevant? She's gone!"

"I know."

We broke for a moment to order our entrees and a second round of drinks before Josie said, "And the laptop was never found?"

"No. If Marsh had finished the story a day later, or if the killing had happened a day sooner, the story might never have come out."

"Why is that?"

"Because Marsh was the only one with all the source materials and he didn't give them to Ted until the story was finished."

"That was the big story that ran Saturday? In the *Torch*?"

I nodded.

"What they did." She shook her head. "It was terrible."

"I imagine the wheels of justice are grinding toward them as we speak.

"And the judge really didn't let any of that in?"

"No. She told us Sunday."

Against all odds, Josie still seemed interested, so I told her about the closing, about Winford's arguments and mine and about the jury verdict.

"So Logan will still be going to jail?"

I nodded. "He still broke in and stole Marsh's stuff. Well, technically the jury found that he didn't necessarily break in but that he entered unlawfully and stole Marsh's stuff. He's looking at quite a bit of time for that still."

"But not for murder."

"But not for murder."

"Are you glad?"

I saw she was serious about the question, and I figured it was as much to learn about me as anything else. "I'm glad to win, just because I'm glad to win. But I also don't think he did it."

"No?"

I shook my head. "I could be wrong but Logan is pretty...straightforward. I don't think he has that kind of deception in him."

Josie smiled and raised her glass. "Well, if you're glad, I'm glad."

"Thank you." We clinked.

"So where in all of this did you have time to take your car into the shop?"

"I didn't have much choice. I had it towed Saturday night."

"Oh no! Did you break down?"

"No. I was in a little accident."

"An accident?"

"Some jerk ran me into a ditch."

"What?! Were you hurt?"

"I was fine, I am fine. I think I'm going to be shopping for a new Jeep though, I'm afraid the frame's bent."

"What did you do?"

"I was kind of out in the middle of nowhere so I called Cade and Olivia."

"Yeah, where were you?"

"I was coming back from my brother's house out on County Road 393."

Josie's face went blank. "Is that where your accident was?"

"Yeah. Between Middle Branch and Forest."

She wiped her mouth with her napkin, at the corners so that it wouldn't smear her red lipstick. "Near the curve?"

"Right on it."

She nodded and put the napkin in her lap then folded her hands. "Did the other guy get cited?"

"He would have if he'd stopped. It doesn't really matter with no-fault insurance but still."

Josie nodded, then put one hand to her stomach. "I'm sorry, Nate, but I'm not feeling well at all. I think I'd like to go home."

"What?" I looked more closely at her. "Really?"

She nodded. "Please. I don't want to get sick in here."

"Sure, let me just take care of the bill."

"Could I have your keys and wait in the car?"

"Of course, here."

The moment I gave her the keys, she left.

It took me a few minutes to get a bill, pay, and get out there. Josie was sitting in the car, engine on, waiting. I climbed in.

"Are you any better?"

"No. A little worse. I need you to take me home."

"Do we need to go to the hospital?"

"No. I'm sure it's something I ate."

As we drove back to her place, I tried to engage her, but she didn't respond. I thought back to when she changed and, although I knew it sounded guilty and needy, I said, "You're not upset that I called Olivia and Cade, are you?"

Josie kept looking out the window. "Not at all."

"What is it?"

"I told you. Something disagreed with me."

We pulled into her driveway and I came around to help her out, but she had already opened the door and was headed up the walk.

"Let me get you settled—"

"—That's not a good idea, Nate."

She didn't look back as she put her key in, turned it, and opened the door. "Good night, Nate," she said without looking back. "I'm sorry."

"Josie! What's going on?"

She turned her head to the side but didn't look at me. "I told you; I'm going to be sick."

I touched her arm. I didn't grab or pull or yank, I just touched it.

She didn't turn around. She just went in and closed the door.

I stood there for more than a minute, but no lights came on and the door didn't open again.

CARNAVAL DE CARREFOUR

70

"Before work?" said Olivia as I walked into the Brickhouse. "Yes, I do believe in miracles!"

"Morning, Liv."

She cracked a water, drank, and set it on the front desk. "I figured you'd be sleeping in after the win."

"No, I had an early night."

"Weren't you supposed to go out with Josie?"

"I did."

"And you had an early night? Is that what the kids are calling it these days?"

I shook my head. "I think I'm in a fight, but I don't know why."

Olivia grinned and made the "come on" gesture with both hands. "Tell Dr. Liv."

I hesitated.

Olivia sighed. "You're right, it's a total coincidence that you came to see your friend right after she finished her early morning classes but before the school moms arrive."

"That's annoying."

"But true. Spill."

"We were at dinner, and she wanted to know about the trial and I told her, and then the accident came up and as soon as I told her where it happened, she—"

Olivia swore.

"What?"

"I am so fucking stupid. Come with me."

I was still standing there, so she reached back, grabbed my arm and dragged me toward her office. When we got there, she darted behind her battered desk and fired up her air-traffic-control-looking set up. As the screens flashed on, she said, "I really didn't even think about it until just this moment."

"Liv, what are you talking about?"

"So let's just start with the premise that I have a tendency to check up on people you spend a lot of time with."

"No kidding."

"I don't do a deep dive or anything invasive, just a quick once around the block to make sure there's no 'psychos are us' signposts."

"Thanks, I guess?"

"By all accounts, Marie-Josée Lacombe is just as sweet as she appears. Certainly nothing there that raises a red flag."

"But?"

"There's no but. Not with her."

"But?"

"Except—"

"—Same thing!"

"Is not. *Except* her greatest grief is right out there for anyone to see." Then Olivia tapped the screen.

I leaned closer to the headline of an article which said, "Local Accountant Dies in Crash."

"Sure, I mean, we've talked about her losing Peter in a car accident."

Olivia tapped the screen. "Keep reading."

The article continued. "Prominent local accountant Peter Hall was killed in a single car accident on County Road 393 last night." I stopped.

"County Road 393?"

Olivia nodded and pointed to the next paragraph. "Mr. Hall lost control of his vehicle and went into a ditch where he is believed to have drowned while unconscious. The accident, which occurred between Middle Branch and Forest roads, remains under investigation."

"That's where my accident was."

Olivia shook her head. "I knew that but I just didn't put it together."

"There's no reason you would have. What did the police investigation show?"

"I didn't see a need to follow up. Want me to?"

"No. I'll follow-up on my own. As soon as I figure out what the hell it means."

"Not too hard to figure out, Shep. I'm sure it scared the hell out of her." Olivia checked the time. "I have to get ready for my next class. Talk later?"

"Sure."

I worked out then because I was already there. It also gave me time to think.

Josie had been surprised when I told her about the accident and, in retrospect, straight up traumatized when I told her where it happened. Understandable. Also strange beyond the bounds of coincidental. I noodled it the whole time I was working out but didn't have an explanation. Olivia gave me a wave from her class on my way out; I waved back then changed my plans and decided to go home.

I searched the death of Peter Hall and didn't find much that I didn't already know—survived by Marie-Josée Lacombe, his parents, and two sisters, partner in the accounting firm of

Gaines & Bennet, which mourned his tragic passing but vowed to work tirelessly with their clients to fill the void of Peter's loss. I did find a small article seven weeks later that was easy to miss—the Sheriff's office found that toxicology was negative in the Peter Hall accident and that the cause had been determined to be loss of driver control caused by excess speed. I reminded myself to let Olivia know about my superior research skills.

But the finding wasn't a surprise and it was consistent with what Josie had told me, that Peter had been in a hurry to get home when he died.

I thought a little longer, then picked up the phone and called Sheriff Dushane. To his credit, he answered.

"Not calling to gloat now, are you?"

"I've got nothing to gloat about. You're going to have my client for a good, long time."

"Not me. We'll be moving him to Jackson after sentencing." He paused, then said, "Silas Winford told me about the evidence that didn't come in. About Paxton and the person who suggested Marsh's house. We'll look into it. Of course, all hell is breaking loose with the *Torch* article; state and fed enforcement have already parachuted in here, so we'll see if they find anything."

"This Peyton Rush might be a link too."

"The woman who disappeared months ago?"

"That's the one."

"We'll look into it." His voice was heavy when he said it.

"No breath-holding, I understand, but I appreciate it."

"So if you didn't call to gloat, what can I do you for?"

"I had a question about an investigation your office did some years ago."

"Shoot."

"The car accident that killed Peter Hall. Do you remember it?"

"Oh, I remember it. The Lacombes were a colossal pain in

my, well, they were very interested in the result and wanted me to see to it personally."

"What did you find?"

"Nothing really. One car accident, negative toxicology, poor bastard flipped his car and drowned in a ditch while he was unconscious. Took a curve too fast out on County Road 393...hey, hold on Nate, you were involved in an accident out there this weekend. I just saw the report."

"I was."

"Listen, are you soft-pedaling me before you sue the County for that road design? Because we settled with the Lacombes after that accident and made all the changes—"

"I'm not suing the County, Sheriff."

"We added the 'reduce speed warning' and the reflective arrows—"

"Sheriff! I'm not suing the County. Someone forced me off the road, remember?"

"Oh, right, the report mentioned that. I guess you'd sue him, wouldn't you?"

"The Lacombes sued the County? Over the road design?"

There was a pause and a hrumph then, "I suppose that's public record and the increased signage is clear enough to see. He was still going too fast though."

"That's what I understand."

"You were lucky—another fifty yards and you'd have been up where the ditch is deepest. If you're not suing us, why do you care?"

"Josie Lacombe is a friend. She was upset when I mentioned my accident."

"I'm not surprised. I know the family took it pretty hard. I never met her, but I'd expect she had it the worst."

"You didn't meet her, with the suit?"

"It never got that far. I only saw the family lawyers at deposition. Do you know they had me buried in more than fifty exhibits? Fatality statistics, prior accident reports, I've never seen anything like it."

That triggered a thought that would give me an excuse to call Josie. "Hey, that reminds me, Josie's dad, André Lacombe, is waiting to get his journal back. Actually, it's his grandfather's journal, but he'd given it to Marsh for his profile article and it was being held by your department in inventory until the trial is over. Can they get that back now?"

"If it was an exhibit, Winford's office would have it."

"No, it was just kept as part of the inventory from his house."

"Alright, that's us then. Shoot me the inventory number and case number and I'll have it released."

"Thanks."

We talked a little longer, mostly about the fact that the ice had never gotten thick enough for long enough for him to get the shanty out on the lake with my dad and their buddies, until finally I thanked him and hung up.

I called Josie, and I texted her, and I didn't get a reply to either. After a while, I gave up and went to work.

71

I f you go into the office of a trial lawyer, you might see a stack of files in the corner and ask what they are, only to be told they were from a case he'd handled four years ago. It's a common affliction, one I'd suffered from more than once, so when I went into the office, I resolved to clean up the Carver file.

We had scanned everything, but I was still just paranoid enough to want the hard copy too, just in case, so I gathered all the loose pleadings scattered about my desk and put them in one folder, correspondence into another, and research into a third. That last one was by far the biggest as I had the expert materials with all of Devon Payne's blood spatter analysis, Marsh's materials on PFAs and pesticides and pharmaceuticals (all of which made me consider taking up bottled water), and reams of cases we had used to argue that the Paxton evidence should be admitted.

I'd made a fair bit of progress when Ted Ringel called.

"We're running another story tomorrow. The EPA is filing a criminal enforcement action against Paxton."

"That's good news."

"The new owners have volunteered to temporarily shut down the facility while the government inspects its current wastewater process."

"That's surprising."

"They must expect it to be up to snuff or they wouldn't have done it. And we're hearing that they're going to cooperate fully to help the feds go after the old owners."

I chuckled. "I imagine all this would have affected the sale price."

"Exactly. Thought you'd want to hear about it."

"I did, thanks. I was just thinking about the water in my coffee pot."

"There's going to be a full analysis of that too. They're going to check the river of course but also some different ground water locations."

I shook my head. "I can't imagine what all's in there."

"What do you mean?"

"It sounds like PFAs aren't the end of it. Christopher had research on pesticides and pharmaceuticals too."

"Did he? That must have been when he first started to research all the pollutants. I only have the PFA stuff from when he narrowed it down to Paxton. Anyway, wanted to let you know." He paused. "Hey, while this case was going on, I said some things—"

"—Stop it, Ted. Christopher was a good man. You had a hard choice."

"Thanks, Nate. I'll talk to you."

I kept cleaning until I hit a wall of apathy and a realization of why those stacks of files accumulated. I texted Josie, this time mentioning that I'd talked to the Sheriff about getting her dad's old journal back and hoping, again, that she was feeling better. There was a flash of three dots that disappeared as soon as they came.

I texted one more time, asking if she wanted to meet after work, but I didn't hear anything. I didn't even see any dots.

Eventually, I left. As I drove, I decided what to do next.

I WAS STANDING across from Josie's car when she came out of St. Wendelin's hospital that night. She stopped when she saw me, about twenty-five feet away, then put her head down and made toward her car.

"I know my accident was on the same road as Peter's."

She stopped but didn't look at me.

"Same curve. Same place."

She bowed her head, back to me.

"It must have brought up horrible memories for you. I'm sorry I didn't realize what was happening, but I didn't know."

"It's just like him," she said quietly.

"It's not, Josie. I talked to the Sheriff. I know about the lawsuit, about the measures you took to fix the curve. But someone hit me."

"I can't lose you too, Nate."

"You didn't, Josie. You won't."

She stood there, head bowed for another second, then put her hand on the door.

"Josie, what can I do?"

She turned, blue eyes under a black stocking cap with blond hair peeking out underneath.

"Stay away from me."

Then she got into her car and I stepped away as she backed out.

Josie never looked at me as she shifted gears and drove away.

72

I drove around for a while, going nowhere in particular, until I remembered that I had to pick up Roxie, so I drove north to Mark and Izzy's. Roxie wagged and my nephews wailed as I came in to collect her. As we packed Roxie's things, Mark congratulated me on the win and Izzy told me, three times at least, to make sure that I got some rest. When she said it a fourth time as we pulled away, I looked in the rearview mirror and noted dark circles that hadn't been there Monday morning.

I was going to head for home when I realized I was already halfway to someone who might understand. So I turned north instead of west and Roxie rested her head on my shoulder as we drove.

~

"NATE!" said my mom as she opened the door. "Aren't you in trial?"

"We finished yesterday."

"Come in! Oh, and Roxie too!" She gave Roxie a scratch and

me a hug, then immediately stepped back. "You've lost weight again. You didn't eat those meals, did you?"

"Of course I did."

"Nathan Shepherd, I will not have you lie about my food."

Try to explain to your mother that you don't have time to eat during a trial, that you always lose a little weight but that it snaps right back, probably too quickly. Go ahead, I dare you.

"Honestly Mom, it was delicious."

"More lies and straight to my heart. You and Roxie get in here, I'm going to throw together some lasagna that you can put in the oven tonight. It won't take but a minute."

I hadn't seen her in a couple of weeks what with everything going on so I spent a few minutes with her catching up and getting out a tin pan and some of the ingredients so she could "throw together" a lasagna that was big enough to choke a horse.

After a while, I said, "Is Dad around?"

"He's out 'winterizing.'" She put it in air quotes. "He says there's all sorts of things he needs to lock up and put anti-freeze into out in that barn before we leave for Florida, but the only antifreeze I've seen is in that refrigerator of his." She smiled. "He'll be happy to see you. You can leave this good girl with me."

I gave her a kiss and went out to the barn, which was actually one of those all-metal outbuildings that are perfect to handle the boats, recreational watercraft, trailers, fishing gear, plows, tools, and other you-name-its that accumulate when you live on a lake. My dad had run heat and electricity out to there so that he had a workspace and refuge all in one. I found him organizing fishing lures on his workbench, pulling out the tiny plastic drawers, inspecting them, and moving them around. He glanced up and smiled with those white teeth. "Hey, son."

"Hi, Dad." I looked over his shoulder. "Did you warn those Florida fish you're coming?"

"I like to surprise them before word gets out. Aren't you in trial?"

"Finished yesterday."

"Did you win?"

Explaining to your father that your client was convicted but that you won on all of the important charges can be like explaining to your mother that you did not actually lose weight, so I said, "Yes."

"Congratulations."

"Thanks. Anything left for you to do out here?"

"Not much. I still need to top off the plow with new gas and empty the garbage can back there but most of it is done."

I walked over to the gas can, shook it to feel that it was full, and went over to the little John Deere plow. As I turned the gas cap and buried the nozzle in the tank, my dad said, "So what's on your mind?"

"Can't I just visit my dad?"

"On a Tuesday? No."

I paused, then plunged in. "Why did you and Marie-Faye Lacombe break up?"

The gas can glugged in my hands, releasing air like a beating heart as the fuel flowed out. I was done and had recapped both before my dad said, "That's pretty personal, son."

"I know. But it's important."

"Does this have something to do with Josie?"

"Yes."

My dad opened one drawer of his tackle box, then another, before he pulled out a lure and picked up a pair of needle-nose pliers. He eyed the barbed hook for a moment before he said, "It turned out she wasn't who I thought she was."

"What do you mean?"

"That seems pretty self-explanatory."

"Please tell me."

He worked the snub end of the pliers into the hook and tightened the bend. "You've met Marie-Faye?"

"I have."

"We probably seem like a strange pair now."

I shrugged.

"People always said she was beautiful but I don't think that's the right word. She was vital. Vital and wild. It didn't matter if we were out on the water or stuck at one of her family's stuffy parties, she made it more fun." He paused. "Made it more *everything*. So after two years, I figure that's what I want and I ask her to marry me. I'm not sure how that's going to go but she seems even happier about it than me."

He swore at the hook, which he'd bent too far, and worked the pliers in again.

"One night, maybe two weeks later, she asks me if I'd be willing to drive her to one of her dad's aggregate sites to pick up a truck. It's about two hours away, down in Indiana, but it's two hours with her so I don't mind at all, and I say, 'Sure.' We get down there and I'm expecting a dump truck for sand or stone but instead it's one of those U-Haul type moving trucks with a roll-up shutter door. She says she didn't realize the truck would be that big and asks if I mind driving it back. I told her I actually preferred it that way so that's what we did."

"So we drive the couple of hours back up here and drop it off at her family's milling plant. She tells me to leave the keys in it, that her dad's guys will get it in the morning, so I do."

"She's all jazzed up and wants to take me to Jed's in thanks and a beer sounds good so I say, 'Sure' and hop in the passenger seat. We're just leaving the milling plant and I see the truck's lights come on and the door go up and guys taking stuff out of the back. I tell her and she just says, 'Oh the guys must have decided to do it tonight,' and I say, 'Do what?' and she says,

'Their jobs.' I say, 'What's that?' and she just smiles and says, 'Jed better have iced the mugs.'"

My dad worked on the hook's barb, prying it out so that it would stick deeper into the fish's flesh.

"I almost let the whole thing go on the way there. It was a warm night, and I was thirsty, and the windows were down so the wind blew her hair around like it was alive. She was happy too; she whooped as we skidded into Jed's gravel lot, gave me a big kiss and says, 'It's on me.'"

My dad stared at me for a moment, then returned to the hook. "She gets a pitcher and I get the mugs and she slides into the booth right next to me and I almost leave it alone there too. But we'd taken a cargo truck from an aggregate quarry to a grain mill, so I say, 'What was in the truck?'"

"She says, 'Who cares, *mon loup*, it's delivered.'"

"I say, 'Marie-Faye. What was in the truck?'"

"'Nothing bad.' she says."

"'So tell me then.'"

"She starts getting irritated, in a way I hadn't seen before, and says, 'Something your future wife asked you to get.'"

"I could've handled the next part better but..."

I smiled. "We've met, Dad."

"Right. So I say 'Maybe.' And she says, 'Maybe what?' And I say, 'Maybe my future wife.'"

He put down the pliers and held the lure in both hands.

"She faced me then on the same side of that booth at Jed's and she stares at me with those light blue eyes, one hand on the back of the booth and one hand on the table, and she leans close and she's not mad and she's not scared, but she's intent as all hell and she says, 'It was cartons of cigarettes and I love you.'"

My dad put the lure into the small plastic drawer and shut it. "I don't know exactly what's going on right then, but I know something's not right and, even worse, I know she's used to doing it. So I say, 'I love you too' and I kiss her, and she wraps her arms around me tight like she's not going to let go and I pull away and I say, 'But I'm not going to marry you.'"

"And slowly she hears me and she unwraps and she lets me slide by her, gentle, out of the booth so I can stand. She stands with me and while I put money on the table for the beer, she says, 'I'll change your mind.'"

"And I say, 'I'm sorry, Marie-Faye, you won't.' And I left."

He smiled. "Turns out it was a long walk home, but I had a lot to think about."

"I bet."

"Mostly, I regretted the last thing I said to her."

"That you wouldn't change your mind?"

"No. That I said I loved her. Because that wasn't right, and I gave her the wrong idea. What I meant was I loved who I thought she was. But you're the one who works with the words, not me."

I connected something he had said a couple of months ago. "That's why she kept turning up around you and mom."

My dad nodded. "It was my fault. Marie-Faye only knew what I'd said, but once I met your mother that was it, it wasn't even a close call. She, your mom, was exactly who she appeared to be, and I love her more than anything." He smiled again. "Sometimes it's better to be lucky than good."

"When did Marie-Faye finally stop?"

"I never really kept track of her, but it seemed like she stopped showing up once Tommy was born. She got married to that George guy the next year and I never saw her again after that."

"Did you ever learn any more about what her family did?"

"I stopped caring about that the minute I walked out of Jed's."

My dad turned to face me directly. Shaggy white hair

surrounded his weathered face and his hazel eyes, green with flecks of yellow and brown, bored into me. "I know you must've had a reason, son, but I don't want to talk about this again. I hate to think of the mistake I almost made, but I hate the doubt it causes your mother even more. She's my life and I won't have her thinking otherwise."

"I won't, Dad. And thank you. I appreciate it."

He nodded, hung the pliers on the pegboard, and said, "That garbage isn't going to empty itself."

"I suppose not." I gave him a hug, then pulled the great black bag out of the trashcan, tied it off, and took it out to the bin.

As I walked, I figured my dad had never told that story to anyone, and he never asked me why I needed to know.

It was enough that I'd asked.

I threw the bag away then went in the house. I gathered Roxie, gave my mother a hug and a kiss goodbye, and left with a pan of lasagna and an insight into what was happening.

I hurried home.

73

As soon as I walked in the door, I slid the lasagna onto the island and opened my laptop. The first thing I checked, just to be sure, were Christopher Marsh's research notes from the Lacombe Distillery article. There was André Lacombe's contact information, the dates the current distillery had opened, a link to the Lacombe Distillery website and another to the history section tracing its lineage from Josie's father André back four generations to Jean-Leon, his great-grandfather and founder of the Carrefour Lacombes.

There was no mention of André's sister, Marie-Faye, or of her sons JP and Maxime, or any of the other many Lacombe relatives and businesses. It was just a pleasant article about the revival of the family's rye whiskey recipe. It was nothing I hadn't read before, and I didn't discover any new facts. But now I read it through the lens of what my father had told me, and I looked for more.

I went back through Christopher's notes on Paxton, his documentation of the dumping and the cover-up. Then I went farther back to his research on PFAs and the plating industry. He listed site after site linking to articles about PFAs—what they were made from, how long they survived, the hazard of their presence in the water and the wildlife, of how the plating industry created PFAs, the histories of other site contaminations, and the governmental regulations that tried to regulate it all.

He had another section of research related to general water quality that was even older, where he had collected listings of common contaminants in Michigan ground water and where they'd been found. Ted had told me that this was what had put Christopher onto the story in the first place, the concern that trace amounts of PFAs were in the local river. Which meant he would have done any general research on common water pollutants, things like pesticides and pharmaceuticals, months ago.

In other words, there was no reason for Christopher to have general water pollution research in his printer on the night he died.

The difference was my father. I never, ever, would have made the connection without him. Even with his story, my guess was a tenuous, frayed thread.

I did some research on my own for the rest of the night. I had the advantage of my father's story, so I'd guess I made faster initial progress than Christopher Marsh had, but then I hit a wall.

I had zero proof. None. I had an educated guess on an outrageous speculation that I had to decide what to do with.

A little later, I received an email from Sheriff Dushane about the evidence inventory, which really didn't surprise me but also didn't move the ball forward at all.

I thought. I thought about a lot of things, including reaching out to Sheriff Dushane or to Olivia. But in the end, I didn't do either.

74

About two weeks later, I was on the sprawling grounds of the home of Marie-Faye Lacombe for her celebration of the Carnaval de Carrefour. Known as Mardi Gras elsewhere, her Carnaval was more like the one held in Québec, a celebration of winter, charity, and traditional French-Canadian food and drink. A twenty-foot-tall Bonhomme, complete with red hat, black buttons, and a traditional arrowed sash, served as a center landmark for an array of fire pits and open-sided tents, stations for hot food and drink, and all manner of winter amusements, including a stage for a band at one end.

Hundreds of people milled about in pursuit of food, drink, and company. I don't have the vocabulary to describe the fashion except to say that the default appeared to be ski-slope chic with an occasional emphasis on obliviousness to the cold. There was a lot of goose-down and fleece with toques of all shapes and sizes. More than one woman sported white fur, faux I'm sure, but then again, maybe not, with a smattering of muffs and boots to match.

The purpose of the Lacombe's Carnaval de Carrefour was to

raise money for charity so most of the people wandering around Carrefour's biggest winter party had paid the steep admission, all of which went to the Carrefour Community Foundation. I ignored it all, made my way around the giant Bonhomme, and walked straight to the only enclosure in the area, the Queen's Tent.

It was a fully enclosed white tent, draped along the roofline with garlands of pine, that had one entrance monitored by two large men in black wool coats and black Cossack hats. They checked a list and let people in or rejected them. I waited my turn, then gave them my name.

The man looked at the list. "I'm sorry, Mr. Shepherd, I don't see..." He put his finger to his ear. "Come in, Mr. Shepherd. Welcome."

I thanked him as he pulled aside the heavy flap designed to hold in heat and entered the damnedest tent I'd ever seen.

There was a wood floor like you see at weddings, only it was made of actual hardwood and covered the whole space. A Bonhomme carved entirely from ice stood in the center surrounded by intricate ice fountains dispensing vodka and whiskey and the traditional drink, caribou. Groups were gathered around tall gas heaters, and I noticed an increase in overcoats among the men and furs among the women with more than one who'd decided to replicate snowflakes with diamonds. Which shouldn't have been surprising, I suppose, since the cost of entry to the Queen's Tent was a ten-thousand-dollar donation to the Foundation.

I hadn't crossed more than half the distance to the Bonhomme when Maxime Lacombe appeared, wearing his own black wool and Cossack ensemble. "Good evening, Nate."

"Hi, Maxime."

Neither of us offered our hands.

"My mother would like to see you."

"I was hoping so."

He gestured and I followed, and we made our way around the ice fountains toward the stone fireplace at the other end of the tent. I'm not kidding, they had assembled an enormous fireplace made entirely of stone in which two very large and very real logs were burning.

Marie-Faye Lacombe stood in front of the fireplace. I don't know what I expected—a full-length black fur or long diamond earrings, maybe—but she wore a black wool coat with a white fleece lining over a white turtle-neck sweater and black pants. A patterned black-and-white toque covered her head, with her white hair trailing out beneath. She was sipping from a steaming mug when she saw me and smiled. "Nathan. I was surprised to hear your name at my door. I understood that you and my niece were no longer seeing each other."

"No, I'm afraid we're not."

"Pity. It was nice to have a Shepherd around again."

"There were…insurmountable obstacles. You know how it is."

Her dark eyebrows twitched. "Well, if you're not with her, I don't recall seeing a check for the Foundation."

"I didn't send one."

"Then why are you here?"

"I wanted to catch up with you." I smiled. "And you're hard to catch."

Marie-Faye Lacombe gave me that almost smile. "I wonder if you might take a walk with me, Nathan? I can't bear all these precious flowers huddling in the heat."

"Sure."

"We'll be fine, Maxime," she said as she wrapped a scarf loosely, buttoned her coat, and pulled on her fleece-lined mittens. Maxime nodded and turned his back.

"Nathan?" She held out her hand to take my arm. I offered it and we pushed aside a flap next to the fireplace.

There was a brace of cold air as we stepped out onto a shoveled flagstone path that was part of a private courtyard interspersed with lines of evergreen bushes and small, bare trees. A stone firepit burned in the center. It was dark but the night was clear and there were strings of white lights scattered at intervals along the way.

As we slowly walked along the path, Marie-Faye Lacombe, still holding onto my arm, said, "I don't object, you know."

"To what?"

"You and Marie-Josée."

"I don't either. She does."

"Why?"

"You can ask her if you like."

"I know it can be difficult to let someone in again after a bad experience. Are you certain how she feels?"

"She was very direct."

Marie-Faye straightened. "Too bad."

"Could you give her a message for me?"

"Perhaps."

"Tell her the Sheriff has lost your grandfather's journal, the one with the whiskey recipes and family history and such."

Marie-Faye Lacombe's fingers did not so much as twitch on my arm. "What do you mean?"

"André had given it to Christopher Marsh for background on the Distillery story. The Sheriff's department picked it up when they inventoried the house after his death."

"I didn't know that."

"I tried to help Josie get it back after my trial, but the Sheriff emailed me that it was gone."

"Well, where is it?"

"They don't know. I'd tell her myself but…" I shrugged.

She shook her head. "We'll sue them if they've lost it. That journal is priceless. Thank you for checking."

"Sure."

"On that score, I understand congratulations are in order for another trial victory."

"It was a mixed bag."

"That's not how I hear it. I understand you were at quite a disadvantage."

"How so?"

"All of the Paxton evidence that was kept out?"

"These things happen."

"Modesty is a family trait, it seems. Fortunately for Mr. Carver, he had a great attorney."

"Mr. Carver's attorney got lucky."

We reached the fire pit and at last Marie-Faye let go of my arm. We took opposite sides, the fire between us, and though the cold wasn't overwhelming, we both held our covered hands over the flames.

"I've enjoyed this chance to catch up, Nathan, but it hardly seems worth crashing my party."

"Word is that Paxton is done around here."

"I've heard the same."

"I think their former officers are looking at prison."

Marie-Faye Lacombe nodded. "In cells that last as long as the chemicals they dumped, I hope."

"Christopher Marsh nailed them."

"He did. It's too bad he didn't see it."

I turned my hands over against the flames. "There's no evidence of what else he was investigating, you know."

"No?"

"No. The *Torch* produced all the research files it has. There was nothing else that I could see that he was working on."

"Are you sure? He seemed so industrious."

"If he was working on anything else, it's gone with his laptop. Paxton's people were very thorough. Just unlucky. A day either way and they would have pulled it off."

"You think it was Paxton then?"

"I know it wasn't Logan. Who else could it be?"

Marie-Faye Lacombe shook her head. "Such a terrible thing. Poor boy. And his poor family."

"His father was pretty torn up at trial."

"I can only imagine."

"I saw Maxime inside," I said. "Is JP here?"

"No, he had to stay in Lansing."

"Working hard on his health and safety agenda?"

Marie-Faye Lacombe almost smiled. "He's tireless."

"I'll say—higher inspection fees on fertilizers and pesticides, increased regulations and fees on antibiotic use with livestock, the vaping ban and cigarette tax increase. His agenda is full as our new Speaker."

Marie-Fay Lacombe nodded. "He's always pushing for a safer Michigan."

"And he's doing it. We're already far safer than places like Indiana."

Marie-Faye Lacombe didn't bat an eye. "Are you taking up journalism, Nathan?"

"Journalism never interested me. I'll stick to law."

"One should stick to what one knows."

"Besides, I'd hate to look in my rearview mirror every time I take a dark curve."

Her blue eyes didn't blink. "That's a strange analogy. You should always be cautious when driving. But I imagine someone who stays in their lane usually has clear roads."

I nodded.

"They do say, though, that distracted driving is a hazard. If you're looking around, at your phone, at a farmer's field, then you might never see a dark curve coming. And that would be a shame."

A log popped and sparks spiraled up and Marie-Faye Lacombe tilted her head to watch as they drifted away before she said, "Of course, busy people rarely have time to be distracted."

"Oh?"

"There are a lot of opportunities for repeatedly lucky attorneys, you know. So many companies looking for legal talent these days." She almost smiled. "Take the Lacombe companies for example—Logistics, Capital, Agriculture and Milling. A good lawyer can find just about any type of work that interests him."

"I'm enjoying it on my own, thanks."

"I can see why you'd think so but sometimes you can't see opportunities that are right in front of you. Why, take our own Agricultural and Milling company, Lacombe A&M. We've recently expanded into nurseries. Through subsidiaries, mind you, but it's all us."

It was my turn to keep a straight face. "How exciting."

"It is. Of course, all those entities can be very hard to keep track of. I don't know how you lawyers do it with all these strict ethical rules that govern every single communication you have with clients. It's amazing you're able to keep your licenses at all."

"It all gets sorted out eventually, I suppose."

"I suppose it does. I can see how you like your autonomy but scale has its advantages, Nathan. You should think about it."

"I like where I am, Marie-Faye. I plan on sticking to my practice so long as nothing else jumps out into the road."

"So long as you're careful I'm sure that will work."

We stared at each other then, Marie-Faye Lacombe on her side of the fire, me on mine. At some point, we'd both stopped reaching out over the flames.

"I'll be careful then," I said, and started back down the flag-stone path.

"There will always be a place for you here, *mon jeune loup*," she said. "For as long as your father lives."

I stopped, turned. "I'm not your wolf, Mrs. Lacombe. And neither is my dad."

Marie-Faye Lacombe smiled. "We'll see."

I left Marie-Faye Lacombe tending her fire. When I re-entered the Queen's Tent, Maxime was waiting. As he passed me to go into the courtyard, I said, "I know a good body shop for your truck."

Maxime cocked his head but didn't respond.

He didn't ask what I was talking about either.

Lucky guess for me.

I decided my run of luck had gone just about as far as I could expect and left the Carnaval de Carrefour behind.

I gave everyone a different version of the end of the Logan Carver case.

I told Olivia and Cade everything I knew and everything I guessed. I knew the Lacombes were a distilling family who somehow grew rich during Prohibition and after. I knew, in my dad's youth, the Lacombes were smuggling cigarettes from low-tax Indiana to high-tax Michigan. I knew, now, that there was a monstrous black market in agricultural products and pharmaceuticals, especially antibiotics used with livestock, and I knew that newly elected Michigan Speaker of the House, JP Lacombe, was pursuing policies that drove up the costs of all those goods here. And I knew, from state filings and corporate licenses and news articles, that the Lacombes had a vast network of legitimate business that generated wealth which had grown with each generation.

I guessed that there were keys to untangling that web. But I knew that the laptop of Christopher Marsh and the journal of Jean-Jacques Lacombe were gone.

Together, the three of us developed a working theory that a

family with that history would have no trouble directing an intermediary to guide an unsophisticated thief to rob the house of a troublesome reporter for cover. We didn't know whether the original plan was to steal the laptop to see what Christopher had or to kill him. We did know, though, that if Logan was convicted of the murder, no one would look any further. Especially if the loose end, Peyton Rush, disappeared.

What was more troubling was that a back-up plan had been in place, that suspicions of a conspiracy had been thrown onto Paxton Plating. And when I realized that the multi-million-dollar company that was being destroyed had also threatened the water supply of the Lacombe family property with its dumping, well, that revealed a subtlety which caused me concern.

It was Olivia, though, who came up with the theory that really gave me the heebie-jeebies—what if Marie-Faye Lacombe had obtained a job for a sitting judge so that the current prosecutor could take his seat, allowing a ringer to be brought in to ensure Logan Carver's conviction?

Attracting the notice of someone with that kind of influence made me more than a little nervous. Sure, Marie-Faye Lacombe had implied that we weren't in conflict right now, but she'd also pretty much said that I was safe so long as my dad was alive; and if that seems like a double-edged fucked up thing to say to you, it does to me too. For now, though, I didn't have actual evidence of anything, so I'd drive straight and keep my eyes on the rearview mirror.

I had a hard conversation with Danny. I explained that Tri-State Nursery and its subsidiaries ultimately ran back to the Lacombe family and that I wasn't comfortable doing business with them. Danny didn't understand at first, so I eventually had to tell him more than I was comfortable with, including my suspicion that as part of shipping its plant stock from state to state, the nursery might be shipping agricultural products that were escaping taxation. Danny figured that I'd gotten a tip from Olivia, and I let him keep thinking that as we spent the next week unwinding ourselves from the Tri-State Nursery transactions. It became clear that firing Tri-State was going to collapse our revenue for the first half of the year and we had a brief argument where Danny tried to give back his partnership since those revenues were such a big part of his contribution. I argued that demonstrated why he was the perfect partner, then, when he persisted, told him to shut up.

I told Emily even less. She didn't really care why we were getting out of the Tri-State deals; she was just thrilled that she didn't have to do any more due diligence and wondered if I had any more murder cases lying around. I told her I didn't, but not to worry—one would come up.

I let Emily take the lead in the Logan Carver sentencing hearing. She argued that he should get the minimum for his burglary-related offenses. Judge Wesley said Emily was eloquent, but ultimately found that Logan's multiple prior offenses required her to impose the high end of the spectrum.

Logan was not bothered by the sentence because he *had* stolen things and he now had friends. Wendy Carver was resigned, knowing it was inevitable, but when she heard the actual number of years, she squeezed an unused tissue in her hands, said goodbye to her son, and left to catch her shift at the Open Grill.

I SPOKE one more time with Josie, about two weeks later. By then, Olivia had concluded that Josie and her father André were exactly what they appeared to be, a respiratory therapist and a farmer with a budding distillery. So I decided to try one last time to talk to her.

It seemed too stalkery to wait by her car again, so I texted. *One short call please.* Two days later, she texted back. *I have five minutes now.*

She picked up on the first ring.

"I've wrapped a bunch of things up," I said.

"That's good."

"I don't expect my cases to cause any more accidents."

"Your case didn't cause any accidents."

"I mean, I'm not planning to do anything that—"

"—It had nothing to do with you, Nate."

That surprised me, so I was silent.

"It was a warning not to let someone inquisitive in the side door. Again."

I thought about how much deeper the ditch was fifty yards on either side of the curve.

"I'm just glad she loved your father. Goodbye."

Josie hung up before I could say it back. I haven't spoken to her since.

MY PARENTS RETURNED from Florida at the end of the following month. If you know my dad, you know he wanted his dock in right away, so I went up to their house on Glass Lake to see how the preparations were going.

My mom answered the door. "Nathan, what are you doing here?"

"Thought Dad might want some help getting things ready for tomorrow."

"You know how that is. He'll welcome the company anyway. And what's this?"

"Thought I could join you for some steak, salad, and potatoes."

She beamed. "That would be wonderful. What do you want?"

I laughed. "Can't a son welcome his parents back from Florida?"

"When he wants something, certainly. Thank you, dear." She gave me a hug. "I'll put the steaks in the refrigerator and you two can cook them when you're done. Is Josie joining us?"

"We broke things off a few weeks ago."

"I—I'm sorry. I know you liked her."

I smiled. "Thanks. Dad in the barn?"

"Where else?" She looked under my other arm. "Do I want to know?"

"Can't a boy bring a gift for his dad?"

"Boys can. Untrustworthy adults cannot."

"See you in a bit."

I walked out to the barn where my dad was busy sliding decking and posts and stairs out from storage slots. "Hey, son."

"You know the three of us will help you do that tomorrow."

"The sooner we're ready, the sooner we'll be done."

There was no arguing with that kind of logic, so I handed him the bag. "I thought I'd bring a welcome home present."

He slipped the bottle out of the bag. "What's this?"

"Old Pogue. Judge Gallon picks up a couple of bottles every time she passes through northern Kentucky."

"Thanks, son."

"I still owed you one from back last fall."

"You don't owe me anything."

"Yes, I do."

He tilted the bottle against the light. "Why don't I pour and then we'll pull out those stairs?"

"Lead the way."

He poured; we drank.

I stood there for a moment as the heat filled my chest. "That's definitely better than the first bottle."

My dad nodded and set down his glass. "That's the way of it sometimes. Grab that rail, will you?"

THE NEXT NATE SHEPHERD NOVEL

Swift Judgment is the next book in the Nate Shepherd Legal Thriller Series. Click here if you'd like to order it.

FREE SHORT STORY AND NEWSLETTER SIGN-UP

There was a time, when Nate Shepherd was a new prosecutor and Mitch Pearson was a young patrol officer, that they almost got along. Almost.

If you sign up for Michael Stagg's newsletter, you'll receive a free copy of *The Evidence,* a short story about the first case Nate Shepherd and Mitch Pearson ever worked on together. You'll also receive information about new releases from Michael Stagg, discounts, and other author news.

Click here to sign up for the Michael Stagg newsletter or go to https://michaelstagg.com/newsletter/

ABOUT THE AUTHOR

Michael Stagg was a civil trial lawyer for more than twenty-five years. He has tried cases to juries, so he's won and he's lost and he's argued about it in the court of appeals after. Michael was still practicing law when the first Nate Shepherd books were published so he wrote them under a pen name. He writes full-time now and no longer practices but the pen name has stuck.

Michael and his wife live in the Midwest. Their sons are grown so time that used to be spent at football games and band concerts now goes to writing. He enjoys sports of all sorts, reading, and grilling, with the order depending on the day.

You can contact him on Facebook or at mikestaggbooks@gmail.com.

ALSO BY MICHAEL STAGG

Lethal Defense

True Intent

Blind Conviction

False Oath

Just Plea

Lost Proof

Swift Judgment

Printed in Great Britain
by Amazon